TRESPASSES

TRESPASSES

Caroline Bridgwood

CROWN PUBLISHERS, INC.
NEW YORK

Published by Crown Publishers, Inc., 201 East 50th Street, New York, New York 10022
Originally published in Great Britain by The Bodley Head Ltd. in 1989.

CROWN is a trademark of Crown Publishers, Inc.

Manufactured in the United States of America

Library of Congress Cataloging-in-Publication Data

Bridgwood, Caroline.
    Trespasses / Caroline Bridgwood.
        p.   cm.
    I.   Title.
    PR6052.R442T7   1990
    823'.914—dc20   89-9875
                                                        CIP

ISBN 0-517-57468-3

10   9   8   7   6   5   4   3   2   1

First American Edition

*For my parents, with gratitude
for their unfailing love and
support*

Part ONE

Childhood

One

We didn't know we were an odd family.

I'm including myself in that statement, although strictly speaking I wasn't one of them. I was a Conway and not a Winstanley.

But I did my growing up with them; I laughed and, later, suffered with them. Their ways were familiar to me. They were my family.

I was orphaned in 1929 at the age of eight, just like a child in a storybook. The Reverend Harold Conway was a missionary from the zealous Victorian mould, and as his daughter it was my fate to be born in a tent in the bush on the continent of Africa. A few weeks later my mother died from a particularly virulent strain of malaria and I was despatched back to England like a parcel. My destination was our Lincolnshire rectory and the bosom of Mrs French, who had been hired to supervise my upbringing in the way that a land agent might be hired to manage an estate for an absentee landlord.

Mrs French was a kind, friendly person. The usual adjective, I realise now, is 'motherly', but since I had no experience whatever of mothers, I didn't know this at the time. It was Mrs French who broke the news – shortly after my eighth birthday – that my father, too, had succumbed to the fever. This time it was the sinister-sounding 'denghi fever'.

I remember feeling deeply disappointed. All I knew of my father were his long, dutiful weekly letters about the exploits of the Africans, but these had always ended with the assurance that one day he was coming home to be a real father to me. I had looked forward to his being made flesh with the sort of excitement that I was later to feel about Christmas, as an event which was certain to happen one day soon. Now it never would.

This sense of disappointment and anti-climax was about all I was capable of feeling on the demise of a parent I had never met. And indignation. In the depths of my eight-year-old mind lurked an embryonic sense of right and wrong; I felt it was rather selfish of these people who had produced me to go and drop dead of the fever as if it didn't matter what happened next.

Mrs French did her best to raise my spirits. Her speech was littered with those sentimental maxims the Victorians were so fond of embroidering on samplers.

'Now, Kitty,' she said, stooping a little so that her face was on a level with mine. 'When you're older you will realise that Into Every Life Some Rain Must Fall. But I've just had word from your dear father's solicitors, and it seems that There is No Great Loss without Some Small Gain. You're to go and live with your dear mother's brother and his family.'

My eyes opened wide. 'For ever?'

'Well, I should think at least until you've come out.'

Come out? Like a rabbit from a burrow? I didn't understand what Mrs French meant, and I felt my insides contract with panic.

'I don't want to go,' I said.

My uncle, Sir Ernest Winstanley Bart., lived with his wife and six children in Russington Hall, near the Cotswold village of Russington Without.

Because of my circumstances I had no sense of family at all, and it was with awe and dread that I rode in the large and impressively shiny motor car that was sent to meet me at Finstock station. Had I been old enough to make an acquaintance with better-known works of English literature, no doubt my thoughts would have been on Jane Eyre or Fanny Price. As it was I had read very little other than my *Child's Companion*, but my imagination was already conjuring up a palatial dwelling full of stiff, shiny furniture and a superior tribe of people who ate breakfast in their ballgowns.

The car rounded a bend and turned through iron gates into what was either a very large garden or a very small park. The house itself was a disappointment: square and substantial and built from ugly grey stone. The front door and most of the tall sash windows appeared to have been flung open.

And the sight of the garden filled me with alarm. It was late

August, with a hint of autumn in the early-morning air, and the herbaceous borders bristled with snapdragons, asters, dahlias ... all spewing forth in an uncontrolled profusion on to the lawns. These lawns descended in a series of stepped terraces away from the house and down to a small ornamental lake. Azaleas, camellias and rhododendrons cavorted along the edge of the drive in wild abundance. There seemed to be no rhyme or reason in the way they were planted or directed their rapacious growth. From among the brightly coloured blooms rose sinister shoots with fungal leaves. I was later to learn that these monsters were rhubarb plants and their odd, purple neighbours were beetroot. In front of the house, slightly to one side, stood a monkey puzzle tree, its outline strange and threatening.

No: I wanted it to seem strange and threatening, but in fact it only looked awkward and ungainly.

Still disturbed by the phantasmagoric appearance of the garden, I was led up the steps by the chauffeur and deposited in the front hall with my suitcases. The shiny black car then slid out of sight somewhere around the side of the house.

The interior of Russington Hall was rather a surprise. The polished parquet floor was inscribed with scrapes and scuffmarks, like hieroglyphics. In one corner lay a pile of tennis rackets, in another a dirty gym shoe. A pile of jackets and coats was tossed over the wooden balustrade. The hall was deserted apart from a fat, pale labrador who shuffled into the centre of the floor, regurgitated the contents of its stomach, sighed and shuffled out again.

'*Oh, Jack! Don't be such a mean pig!*'

Suddenly there was a cacophony of children's voices at the top of the stairs, the sound of running feet and doors slamming.

Then a woman's voice: 'Not at all nice, darling, I don't think, to call poor Jack a pig ...'

The owner of the voice materialised on the top landing, and when she saw me she gasped, 'Oh my goodness gracious me!' and hurried down the stairs.

'Oh, but you're *here* ... we didn't expect you yet ... or, what's the time? I'm not late, am I?'

I stared back at her surprise. This, I guessed correctly, was Lady Winstanley, my Aunt Beattie. She was a small, plump person with a very pretty face, dressed in dingy, shapeless tweeds.

She fell on me with a great cry and embraced me tightly. 'Oh darling! Poor Kitty! Oh you *poor* girl, poor child, poor darling ...'

Aunt Beattie stepped back a pace and examined my face. 'You're not going to cry, are you?'

I assured her that I was not, and she looked much relieved.

Mrs French had drummed home the importance of Polite Conversation, so I searched for something to say. 'I saw your garden,' I offered.

'Ah yes, the *garden*,' said Beattie in a weighty tone, as though I had uncovered a great mystery. 'It is a little lively, isn't it? It's poor Tyler, you see, the gardener. He sometimes gets the seeds a little muddled.' She beamed at me. 'He's blind, poor darling ... still, it makes it all so much more *fun* when things come up, don't you think?'

I was wondering whether or not it would be polite to mention what the labrador had done on the floor only inches away from my aunt's small, plump foot. In the end I was relieved of this duty. A row of curious faces was peering over the top of the banister.

'Mum! Oh, Mummy! Flash has puked on the parquet!'

'Please don't say that word, dear, it's not at all nice.'

'What – parquet?'

'You *know* which word I mean,' said Beattie sternly. She turned to me. 'I expect you're hungry. Children are always hungry. You shall go into the kitchen and have something to eat.'

I was escorted into the kitchen and handed over to the cook, who seemed to be very preoccupied feeding three cats with a smelly mess of cod. The cats stared at me over their food with baleful eyes. I wasn't used to the presence of animals in a house, or to the dirt and grime in odd corners around the kitchen; jars sticky with jam, odd bits of half-eaten cheese on plates.

As I had half hoped, half dreaded, my Winstanley cousins trooped in after me *en masse* and stood around the table staring covetously at my glass of milk and slice of pie. I looked up at them, and my nervous smile was greeted by a unanimous grin of encouragement before their gaze returned to my meal. Much later I was to learn that this was a standard Winstanley ploy; if ever a guest was offered or brought food, the children would fix the object in question with an unwavering stare until their victim succumbed and relinquished the spoils.

I merely felt too intimidated to eat.

'What's wrong?' they asked. 'Don't you like pigeon pie?'

'It's awfully good. Nim sends us out to shoot the pigeons.'

Once more I was searching for something to say. 'It's my plate,' I mumbled. 'It's got something on it.'

The gasps of horror were quite genuine enough when they saw the rim of dried yolk on my plate, though this sympathy did not stem from a shared sense of fastidiousness. The rectory in Lincolnshire, the only house I had ever known, had been spotlessly clean, whilst the Winstanleys had always thought that the disorder of their kitchen was quite normal.

'Oh dear, poor you!' said one of them, rushing to the cupboard to find me another plate. I wasn't being teased, this concern was quite real.

'Poor Kitty!' said a girl of my own age, who I was later to discover was Francesca, or Frannie. '*Poor* Kitty, we must make sure that she always has the cleanest plate!'

Equipped with a clean, but cracked, plate depicting pheasants and woodcocks, I was nonetheless dreading eating my meal in front of an audience. I was rescued by Aunt Beattie, who swooped into the kitchen and shooed my cousins away, promising that they could be introduced to me properly in the drawing room later.

At first I found it difficult to remember which was which.

It wasn't that they all looked alike, but that they presented an alarming uniformity of manner: their vocabulary, their shrieks of laughter and howls of protest, their boisterous high spirits. I felt oddly insubstantial in comparison; as though I only had two dimensions while the Winstanleys boasted three.

I was led into the drawing room after I had eaten, for the formal presentation. It was a warm, mellow room, whose faded Aubussons sported darned patches and faint stains where Flash had been sick. A velvet *chaise longue* was bleached by sunlight from the tall windows, and losing its horsehair. The upholstered leather seat on the brass fender was scratched and torn by various animals, the gilt-trimmed early Chippendale mirror above the fireplace was flyblown ... it was a room that achieved the unlikely feat of being at once grand and cosy. The Winstanleys had a keen appreciation of art and history, but the precious artefacts in their house were both revered and *used* in an everyday fashion. A priceless T'ang vase was filled with umbrellas and walking sticks, an elephant tusk was used as a door stop, and an eighteenth-century French *petit-point* footstool bore the imprint not only of dirty shoes, but also some rather dubious stains.

'Now Kitty,' said Beattie, once I was seated on the *chaise longue*. 'These are your cousins ...'

Irving was the eldest: a tall fair boy who seemed impossibly mature and distant at thirteen. Then there was eleven-year-old

Alexandra (always known as Lexi), ten-year-old Jack, Frannie (whose birthday was only a week after mine), and four-year-old Isolde. The youngest, Clement, was still in the nursery and considered too young to count by the others. Jack and Irving were at home for the summer holidays: I was to discover that it would be much quieter when they had gone back to school.

Questions were fired at me from all sides.

'... What's it like to be an orphan?'

'... Did you cry and cry?'

'Hush, dear! It's not polite to ask that sort of question!'

There was unanimous horror when they learned that I had not had any pets at the rectory, and Flash, the smelly old labrador, was sent for at once so that I should no longer miss out on the joys of having a dumb animal to care for. A dog less like its name is hard to imagine. He sat down next to me with a sigh and proceeded to scratch his genitals with a back leg while I gingerly stroked his sad, square head. He did not even look up when the door opened and another dog ran into the drawing room; a small creature with as much hair at its front end as its rear.

'Dearest! You naughty thing!' trilled the elderly woman who was following it. She was addressing the dog, which she scooped up into her arms and kissed with devotion.

'That's Aunt Griz,' said one of my cousins in a tone that implied this was explanation enough.

Aunt 'Griz', Beattie's aunt, was a tall, thin lady dressed in a floating creation of mauves and pinks, trimmed with a soft fuzz of clipped ostrich feathers. She gave me a dazzling smile and said, 'Well, my darling, you certainly look robust enough. You'll need to be.' Then she turned and whispered something to her dog, inaudible but for the word 'Dearest' and drifted out.

'Well, that's it then, dear,' said Beattie. 'You've met everyone.'

'Not everyone!' chorused various cousins. 'She hasn't met Nim yet.'

'Nim?' I asked.

'Yes, Nim. Nimrod ...'

'... Nimble ...'

'...Nimbleshanks ...'

'... Our father, silly!'

I thought of my own father, the florid, distant, ever-correct Reverend Conway, who never signed himself anything other than 'Father'. This, of all the Winstanley perversities, seemed the oddest to me. 'Why's he called Nim?'

'Because he just is, that's all.'

8

'Let's take Kitty to meet him. He's in his lair.'

And they dragged me off down the corridors shrieking '*Nim!
Nim! Nimbleshanks!*'

The noise of the ravening horde could not easily be ignored, and
a door was flung open.

'SILENCE, YOU LITTLE SAVAGES!' roared the tall man who
stood in our path.

I quaked in my shoes, but the others were not at all dismayed by
my uncle's ferocity. 'Are you haranguing the Nincompoop at *The
Times*, Nim?' they enquired with an easy familiarity.

It seemed my uncle sat down at his desk each day and composed
a letter to the editor of *The Times*, complaining about the lies
printed by that particular newspaper. After that he would press on
with his own very idiosyncratic account of the history of the British
Empire.

'Indeed I am, savages,' said Nim, producing the letter with a
flourish and beginning to read.

> Sir: It occurs to me that your wishy-washy leader article on the
> problems of unemployment ignored the following very obvious solu-
> tion. All the unemployed should be drafted to labour camps on the
> south coast of our fair isle, where they would provide a useful resource
> in building a strong coastal defence system. This would prevent the
> damned Hun from ever penetrating our shores. Alternatively, Ramsay
> MacDonald should be shot. Yours, etcetera, etcetera...

He looked around the circle of upturned faces expectantly, waiting
for signs of approval.

'Nimble, this is Kitty Conway.'

'Conway?' he repeated my surname in a puzzled tone, even
though my father had been married to his younger sister.

'Yes! She's come to live with us. Silly Nim – don't you
remember?'

'Can she ride?' he barked.

'A bit,' I said.

'Good. Can't abide a woman who can't sit on a horse.' And he
turned his back, slamming the door in our faces.

I was to share a room with Frannie, since we were the same age. It
was a large room, with plenty of space for two little girls to spread
out their possessions without getting in one another's way. Frannie's corner was already stuffed with a menagerie of elderly soft

toys, pictures painted by various siblings, a battery of weapons made from sticks and bits of string, and a grisly set of mementoes from the animal kingdom, which included one of Flash's teeth and the skull of a fox.

My side of the room, in contrast, was empty but for my little bed with its candlewick cover; my character yet to be imprinted on it.

I was sitting there alone on the edge of my bed, trying to take it all in, when a figure appeared in the doorway. It was Jack.

'Are you going to cry tonight?' he asked. He was curious, not callous. The Winstanleys seemed to regard me as a member of a separate species, with emotions and manners quite different to their own.

'No,' I said, turning to him shyly and studying his face. I thought he had the most wonderful face I had ever seen in my life. It wasn't his thick, waving dark hair, the brilliant blue of his eyes, the girlish luxuriance of his lashes. At the age of eight I had little notion of conventional good looks. What attracted me was the laughter in his eyes, the smile that never seemed to be absent from his face for long, the look of someone who was completely at ease with his own nature and never knew a moment's self-doubt.

'I know,' he said. 'I know something that will cheer you up.'

He led me down the stairs and into the kitchen. It was now deserted except for Flash, who was sighing over a tea tray of dirty dishes.

'D'you like condensed milk?'

'I've never had it before,' I confessed, conscious of what a dull creature I must sound.

Jack was in the larder, rooting amongst the tins, with a hopeful Flash at his heels. He selected a tin and with a deft, expert movement pierced it in two places with his pocket knife. He handed it to me.

'Here – we suck it out. You use that hole and I'll use the other one.'

I took a tentative drag. 'Mmmm – lovely.' I gulped down the thick, sticky liquid and handed the can back to Jack. We passed it between us until it was all gone, tipping our heads back so far to drain the tin that it felt as though our necks would snap. Flash noisily hoovered up the drops that spilled on to the floor.

Jack let me drink the lion's share. 'I don't mind . . . if you've never had it before,' he said magnanimously. We hid the tin at the bottom of the waste bucket and sneaked out of the kitchen wreathed in conspiratorial smiles.

'Jack! Jack – come here you young . . .'

10

Flash had given us away. Cook had caught sight of him lumbering behind us with a look of dreamy contentment on his face and a dribble of condensed milk on his muzzle. She came running after us.

'Jack Winstanley, have you been in the larder again? After – '

'No.' Jack gave her an innocent, bemused smile. 'We haven't, have we, Kitty?'

I was so taken aback by Jack's shameless fibbing that I was incapable of uttering a sound. Cook mumbled a curse under her breath and turned on her heel, letting the green baize door flap to and fro wildly.

I was on shaky ground. A newcomer in the house and uncertain of its rules and customs, yet I felt I ought to venture some sign of disapproval.

'Jack, you shouldn't have said that ...'

He was still smiling. 'Who had more condensed milk, you or me?'

'I did, but – '

'Well, I'm doing it to protect you.'

Not an inkling, not a flicker of shame or conscience. Jack was a complete rogue, I understood that at once. I was a rather priggish child after Mrs French's upbringing, and I felt I ought to be repelled, but I found that I liked him as much as ever. Despite the fact that he was a liar and a cheat.

Frannie's bedtime ritual was fascinating.

I had had a long, exciting and largely overwhelming day, and after cleaning my teeth I was ready to fall into bed and go straight to sleep.

'It's all right,' Frannie offered generously. 'You can turn the light out. I'll say my prayers in the dark, I don't mind.'

She proceeded to kneel beside her bed and vent forth an incredibly long and complicated series of requests.

'... Dear God, if you can, please make the mare at Chudleigh Farm drop her foal while Irving's still on holiday, because he said he'd take me over there to see it when it comes ... please make Kitty like it here so she'll stay ... please try and stop Jack being such a fibber ... thank you for rescuing Aunt Griz from the fencing master ...'

After she had finished, she hopped up on to her bed and burrowed under her covers, gathering them over her head in a tent-like arrangement. From the glow of light seeping out around

11

the edges of this hump, I could tell that she was using a flashlight.

'What are you doing?' I asked.

'Writing my play.' She popped her head up from under the blankets. 'I've been writing it since I was seven. It's about the lives of the saints.' Frannie disappeared under the covers again. 'The trouble is, I don't know when I'll ever be able to finish it, because I keep changing it ...'

She tried to explain the plot to me, but she had jumbled together so many different periods of history and so many geographical locations that I had trouble following.

'... I can't decide whether or not Saint Aloysius is going to appear to Julius Caesar before the battle ... Saint Winifred and Saint Cecilia are going on holiday together ... but I'm not sure what will happen when they get there ...'

The play was not, it seemed, a finite work but a shifting saga; something like the serials that were popular on the wireless, with the saints as a cast of characters who came and went.

Frannie was a child of boundless energy and was by no means tired out after her creative efforts. She picked up a volume of fairy stories that was next to her bed.

'I'm just going to read for a while ...'

I dozed off, only to be awakened by a loud exclamation from the other bed.

'*Oh no!*' Frannie wailed. 'Oh no, I can't bear it!'

Thinking she might have hurt herself, I sat bolt upright in bed and switched on the lamp. 'What is it?'

'Here, Kitty, let me read it to you ...' She read aloud from the book. '"*And then the good fairy said to her,*" – it's about a poor peasant girl who meets a fairy in a wood and ends up living in a beautiful castle full of wonderful things – "*... The spell is over and you must go back to the woods where I found you. For all good things come to an end, my dear!*" All good things come to an end – is this true, Kitty, d'you think?'

I shrugged. 'I suppose it must be.'

'I don't think I can bear it if it is! "*All good things come to an end.*" How terrible ..!'

And long after we had turned out the light, my cousin Frannie was still weeping noisily at the discovery of this inescapable truth.

12

Two

The next morning I woke to find Frannie in front of the looking glass. She was pulling at the skin around her eyes and grimacing horribly.

'What are you doing?' I asked, genuinely baffled.

'I'm doing my "piggy eye" exercises,' she explained, giving me the beaming smile that was so like Jack's. 'Lexi says I've got piggy eyes, but I can make them bigger if I do these exercises every day.'

Frannie followed her elder sister's advice assiduously for years, much to my amazement. Indeed, the relationship between the sisters was a source of never-ending wonder. They couldn't have been less alike. Warm-hearted, bouncy Frannie with her inventive mind was certainly an attractive child, but her broad, freckled face could not really be described as pretty. Lexi, on the other hand, was unmistakably pretty in a healthy, outdoor way. She had a smooth, peachy skin and a mane of hair streaked with shades of wheat and corn.

Jack once said she reminded him of breakfast cereal. That was his way of disparaging her; he felt that she needed to be taken down a peg or two. For Lexi had the aloofness that often goes with being truly gorgeous, and she positively radiated self-assurance. Frannie was all doubts and muddled ideals, and Lexi played on this in rather a cynical fashion, pointing out her sister's shortcomings to her and – more often than not – telling her what she should do about them. Far from giving Frannie an aversion to Lexi, the effect was a slavish devotion to Lexi's opinions which from time to time I found very irritating.

Breakfast at Russington was taken *en famille*, and by the time

Frannie and I came down, after several false starts while she hunted high and low for a lost sock, a lost Alice band, the others were all assembled.

My nervousness was quickly dispelled by my fascination for the everyday Winstanley badinage; a mixture of squabbling and private jokes that was worlds apart from a soft-boiled egg with Mrs French and her Victorian homilies.

The topic of discussion that morning was friends of Nim and Beattie who were going to be guests at dinner that night; a Colonel somebody-or-other and his wife.

'He's a beastly old bounder!' said Jack with glee, and Frannie and Ysolde (who was mysteriously referred to as 'Shoes' by her siblings) took up the chorus.

'Beastly-Old-Bouncer's coming for dinner, Beastly-Old- '

'Do be quiet .. ! Poor Colonel Price!' admonished Beattie.

Aunt Griz, her feather boa trailing in the Oxford marmalade, looked up from the kipper that she had been feeding to her dog. 'Ah yes ... Herbert Price,' she said dreamily. 'He and I were once ... ' She made a gesture but left the sentence unfinished.

Once what? I wondered. Beattie patted Aunt Griz's hand absently, but otherwise this revelation fell on deaf ears. She was treated as though she were a little soft in the head, and Frannie had already divulged that her family had been forced to step in and rescue her from an unwise liaison with her fencing master.

Aunt Griz pushed back her chair with a flourish. 'I must go upstairs at once, darling Beattie, and decide what I'm to wear!'

Just as Aunt Griz's dog was always Dearest (we never discovered its real name, if it had one), my aunt was always Darling Beattie, as though the endearment were a formal title.

The Winstanleys' cook was a charity case, like the blind gardener, and there were loud protestations from the children about the leaden state of the porridge. Frannie, who had a volume of the *Encyclopaedia Britannica* open on the table in front of her, said, 'Mummy, why can't we eat monkey's brains for breakfast, like they do in China?'

Nim had provided the *Encyclopaedia* with a stipulation that his children should absorb all its information, taking one page each day. Already, having reached the letter 'C', this scheme had proved controversial. 'Bigamy' had been a difficult topic, as was one of the words on the agenda that morning.

'Nim, what's "circ ... circumcision" .. ?'

'Hush, Frannie! That's a very rude way to talk − '

'Can we ask the Beastly Old Bounder when he comes tonight?'

14

'SILENCE!' roared Nim. 'You're very silly children and I don't want another word out of any of you all day!' He glared at each of us in turn. 'And that includes you,' he added, pointing at me.

Frannie gave my hand a sympathetic squeeze but, far from being put out, I was pleased by this conferring of equality. And I waited with bated breath until eight o'clock that evening, only to find that our dinner guest was a sweet-natured and rather plump old gentleman. I could find nothing beastly about him at all. My new family was full of mysteries.

Nim Winstanley was an extraordinary man.

He was not rich, because his small estate was left to run itself, and it did so in a rather haphazard fashion. Nevertheless, he inspired fierce loyalty and devotion in his staff – despite his gruff manner – for he was very thoughtful and good at remembering details. There were many unexpected traits in his character, one of which, I discovered, was a passion for silent films.

When I first arrived at Russington I was always losing my way in the house, which was very large. One afternoon I was wandering down a passage, opening doors on to cluttered boxrooms and cupboards, when I heard a strange noise; a rhythmic whirring sound. I opened a door and found a room that was in total darkness but for a large, flickering screen. Nim had converted the room into a private cinema and he was sitting there alone at the centre of an arc of velveteen seats, puffing on a cigar and watching the screen with a rapt expression. I too looked at the screen, which seemed to be crowded with people in fancy dress milling to and fro in a rather disorganised fashion. I later discovered that the film was von Stroheim's *Greed*. Nim was shaking his head to and fro and muttering in a rather admiring tone, 'Babylon, Babylon ...'

He turned his head when he heard me, but to my surprise he didn't roar. He patted the seat next to him.

'Come and sit down, girl, instead of standing there gaping like a dead cod! I'll put on something more suitable ...'

He went to the projector and exchanged *Greed* for Charlie Chaplin in *The Tramp*. 'You'll like this ...'

And so we spent the afternoon together, my uncle and I, watching Charlie Chaplin films. I was secretly thrilled to have discovered this sentimental side of Nim. For in the flickering half light I could see the silhouette of his angular face and there was a tear running down his cheek when Chaplin fell in love with the little blind flower seller. He treated me as an equal, too, politely asking my opinion of the plot and the acting at the end of each reel. Then the lights would go down again and he would become absorbed in the world of the screen, lifting his cigar from the ashtray to his lips and putting it back again with a slow, measured movement, shaking his head occasionally and smiling at what he saw.

That afternoon was to be printed on my mind for ever with the sensory sharpness of childhood memory – the rough, scratchy feel of the velveteen pile beneath my bare knees, the distinctive smell of Nim's Cuban cigars, the pervasive hum of the projector and the kaleidoscopic images on the screen.

My curiosity had been aroused, and after the film was over I went to look more closely at the photograph of Nim that stood on the long table in the drawing room. It was a formal portrait of a younger Nim in his Great War cavalry officer's uniform. His dark moustache was trim, his glowing eyes – rather like Jack's, I thought – looked straight into the distance. I thought it a dashing and mysterious portrait, and I felt the stirrings of interest in how it was composed and how the glow of light behind the head had been achieved...

After I had studied it carefully I asked Lexi, 'Who's this one?'

Nim's portrait was one of a pair: from a matching silver frame stared a beautiful young woman with soft, smudged eyes and a pale, fragile-looking dress.

'It's Mummy, of course,' said Lexi, without looking up from the task of checking Flash's coat for ticks.

'But . . .'

Lexi wasn't listening.

But it doesn't look anything like her! I said to myself, thinking of Darling Beattie's roly-poly figure in its shapeless clothes, her solid little legs like a teddy bear's. Only her voice seemed to fit with the beautiful young woman in the photograph; it was melodious with a delicious rising cadence that the girls unconsciously imitated.

I asked Frannie what she thought had happened to her mother and she said she didn't know, but she did take me into Darling Beattie's room. It was a very grand affair of lilac and glazed chintz with lots of mirrors. Frannie flung open the doors of a huge wardrobe and said with the eagerness of a conspirator, 'Look . . . look at these!'

The wardrobe was crammed with clothes: not sensible dumpy tweeds but flimsy, frivolous dresses. Debutante's gowns in crêpe and taffeta and organdie. Dresses that belonged to the girl in the picture, just as Darling Beattie's lovely voice did. And there were

16

shoes, too, made from soft suede and kid, and satin dancing pumps with rosettes on the toes.

The clothes exuded a smell of camphor and Jean Patou, trapped there amongst the frothy skirts with Darling Beattie's identity. I wasn't sorry when Frannie closed the wardrobe doors. It was as if the exposure of the abandoned finery had released something other than perfume into the air: a sort of deep and inexplicable sadness.

After the excitement of my arrival had subsided, life at Russington Hall settled into a routine.

Jack and Irving returned to their schools and, for the rest of us, education resumed in the schoolroom. Nim considered school for girls unnecessary, probably harmful and too expensive.

Our governess, Miss Howland, was an extraordinary woman, and added to the list of shattered preconceptions that made up life with the Winstanleys. When Mrs French had told me I was to be educated by a governess, naturally I had visualised a stern and forbidding martinet who would impose strict discipline and whom we would be committed to outwitting at every turn. Not so. Not only was Miss Howland a gentle, mild-mannered person, but also she never seemed to have grown up herself and was an avid conspirator, encouraging us in our most unworthy schemes. She was small and sleek like a plump rabbit and her brown eyes would shine with child-like glee at the latest development in Frannie's play, or Jack's outrageous fibs. Miss Howland was under the spell of the Winstanleys, just as I was starting to be.

If we didn't learn much during lessons, it was because their content was controlled by us children rather than Miss Howland. And no one seemed to care very much what we studied. Nim was too busy berating the editor of *The Times*, while Darling Beattie had very vague notions about the precepts of education. What we did learn, in abundance, was Latin.

Perhaps ours was the only schoolroom in England where Latin was the favourite subject. Frannie and Lexi were far more adept at the language than their brothers, with their expensive, Classics-orientated public school. They insisted on treating it as a living language, and the ever-willing Miss Howland duly conducted Latin conversation classes. No matter that the examples in Kennedy's *Latin Primer* were concerned solely with Roman military campaigns. We battled on.

'*Hostes fugientes vidis?*' Frannie would enquire. ('Have you seen the enemy fleeing?')

I would shake my head vigorously (Kennedy didn't supply the Latin for 'no'). '*Sed cum cives audiverunt, strepitu multi convenient.*' ('No, but when the citizens hear of it, they will assemble with great uproar.')

Most rainy afternoons were devoted to these conversations, in the cosy gloom of the schoolroom, sitting on the capacious window seats whose cushions were covered with the most hideous fabric imaginable. ('Who would have thought they could have invented so many shades of bile green?' mused Frannie.) They certainly didn't match the curtains, which were a frightful sort of sham tapestry covered in dingy leaves and berries. Across the fireplace marched a chorus of porcelain Beatrix Potter figurines, the perfect backdrop to the childish enthusiasms of Miss Howland.

But whenever the weather was fine, we were out of doors and running wild on the estate. Fuelled by a diet of spinach and pink junket, we rode our ponies like little savages, through the dogwood and golden willow around the pond, over fences and into the fields...

A favourite pastime was visiting the farms to watch the calves being born. We all loved the gory bits, especially little Shoes. 'Here comes the afterbirth!' she would shout. 'Look at all the blood, all red – lovely!'

Darling Beattie wasn't at all happy about this aspect of our education. 'Not at all a nice place, the cowsheds, I should think,' she would say with a shake of her head and Flash would look on and sigh. She couldn't really stop us, but she could prevent little Clem from coming with us. As the youngest of the six he was Darling Beattie's favourite and she did her best to shield him from our corrupting influence. He was a sunny-tempered and amenable child and on the occasions when he tagged along behind us, he was treated rather as we treated the pets.

Frannie and I became inseparable. One couldn't help but love her; she was so warm and generous, so concerned with the happiness of others. Even in those innocent days she worried about things like good and evil. We were walking back together from church one day, after the vicar had based his text on the chances of rich men going to heaven.

'Oh dear, Kitty,' lamented Frannie. 'Do you think there's any chance a camel *could* get through the eye of a needle? Perhaps if it was a very, very tiny camel and a huge great big needle..?'

I shook my head. 'I doubt it.'

'Then there's no hope for us, then? No hope of getting to heaven?'

18

'I should think not. Not unless Nim gives it all away.'

'Do you think he might ..?'

We were silent as we considered this unlikelihood.

'Kitty,' said Frannie finally, 'do you think it should be Saint Anselm or Saint Barnabas who fights the dragon?'

And we repaired to our secret hideaway under the branches of the Portugal laurel to work out the plot of Act Three.

The weeks passed and we reached 'F' in the *Encyclopaedia* ('"Fornication" – oh dear, how unsuitable!') and suddenly it was time for the boys to return to Russington for the summer. The noise level rose. For one thing, we teased Irving vociferously. He had reached the awkward threshold of adolescence; we recognised that he was no longer one of us and punished him for it. We started abbreviating his name to Irv, which he hated. Instead of 'NIM – NIM – NIMBLESHANKS!' the corridors resounded with cries of 'IRV – IRVIE – IRVIE BABY!', a title we had adapted from the popular songs we were always hearing on the wireless. We thought we were very funny.

For me, there was an important initiation still to come.

The Winstanleys were devotees of game-playing, but unlike most families they only played games of their own invention. There was the game in which they pretended to be deaf or blind for a day, which resulted in a lot of things being broken. And there was Hunting the Snark, as violent as it was astoundingly simple.

It started when some children came to visit us for the day. ('Some *nice* children,' said Darling Beattie, with feeling.) They were called the Peake-Taylors; the offspring of friends of Nim and Beattie. Their christian names were Fergus, Sarah and James, and they were the same ages as Irving, Lexi and Jack respectively.

I was full of curiosity about them, but the Winstanleys were contemptuous. 'Eugh, the Bleak-Wailers!' they scoffed. 'Beastly dull!'

'Now, you children go upstairs ...' said Darling Beattie when our guests arrived, '... and find something quiet to do ...'

And so we found ourselves facing one another in the nursery; two distinct camps, the Winstanleys and the Bleak-Wailers.

'What shall we play?' demanded Lexi.

This was thrown down as a challenge to the Bleak-Wailers. They did indeed look bleak, standing huddled in their lesser group. They all had the same pale, sandy hair and were as uniformly small and thin as we were large and vigorous.

'Well,' suggested James. 'We could play Animal, Vegetable, Mineral. That's when we choose one of us and the person who's it has to guess who we've chosen from the clues.'

'The clues?'

'Well ...' He was floundering. 'The clues are saying what animal, vegetable and mineral the person's like. So Jack might be like a potato – '

'A *potato!*' growled Jack.

'I've got a much better idea,' said Irving. 'Let's Hunt the Snark!'

There were enthusiastic cries of support from our camp. I must have looked as blank as the poor Bleak-Wailers.

'It's very easy ... one person's "it", and they have to go and hide, and everyone else has to try and find them. And the first person to find them shouts "Snark!" – that's the war cry – and everyone else comes along shouting "Snark" and then they all tickle and slap the person until they beg for mercy.'

The Bleak-Wailers said, 'Is that all?'

'All?'

'Well, it doesn't seem very ... fair.'

'*Fair?*' The idea of fairness had never occurred to the Winstanleys.

'So, we're agreed then?' they said to the Bleak-Wailers, who looked on in mute terror. 'Right, Kitty can be it, since she's never played before.' This was decided with curious Winstanley logic. 'Off you go!'

I ran. The hunting instinct was aroused, my blood was up. I pelted along the corridor and down the stairs, past Nim's study, past his 'cinema' where the light flickered in the dark and the movie projector was making its low drone ... I considered sneaking in and hiding in there, but imagined the resulting massacre taking place under Nim's nose and thought better of it.

But they were coming, the others, closing in. I could hear them. I ran to the very end of the passage and up the back staircase, just as they reached the bottom of the main staircase. We had moved round in a circle, and I was now heading upstairs again to the empty schoolroom where we had started. I prided myself on this brilliant manoeuvre. They'd never think of coming back to look in here, they'd be too busy combing the rest of the house. I hopped on to one of the bile-green window seats and drew the mock-tapestry curtains around me. I was safe. I drew in a great sigh of relief and gradually the pounding in my chest subsided ...

The door of the schoolroom opened. I froze, not daring even to raise a hand and scratch my nose, which was itching terribly. Too late. The tapestry curtains were flung open. I sneezed. And there stood Jack.

20

'I thought I'd find you here.' Giving me his most irresistible grin, he squeezed on to the seat beside me and for a moment I imagined that he would decide not to give me away. He must have read my thoughts.

'Wouldn't it be a wheeze,' he said, 'if I hid in here with you and pretended to the others that I hadn't found you?' His eyes glinted. 'I bet they'd never think of looking in here.'

He smiled at me. I smiled back at him.

Then he jumped to his feet and bellowed at the top of his voice, 'SNARK!'

The others came running, baying for my blood. 'Snark . . ! Snark!' they shouted.

'Come on, Dearest!' enjoined a familiar voice in the midst of the howls. 'Lovely game!'

I disappeared beneath a flurry of punching, pinching, tickling hands, with Aunt Grizelda's dog sitting in triumph on my chest and her feather boa wrapped around my eyes. The more I screamed and struggled, the more those strong little fingers dug in, finding the spaces between my ribs. They did not belong to the Bleak-Wailers – I knew that without opening my eyes. Our visitors hung back and watched the massacre with mouths agape.

I do not know how long it was before I gave in; it may have been five minutes, it may only have been thirty seconds.

'*Stop!*' I cried. '*Mercy!*'

My tormentors stepped back and relinquished me.

'Not bad,' said Irving, rubbing his hands. It seemed it was a matter of pride to hold out against the torture as long as possible.

Later that afternoon, the Bleak-Wailers escaped and went back to their tranquil home, while we indulged in another Winstanley speciality – the Truth Game. Again the rules were simple – everyone had to tell the whole truth and nothing but the truth all day long. This was more of a feat than might at first appear, because my cousins were naturally prone to inventions and exaggeration. The idea was that one tried to catch out the others by springing a question on them accompanied by the ritual chorus of, 'Tell-the Truth, Tell-the-Truth-now!'

'Jack,' asked Lexi on this occasion. 'What did you do with your serving of custard yesterday? I saw you put it in your pocket.'

This fantastical feat was all too possible, since Beattie employed a cook who couldn't cook. Her custard was like yellow India rubber and served in solid slabs.

'I put it in Flash's kennel,' said Jack, 'and he buried it in the garden.'

21

We didn't know whether or not to believe him. Jack always cheated at the Truth Game.

Jack Winstanley was old beyond his years. Perhaps that was the reason he was the only one who had not attracted a nickname – a mark of his self-possession. Jack was just Jack.

I used to try so hard to get cross with him, but I always failed. His disgraceful charm always got the better of me. Besides, he was incapable of shame or remorse. As with the condensed milk episode, he could always rationalise his misdemeanour, or else when upbraided he would pretend not to understand the charge. There was nothing sly about him; he didn't try to hide things, nor was he malicious. Promises weren't broken, they were merely forgotten.

On my ninth birthday, Jack presented me with a four-leaf clover. I was delighted.

'It's not a real one,' said Lexi. 'It had five leaves and he pulled one off. I saw him.'

But that didn't spoil it for me. It was the fact that he had wanted *me* to have it that mattered. I wrapped it up in cotton wool and hid it away in my underwear drawer, beneath my baggy Chilprufe knickers.

Nim had a special present for me, too. He took me to one side and presented me with a brand new Leica camera.

'Since you're so interested in cinematography,' he said gruffly, and gave my shoulder a brief squeeze before he stomped off to his study again. I was touched. This was Nim's way of showing his appreciation of the hours I spent keeping him company in the gloom of his cinema, shifting uncomfortably on the scratchy velveteen seat.

The camera was extremely heavy and looked very complicated. I had not the least idea how to use it – neither did Nim, who told me I would have to find a book in the village library and teach myself.

'Oh dear!' said Darling Beattie when I showed it to the others. 'Not a very suitable present for a nine-year-old, I don't think.'

Nevertheless, I made the entire family troop outside to have their photograph taken. I made them pose on the pillared steps while, below, old blind Tyler fumbled amongst the disorder of clove pinks and sweet geraniums. Jack and Frannie each swung from one of the stone pineapples that graced the end of the balustrades. The picture was a complete blur. I then took one of Flash, which came out a fuzz of white.

The Winstanley children were disgruntled. 'Nim never gives us presents,' Fannie said, adopting a hurt expression.

'You can share the camera,' I said hurriedly. 'It can belong to all of us if you like.'

Nim had given me a wonderful present to make me feel special, to make me know that I was wanted. He wasn't to know that the last thing I wanted was to be singled out from my cousins.

That state of affairs wasn't to last long, however. Darling Beattie decided that we were to learn to dance. A conflict of interests arose at once. She thought it absolutely necessary that we should learn young; we were too young to envisage a time when such a thing could be necessary. We revolted, but in vain. Darling Beattie had an ally in the matter, none other than Mrs Bleak-Wailer. The two of them pooled resources to employ a dancing mistress, a mountain of a woman called Madame Breszinska. She claimed to be conversant with the Keel Row, though how she picked it up in the cafés of central Europe remained a mystery.

Dancing lessons ran thus: Miss Howland played the piano while we lumbered around mournfully to the waltz, the gavotte and the polka. Madame Breszinska barked 'One-two-three' like a regimental sergeant-major and Jack tried to tread on the Bleak-Wailers' toes. There were eight of us: Irving and Lexi, Jack and myself, Frannie and James, Fergus and Sarah. That made four neat couples so there wasn't even a chance to sit out. Clem and Shoes wanted to join in, naturally, but were deemed too young. They used to watch from the sidelines with Flash, jumping up and down with excitement whenever our formations went astray. Sometimes Darling Beattie would come and watch. 'Ah ...' She sighed with satisfaction, seeing the four neatly matched pairs. 'How nice. Aren't they sweet?'

She shouldn't have voiced her approval out loud. From then on, sabotage was in the air.

'Madame,' said Jack one day, sidling up to her with his most angelic smile. 'Wouldn't it be a good idea if we used a gramophone instead of the piano? Our father has one we could borrow.'

Miss Howland's piano playing left a lot to be desired; moreover she was our accomplice and had a glint in her eye whenever we forgot our steps. Madame was only too glad to be rid of her.

Nim would never have agreed to our using his precious gramophone, naturally, but we removed it by stealth, along with several of his records. It was my idea, and I was justifiably proud.

'Hmmm, seventy-eight r.p.m. ...' said Irving. 'We'll have to change that, of course. Clem, fetch me a screwdriver.'

Irving was passionate about any sort of machinery or gadget that had knobs or controls and after fiddling around for a while, with the rest of us craning to see over his shoulder, he managed to rearrange things so that the turntable rotated at one hundred r.p.m. Some of the screws were hanging loose, '. . . But don't let's worry about that,' said Irving.

Oh, we were so pleased with ourselves when Madame gave the command, 'Take your partners, plees!' I usually danced with Jack, but on this occasion, for our scheme to succeed to its best effect, I chose James Bleak-Wailer. Jack partnered Sarah and Frannie latched on to Fergus.

'Ready now children *and* . . . one-two-three . . .' Madame dropped the needle on to the record.

'*Take-a-Pair-of-Sparkling-Eyes!*' it screamed at one hundred revolutions per minute, like a demented piglet.

At this signal we spirited our innocent partners into a fiendish polka, careering around the schoolroom at speed, bumping into the walls, into chairs, into each other.

'*Take-a-Pair-of-Rosy-Lips,   Take-a-Figure-Neatly-Planned!*' shrieked the gramophone.

'*Enough!*' barked Madame.

Attracted by the commotion, Darling Beattie stood in the doorway. 'Goodness, you naughty children!' she said.

And then there was a blinding blue flash and the gramophone exploded.

Nim devised our punishment himself.

We were lined up in his study to receive sentence.

'You're savages!' he shouted. 'D'you hear me? Savages! I've a good mind to write to that nincompoop at *The Times* and offer you as fodder for the White Slave Trade!'

Jack showed signs of interest at this prospect, but Nim went on, '. . . Of course, no self-respecting White Slaver would touch you rabble. So I'm putting you to work m'self. I've given the stablehands a week's paid holiday and you're going to do their work for them. Up at five! Mucking out! All that sort of thing! And no complaints.'

We looked down at our shoes, trying to seem contrite.

'The biggest scoundrel of the lot of you was the one who thought up stealing my gramophone.'

Sidelong glances, all in the direction of my scuffed button shoes and bagging socks.

'Well – which one of you is a criminal as well as a savage?'

'It was me,' I said, without daring to look up.

'*You!*' Nim blustered. 'Hellfire, you're just as bad as your cousins!'

I was delighted. I was one of them at last.

Three

The four years that followed saw my transformation from a rather lonely little child into a loud, boisterous Winstanley.

They also saw the emergence of two new centres of interest within our closed circle: sex and money. This growing preoccupation with sex was reflected in the development of Frannie's play about the lives of the saints. Saint Anselm was now having a torrid affair with Saint Catarina of Siena, and they eloped together. A lot of time and effort went into the dramatisation of the elopement; an attempt to ensure that it was realistic in the face of our complete lack of experience.

'Do you think he'd kiss her at the station, or d'you think he'd wait for the train to arrive?' Frannie would ask as we lay tucked up in our candlewick-covered beds, amid her collection of sheep's skulls and Clem's milk teeth. 'D'you think they'd ask for a sleeper?'

We didn't call it 'sex', of course. We referred to it as Experience, with a capital 'E'. So desperate were we for Experience that the quest took on a competitive edge. Lexi and Frannie and I formed a secret society, specifically to compare notes. We used to meet in the schoolroom, squeezing our six arms and six legs into the impossibly constricting space of the window seat, and pull the curtains around us. But Jack became too good at sneaking in unheard and listening to our confessions.

Then I seized on the brilliant scheme of using the Motor. Nim's old car was a large black museum piece, lavished with as much love and care as one of the family, and only taken out on special occasions. We would open the door and climb into the back seat, marking the walnut trim with our grubby fingers, making the springs squeak in the soft, hide-covered seats. They had a clean, dry smell that was – to our questing nostrils – intensely masculine.

'Mmm ...' said Lexi dreamily, stroking one fingernail up and down the back of the driving seat. 'To think that *he* sits here every day!'

'Not every day,' said the literal-minded Frannie. 'Only about six times a year, in fact.'

'He' was Nim's driver, Tony, a swarthy young Anglo-Italian with the look of a dangerous animal about him. Tony had the dubious honour of being the object of our girlhood lust.

The idea of our meetings was that we were to confess any and every Experience we might have had. Since our daily life at Russington was devoid of romantic assignations, we were forced to invent and embroider, to read momentous significance into the tiniest gesture.

'I saw Tony washing the Motor this morning,' sighed Frannie, curling her legs underneath her on the squashy leather seat. 'He was rinsing out his chamois in a bucket ...'

Sighs of wonderment.

'... And he sort of lifted it out of his bucket ... all soapy and dripping ... and he flapped it at me!'

'*Flapped* it at you?'

'Yes, you know, as if he was beckoning me to come over to him ... and he smiled ...'

'And?' demanded Lexi.

'Well, I didn't go, of course. Remember what happened to Aunt Griz! I couldn't possibly have given in to the whim of a chauffeur.'

'Driver,' said Lexi sourly. There was a great debate raging at the time over whether it was common to say 'chauffeur'. Darling Beattie maintained that it was *nouveau-riche*. Heaven forbid!

'Driver.' Frannie corrected herself, anxious as ever to please Lexi.

'Anyway, how about you, Kitty? Have you had any Experiences this week? Any stolen rapture?'

'Not unless you count a kiss on the lips from Miss Bean,' I said gloomily. Miss Bean was the village librarian, a square woman with cropped hair and a loud voice who was fond of wearing cast-off men's clothes.

'Eugh, beastly old lesbian!'

'It must be awful being a village spinster,' I mused. 'Mind you, I shall probably end up being one myself.'

Now that I was thirteen, I was very sensitive about what I saw as my irredeemable plainness. My hair was an ordinary brown, my

nose, mouth and brows all sat on my face in unfeminine straight
lines.

'Oh no!' said the faithful Frannie. 'Aunt Griz was saying only
yesterday that she thought you'd turn into a beauty one day.'

'She's so old she certainly won't be here to see it – if such a day
should ever come!'

Lexi could afford to scoff. She grew prettier and riper by the day,
as Frannie and I grew more awkward and ungainly. She had also
become very vain. Frannie and I used to troop into her room after
her and watch her practising with cosmetics. This activity was
strictly outlawed, and we were only granted the status of witnesses
if we swore on every imaginable sacrament that we wouldn't tell
Darling Beattie. She maintained that, at sixteen, Lexi was much too
young for such things.

We would lie on the bed while Lexi sat at her dressing table,
narrowing her eyes and sliding her lips to and fro to blend the
lipstick, enticingly named 'Blood Roses'. The first layer was blotted
carefully, dusted with powder and a second coat applied. Then she
held up the heavy silver handglass and turned her head this way and
that in order to see herself from every possible angle. She even faced
the dresser and held her handglass behind her head so that the two
mirrors reflected the back view.

Frannie and I were scathing. 'Imagine wanting to know what the
back of your head looks like!'

We were sceptical about the whole operation, because Lexi had
such gloriously healthy looks, with her hair like glossy wheat
kernels and her pink-and-white scrubbed skin, that she did not
need the enhancement of cosmetics.

I said, 'Lexi, your lips are rosy enough already. You ought to save
that stuff for people who need it. Like us.'

'Oh, but I read somewhere that if you want to make an
impression when you walk into a room, it's important to be
wearing lipstick. You never know when you might need to make an
impression,' Lexi said darkly.

She lifted the Blood Roses to her lips again, only to be interrupted
by a high, ear-splitting sound.

'Damn and blast it, they're at it again!'

Clem and Shoes had recently learned to whistle, and they did so
incessantly, prowling the corridors of Russington Hall and giving
their own renditions from *Hymns Ancient and Modern*.

'I can't concentrate on this, not with that racket! Fran, can't you
go and tell them to shut up?'

Frannie was leaning back on the pillow, doing her piggy-eye

28

exercises. 'I could, but it wouldn't be any use, not today. They're playing at Being Deaf.'

Our second abiding preoccupation was money.

Nim gave us pocket money, but it wasn't enough to buy anything with. We tried everything: selling eggs from the farms on the estate, pawning antiques from the house. Lexi was so desperate for new clothes that she even begged Nim to sell her pony and give her the proceeds.

Eventually we hit on a money-spinning scheme.

'... So simple,' said Jack smugly. 'All we need is a couple of wooden crates, a signboard and some paint, some old dusters ...'

Lexi, Fran and I helped him carry these items down the drive to the gates at the entrance of the park. Clem and Shoes ran along behind, picking up the things that we dropped and whistling 'When I Survey The Wondrous Cross'. Irving wasn't with us — he had left school that summer and considered himself too old for our schemes.

We upturned the crates and set to work painting a sign — 'SHOE-CLEANING DONE HERE'. Then we sat down to wait.

Before long, a group of curious villagers had gathered, but they seemed reluctant to have their shoes cleaned.

'Perhaps they think it's a trick!' hissed Frannie.

It was more likely that they doubted our ability to clean shoes. They stood in a little gaggle on one side of the lane; we sat on our crates at the park gates. The two camps stared at one another. Then one of the village men, Ned Hawkes, who had worked on the estate for years, stepped forward.

'Reckon my boots could do with a clean.'

He stumped over to our side of the lane and sat down heavily on the crate opposite Jack. Jack lifted Ned's foot gingerly, clad in its rough, mud-spattered boot, and placed it between his knees. Then he applied the polish and set to with gusto, rubbing the stubby toes of Ned's boots until they had a dull gleam. Ned appeared to be delighted with the results.

'That will be thruppence, please,' said Jack.

'It doesn't seem right, somehow,' I whispered to Frannie as Ned stamped off down the lane, getting mud all over Jack's handiwork. 'Taking money from people like Ned.'

'Especially since he used brown polish, and Ned's boots are black.'

It seemed as though Ned might be our first and last customer, but

29

then the village policeman stopped to have his boots polished, and we managed to catch the eye of a group of Oxford students who were driving out to spend a day in the countryside. There were six of them squeezed into an Austin Seven, and they all decided to have their shoes cleaned. Jack didn't register a flicker of conscience as he charged them one shilling apiece.

Clem and Shoes had decided to make themselves useful by providing a musical accompaniment. They formed half a barber's-shop quartet and since they couldn't sing, they whistled their way through 'The Last Rose of Summer' and 'I dreamt I dwelled in Marble Halls'. Miss Howland came to cheer on our efforts and gradually quite a large crowd gathered. The box full of pennies grew heavier.

'I might even buy an organdie blouse ...' Lexi was saying, 'or perhaps a cashmere sweater. Do you think they sell cashmere in Gorringe's ..? Oh, God! Look!'

The Motor was coming down the drive; long, gleaming and menacing.

Tony brought it to a halt in front of the sign and Nim's angry red face shot through the window, moustache bristling.

'What the devil is the meaning of this circus?' he shouted. '"SHOE CLEANING DONE HERE"! You'll be turning the place into a hotel next! Inviting people in to bounce on my bed, no doubt! You horrible little savages!'

Our potential customers fled and we were ordered to foreclose our business at once. Only Clem and Shoes were satisfied with its outcome. The nine shillings and sixpence we had made was confiscated and donated to Parish Council funds, but by then the two of them had already run down to the village shop and spent their share of the profits on an orgy of liquorice.

Back at Russington, the rumpus carried on for the rest of the day. We were lectured on our Responsibilities and our Position, while Lexi mulishly argued that we might as well be paupers for all the benefits we derived from them. Nim launched into a tirade on ingratitude that would have done credit to Lear, and Flash was just starting up a mournful howl in sympathy when Darling Beattie stamped her solid little foot and intervened.

'Really, we can't carry on like this, you know, not when we have a house guest coming.'

'A house guest?'

We gathered around Darling Beattie, anxious to hear more, but she was frowning.

'She's a cousin of your mother's,' said Nim.

30

We bombarded Darling Beattie with questions but she said we would have to wait and see. We groaned in frustration.

'... Though I'm really not at all sure it's a good idea. You know how Cook is.'

With this obscure remark Darling Beattie turned round and went back into the kitchen with Flash at her heels.

'She's from Europe,' said Nim, 'so perhaps she'll be able to drill some manners into you young Hottentots!'

Europe! The word had the same effect as a match on touch paper. To us Europe was the epitome of glamour and Experience: it conjured up Greta Garbo and French cigarettes, dubious assignations in dimly lit bars. We had seen it all on the flickering screen in Nim's cinema.

'And you lot had better look lively,' said Nim with some satisfaction. 'Because tomorrow night we're giving a party to celebrate our visitor's arrival.'

'Oh no!' groaned Lexi. 'What on earth are we going to *wear*?'

'My goodness, I bet *she's* had some Experiences!' whispered Frannie.

'With a name like that!' I added.

We were leaning over the banisters watching Darling Beattie's cousin make her entrance in the hall below. I was reminded of a similar scene at my own arrival, five years ago.

'*Where's Flash*?' I hissed.

'It's all right, he's locked up in the kitchen.'

Her name was Mireille de Vere and she was lovely, quite lovely to look at. She was aged somewhere between thirty and forty but her skin was still pale and creamy, her red-blonde hair thick and curling. The lids over her great, dark eyes seemed to droop slightly, as though they were a little too heavy for her to open them fully.

And, of course, she was exactly as we had imagined, even down to her improbable name. Even if she had looked like Miss Bean the librarian she couldn't have disappointed us. She wore a pale linen coat over a pale linen suit, and a pale hat with a dotted veil. The effect of the chalky linen and the ivory skin was dramatic; she seemed to have no colour at all except for the faint red of her hair. And over her arm she carried a fur travelling wrap.

'Oh my God!' Lexi exhaled a long sigh of envy, like a balloon deflating. 'I don't believe it! It's sable. *Sable*.'

Tony carried in a fleet of pigskin cases and put them down at the foot of the stairs. Mireille's gaze swept upwards.

31

'Come on,' said Lexi. 'We'd better make ourselves scarce. We've got to find something to wear tonight, remember?'

Since we had no money, and since we couldn't compete with the glamour we'd just seen, we were forced to take an inventive approach.

'I think I have an idea,' I said. I led the way into Darling Beattie's room and flung open the doors of the wardrobe with a flourish.

'There,' I said, pointing at the soft pinks and blues, at the satin and kid dancing pumps with their dainty rosettes. 'We can borrow something.'

Lexi and Frannie exchanged glances, and Frannie shook her head. 'No,' she said. 'Mummy doesn't lend her dresses, not ever.'

'She doesn't like them to be touched,' said Lexi.

We resorted to raiding the dressing-up box in the schoolroom, where I found an ancient shift of grey silk organza that had holes in the armpits and did nothing to flatter my colouring. I also salvaged some strings of beads and a pair of purple shoes with Louis heels.

Frannie picked on a hideous brocade curtain which she draped around her chubby form in a sheath-like arrangement, instructing me to trim off the few inches that dragged on the ground, and wind them round her head in a turban.

All eyes were on Lexi now.

'Hmmm . . . ' She curled her lip at the tired-looking remains in the dressing-up box, then began casting around for something different. 'I know!' she said, 'Aunt Griz. Why didn't we think of her before? She's got simply heaps of old dresses from when she was young. Come on!'

We waddled after her like two jesters in their motley, Frannie wobbling awkwardly in her brocade sheath while I swayed and staggered in my high heels, which were two sizes too large. As we followed Lexi down the corridors I reflected that I had never been in Aunt Griz's room before. I was not even sure where it was, and now felt overwhelmed by curiosity.

'Dearest, look! We have visitors!'

Aunt Griz was lying on her bed reading, propped up against a pile of pillows with her dog on her lap. 'How lovely! Do come in, dears.' Then she looked slightly nervous. 'Has Darling Beattie sent you?'

We explained our purpose and Aunt Griz wafted around the room in a flurry of feathers and gauzy scarves, searching through drawers and cupboards. Her room was quite a contrast to the rest of the house, which was largely shabby and bare and rather drafty. Aunt Griz's room was thickly carpeted and everything seemed to be cushioned and padded and soft, as if it was protecting her from the real world outside.

Next to the rather grand looking-glass there was a photograph of a dashing, dark-eyed young man dressed in white tie. His hair was combed back in waves from his fine forehead and he was smiling confidently, one hand on his hip in the arrogant stance of a bull-fighter. Next to this portrait was something which I thought Flash must have regurgitated but, no, it was a corsage of flowers, dry and stiff and purple-grey like a dead mouse.

Aunt Griz saw me looking at the photograph.

'Oh darlings!' she said with a girlish wave of her bejewelled, liver-spotted hand, 'yes indeed, it is Him. The love of my life!'

We looked at one another and sniggered. We were only too accustomed to hearing Aunt Griz boast of how she had been in the grip of a Great Love. I looked at the photograph again.

'I know exactly what you should wear, darling Alexandra,' announced Aunt Griz, dropping her dog on the counterpane and drifting over to a wardrobe. 'Black. It's perfect with your colouring.' She pulled out a long, tubular affair made of black velvet.

Aunt Griz was quite right about the colour. The dense, inky blackness was perfect with Lexi's rosy complexion and streaky blonde hair. Aunt Griz arranged a twist of black velvet around her head, entwined with a string of pearls.

'Real pearls,' said Lexi with satisfaction. She looked very beautiful. The elegant dress seemed to have brought out some mysterious quality in her. The nearest word I could find to describe it was worldliness, but it wasn't that exactly. She could have been anything between sixteen and thirty.

We were all immensely proud of ourselves. I had become quite skilled with my camera over the years and I insisted that the others wait while we all posed in our finery at the top of the stairs; setting the timing device then hobbling round as fast as I could so that I could be in the picture too. Then we minced our way down the main staircase.

Jack burst out laughing as soon as he saw us. I dare say we looked quite ridiculous.

Darling Beattie came into the hall. She was dressed in a dull-green wool gown which made her look more roly-poly and teddy-bearish than ever.

Her brow furrowed when she beheld us in our splendour. 'Oh, you dreadful children, what can you have been thinking of! You look like the raggle-taggle gypsies! Go upstairs at once and take off all that nonsense!'

There were groans of protest, but Darling Beattie was not in the mood to be crossed. 'That's enough! Upstairs with you at once and come down in something *suitable*.'

'Oh, please don't send them back!'

A cool melodious voice spoke from somewhere behind Darling Beattie. 'They look so charming!'

Mireille stepped out of the shadows, dressed in bone-white crêpe de Chine with some very old and foreign-looking jewels at her throat and wrists.

Darling Beattie frowned again. 'Very well.' She didn't sound as though she meant it. 'Since Mireille is a guest ...'

I couldn't see why she was so doubtful. The rest of us were all captivated by Mireille. In fact, 'captivating' was the perfect word to describe her. Or perhaps 'alluring'. To our adolescent eyes she was the epitome of glamour, but it wasn't the hard, brittle boyish glamour one associated with women of the twenties and thirties. Mireille had a substantial womanliness. The rather Edwardian qualities of dignity and gravity were there in force; in fact Frannie was to say later that Mireille reminded her of Irene in John Galsworthy's Forsyte novels. She only had to sit in a corner of a room, in perfect stillness, and you knew that someone would be sure to ask, 'Who *is* that lovely woman?'

And yet she was one of those people with the gift of drawing others into their confidence, by patting a seat very close to her and asking them to tell her all about themselves.

'She's lovely, isn't she?' I said to Jack after we had all gone through into the drawing room and Mireille had engaged Lexi in a long series of mutual compliments about their toilettes. He was looking at her very intently.

'Mmmm,' said Jack. He smiled, but it was the sort of smile you wear when you are having a private conversation inside your head.

There was a big fire in the drawing room, even though it wasn't cold. Darling Beattie thought it made the room look brighter. The furniture had been arranged to hide the worst of the stains on the carpet, and there were bowls everywhere spilling over with the confused contents of the garden.

The dinner guests were arriving, mostly what we called the Old Faithfuls; the village elite of retired colonels and red-faced huntsmen. Nim stood in front of the fire in his well-worn tailcoat that was green with age, and barked orders at them as they arrived, indicating exactly where they should sit.

In addition to the Old Faithfuls there was a couple called the Cawardines. Bruce Cawardine was like the stock seducer of Noël

Coward plays, big and hearty with a roguish ginger moustache. His wife Marjorie was wearing a lilac-coloured dress that clashed terribly with her pink face. Clutched to her plump bosom was a box of chocolates, the expensive hand-made kind. She put them down on a table and immediately Jack and Frannie materialised out of nowhere. They fixed the box with an unwavering stare.

'Go on, dears,' said Marjorie Cawardine weakly, 'do have a chocolate.'

Mireille had now cornered Irving. She had an evening bag with her, a fascinating beaded purse with two little balls of ivory that clicked it open and shut. From out of the bag, like a conjuror, she pulled a small ivory tube, about two inches long, which turned out to be a collapsible cigarette holder that pulled out into sections until it was at least three times its original length. I was hypnotised by that cigarette holder; so much so that when I was eventually to take Mireille's picture I made sure that the cigarette holder was in the photograph.

Mireille was fixing a Balkan Sobranie into one end of it, handing her lighter to Irving and leaning forward so that he could light the cigarette. Poor Irving was covered in confusion at this intimate gesture, and Lexi and I exchanged smiles when we saw his blushes.

Mireille had been the centre of interest for my cousins that evening, but Lexi was certainly attracting her fair share of attention. She looked irresistibly fresh and pretty. Seated between an Old Faithful and Bruce Cawardine, she leaned over the table and hissed, '*Meet me in the Motor tomorrow – he's put his hand on my knee!*'

I glanced up at Bruce Cawardine, who wore a faint smile beneath his ginger moustache and looked extremely pleased with himself. I was shocked. We talked all the time about 'affairs' but with an implicit recognition that it wasn't at all the sort of thing that people one *knew* did. The thought that the would-be perpetrator of actual marital infidelity was sitting a few feet away with his hand on Lexi's knee was enough to make the pulse race. Our own examples of the married state were Nim and Beattie, and of course they were quite content.

Our talks about Experience were full of conjecture about these details. Darling Beattie had explained the facts of life with a vague precision: '... You really must be careful, darlings, it can all happen so quickly. You meet a man, you are attracted to him, you give in to him ...'

What did that mean, to 'give in to' him? We weren't entirely sure. For a long time we had thought that women gave birth through the navel.

We had agreed before dinner that we would try to steer the evening's conversation on to topics that would enrage Nim. His political views (so generously imparted to the long-suffering editor of *The Times*) were right-wing in the extreme; dangerously so, perhaps, given the mushrooming of fascism in Europe. He wasn't an unkind man: his devotion to his staff and servants bore witness to that fact, but he had led a very narrow life and there were many things he simply didn't understand. When he read of hunger marches and riots in what were known as 'distressed areas', he would shout, 'Shoot the lot of them!' and march off to his cinema to watch Buster Keaton.

'Oh dear,' Darling Beattie would sigh. 'Ernest is a tiny bit intolerant.'

That evening, Nim was professing to admire the work of the newly elected Adolf Hitler. 'Wonderful work they're doing over there, the National Socialists!' he told a shocked-looking Marjorie Cawardine. 'We could do with someone like that to clean up over here.'

Jack caught my eye and then remarked casually, 'Oh yes, but what a shame about Great-granny Bloomensteiner.'

Marjorie Cawardine looked as if she might faint. From the end of the table, Darling Beattie was trying unsuccessfully to freeze out Jack with one of her looks.

'Oh, didn't you know?' said Jack cheerfully. 'We're one-sixteenth Jewish.'

There was silence at the table.

Then, with perfect timing, Mireille began to laugh.

'Only a joke!' said Jack. 'Of course we're not really!'

Several other people began to laugh, more with relief than mirth. I looked at Mireille admiringly. It had been very clever of her to guess that Jack was only joking and defuse the situation. Lexi looked preoccupied and I began to wonder what was going on underneath the table.

'Perhaps Mireille would care to play for us?' said Darling Beattie. 'Didn't someone once tell me that you were rather musical?'

She was taking pains to make Mireille feel like one of the family, though it seemed the connection was rather vague and she had to prompt Mireille into explaining it to the rest of us over dinner. Mireille's mother had been married briefly to Beattie's second cousin, but had been widowed within a year and had taken her infant daughter to live with her own family, by then in America.

36

Without comment, Mireille walked over to the piano and started to play. Her performance was a revelation to those of us who could just about stumble through 'Für Elise'. For at least forty minutes she played her way tirelessly through Brahms' Hungarian dances and some romantic *lieder* with an exotic, European air, full of melancholy peaks and cadences.

Everyone was listening with their full attention except, perhaps, for Lexi. She had a faraway look as though dreaming of some sublime Experience. Nim stood straight and still beneath the big window, his hands folded behind his back. Darling Beattie was frowning, and the longer Mireille's playing went on, the more she frowned, as though she wanted it to stop. She fondled Flash's ears so firmly and rhythmically that he walked away in protest. I could just see him out of the corner of my eye, rooting around beneath the sofa for Marjorie Cawardine's hand-made chocolates.

Finally the music stopped. Some of the Old Faithfuls clapped and murmured, 'Hear, hear!'

'How lovely!' said Marjorie. 'Did you learn to play like that in . . . where was it you grew up, again . . ? Switzerland?'

Mireille's answer was forestalled by Flash. He was leaning heavily against Marjorie's lap, and as she finished speaking he jutted his big, square head forward, sighed, and regurgitated the chocolates she had brought on to her skirt.

With Nim roaring at Flash and glaring at us lest we have the bad taste to laugh, Darling Beattie rushed across the room to the scene of the accident, brandishing her handkerchief. She dabbed at the stain and apologised repeatedly.

'Let me, Beattie,' said Mireille coolly. She rose from the piano stool and led the whey-faced Marjorie from the room. 'Come up to my room and I'll find a dress you can borrow. I think we're about the same size . . .'

Nim sent for more brandy, but my aunt had decided that for us children the party was over, and sent us off to bed.

'It's always the same,' grumbled Jack, as we walked up the staircase together. 'As soon as something interesting starts to happen, we're shooed away. And if they'd had the sense to let *us* finish off the chocolates, it wouldn't have happened anyway.'

I remember smiling at this characteristic piece of logic, and then pausing on the landing to catch a last snippet of adult conversation. Marjorie Cawardine was in the hall below, radiant in a spotless dress of silver crêpe de Chine. Darling Beattie was with her, still apologising for Flash's offensive behaviour.

'Please don't worry, Beattie dear,' her guest replied. 'Your dear cousin has already done everything that needed to be done.'

37

Four

Mireille de Vere stayed on at Russington.

'Of course, Mireille probably won't want to stay past the weekend,' Darling Beattie said the morning after the dinner party. 'She'll want to go up to Town and see friends, I expect.'

'*Oh!*' wailed Frannie. 'Tell her to stay, Mum! She's so lovely!'

'I won't *tell* her any such thing; it would be rude. Besides, I don't really think we're up to catering for a house guest. It's a busy time on the estate and your father and I both have things we ought to be doing.'

'Oh, please!' wailed Frannie again. 'Ask her!'

Mireille expressed enthusiasm for the idea of an extended visit, and Frannie and I were detailed to unpack some of her larger pieces of luggage. We spread her clothes out on the bed and examined them, sighing and exclaiming by turns. There were fine cambric nightdresses, so different from our regulation Viyella, cashmere sweaters, and gloves and belts made of leather so fine it felt like silk. And in one of the largest cases the shimmer of moiré silk and toile de Jouy revealed a vicuna coat, soft as a puppy's fur.

'Imagine!' said Frannie. 'Imagine owning *things* like these!'

In the days that followed, we talked endlessly about Mireille's 'Beautiful Things', as we termed them, and when Darling Beattie announced that she was taking us in to Oxford to buy clothes, it was to these dizzy heights of elegance that we aspired.

'We don't do Vi-coona here, miss,' said the sales assistant at Gorringe's department store, when I asked. 'We find there's not much call for it.'

She was old and gnarled, with smudged lipstick and a whisker on

38

her chin. I looked at her, then at Lexi and Frannie, who shrugged sympathetically. I was to have a new winter coat, but Darling Beattie, who had been in one of her moods for several days now, was not going to let me choose it.

'Oh, Mother!' said Lexi as the shop assistant trotted out several hideous garments. 'You can't possibly – '

'I think you girls are being very silly indeed,' said Darling Beattie tartly. 'I've had enough of your nonsense. Now, Kitty, how about this one?'

'I quite like that camel coat,' I said, looking in desperation to the rack on the other side of the sales floor. 'Could I – '

'No, I think that one is rather too grown-up for you, darling.'

'Quite so, Lady Winstanley,' said the toady of a sales assistant. 'My own thought exactly. But might I recommend the green for your daughter?'

I was not Darling Beattie's daughter and at that moment, faced with her taste in winter coats, I did not feel much as though I wanted to be. However, she had the good grace not to point out the assistant's mistake, merely smiling and saying, 'Yes, I think we should have a look at the green.'

I put the coat on with reluctance. It was made from tweed of the same bile green as the nursery seat covers. It had a velvet collar and leather buttons and was the same style of outer garment that I had been wearing for the last four years, and that Clem and Shoes still wore. I clenched my teeth when I saw my reflection in the full-length glass.

'Eugh!' said Lexi, who was not given to sparing the feelings of those around her.

Darling Beattie ignored her. 'I think that's very nice, don't you?'

The question was addressed to me, but the shop assistant answered, 'Very nice, yes. Very suitable. Such a good colour for autumn.'

I pictured myself strolling through crisp autumn leaves in my bile-green tweed. My jaw wobbled. I hated it.

'Well, Kitty?'

'She hates it,' said Lexi.

'No ... no, I don't *hate* it, it's just ...'

What could I do? My aunt had taken me into her home and treated me as her own, out of the goodness of her heart. Frannie or Lexi could voice objections, but I couldn't. I had to be grateful.

'... I'm not sure that green suits me, that's all.' I was thinking of Mireille, of course, in her bone white and magnolia and ecru.

'Of course it suits you, silly girl! You've got brown hair ... So! That's decided then, is it? We'll take it ... Kitty?'

'Hmm,' I mumbled.

'Right! What's next?' Darling Beattie consulted her list. 'Underthings. And before you open your mouth, Alexandra, don't even think of silk! There's nothing wrong with lock-weave cotton ...'

It was part of the post-shopping ritual that we were obliged to parade our new clothes for the rest of the family and earn grunts of approval or roars of rage from Nim. Undergarments were excused. Jack saw me in my coat and said I looked like a middle-aged pixie.

I laughed with the others, then went upstairs to my room and slammed the door behind me. I removed the offending garment and threw it across the floor. I stamped on it. Then I thought of Darling Beattie's good intentions, and the love she had shown me over the years, and burst into confused, adolescent tears.

There was a polite tap on the door, which meant the person outside was not a Winstanley.

'May I come in?' asked Mireille.

She could see the tears in my eyes, but had the good taste not to comment. She pointed at the discarded green heap, instead.

'Your new coat?'

I nodded.

'Oh dear ...' She picked it up, and examined it. 'Oh well ... I suppose Beattie knows best.'

Had I imagined it, or was there the tiniest bit of spite in this statement? But no, the voice was as cool and melodious as ever.

'Come on ...' Mireille took me by the hand. 'I think you need a bit of cheering up ...'

She led me to her room and opened the wardrobe where Frannie and I had hung her clothes with such reverence. She started to slide the hangers across the rail, slowly, gracefully.

'It occurs to me, my darling, there is a time in every girl's life when she needs to feel a little special, a little ... how shall I say ..? sophisticated. So I was thinking ...'

As she spoke she pulled one of her furs from the wardrobe, a three-quarter-length jacket in pale, strawberry-blonde fox fur that matched her hair. '... I don't wear this any more. To tell the truth it was always a little short for me. Here – '

She tossed the jacket at me, as if it was a mere rag. 'I want you to have it!'

'But Mireille ... oh, my goodness, a fur! Oh, I don't think I could ...'

But I was already burying my face in the golden pelt.

Lexi and Frannie were outraged at my acceptance of the gift. I was unprepared for their reaction, since they admired Mireille's Beautiful Things, and disdained the green tweed just as I did.

'It's vulgar!' said Lexi, picking up the jacket and sniffing at it. 'Mum says you should only wear a fur if it's dark, like sable or mink. And full-length.'

'You're just jealous,' I said.

'D'you really think you should accept it, though?' Frannie asked hesitantly. 'It must be worth an awful lot of money. And Mummy ... well, it might look a little bit disloyal ...'

I snatched the jacket from Lexi and held it against my chest.

Jack had come into the room and stood between his two sisters. 'I think you should give it back,' he said, fixing me with a direct gaze.

We faced each other and momentarily I didn't feel like a Winstanley at all. 'Well, I'm not going to,' I said. 'It's a lovely present and I'm keeping it.'

It was the first time there had ever been dissension between my cousins and myself.

The gift of a fur mollified my resentment towards my aunt, and I smiled at her benignly when I found her in the drawing room, darning one of Clem's sweaters.

Mireille was also in there, glancing around the room as though waiting to be entertained. Darling Beattie ignored her, snapping a piece of thread viciously with her teeth. The two women, far from behaving like long-lost relatives, did not have a word to say to one another.

I knew instantly that I had stumbled into a sensitive situation. What was more, I was terrified that Mireille would mention the delicate subject of her gift in front of my aunt. I withdrew to the window seat and pretended to study the front cover of *The Field*.

'Oh well ...' Mireille sighed and stood up. 'I'd better make myself useful. Perhaps I'll go along to the kitchen and see if I can teach that cook of yours a thing or two ...' She floated out.

'The nerve of the woman!' muttered Beattie.

When Nim came in, searching for his newspaper, she glanced up at me and said, 'Kitty, dear, would you mind running along for a minute ..?'

41

The look she gave her husband confirmed that what she had to say was not for the benefit of small ears.

I lingered outside the drawing room for a while, long enough to hear most of the taboo conversation.

'... the presumption of the woman!' Darling Beattie was saying. 'It's not as if I *know* her! Her mother was only married to Howard for five minutes; it's a flimsy connection if ever I heard one ... And you know, if there's one thing I can't stand, Ernest, it's people who invite themselves to stay! Telephoning like that! She just wants somewhere convenient to rest her head until she's something better to do!'

'Nevertheless, she is our guest – '

'Our guest! She's *my* relative – *I'm* the one who has to go through the embarrassment of introducing her to my friends as a cousin when I don't know the first thing about her. And by all accounts her mother was a frightful woman – Swiss or something, and didn't speak a word of English.'

'Well, I find her quite civilised for a foreigner. In fact, I can't see what all the fuss is about. She seems to like the little savages, which is quite extraordinary. I find her quite charming, actually.'

'Well you would!' my aunt commented sourly, then added something I couldn't quite hear.

'And the woman's no trouble. Looks after herself – '

'That's precisely what I mean about her being presumptuous! She acts as if she owns the place, while I'm the one who's supposed to be responsible ... Well I don't intend to be any more. *You* can entertain her if you like. I don't want any more to do with the whole business!'

The first of the entertainments that Nim laid on for our unwelcome house guest was a picnic for the entire family, at some unspecified site in the Windrush valley. Darling Beattie's suggestion that we could quite easily carry a hamper into Russington's own grounds and picnic there was shouted down by her offspring. Such a picnic would be tame and unadventurous, they claimed. Consequently the Motor was to have one of its rare outings, with the overspill who could not squeeze on to its well-tended hide seats being transported in a hired charabanc driven by young Tyler, son of the blind gardener.

Frannie, Lexi and I ran upstairs after breakfast to don our finery for Tony's benefit. Being the least smitten, I was beautified and heading for the stairs first, when I tripped over Jack. He was leaning over the banister.

'Look ...' he said, putting out an arm to stop me. 'Mireille's using the telephone.' He pointed down to the hall below.

I was about to ask him why on earth she shouldn't, when something stopped me. The way Mireille was standing there, hunched towards the wall with the receiver cradled under her chin, made it plain that she didn't want to be overheard, or even seen. But the thing that surprised me most was her voice. It was completely different; harsh and guttural and the language unrecognisable. Mireille had said that her second language was French, but this sounded more like German.

She appeared to be pleading, or remonstrating, then her tone became angry.

I was baldly curious, all the more so after overhearing the uncharacteristic outburst from my aunt.

'D'you think she's calling overseas?' I whispered to Jack.

'It wouldn't surprise me.' He curled his lip.

'You don't like Mireille, do you?'

'It's not a question of like or dislike. I don't trust her. She's stayed on here for a reason.'

I wanted him to explain, but he turned and ran down the stairs before I had a chance to ask. Mireille hastily hung up the receiver.

We were all kept waiting by Lexi, who finally appeared to a chorus of grumbles wearing a bewitching straw hat and the merest hint of Blood Roses on her lips. She positioned herself at the centre of the Motor's back seat, in full view of Tony's driving mirror, between Mireille, Darling Beattie and Miss Howland. Nim sat at the front with Tony, and the rest of us climbed into the charabanc, which was cramped but a lot more fun to ride in on a glorious July morning.

Nim insisted on a maximum speed of thirty miles an hour, so we made our way like a stately royal progress along the ridge of the Cotswolds. Halfway between Burford and Minster Lovell we turned off the main road and wound our way down bumpy tracks to the bottom of the river valley, until Nim told Tony to come to a halt.

Arguments ensued, inevitably.

'Not here!' complained sundry Winstanleys. 'Not in a field. So dull!'

'Lots of lovely shade,' pointed out Darling Beattie, and Miss Howland sighed in agreement.

43

'But we want to swim!' said Jack.

'I really don't know, darling, the river bottom is so very muddy and damp. Not at all a good idea, when Mireille's in her good shoes ... and white ones, too.'

Mireille moved her spotless parasol slightly so that the sunlight fell across her pale face. 'I think we should go down to the river,' she said.

'Very well,' agreed Darling Beattie, tight-lipped. 'Ask Tony to motor as far as that gate, Ernest dear, then we can carry our things down to the bank.'

Tony carried the hamper, and a rug, which he spread out in the shade of a horse chestnut. The rest of us ran behind with shooting sticks, a gramophone and cushions. I carried Flash's water bowl and my camera.

'Well, this is nice!' Darling Beattie sat down self-consciously on the rug and patted it. Mireille placed a folding canvas chair in the tallest grass and sheltered beneath her parasol, looking like a participant in a big game shoot. Jack and Irving tried to coerce Flash into chasing moorhens, but he flung himself, panting, on to the rug between Frannie and Darling Beattie and closed his eyes. His nose twitched slightly as Miss Howland opened up the hamper and started to reveal the horrors that Cook had in store for us.

'Time for luncheon, I think,' said Darling Beattie, who had been stroking Frannie's hair in a distracted fashion. '... Ginger beer anyone .. ? Put that camera away, Kitty dear. Not very nice to have pictures of us eating ...'

We drank ginger beer and pink lemonade and chewed our way through Cook's leathery sandwiches and cement-like pies in near-silence. There was a tension in the air, as though the strong sunlight was making everyone's moods and feelings obvious to the naked eye. Darling Beattie fidgeted and fussed more than usual, and Nim seemed unable to sit still, pacing up and down the river bank, raising imaginary sights at any waterfowl that stirred. Irving, still in the grip of his adolescent crush, positioned himself in Mireille's orbit and pretended so hard not to be staring at her that he quite failed to notice the piece of game pie he had dropped on her pristine white shoe.

Jack noticed it. Jack noticed everything. He leaned against the trunk of a rowan tree and he stared at Mireille, too, only his was a hostile, watchful stare.

I took a photograph of him, then one of Mireille. I was just lining up a shot of Clem and Flash together when Lexi materialised at my elbow.

44

'*Tony*!' she hissed.

'What?'

'Tony – he's disappeared!'

I frowned. 'Well, he'll be back, won't he? He's probably just gone to stretch his legs.'

Lexi raised a finger to her lips, flinging a warning glance in the direction of Darling Beattie. 'Let's see if we can find him. And bring your camera ...'

'*Shhh*!'

After some frantic eyeball rolling and beckoning we managed to summon Frannie, and the three of us set off down the towpath. Behind us we could hear shouts and splashes as Irving and Jack plunged in for a swim.

'Wait a minute!' said Lexi, stopping us dead. She reached into her pocket and took out a compact and her Blood Roses. Holding the mirror up to the sun, she daubed the lipstick expertly on to her mouth. I looked on in disgust at this display of vanity and Frannie said, 'Can I try some?'

'No,' replied Lexi firmly. 'It would look completely silly. Your nose is all sunburnt.'

'Sorry,' said Frannie.

We walked on further until we spotted Tony, on the other side of some weeping willows that trailed their leaves in the water. He had unfastened his tie and top button, and was rubbing his hand across the back of his neck as though trying to dispel the heat. He took rolling paper and tobacco from his waistcoat pocket and rolled a cigarette.

We hung back, screened from him by the leafy fronds of willow.

'D'you think we should go and talk to him?' asked Frannie.

'*Shhh*!' hissed Lexi. 'Don't be ridiculous!'

Tony took the cigarette from his lips, pinched it with two fingers and threw it into the river, where it floated conspicuously on the brownish water.

'Naughty, naughty!' commented Lexi.

'Look, he's taking his tie off,' whispered Frannie. 'He must be awfully hot in his suit. I wouldn't like to be a chauffeur in this weather.'

'Driver,' said Lexi.

Tony draped his tie carefully over a bush, then took off his jacket and dropped it on to the grass. He stared at the water for a moment, then seemed stirred into action. He started to unbutton his shirt.

I said, 'He's going to swim.'

Frannie said, 'Look at his chest!'

Lexi said, 'Take a photograph quick!... OH!'

Tony had now removed his trousers and was standing on the very edge of the bank in his baggy cotton undershorts. Then, before our bedazzled pubescent eyes, he hooked his thumbs into the waistband of his shorts and pulled them down, revealing muscular buttocks that gleamed bluey-white in the strong sunshine.

It hardly needs saying that none of us had seen a man's naked rear before. Or his front.

'What if he turns round?' whispered Frannie faintly.

'I hope he does.'

'*Lexi!*'

'Well, I want to know what *it* looks like, and so do you, I bet, if only you'd have the nerve to admit it. Take a photo, Kitty ...'

I was in the middle of explaining how I couldn't possibly ask Mr Munson, the local photographic expert, to develop pictures of a naked man, when Tony sprang up on his toes and dived into the water. We stared expectantly at the muddy swirls. He surfaced a few seconds later, his dark hair made black and sleek by the water, clinging to his temples.

'He's beautiful,' I said.

'I'm in love with him,' said Frannie.

Tony raised his chin and spat out the river water in a fountain.

'He'll have to get out some time,' observed Lexi, a smile of pleasurable anticipation playing round her Blood Rose lips. 'And then we'll see everything.'

'Not necessarily,' said Frannie. 'Not if he gets out on the other bank.'

'Why would he do that, stupid? His clothes are on this side!'

'Well ... he might climb out backwards.'

Lexi laughed, as though she already had some deep insight into masculinity that the rest of us lacked. Tony splashed around for a few minutes longer, then quite abruptly, stood up and waded to the bank.

Water streamed down his chest and from his armpits, the backs of his knees. I remember noting the way it ran in two neat rivulets to the dark hair of his groin, then I instinctively averted my gaze. Frannie gasped and shut her eyes tight. Only Lexi really looked. She even tilted back the brim of her straw hat so that she could see better. Her gaze was curious, steady. But then that was what I would have expected. I had never once seen her lose her composure.

'It looks so small,' she said finally, 'from here.'

Tony, rubbing himself down with his handkerchief, glanced in

46

our direction. We edged back a bit then started to hurry back along the path. My camera was thumping against my chest, and I started to giggle. So did the others, and soon we were flinging ourselves down on the grass laughing uncontrollably.

'Well,' said Frannie when we had calmed down, 'that's what I call real Experience!'

Jack strolled towards us, his hair damp with river water and a towel slung around his neck. 'What have you been up to?' he wanted to know, and looked annoyed when our only response was more giggling. Nim was asleep in the grass with his sola topi over his eyes, and Darling Beattie and Miss Howland looked as though they would do the same if this could be achieved without loss of dignity. Clem and Shoes buzzed around them restlessly, like flies.

'Why don't you play a game, dears?' asked Darling Beattie. When she saw the look that crossed one or two of our faces she added, '... A nice, quiet game. Irving, you think of something, darling.'

'Don't look at me,' said Irving. 'Games are for kids.'

From the shaded sanctum of her parasol, Mireille smiled slightly. 'I think playing a game is an excellent idea.'

'Well, some games are all right,' said Irving.

'"Tell a Sad Story"!' cried Shoes, who had always had a morbid streak. 'Let's play "Tell a Sad Story"!'

This rather curious game was a Winstanley invention. The players took it in turns to volunteer a story, and each narrator was to dwell on the horrific or pathetic elements of the story. When he stopped or was interrupted, the next player in the sequence had to add a piece of embroidery to the tale, and this 'tragedy capping' continued until the story reached its logical end.

Lexi started. 'A jealous husband once caught his wife with a lover. But he didn't kill her. He shut her up in a cupboard that was shaped like a coffin, just off his own study, and he fed her the minimum amount of food required to keep her alive ...'

'He kept her dressed in rags,' went on Frannie. 'And every day he forced her to mend the silk dress that she had been wearing on the day she was caught with her lover ...'

'She turned the seams so many times that the dress was almost worn away to nothing,' I added, 'and the silk was stained with her lover's blood.'

'All brown stains, all horrid,' said Shoes.

'... And the reason that she never cried out for help was her husband had cut out her tongue!'

'Goodness me!' Frowning, Mireille lit a cigarette, and the

pungent tobacco mingled with the scent of sun-warmed grass. 'I'm not sure that I like this game.'

'Here's another one,' said Irving, chewing on a stalk and trying not to look at Mireille. 'A husband is so devoted to his wife that he goes out to buy her cigarettes while she's in bed . . .' He cleared his throat and blushed. '. . . With her lover.'

' – in the pouring rain!'

' – in a blizzard!'

' – and one day she asks him if he doesn't mind waiting outside on the street until her lover has left,' offered Jack. 'The wife and the lover forget all about him and he's out there so long, he dies of cold . . ! Right, let's play something else. The Truth Game!'

Miss Howland had lit the gas primus and was heating water for tea. The kettle made a pleasant, sleepy hum as it reached the boil.

'The Truth Game, the Truth Game!' chorused Clem and Shoes.

'Right,' said Jack, straightening up from the position he had been lying in, with Flash's comatose body as a pillow. 'We now have to tell the truth, the whole truth and nothing but the truth, for the rest of the day. Starting with you, Lexi. What were you three doing when you disappeared after lunch? Tell the truth now!'

'We were – '

'*Lexi*!'

I hissed a warning as Darling Beattie approached with a tray. 'Tea anyone?'

Lexi took a cup and passed it to me, whispering in my ear. 'We don't have to say anything about his you-know-what!'

'Come on, Lex!'

'We were watching Tony take a swim,' said Lexi. 'That's all.'

So much for the whole truth.

Jack seemed satisfied, but I noticed a look in his eye that was all too familiar. 'Your turn now, Mireille. Who were you talking to on the phone this morning?'

There was a second's silence.

'Jack!' said Irving, blushing at his brother's insensitivity to his heroine. 'Steady on!'

'It's all right,' said Mireille. There was a moment's tell-tale hesitation as we waited to hear what her answer would be. 'Marjorie Cawardine very kindly asked if I would like to join their bridge game, and I was telephoning her to refuse. That's all.'

'That's not true,' Jack said coldly. 'You're supposed to tell the truth!'

'*Jack*!'

Mireille stood up, looking hurt. She took down her parasol and

48

shook its lace-trimmed folds. 'I've told you the answer. I'm sorry. I'm afraid I don't really understand what you want me to say.'

'It's only a game,' said Irving.

Mireille had moved away and was offering cologne and tablets to Miss Howland, who had suffered a touch of heat stroke.

'She wasn't talking to Mrs Cawardine,' Jack insisted, raising his voice so that everyone would hear. 'Was she, Kitty? You were there ...'

I was reluctant to get involved, and waited for Darling Beattie to intervene with a reprimand before I answered. But it was Nim who called a halt to the proceedings. He had been studying the horizon with his field glasses and it wasn't possible to tell whether he had been listening to us or not. Suddenly he rose from his shooting stick, and said, 'I can see Tyler coming with the charabanc, to take some of you away. Good. The rest of you savages had better go and get into the Motor!'

'I don't really care about her not telling the truth,' Lexi confided as we bounced our way back to Russington in the charabanc. 'But poor Mireille, she doesn't really have a sense of humour, does she?'

She hadn't, and it made her stand out from the rest of us like a sore thumb. But then Jack hadn't displayed much humour when we were playing the Truth Game that afternoon. As I was lying in bed that night, I found myself thinking about this, and about his claim that she was untrustworthy. He was the most quick-witted of us all: he must have seen or heard something the rest of us had missed.

And I was feeling guilty. Mireille had been kind to me and I had eavesdropped on her.

I even worried that she might ask me to give back the fur jacket. I climbed out of bed and looked at it hanging in my wardrobe. I stroked a sleeve. Through the darkness I could hear Frannie's heavy, rhythmic breathing, but I was too restless to sleep myself. It was a warm night and I felt thirsty. I set off in search of a drink.

Half way along the landing, I stopped dead. Darling Beattie had accepted Marjorie Cawardine's invitation to play bridge, and had gone out; I had seen her with my own eyes. But the light was on in her room and she was in there, moving about.

I looked round the door. There was Mireille, standing in front of the big wardrobe with her back to me. She was stripped down to her duchesse satin petticoat, and her dress had been tossed carelessly on to the bed. And, as I had done when Lexi and Frannie first took me in there years ago, she was staring at Darling Beattie's collection of gowns.

She lifted one out, a complicated creation of crunchy pink tulle sewn with beads. It was not a Mireille-ish sort of dress but, even so, she held it out in front of her and stepped into it, into Darling Beattie's dress. It fitted her slim figure closely, but was a little too short. She sniffed at it once it was on, as if acknowledging that it wasn't her own.

The ivory cigarette holder had been left on the edge of the dressing table, with a cigarette smouldering away in it. Mireille picked it up and flicked the tell-tale trace of ash away with her fingers. She sucked hard on the thin ivory tube as she contemplated her costume in the looking glass. She was smiling a mocking smile as she did so, as though the borrowed dress was part of pretending to be someone else . . .

The idea of her looking as my aunt must once have looked made my spine prickle. It occurred to me that I ought to warn her, before anyone else saw her, that no one was allowed to touch those dresses. But I didn't want her to think I was a habitual snoop. I stepped back and pulled the door to very gently, so that the light wouldn't be so obvious.

Irving was on the landing.

'Is Mother back?' he asked. 'I didn't hear the Motor.'

'Just closing the door to keep the moths out,' I answered. 'I'm on my way to get some water.'

Irving walked past the door in question and headed for his own room. I felt great relief, not least because in protecting Mireille I felt that I had somehow made up for overhearing her phone call.

I tiptoed to the kitchen, and as I passed the drawing room I saw that the French windows were opened wide on to the terrace. I could just glimpse a blob of white at the top of the steps. I blinked at it until I could discern that the white was Nim's dress shirt. I remember being deeply shocked by the fact that his sleeves were rolled up, but then the night was hot and close. One hand was resting on a stone pineapple at the top of the balustrade, the other held the ubiquitous cigar. He seemed to be staring towards the park gates, waiting for something – or someone.

Five

'I wish I was older', Frannie lamented to me as we lay in the shade of the Portugal laurel a few weeks later. 'I wish I wasn't thirteen.'

It was a baking, windless day in early August, and we had been allowed to concede some of our modesty and wear shorts. They were made of pink gingham and shaped like babies' rompers. We leaned against the trunk of the tree with our naked legs stretched out before us. I was studying them thoughtfully. They looked like four uncooked sausages, I decided. Chubby and plumpish and faintly mottled. And too pale. Lexi said it was ghastly and unsophisticated to have pale legs.

'I wish I was twenty-one,' I said, 'and I could do anything I liked.'

'What would you do?'

'I'd make a bowl of cake mixture and eat it all raw. All of it.'

'If I was twenty-one, I'd have as many pets as I liked,' said Frannie. 'And they'd all be allowed to sleep on my bed.'

'I'd have a new dress made every week, by a couturier.'

'So would I.' Frannie sighed, examining the freckles on her forearms. 'And do you know how I'd test them out? I'd ask Tony up for cocktails in my room, and ask him what he thought of them!'

'How old would *he* be, then, if we were twenty-one ..?'

Frannie and I were feeling our age, acutely. A small dance was being held at one of the houses in the district and only Lexi was allowed to go, because she was sixteen, and almost old enough to be 'out'. The rest of us were very much 'in'.

To make matters worse, Lexi was being allowed a new dress. Not from horrible old Gorringe's in Oxford, but from a proper dressmaker, in London. She was going up on the train for a day, just to be fitted. *Unaccompanied.* Darling Beattie was prevented from going by an important meeting of the parish council, so she had given her daughter strict instructions to take a taxi to the dressmaker, who would duly escort her back to Paddington afterwards.

'It's not fair,' I said, for the tenth time that day.

'At least Lexi will be able to tell us all about it when she gets back. She might even have had some Experiences. I hope so, because I'm running out of material for my play.'

Lexi returned at seven o'clock that evening. She strolled into the front hall with her jacket over her shoulder and started up the stairs, cool as a cucumber.

The others were all playing British bulldog on the croquet lawn, but Frannie and I had been lying in wait for hours, in the drawing room, to ambush Lexi and indulge in a feast of vicarious thrills.

'Oh, hullo,' she said when she saw us, and continued to walk up the stairs.

'*Lexi!*'

We pelted up the staircase after her. She was trying to be cool and grown-up, as always, but I saw the tell-tale twitching round the corners of her mouth, which signalled her suppressed excitement.

'Lexi – what happened? You've got to tell us!'

She stared at us frostily for a second, then broke into a grin. 'Oh, all right! Come into the schoolroom and I'll tell you all about it!'

The sun had been beating down on the schoolroom windows all day, and the air trapped behind the tapestry curtains had a stale, baked feeling to it. Nevertheless, the three of us climbed on to the window seat and pulled the curtains around us, to make a hot, stuffy little cave. The Winstanleys were fervent respecters of their own traditions.

'Tell us about your dress!' said Frannie. She blew upwards at her fringe, trying to stop it sticking to her forehead.

'Never mind about the dress, ask me what happened on the train!'

'What happened on the train?'

'I met a man!'

'You mean ... an Experience?'

Lexi nodded slowly, lifting her blue velvet Alice band forward and using it to push back a few stray blonde strands from her forehead. Not that she was sweating, like we were. Lexi would never sweat.

'Tell us!' we pleaded.

'Well ...' Lexi leaned back so that her head was resting against a wood-panelled shutter. 'Mum said I mustn't sit in a carriage on my own, or with a man. She said I was to choose a respectable-looking lady and sit near her.'

'Preferably a married lady, over the age of forty-five,' said Frannie, who had overheard this conversation.

'Yes. But, really, all the married women looked so horribly dull, as if they were on their way to the public library or something! And I couldn't always see whether they were wearing a wedding ring, so they might not have been married at all.'

'Like Miss Bean?' I said, and we all shuddered.

'Beastly old lesbian ... anyway, married women always seemed to be with other married women, so there wasn't any room. I shouldn't think Mum wanted me to sit on their laps ... So, I walked right down the train, and in the last carriage there was a respectable looking man, and a nun.'

'Perfect!' said Frannie. She had taken out her notebook and was making notes for the elopement scene of her play. I privately doubted the existence of the nun.

'... Anyway, the train stopped at Reading and guess what?'

'The nun got out?' I suggested.

'*Exactly* ... I took out my book and started to read, but the man leaned forward and spoke to me.'

'What was he like?' asked Frannie, pencil poised.

'Handsome!' said Lexi without hesitation. 'Oldish, but handsome. Sort of like Mr Rochester – you know, dark and brooding – but wearing a chalk-stripe suit and black shoes, the ones with a pattern of holes punched in the toes.'

'Slow down a bit, I'm still on *"the nun got out at Reading"* ...'

One was forced to admire Lexi's power of total recall. She made sure she had our attention, then went on. 'He said wasn't it hot in the carriage, and did I mind if he opened the window a bit? Then he looked at my book and said he'd always found Mrs Gaskell such a *passionate* writer.'

'Imagine that,' whispered Frannie, scribbling away. '*Passionate.*'

'... I pretended to be reading my book, but I could see him staring at me, out of the corner of my eye. All the way to London. When the train came in to Paddington, he leaned forward and put his hand on my knee and said, "I shall be procuring myself a cab. You must let me convey you to wherever you wish to go." I wasn't going to say "yes", then I thought that if I saved the taxi fare Mummy had given me, I could buy myself some of those lovely *peau d'ève* knickers that Mireille wears. I said, "Yes, please, I will.

Be kind enough to drop me at Mrs Moira Soames's salon in Farm Street." We drove off – '

'Were you sitting next to him?' Frannie interjected.

'Of course I was sitting next to him, we were in the back of a cab! Don't interrupt . . ! Then he told the driver to stop, and I said, "Oh, are we in Farm Street then?" And he said, "No, this is my house." It was rather a grand place, Kensington or somewhere I think.'

'Oh my goodness!' Frannie and I exchanged gleeful looks and hugged our knees tighter. 'Weren't you scared?'

'Of course not! I remembered what Mum says about a lady never forgetting her manners, whatever the situation. I pretended to myself that he'd just offered me a cup of tea, and I said, "If it's all the same to you, I'd rather go straight on to Farm Street. If you don't mind." And he sort of looked at me, then he kissed me smack on the lips. And bolted from the cab like a frightened rabbit. I ended up having to pay the driver so I couldn't buy any new knickers after all. Pity, really.'

'Wait a minute, wait a minute . . . ' complained Frannie. 'Go back to when he kissed you. What was it like?'

'Rather awful, actually. He tried to put his tongue inside my mouth.'

'Oh!' said Frannie. Then, 'What for?'

Two days later, Lexi set off on yet another Experience-culling trip, to the dance. She was dressed in Mrs Soames's best work; a flowered chiffon with a shirred bodice. Once more we lay in wait for her, notebook at the ready, and did our best to drag information from her.

'What was the dance like?' She repeated our question as she flung her stole down on to her bed. 'Oh, that. Boring. Fergus Bleak-Wailer treading on my feet all evening.'

But she was smiling. We waited, patient, in the hope of new revelations.

'Shall I tell you what the best part was?' She sat down on the edge of the bed and eased off her high-heeled dance pumps with a grimace of pain. 'It was when Tony came to collect me afterwards. He stopped the Motor on the way back and we had a cigarette together.'

'A *cigarette*!' I almost fainted with shock.

'It's not fair!' moaned Frannie. 'A cigarette, with Tony!'

Later, when we crept back into our own bedroom, Frannie flung herself on to her knees and clasped her hands together.

'What are you doing?' I asked, as if it wasn't obvious.

'Praying,' she replied. 'Praying that something interesting happens to us.'

With amazing speed, her prayers were answered. Nim announced, as if it was no business of ours, that he was taking us all off to Rome for a month. Then he returned to reading his copy of the *The Times*, leaving us all agog. We were going to be Abroad, a state of affairs even more exciting than being 'Out'.

'Just a quiet family holiday,' said Darling Beattie. She turned away from the table to offer Flash her porridge bowl to lick. There was a pause, then without looking up she added, 'You will come with us, of course, Mireille?'

'Yes, thank you, I'd like to very much. I have friends in Rome.'

'That will be very pleasant for you then.' Her tone was cold. 'And very convenient. One would be able to take a train directly from there back to Lausanne, I shouldn't wonder.'

'Yes,' said Mireille, smiling. 'One would.'

Nim had sold off a few portraits of liverish ancestors in order to pay for our summer accommodation. He had rented a secluded villa on the Aventine hill, a few miles outside Rome on the road to Viareggio. The grandeur of the situation was enhanced by the grounds, like an oversized garden planted with elms, chestnuts and cypresses, bays, myrtles and pomegranates – in whose shade stood statues, fountains, grottoes and pavilions. The villa itself had porticoed colonnades and a long pergola covered with vines, jasmine and pink, white and red climbing roses.

'Listen!' said Frannie as we sat under the pergola on our first evening. The air was humming with a thousand cicada wings. 'Isn't it magical! It's the sort of place where one ought to fall in love, I should think!'

'Pity *he's* not here,' sighed Lexi, *sotto voce* so that Darling Beattie wouldn't hear.

Tony had been left behind, as had Aunt Griz and Miss Howland, who travelled very badly, and whose ankles swelled in hot weather. To take her place, Nim had hired an Italian chaperone to oversee our activities; a local girl called Grazia. She was short and plump with coarse dark hair and a round, cheerful face, and her earnest attempts to acquaint us with Rome and its culture endeared her to us at once, though had she not been there, we would probably

55

have been content to sit around in the shade of the statues and gorge ourselves on squashy green figs. Grazia was serious about her education and intended one day to teach at a college or university, a fact which made her something of a maverick in her own community. Rough, ignorant pre-unification Italy was not ready to acknowledge members of her sex anywhere but in the kitchen.

Grazia took us walking in the Borghese Gardens, where our cotton sunhats and sensible sandals must have made us seem a sombre little group in contrast with the handsome, frivolous Romans. Then she would lead us through narrow side streets so that we could see bourgeois, fascist Rome betraying its peasant origins in the *trattorie* and *osterie* that still had drifts of sawdust on the floor.

One day we wandered as far as Trastevere, the uncharted territory on the left bank of the Tiber, which had a wonderfully outlawed, gypsy feel to it. Through ground-floor windows defended by stout iron grilles we could see big fireplaces with blackened country cooking pots suspended over fires, and we would sigh and lick our lips at the wonderful smell of garlic. Darling Beattie wouldn't countenance garlic at the villa, and we decided this must be out of fear of its aphrodisiac powers, duly noted when we reached 'G' in our study of the *Encyclopaedia*.

With our wholehearted approval, Grazia hitched a ride for all of us on a wagon bringing wine from the Castelli Romani and we squeezed in among the barrels. The carter then fell asleep, and the horse plodded on regardless.

Once we were back on the right bank, Grazia took us to see a place called the Cellata. 'This hospital was founded in 1770,' she told us.

'I didn't know they had hospitals in those days,' said Irving. 'I thought they just died at home.'

'It was a lying-in hospital, for unmarried mothers.'

A ripple of interest went through Grazia's audience as we caught a whiff of scandal. She went on, 'The mothers were not required to give their names. They could wear a veil over their face so that no one would ever know their identity, and they were known by a number. It was rumoured that some of the women were very well born ... They couldn't keep their babies, of course – '

'Oh no, how sad!' said Frannie.

' – they were given to the orphanage of San Spirito. Or if the baby or the mother died, they were buried in unmarked graves.'

Grazia couldn't have calculated for the Winstanley taste, but even if she had known us for years she could hardly have picked a more suitable piece of history. This was exactly the sort of thing we loved.

'Clever Grazia,' said Shoes. 'Just like "Tell a Sad Story".'

Mireille didn't join us on these expeditions. She preferred to go shopping in the Corso or to pay visits to friends, faded members of the Roman aristocracy whom we never met.

'I think she's got a lover,' Lexi announced one evening, when she and Jack and I were sitting on the veranda. Or lying, in Lexi's case: she was in a hammock. We were feasting on hard, sweet Pratese biscuits, dipping them into red wine until they turned pink, then sucking the liquid out of them.

'But seriously, haven't you noticed the way she's been behaving?' Lexi persisted.

'Perhaps the climate suits her,' I said, ever reluctant to take sides, but privately I agreed that Mireille's behaviour was rather odd. Whereas in England she was cool and languid, content to sit around for hours and read or play the piano, in Italy she seemed charged with energy, playful, almost flirtatious.

'You should have heard her singing yesterday when she was getting dressed up to go out. She *must* have been on her way to a secret assignation!'

Jack had been sitting silently for a while, listening. Then he grinned and said, 'Well, don't let old Irvie baby hear you talking like that, will you, Lex! He's still mooning over her; that's something else I've noticed.'

Lexi gave her sweet biscuit a long, thoughtful suck. 'It's his age,' she said with sisterly condescension.

Whatever the reason, Irving had certainly been moody and bad-tempered. And when squabbles had arisen, there had been no one there to adjudicate. Mireille was not interested, Darling Beattie suffered from the heat and spent most of the day in her room, and Nim was preoccupied with errands of his own. When we weren't going on cultural expeditions with Grazia, we tended to split up and go our separate ways in a natural attempt to defuse tension. And for the first time in several years, I found myself spending time alone with Jack.

It started one afternoon when I was bored. Frannie and I were sitting under the pergola and Frannie was reading aloud from a book about the history of Rome.

'"... *At the Mamertime prison, prisoners were thrown in by a hole in the floor, where they waited death by starvation, or at the hands of an executioner in the charnel house below"* . . . Oh, Kitty, how dreadful, don't you think . . ?'

'Mmm . . .' I said, fiddling with the lens on my camera, holding it up to my eye and focusing it to different distances.

' . . . It's just like a Sad Story, listen to this: *"Jugurtha fell naked through the hole exclaiming, 'Oh Hercules, how cold your bath is!'"* . . . Is that correct English, Kitty, *"How cold your bath is!"*? . . . Shouldn't it be *"How cold is your bath!"*? . . . Anyway . . . *"He died of starvation six days later."* Goodness, poor Jugurtha . . !'

I wandered off into the garden, holding up my camera every so often and lining up imaginary shots. My favourite place was the kitchen garden, which smelt how I imagined heaven must smell. The air was heavy with sun-warmed basil and the spicy, faintly sweet smell of *rugetta*, a salad vegetable. I went there now and watched the tiny lizards darting about on the south-facing wall that ran along its perimeter. The lizards fascinated me, but they were not easy subjects for a would-be photographer. They moved so quickly, and unpredictably.

After a few minutes I abandoned my attempts at photographing the wildlife and concentrated on eating instead. There were large, ripe tomatoes growing in rows, their scarlet flesh slightly dusty. I picked one and held it against my cheek; it felt warm.

A split second before I looked up, I was aware of someone watching me. It was Jack.

He gave me a strange little smile and his voice was gentle . . . 'Shall I tell you something?' he said. 'Standing there like that, you look quite pretty.'

I felt colour flooding into my cheeks and I stared fixedly at the tomato, as though there were something quite riveting about it. I had never thought of myself as pretty before, and certainly no one had ever told me I was.

'Not very pretty,' Jack added hastily. 'Just quite.'

'Oh.'

'I think it must be the tomato. It makes your cheeks look a nice colour . . . wait a minute . . .'

He strode over to the fig tree and pulled down a couple of figs. ' . . . Let me do a controlled experiment.' He sat me down on a low wall and held the greenish figs against my cheeks. 'No, that doesn't look the same at all. Looks sort of sickly.'

Unable to think of anything else to do, I ate one of the figs, then the other. Jack was wandering away again, seemingly having lost interest. 'Don't eat too many of those,' he called over his shoulder. 'Bad for the bowels.'

'Bloody Huns!' said Nim at breakfast the next morning. 'they've got a damned nerve, I'll say that for them!'

He was referring to an article in *The Times* about Hitler's proposed Nuremberg Laws outlawing the Jews.

The housekeeper, Angelina, offered him *espresso* and he waved it away in disgust. 'Take that filthy muck away, and bring me some tea, for God's sake. Tea's the only drink fit for an Englishman!'

I suspected that Nim rather enjoyed the pose of the eccentric Englishman abroad, and played up to it. Certainly, when he was out and about in the city he made a big show of not understanding anything that was said to him, and cursing publicly any and every un-English habit. 'Can't think who said that nonsense about "When in Rome ... "' he said when Lexi and I were in town with him one afternoon. 'Load of old rubbish.'

We were strolling down the Via Fratini, looking in the windows of the fabulous shops. Lexi and I sighed with longing over the lovely clothes and shoes, and Nim roared with indignation at the prices.

'Thieving bloody foreigners!' he said. 'Sharp operators! Infernal weather!' He seemed to be enjoying himself enormously.

We turned into the Via Condotti and passed a smart gentleman's outfitters. Lexi looked in the window at the display of fine silk cravats in brilliant colours. 'Oh look, Nim, for you! Do let's go in!'

Nim snorted with contempt. 'Italian men dress like gigolos!' he said. But he followed us into the shop.

'Something for milord?' murmured the sales assistant with the sort of continental oiliness my uncle most despised. 'A fine figure of a man, if I may be so bold.'

'Not at these prices, you mountebank!' growled Nim, but I caught him glancing at his reflection in one of the tall looking-glasses. He picked up a panama hat and balanced it thoughtfully on his head. 'How do I look?' he asked Lexi.

'It suits you,' she said, trying to catch my eye. 'I think you should buy it, don't you, Kit?'

'Oh yes,' I said. 'And a cravat.'

Nim seemed to have been sidetracked by the spirit of Rome, finally. He allowed the assistant to bring out a selection of the cravats and arrange them fussily around his neck. In the end he bought the hat and a sapphire-blue cravat and wore them out of the shop. He looked at himself in the mirror again as we left, smiling this time.

'What do you think?' he asked.

I was surprised. Not because he had actually parted with money for the goods, which was surprising enough in itself, but because it had never occurred to me before that Nim was vain.

A few days later, Nim dressed himself up in his new hat and cravat and announced that he was going into the city directly after lunch to attend to some business. He telephoned for a taxi and we sat on the veranda and watched the taxi disappear down the hill in a cloud of fine, yellowish dust.

Directly the taxi had disappeared, Mireille jumped to her feet and began to pace up and down as though charged with an invisible source of energy.

Her restlessness irritated Darling Beattie, who was sitting with her feet up and a damp towel draped over her temples. Clem was fanning her with a copy of the *Boy's Own Annual* as she sipped cold lemonade.

'And you, Mireille, dear? Shall you go into town? Do you have friends to visit today?'

She opened her eyes wide enough to fix her cousin with an inquisitorial share.

'No, no, I don't think so.' Mireille made a big show of looking for one of her gloves. 'I think I shall go and write some letters.'

She retreated to her room.

A few minutes later, Darling Beattie fell victim once more to the strong afternoon sun, and announced that she was going to lie down in a darkened room. Clem followed in her wake like a single chick behind a hen. Frannie and Lexi were reading in the shade of the pergola.

'Looks like it's just you and me then,' Jack said to me. 'Feel like a game of cards?'

We played several rounds of Beggar my Neighbour, and then I asked rather shyly if Jack would let me take some photographs of him. He agreed, and made a very good subject because of the quality of stillness about his face when he was thinking his own private thoughts.

'Move over and sit on the wall, will you, so that I can get the sun behind you and the hill in the background ... Oh, goodness!'

I had spotted something in the viewfinder as I adjusted the focus on the shot. A small dark shape moving around in the background.

'Look, Jack!' I put the camera down and pointed. He followed my finger with his eyes, screwing them up against the sun.

'It's Mireille.'

Quickly, I put the telescopic lens on the camera and looked

through the viewfinder again. It *was* Mireille, dressed in a suit and large black hat. She was walking quickly down the path to the main road, glancing over her shoulder every now and then. Finally a car came into view and stopped for her. She climbed into it and it disappeared in the direction of Rome.

I waited for Jack to make some snide comment. But he jumped off the wall, his lips pressed together as though he were angry, and walked into the villa.

It was Grazia's day off, and the task of assembling everyone for supper fell to Darling Beattie. At half past six she came on to the veranda, where I was still sitting, reading and slapping at the occasional mosquito. It was dusk and the noise of the cicadas was deafening.

'Has your uncle returned yet?' she asked.

'No, I don't think so.'

'Goodness, how annoying! We may have to start without him . . . I take it Irving has gone for a bath?'

'Irving?'

'Yes, dear, Lexi said he was with you, outside.'

I put down my book. 'I don't know what made her say that. The only person who's been out here with me is Jack . . . '

Darling Beattie went inside again, looking harassed, and a lot of noise ensued when Irving could not be found, not anywhere.

Discussion of possible errands he might have undertaken was interrupted by Darling Beattie saying suddenly, angrily, 'He's with *her*, I know he is!'

'With who?'

'With *whom*, you mean . . . '

'With Mireille, of course!' said Darling Beattie fiercely. 'I've seen the way he looks at her, and *she*, well – '

'Is there a problem, Beattie dear?'

Mireille's cool voice, from the doorway. She stood there in her linen suit, immaculate as always. The hat was gone. I noticed a greyish smear of dust on the toes of her shoes.

My aunt looked as though she had seen an apparition, and was too overcome to speak.

'It's Irving,' explained Frannie. 'He's disappeared.'

Mireille took charge at once, organising us into search parties, insisting that there was a perfectly logical explanation. Then she stayed with the near-hysterical Beattie while the rest of us went to look outside.

'He's probably drunk too much wine and fallen asleep under an olive tree somewhere,' said Jack, who was my partner in the search.

There was a farm in the grounds of the villa, supplying it with produce, and we had volunteered to search its buildings.

'Listen!' said Jack, as we skirted the edge of the barn. 'Do you hear that?'

There was a rustling sound coming from inside.

'Mice,' I said, but Jack laughed in my face. He switched on the flashlight, and opened the barn door slowly. There was a large heap of clothing on the straw bales, which moved around and turned out to be Irving and Grazia, locked in a close embrace. Grazia's skirt was twisted around her thighs and I noticed what a pretty brown colour her bare legs were, and how the flashlight seemed to make them shimmer.

'Oh,' I said. Then rather foolishly, 'We found him.'

Jack and I would never have told tales on the lovers but when we returned to the villa, instead of making up some story, Irving calmly told his mother that he had been with Grazia.

I could see little point in this piece of adolescent defiance, except for the rather dubious proof of Irving's manhood. Darling Beattie was embarrassed and shocked, and this made her garrulous. She ranted about honour and decent behaviour until her face turned red, and then she said that if the village men found out that Grazia had been 'interfered with' they would come up here with pitchforks and torches and we would be pillaged and very likely burnt into the bargain. Besides, Grazia was supposed to be working for us, and how could she be trusted under the same roof with us all if this sort of thing was going to go on?

We stared in disbelief at this outburst, and I was afraid to catch Lexi's eye in case she made me laugh. It was Mireille who supplied the oil for troubled waters. She poured Darling Beattie a glass of sambucca, and said that she would go and find Grazia and make sure she wouldn't speak to anyone about this matter. She returned an hour later not only having done this but also having arranged for Grazia's cousin Titiana to stand in during our final week.

We were all grateful to her for restoring calm before Nim returned to the villa, and sparing Irving an uncomfortable few days. So grateful, in fact, that no one thought to ask Mireille where she had been that afternoon.

Six

Mireille continued to make herself indispensable for the rest of our stay in Rome, and after that there was no question of putting her on a train to Switzerland. Darling Beattie was shamed into quelling her own reluctance and inviting her back to Russington with us.

And one month after our return there was to be a dance for Lexi's coming out, so naturally Mireille would have to stay until then.

For the moment, at least, Darling Beattie forgot all her other concerns in a headlong clash with her eldest daughter. It was her job to go with Lexi to London and with the pair of them in formal court dress, accompany her daughter to Buckingham Palace and present her at court with all the other debutantes. Then, like all the other debutantes, she would be given a dance in her honour at some rented, flower-filled ballroom in London, and a lot of Suitable Young People would be invited.

Not so, said Lexi. She didn't want a boring, formal dance with a lot of gormless young women in white frocks who had nothing to say for themselves. Like many exceptionally attractive women, Lexi had little time for members of her own sex. What she wanted was a big party at Russington; a costume ball with fancy dress and fireworks.

It goes without saying that we supported Lexi's scheme. A dance in London would be out of bounds to those of us who were still 'In'. A dance held at Russington would be open to all of us, even if it meant sliding through our bedroom windows on ropes made from sheets.

Nim took no part in the debate, locking himself away in his office to write and suggest that the readers of *The Times* pay close attention to the emergence of the new regime in Germany. In fact, he kept himself to himself more than usual after our return from Italy, and we saw little of him. It was left to Darling Beattie to make a decision, and in the absence of anyone else, she was forced once again to turn to her cousin.

Russington had many advantages, Mireille pointed out. It would be much cheaper, for a start, and would obviate the necessity of renting a house in London for the duration of the season. And, of course, it would prevent arguments about which of the children were to be excluded from the festivities.

Darling Beattie could see the sense in this; moreover she knew when she was beaten. She had the good grace to devote herself wholeheartedly to the arrangements, and even found a specialist firm in Banbury who would undertake a magnificent firework display in the grounds.

'I'll speak to Mrs Pruitt in the village,' she announced one afternoon, 'and if she's not too busy with her sewing for her other ladies, she can come up here and give us a hand with the costumes. I thought a pastoral theme, something pretty. Shepherds and shepherdesses, perhaps .. ?'

We exchanged looks which said '*Shall I tell her, or will you?*'

'It's all right, Mummy,' said Lexi quickly. 'You're probably too busy with the food and things. We'll organise our own costumes ...'

We had already taken steps in this direction, and had no intention whatsoever of dressing up like shepherds. Irving had discovered a wonderful theatrical costumier in the backstreets of Jericho, a run-down area of Oxford, and we planned to take a bus in there one afternoon and raid their sources of chain mail, viking helmets and hideous masks.

Lexi had firm ideas about how she wanted her dance to be, and she started to make the necessary preparations. Frannie and I were out walking Flash one day when he disappeared into the bushes and started to bark. This was not his usual behaviour. He was one of the few dogs in Britain who was too lazy to enjoy being taken for a walk, and we had to search under all the beds and drag him by the collar from his place of safety all the way down the stairs and into the garden. From there, with much calling and coaxing, he would waddle as far as the pond, then turn round immediately and start back before anyone tried to change his mind.

There were sounds of struggle from the bushes and a familiar voice said, 'Flash! Get off me, you stupid mutt!'

We found Lexi in there, surrounded by coils of wire and the coloured lights and paper lanterns we hung up at Christmas.

'I'm making a grotto,' she announced after we had dragged Flash to heel.

'A fairy grotto, you mean?' asked Frannie eagerly.

Lexi gave her a look dripping with disdain. 'Not a fairy grotto, stupid! Fairy grottoes are for children. This is going to be a mystical grotto. A private grotto.'

It was obviously something to do with the party, but neither Fran nor I wanted to appear stupid by asking what it was for.

'Guests. You know how they are . . .' said Lexi, reading our thoughts. She snapped off a length of wire and used it to attach a Chinese lantern to a branch of dogwood. 'They can be the most infernal bore. In fact parties would be a lot nicer if one didn't have to have guests at all, don't you think?'

'Oh yes!' said Frannie fervently, a Winstanley to the last. Outsiders were not tolerated gladly in our tight little community, and it was quite typical of the family to feel the need to escape from their own guests.

'There are going to be an awful lot of boring people wanting to talk to us, and dance with us, and if the party's for me then it's going to be very difficult to avoid them. So I thought I'd have a place they don't know about that would be just as much fun. Or . . .' A glint came into her eye. 'If there are any especially handsome guests, then it could be a place for Experiences . . .'

'*Lexi*! You wouldn't . . .'

'I might even ask Tony to meet me down here,' she said casually, placing a pair of pliers between her teeth.

'For a cigarette, you mean?'

'Possibly . . .' she said, through the pliers.

The finishing touches on the grotto were now complete. The branches had been bent and tied to make a low, green ceiling punctuated with colourful paper decorations. Around the cave-like entrance, Lexi had fixed a string of coloured lights. She attached the end to a voltmeter and turned the switch. The lights came on, their gaudiness muted by the daylight.

'There!' she said. 'A party within a party!'

Poor Beattie! When her flock descended from the upper regions of the house, radiant in their finery, it was not as a troupe of whimsical nymphs and shepherds. Our tastes were more baroque. It didn't matter one jot to us that the garments we had hired from the theatrical costumiers were grubby and yellowing and had dubious stains in the armpits. To us they were desirable because they were made from vivid, shining fabrics and resplendent with flashing sham jewels.

Jack was a pirate, Irving a viking with a silver papier-mâché helmet and bits of mangy fur hanging from his shoulders. Frannie and I were Elizabeth I and Mary, Queen of Scots respectively. And Lexi, the centrepiece of the whole occasion, was a magnificent Queen of the Nile in a black wig and a diadem encrusted with artificial rubies, pearls and diamonds.

'Rather vulgar, dear, don't you think?' murmured Darling Beattie when she saw us assembled in our tawdry splendour. She was rewarded with a black look from Lexi and sniggers from the rest of us. Together we descended the staircase into the hall, accompanied by Clem and Shoes whistling 'When the Saints Come Marching In' from the landing. A few of the guests clapped; one or two of the more daring ones whistled. Cheering loudest of all was a nun in a wimple, who turned out to be Aunt Griz, with Dearest secreted inside one black sleeve. ('Most inappropriate!' was Darling Beattie's verdict.)

In the ballroom, the Windrush Valley String Symphony was already hard at work, and dancing had begun. The musicians were a rather mournful bunch of geriatrics in mouldering dinner suits and socks that didn't match, as Frannie pointed out gleefully.

'I wish we could have had a jazz band,' said Irving.

'Can we start the fireworks now, please?' demanded Lexi.

'No, you can't! Now don't be such dreadful ungrateful children and go and dance with your guests!'

My aunt (a short, plump Queen Alexandra) went off to dance with Nim (The Iron Duke) and the two of them blended into the crowd of well-bred, over-fed county folk. I stood on the edge of the dance-floor watching them all shuffle around to 'The Blue Danube'; elbows touching elbows, horsewomen's thighs and backsides straining the thin fabric of their costumes. Their general lack of elegance made my thoughts turn to Mireille, and I found myself instinctively looking out for her among the dancers.

There she was, standing near the band. She was dressed as the Muse of Poetry in a shroud of death-white silk that flowed like a waterfall from her shoulders to her naked feet. Her pale red hair was pinned close to her head and a few tendrils of ivy clung around her temples. She started to come towards me and I thought perhaps she wanted to speak to me, but she drifted past as though she scarcely saw me. A white silk streamer, draped from her shoulder, fluttered across my face as she passed. It had a strange scent.

'God, look at that, would you believe it?' Jack was at my elbow suddenly, turning me round to face in the direction of the door. The Bleak-Wailers had arrived, and they were not dressed in costume. Fergus and James were in white tie and their sister was wearing a frumpy dance dress.

'... Typical of them, isn't it?' Jack was saying. 'They haven't got the gumption to make idiots of themselves. Imagine coming to a fancy-dress ball in white tie ...'

I wasn't really listening to him. The smell given off by Mireille's clothes had disturbed me. I couldn't place it, yet it was very familiar. The thought filled me with a sense of foreboding.

I danced with Jack.

We danced, oh, how we danced! So close I could measure his breathing against my cheek, in ... out, in ... out, and feel the slight dampness of his lips against my skin. We twirled round and round until we had danced out of the ballroom altogether, on to the terrace and down the stone steps on to the lower lawn.

We stopped, and for the merest second examined one another's faces. For the first time in my life I knew what it was to want time to stand still. Then we walked back into the house and Jack made a joke about the string-players' socks and everything was ordinary again.

'Now is the time,' Darling Beattie had announced to us earlier with great satisfaction, 'for you to appreciate all those dancing lessons you had!'

She was right. The hours lumbering about the schoolroom had paid off. None of us was especially graceful, but we were competent, and for three hours our skills were in constant demand. I felt as though I had danced with everyone. I danced with James Bleak-Wailer and felt annoyed by the way he clutched me. To distract myself I looked at his right hand, wrapped around mine. He had thin, pale wrists covered with dark hair.

All of the time I was dancing I was tensed, waiting for some signal from one of the others, waiting for the party to begin in earnest. Eventually it came. We were dancing to a fox-trot, and it was a gentlemen's excuse-me. Irving, who had been dancing with Lexi, cut in on the Old Faithful who was partnering me. 'Come outside,' he whispered, and guided me towards the doors to the terrace. And there – of course – were Jack, Lexi and Frannie, their finery only the merest bit bedraggled.

'We thought we'd play Hunting the Snark,' Lexi explained. 'There's just time for a game before the fireworks begin.'

'Who's going to be it . . ?'

Some instinct made me say it. 'I will.'

I ran off into the darkness. Where else was I to go but the grotto? It was an obvious hiding place, and yet I could not avoid it. I could have disappeared to some obscure lair within the grounds, but I would have risked not being discovered at all, and what would have been the point of that? Hunting the Snark was all about being found. It was about making oneself suffer.

I had been given a head start, but the costume was an instant handicap. Mary, Queen of Scots had probably never played anything more energetic than the lute. It was so difficult to run in my spangled, grubby farthingale that by the time I reached the site of the grotto I was doubled up and breathing noisily.

My breathing calmed. It then almost stopped as I realised there was someone else already there.

Nim and Mireille were in the grotto. Not the beast with two backs, writhing semi-naked on the earth together. Not that. They were in an attitude that seemed profoundly more disturbing to my shocked perception. Mireille was sitting on Nim's lap. He had her hands clutched in his, and he was kissing her tenderly.

I could not move, I could not even close my eyes, so I witnessed that kiss. And as I did so many things fell into place. That smell, from Mireille's dress. It was the smell of Nim's cigars, etched into my consciousness by the hours spent sitting in his cinema. Mireille's behaviour in Rome. The veiled sneering in her attitude to Beattie.

I felt sick but I also felt, as I had before, an urge to protect Mireille. If only I'd been alone, I could have turned and run away. But in this family, this close family, no one was ever alone for very long. The others were already behind me; the boys – unrestrained by long skirts – arriving first. I closed my eyes at last.

The sky had become a paintbox of colour. Countless tiny points of light rocketing upwards in the wake of each muffled explosion, then cascading down again, dying just before they touched the earth.

'Oh no!' said Lexi as we ran towards the terrace. 'They've started the fireworks without us!'

'They're bound to ask where we've been!' wailed Frannie, tugging up the skirts of her farthingale to keep them out of the mud. 'What are we going to say?'

We paused under a green and red sky to consider this question.
'It doesn't matter,' said Lexi firmly. 'We can't stay away.'
'What if she asks where Nim is?' I ventured. 'She might – '
'We're not leaving Mother on her own!' said Irving. 'We've got to be with her.'

We ran on again. With my more conventional soul lurking somewhere within me, I was full of trepidation about how our sudden arrival would look. But I decided to say nothing more all evening. I had been frightened by my cousins' reaction to what they had seen. Unanimous, undiluted hatred. Not of their father, but of Mireille, the outsider, the viper in the bosom. Jack had disturbed me most of all. He had said nothing, but looked straight from Nim and Mireille to me, as though what had happened was somehow my fault.

Darling Beattie was standing on the steps. Aunt Griz was somewhere nearby, and the other guests were grouped around in a respectful arc.

'I'm sorry you weren't here,' my aunt said, 'but the gentlemen from Banbury said they couldn't wait any longer. They say they have to get packed up and go home.'

My aunt knew her children too well to be surprised by their untimely absence. But then she added in a tight little voice, 'I don't know where your father can have got to.'

Two Roman candles shot across the sky, one heading west, the other east. They touched, embraced almost, then mingled in a shower of blue stars before fading into nothing. The guests cheered and clapped and smiled at Darling Beattie, eager to share in this celebration of her united family. I stared up mechanically at the sky, and thought of nothing but fireworks; their shapes, their colours. I didn't want to think about anything else.

Behind me, Lexi and Irving were whispering.
'We'll say nothing for now, all right .. ?'
'All right. But we must talk.'

They danced until dawn.

That phrase came unbidden into my brain and stuck there. *They danced until dawn ... they danced until dawn ...*

The ball went on interminably, long after we wanted it to stop. The arrival of dawn found us all in the schoolroom: Jack, Frannie, Lexi, Irving and I. Flash waddled in after us, and lay down next to me with his sad, square head on my foot.

Irving had removed his helmet. Lexi took off Cleopatra's diadem and her wig, and laid them on Miss Howland's desk, where we all stared at them. The plastic rubies and pearls looked drab now that the silvery light of day was beginning to filter through the tapestry curtains. As I looked at them I was imagining Nim and Mireille. Where were they: what were they thinking? They must have known they'd been seen. They must have heard us, even though we turned round and went back to the house without saying anything...

I drifted back from my own thoughts and became aware that the others were discussing their mother.

'We have an obligation to tell her,' said Irving pompously. 'She has a right to know.'

'No!' I said, suddenly breaking my resolve not to speak on the subject. 'I don't think you should.'

Without raising my eyes from Cleopatra's crown, I knew that they were all looking at me. 'Mireille knows what she's done.' I continued. 'It's up to her to decide what should be done now. She may think it's better that Darling Beattie knows nothing.' I took a deep breath. 'And anyway, Mireille's not entirely to blame. Nim's involved in this too – '

'*Not to blame!*' I can't remember which of my cousins said this; it could have been any of them. 'Not to blame? Of *course* she's to blame! Mummy and Nim were perfectly happy before *she* came along!'

I couldn't bear this blind self-righteousness any longer. 'They can't have been!' I shouted. 'Don't you see?'

'I tell you what I see.' Jack spoke up. His voice was calm and there was the familiar half smile on his lips. 'I can see that it doesn't take much to buy your loyalty. You've stuck up for Mireille ever since she gave you that fur coat ...'

The others were nodding.

'... If you take her side, you're nothing but a traitor.'

I stared at them, wild-eyed, waiting for Frannie to defend me. But she bit her lip and looked down at the floor.

I jumped to my feet, pushing Flash roughly away. Even Flash was one of them; foolish, unthinking Winstanley creature. 'Get off me, you stupid dog!' I could hear him whining as I reached the door. '... And you're nothing but a bunch of ostriches with your heads buried in the sand!'

In my room – not even that was mine, I still shared with Frannie – I sat on the bed and reflected. Shocked tears at my first conflict with my cousins soon dried and I felt calm. I wasn't really one of the, I knew that now. At first I had so wanted to be, but now I knew it had been proved that I was of a different make-up, I didn't mind. I was no longer sure that being a Winstanley was such a good thing.

Their way of looking at the world was dangerous, I had decided. For all their curiosity and lust for new experience, they had built themselves a fortress and they were afraid to abandon it. As long as they could laugh at the outside world, as long as they could approach life as if it were a game, they were safe. But they feared ugly situations, and real emotion. And I feared for them.

Mireille de Vere slipped from our lives like a fox. She just disappeared the day after the ball, with all her Beautiful Things, without saying goodbye. The photograph of Nim disappeared with her; the one of him in uniform that made a matching pair with Darling Beattie's picture.

Beattie *knew*, of course she knew. With our childish arrogance we had assumed the necessity of someone informing her of her husband's infidelity. But for all her vague exterior, and her indulgence towards her offspring, she was no fool. For a few weeks after the ball she walked around with a pained smile on her face and a sadness around her eyes, but she seemed much calmer than she had been during Mireille's visit. Gradually, as the memory receded, she reverted to her normal self.

Nim shut himself in his cinema and watched all of Charlie Chaplin's films, several times over. I didn't go and join him this time, but I did wonder about the pain he was feeling. Had he loved Mireille? Aunt Griz (who had dropped some obscure remarks about how Nim was 'pining') and myself were the only members of the family who were prepared to concede this possibility. In future years I was to overhear people gossiping discreetly about the affair, at parties.

'Of course, he was *such* a beautiful man,' one woman said. 'So handsome. Quite irresistible ...'

Was that our mistake, I would wonder, failing to realise that Nim, our old Nimbleshanks, was attractive?

On the morning of Mireille's departure, just after I had noticed that the photograph was missing, I went upstairs to our bedroom. Frannie was in there, scribbling away at her play. I walked past her to the window and looked out, following the driveway with my eyes.

Frannie eventually broke the silence. 'We'll never have to see her again, will we?'

'No, we won't.'

Without turning to look at her, I knew that Frannie and I had just called a mutual truce. And I also knew that we would both remember that moment. It was the end of childhood.

Part TWO

Growing Up

One

The following year, 1936, saw Frannie and me achieve the grand old age of fifteen. Frannie's dramatisation of the lives of the saints reached its fifth and final act. Clem lost his milk teeth. Irving won a place at Oxford and deliberated between academia and a career in the forces. Lexi continued to develop at a precocious rate into a beautiful and poised young woman. Jack, of course, stayed exactly the same.

1936 was also the year of the eleventh Olympic Games, in Berlin. To our utter amazement Nim, that opponent of the barbaric Hun, announced that he would be taking the five of us older children to spend a few weeks in Berlin for the Games. Since Mireille's departure his behaviour at home had been of a more docile nature, and he seemed anxious to compensate for the distress caused to his family. The cause of this distress was naturally never alluded to openly – that would have been in very poor taste.

There was outrage from Clem and Shoes, who considered themselves mature enough for the education a sophisticated city like Berlin had to offer.

'Never mind, my lambs,' said Darling Beattie. 'We'll have a wonderful time here, just the three of us.'

My aunt was not to make the trip with us either. She said that the thought of sitting all day watching foreigners running about beneath blazing sunshine made her feel quite ill. I was not sure if this was true, or whether Darling Beattie was still trying to punish her husband. Although the year had passed calmly enough, I had noticed undercurrents and tensions, a polite distance between the two of them.

There had been changes in my relationship with my cousins as well. They were of the slightest, subtlest kind, like flickering pulses in an electric current. We were still close companions and confidants, but the Winstanleys seemed less anxious to suck me into their way of thinking, more content to let me take a different stance. We were growing up.

On a warm day in July we took the Pullman to Berlin and checked into the Excelsior Hotel. My first memory of that city is of the half-lifesize colour portraits of Hitler, Goering and Goebbels that graced the reception lounge. I felt a sense of unease whenever I passed them, as though their eyes were following me. In a sense this was true; for Berlin was well and truly under the boot of the National Socialists. Everywhere we turned we saw uniforms; Hitler Youth in shorts, brown shirts and Sam Browne belts, SS men in black, the army in grey and the labour corps in ochre. Worst of all, and a sight that made Frannie and me shudder, was the sight of the *pimpfe*, cub scouts of the Nazi movement dressed as mini-SS men. The youngest of them was six years old.

Nim expressed his approval of all this uniformity. 'Sign of good discipline,' he said. 'Could do with more of that in England. Especially amongst the work-shy communist rabble.'

But even the oppressive influence of Hitler could not damp our spirits for long. We were thrilled to be staying in a hotel, something which we had never experienced before. To us, hotels meant the excitement and glamour of anonymity. The idea of walking in whenever you pleased, picking up your keys and riding up in the lift to a corridor of beckoning identical doors ...

Not that the Excelsior was a place designed to cater to the romantic appetite. Despite their high ceilings and large windows, the rooms still seemed gloomy, filled as they were with solid, ugly furniture too heavy to be rearranged. There were ungainly Gothic washstands and cavernous closets with stained-glass windows. On the table of each sitting room was a small brass dish filled with chocolates, which we obligingly emptied each day so that it could be refilled. To us, these sweetmeats were emblematic of the Berliners' obsession with food, drink and tobacco.

Our fellow residents were a mixed bunch. There were journalists covering the Games, who seemed to be forever rushing in and out through the revolving doors and arguing with the staff on reception. Then there were a handful of Russian émigrés, young men in blue serge suits and knitted silk ties who smoked their way endlessly through *papyrossi*, thin cigarettes with blue smoke that drifted in clouds to the ceiling of the piano bar. Jack particularly liked to make fun of a fat Hungarian countess whose corsets squeaked as she walked. She was accompanied everywhere by a young female companion to whom the countess spoke energetically in French but who never, as far as we could discern, made any reply. Finally there was a group of our own countrymen not unlike the Old Faithfuls back in Russington. They were 'People Like Us' who spoke in loud confident voices, wore tweed even though it was summer and insisted on airing their own prejudices on any subject that arose.

Though not gregarious, Nim also liked to air his prejudices publicly, and he soon got into the habit of sitting in the bar with his fellow English tourists, taking it in turns to order gin and french and airing his views on the work of the National Socialists. To our mingled surprise and relief, he made no attempt at any time during our stay to chaperone us or police our activities. At twenty, Irving was considered old enough to take responsibility. And it was as if he was admitting to us that he was no longer fit to set us a moral example.

Despite Germany's new Reich's Chancellor, and the patchwork of uniforms that covered the streets, Berlin still had a reputation for light-heartedness and *joie de vivre*. As in Rome, we were eager to immerse ourselves in a new city and since we had no guide we were forced to find our own way around. Which was much more fun, if a bit random.

At first we confined ourselves to the hotels, bars, cinemas and shops that made a sparkling nucleus of light around the Memorial Church. Then we became more adventurous and took trams into the civic centre, with its grave, grey façades, and took stock of the cathedral and the opera house. Much of the time we sat in cafés and drank fiendishly strong black coffee from hissing machines, thinking ourselves very European and sophisticated.

Lexi bought a slope-brimmed hat from the famous milliner Berthe, in Lennestrasse, and in it she looked the epitome of beautiful Aryan womanhood. Every now and then she would light one of the cigarettes that Irving had recently taken up, and I would think of her smoking with Tony, and wonder how much practice she had really had. Ever since Nim had given me my first Leica I had been passionate about photography and my camera accompanied me everywhere. I took a photo of her like that, sitting in the

Romanisches Café with her face almost completely obscured by the large brim of the hat and the wisps of smoke that hung around her face.

Finally, when our feet had started to hurt and we could no longer agree on what to do next, our wanderings took us back to the Excelsior, where Nim was taking tea with an Admiral's widow and expounding his methods to restore Britain to full employment with the help of the horse-whip. He looked up when he heard us coming in, and a strange expression crossed his face when he saw Lexi in the hat. I was almost sure he was thinking of Mireille de Vere.

Shortly after the visit to the milliner's, we piled into a charabanc along with some of our fellow hotel guests and were driven out of the city to the new stadium at Pichelsdorf, for the opening ceremony of the Olympics.

We had not discussed the Games much beforehand, and I for one had had little idea of what to expect. Never having attended a school, our experience of organised sports was limited to the meeting of the local hunt. I suppose I had expected something like a circus parade, with the athletes setting the tone in a display of buoyant international friendship. Instead, the Führer dominated the occasion. As soon as he entered the stadium, the German audience leapt to their feet, flung out their arms and started a deafening, brain-numbing chorus of '*sieg heil*'. Hitler did not seem surprised by the response, but stood with a straight-backed resolution which inspired a cold sensation of fear at the base of my spine. The Germans were mad, I thought, to allow such a small, unprepossessing man so much power.

Frannie must have been thinking the same thing, because she leaned towards me and whispered, 'Can you imagine what it would be like if he looked like a film star?'

For those opening few minutes it was impossible not to stare at the Führer, flanked on either side (so the newspapers told us later) by Reich Minister Fuch, Rudolf Hess, Field Marshal von Blomberg and the Crown Prince of Italy, for whom I felt sorry because he was wearing a dark suit and looked very left out. Then the loudspeakers blared out a sombre march, and all the athletes started to march around the stadium. The faces of my cousins told me that, like me, they found the military air of the whole proceedings offensive. Nim, however, was nodding his approval. He took a large silk handkerchief out of his pocket and wiped his forehead, before replacing his sola topi.

'Good turn out,' he commented with grudging admiration. 'Got to admit the damn Huns know how to do these things properly.'

Frannie caught my eye, and leaned across in her seat to whisper to me. 'I think Nim's turning into a fascist!' she said with genuine alarm. 'That's the third time today he's approved of the regime out loud.'

I thought about this piece of political fickleness as the races started, and we watched Jesse Owens, flowing along the track like a sleek black cat, and proving the fallacy of Aryan supremacy right under the Führer's nose. I concluded that my uncle was the originator and arch example of the Winstanley trait of turning a blind eye to any truth that they consider difficult or unpleasant. My cousins had not wanted to admit to themselves that their father could be the willing participant, even the initiator, of an adulterous affair. Nim in turn did not want to think about the fact that so much outward patriotic fervour concealed a more sinister hysteria.

Frannie was nudging me, trying to get me to agree that the New Zealand runner Jack Lovelock, with his black singlet and gleaming golden hair, was 'absolutely *divine*'. Our giggling irritated Irving and Nim, who leaned over and told us crossly that if we didn't shut up, we would have to get up and leave in front of all those people. Frannie raised her arm in a Nazi salute behind his back and we stuffed our handkerchiefs in our mouths to stifle our cries of glee as Jack Lovelock won the fifteen-hundred metres.

Lexi was on my right-hand side, the hat obscuring all but a calm smile as she watched the proceedings. Then she made a great show of opening the picnic hamper and passing round liverwurst sandwiches, which no one really wanted. My sandwich crackled as I bit into it, and I opened it up to find a piece of paper on which Lexi had written me a note.

K. – *Don't* let Nim see you, but take a look at the man sitting two rows behind Jack. *Not* obviously, of course! What Miss H. would call a fine figure of a man, I think.

I waited until everyone had started clapping, then turned and glanced over my left shoulder. The object of Lexi's interest (how typical of her that she had managed to stare without anyone noticing) was a young man, probably in his early twenties, of unmistakably Aryan appearance. He had straight, pale hair smoothed back from a high Prussian forehead, and eyes as grey as the Baltic sea. There was something unexpected about his appearance, and I realised that it was because he wasn't wearing a uniform. He was very neat and tidy, however, in a light-coloured suit, spotless white collar and cuffs and silk socks. Nim only wore silk socks for 'best'. On the little finger of his left hand he wore a heavy gold signet ring.

I stared for so long that it was inevitable that he noticed me. When he did so, he smiled a polite and faintly amused smile, and inclined his head. I blushed and turned back to face the stadium feeling guilty. It was really Lexi he should have been smiling at. I picked up the pad of paper and pencil that were sticking out out of her handbag and, ever eager to promote the cause of Experience, scribbled my report.

Dear L.,
Very nice, and interesting looking. He caught my eye and smiled at me, so perhaps he is bored? Why don't you try it — smiling at him, I mean, I'll nudge you if N. looks. K.

Lexi stared at my note, for a few minutes sitting very still. Then, slowly, she turned her head and looked backwards. I was longing to witness the ensuing exchange of glances but Jack was looking at me crossly, and I didn't dare to turn back again. I could imagine it, though, when I looked at Lexi's face. For the rest of the afternoon she sat as straight-backed as the Führer, but the gleam in her eye told me that she didn't see a single thing that happened.

It was a relief to get back to the Excelsior that evening, away from the flag-waving and marching. After soaking in a hot bath, I changed into an evening dress (my *only* evening dress, acquired after much bargaining with my aunt) and went down with Frannie to the lobby, where Jack and Irving were poring over the evening papers to read their account of the day's sporting events.

'Look at this!' said Jack in disgust. He was holding a copy of Goebbels's paper, *Der Angriff*. 'They call the black American athletes "black auxiliaries to the American team". They've even got the nerve to leave out mention of Jesse Owens's gold medal.'

'Why do the Germans do it?' Frannie wanted to know. 'I mean, why do they scurry after Hitler like a load of mindless ants?'

The idea of people doing what they were told was always incomprehensible to the Winstanleys, but there was a new urgency in Frannie's voice, and she looked quite pale. I knew then that like me she had spent a lot of the afternoon thinking about the implications of what we saw at the stadium.

'They're frightened,' said Irving, lighting a cigarette. 'They're frightened of inflation getting out of control again, and they're frightened of unemployment, so when Hitler says that he can build them a better Germany, they want to believe him. When he tells them that racial purity means strength, they believe that too.'

'But they can't do,' insisted Frannie. 'If they believe that, then they can't be thinking properly.'

'Why think, if it's easier not to?' Jack was as quick as ever to see the Machiavellian point of view. 'Of course the National Socialists aren't thinking. Any more than Lexi was when she started making eyes at that Nazi.'

He dropped in this last remark casually, but his voice was cold with disapproval. Of course Jack would have seen, I realised. He rarely missed anything. I looked at him sharply over the rim of my glass, but he avoided my eyes.

He had been subdued since our arrival in Berlin, his usual jokiness only just masking strong repulsion by much of what he saw. If it surprised me, it was because Jack, with his policy of looking after number one, was the last person I expected to be partisan or politically aware.

His sour mood continued that evening. We left Nim playing bridge with the English guests and set off in search of the most *louche* nightclub we could find. A man we spoke to in a bar directed us to the Salome, an underground cavern painted bright red and gold, stuffed with crimson plush and mirrors. We were so busy trying to give the impression that we were over twenty-one years of age that at first we didn't notice the semi-naked dancer on stage, her breasts clearly visible through a diaphanous dress, her face hard and painted. Even the saxophonist leaned into his microphone with a leer and an innuendo.

When we did notice, we pretended to be so madly sophisticated that we'd seen the same, and worse, before. The rest of the audience did the same; not shifty single men as I might have imagined, but cheerful burghers and their families, registering nothing more than mild surprise as the dancer removed what remained of her clothing and thrust her hips in their direction.

Irving had turned red, and busied himself with looking at the wine list and ordering champagne. Boys dressed as bell-hops, barely more than children, with trays around their necks, moved between the tables shouting '*Zigarren!*' above the noise of the saxophone. They looked bored; they had seen it all before many times.

Since the dancer had now removed all her clothes and the

audience had all taken in what she had to offer, there was little more for her to do but leave the stage. The next performer was a man dressed in embroidered *lederhosen* and climbing boots, his face a burlesque of the simple peasant boy in folk stories, with painted-on freckles and red circles daubed on his cheeks. With a lot of thigh-slapping and suggestive rolling of the eyeballs, he sang a song that was doubtless obscene when translated from the German. The audience seemed to enjoy it, laughing amd smiling to each other, and clapping loudly.

Then the singer left the stage and strolled among the tables, his eyes darting about as he looked for a suitable victim. I wanted to look away, but as he drew closer I became transfixed by the crayoned brown freckles, like the marks of some grotesque skin disease. I couldn't bear to look, but I couldn't not look.

He saw me staring at him and smiled, revealing lipstick-smudged teeth. 'Komm!'

I smiled back politely but started to shake my head.

'*Komm, Fräulein.*'

He had taken hold of my hand and I was being pulled to my feet. Suddenly Jack caught me by the other wrist and jerked me back into my seat. He continued to hold on to my wrist, squeezing it painfully.

'Don't!' he said angrily. 'Don't go up there with him. They only want to make fools of us!'

The singer looked amused, and strolled away to another table.

I pulled my hand away from Jack's grasp, laughing slightly at the expression on his face. 'I think you're overreacting a bit,' I said. 'He wouldn't have done me any harm. He probably wanted me to sing a duet with him, something like that.'

'Well, I don't trust him. I don't trust any of these people.'

Jack continued to scowl, and we didn't have enough money for another bottle of the over-priced champagne, so no one argued when Irving suggested we stroll back to the hotel via some coffee shop. As I stood up, I looked around me for my evening bag, and ended up groping around under the table for it in an undignified fashion. I pulled myself up from my knees and found myself looking straight into the face of Lexi's Prussian. He gave me a smile and a nod of recognition, immaculate in his full evening dress.

The others had almost reached the door.

'Wait!' I said quickly, running after them. 'Lexi, look who's over there.'

She stopped in her tracks. 'Oh,' she said, looking straight at him, and with the intonation of that plain monosyllable, I knew that she desperately wanted to stay behind.

The boys wouldn't hear of it. They shepherded us towards the door, and as we reached it Lexi paused and, with so much grace and naturalness that it would have looked accidental to anyone with less knowledge of my cousin, she dropped her mohair stole. Then we emerged from the stuffy basement into the cool air of the Tauentzienstrasse.

I held my breath and counted.

One . . . two . . . three

We had taken only eight paces before there was a sound of footsteps behind us, almost – but not quite – running.

His hair looked darker in the half-light, but his eyes shone clear and pale, full of suppressed emotion. He held the mohair stole out to Lexi, saying in perfect English, 'I think this is yours, is it not?'

Lexi held out her hand and sank her fingers into the soft wool. The German was still holding it. She didn't smile, but as he let go, a look passed between them.

He clicked the heels of his patent evening pumps, bowed low and kisssed her hand. '*Gnädige Fräulein . . .*'

One only had to look at Lexi's face to know what was going to happen next.

Two

Lexi was desperate to see her young admirer again and, over the next few days, much of our energy was devoted to furthering the cause of romance.

We dragged our reluctant male escorts back to the Salome club the following evening, but even though we managed to spin out one bottle of champagne for two hours, the handsome German did not appear.

Finally we spotted him at the Olympic stadium, watching the triumph of the German rider and his beautiful horse, Nurmi, in the three-day event. Coyness was not Lexi's forte, and two days of frustration had made her bold. Having told her father she was going to find herself a drink of water, she marched straight up to the elusive Prussian and introduced herself. Frannie and I watched the encounter from a safe distance, giggling into our handkerchiefs.

'*What did he say, what did he say?*' we hissed when she sauntered back to her seat, smoothing·her gloves over the back of her hands as though nothing had happened.

'Oh.' She shrugged. 'He asked me out, of course.' Seeing the look on our faces, she added, 'Only for tea, sillies. And I'm not going alone ...'

As usual, Lexi had everything very carefully planned. Frannie and I were to act as chaperones, and she was even going to ask Nim's permission to take tea with a German friend she had made. As it was, he was so engrossed in watching the Argentinians play polo that he scarcely registered the request.

Of course Fran and I were only too willing to take Pandarus's role, but found it difficult to treat the whole procedure seriously.

84

Lexi insisted that she didn't want to be seen out and about in Berlin with a pair of children, so the two of us were subjected to a long grooming session in which our nails were manicured, our faces powdered, our lips painted and our hair set. She lent us each one of her second-rank hats, which made us snort with laughter whenever we looked at each other. Only when she was satisfied that our appearance was almost as immaculate as her own were we allowed to set off – not on the tram, mark you, but in a taxi.

The second thing on which Lexi insisted was not making an entrance too early. So when the cab put us down in the Hardenbergstrasse, outside the Café Berlin, she dragged us round the corner to 'hide' out of sight in an alleyway. Curious passers-by stared when they saw three English girls, in identical gloves and lipstick, cowering behind a Prussian Lottery stand with their hats pulled down over their faces.

Frannie and I were sent in turn to peer through the windows of the café, and it might have turned into rather a hot and tedious afternoon had not the Count Hubertus von Russow been perfectly punctual. I spotted him amongst the glass and chrome, indicating to the waiter with a wave of his hand that he would be placing an order later. Lexi made us count to three hundred and fifty-six (why three hundred and fifty-six? – I never did find out) before she walked in to the café, with her two handmaidens in her wake.

Sensible Hubertus had picked out a table for two, so after being introduced and explaining that we were not twins, but cousins, Fran and I were relegated to a nearly table where we could watch and sigh with envy from a safe distance.

'Can you lip read?' Frannie whispered.

I shook my head.

'Then change places with me, and I'll have a go. We used to practise when we were little, on the days when we pretended to be deaf and dumb.'

Frannie and I switched chairs so that she was facing the courting couple. She peered intently at Hubertus's lips. '... "*I believe the chocolate's very good.*" ... that's what he just said ... wait ... "*Have you been to Germany before?*" ... oh, bother! Lexi's moved and I can't see through her hat!'

My sense of disappointment increased as the afternoon wore on. The Café Berlin was one of the most sophisticated places we had visited, and it was pleasant sitting there sipping on a strawberry frappé and listening to Schulgate and his orchestra playing Russian romances. But it was Lexi, and not I, who was experiencing life. That was the way it had always been, and that was the way it always would be, because of her superior looks and the two-year advantage that would never be eclipsed. She acted and we watched. As I sat there, staring at the back of her head, listening to Frannie's attempt to interpret every gesture, I resolved that I would have no more part in Lexi's schemes. Instead I would go out and partake of Experiences of my own.

I had this in mind when Lexi knocked on the door of my room later that evening. She was in her bathrobe, and her wheat-gold hair was loose.

'Kitty, do me a favour, will you? I'm going out this evening, and I want you to come with me. Just for a while.'

I put down the book I was reading and raised my eyes in enquiry.

'I'm meeting Hubertus.'

'Sorry. I didn't feel like going out tonight. Ask Frannie.' I picked up my book again.

'She's not feeling well ...' Lexi waited for me to soften, then went on. 'But it's all right. I'll just find my way to the place on my own, and if I get lost and end up being assaulted by Brown Shirts, who – '

'All right, I'll come!' I flung down the book. 'Just this once.'

'Good girl.' Lexi kissed me on the forehead. 'I'd do the same for you, Kit darling, you know that. I'm just going to finish dressing – be an angel and meet me in the lobby in fifteen minutes!'

On my way down the corridor to the lift, I was waylaid by Frannie, who was nursing a sore throat.

'You're going? – good,' she croaked. 'I want you to tell me *everything*. Tonight's *bound* to be the night, after all.'

I looked at Frannie more closely. The expression on her face told me that she knew something. And she was bursting to tell me.

'I was watching Lexi get dressed. She put on her *best underwear*!'

I was still turning over the implications of this statement when I met Lexi in the lobby. She smiled and held up a message that the desk clerk had just handed her.

'That's lucky,' she said.

'What is?'

'Irving just telephoned from the stadium. The pole-vaulting's carrying on under floodlights, and it won't be over for another couple of hours. He and Jack and Nim are staying to watch it.'

'Very lucky,' I agreed, unsurprised. Lexi always was.

We took a cab to the Potsdamerstrasse, and then started to walk. To my delight there was a fairground at one end of the street, advertising negro boxers and fat lady wrestlers at ten *pfennigs* a go.

'We're meeting Hubertus at the fair?'

'No, but the place is near here somewhere ...' Lexi had a hopeless sense of direction which she claimed was the reason for her needing an escort. '... A little turning about the third on the right, he said ...'

We continued walking, then Lexi stopped suddenly and grasped me by the shoulder so that she could look straight into my eyes.

'I'm in love with him, you know.'

I nodded and we walked on, until we came to a small and extremely seedy-looking hotel. It was the sort with an electric sign switched on over the nightbell. One where you could hire a room by the hour, if you so wished.

'Well, this is it ...'

I understood at once from the expression on her face that she was not just intending to meet Hubertus there for a drink. I was profoundly shocked. So shocked that for a second I thought my knees were not going to support me.

'Lexi ..!'

She anticipated my question. 'I know what I'm doing, Kit. This is what I want ...'

The Ultimate Experience ... My brain formed the words silently.

Lexi squeezed my shoulder, then kissed me swiftly on the cheek. 'Please don't worry about me, I'll be perfectly all right.' She seemed, for the first time in her life, truly excited. 'Here's five marks. I'll ask the man on the desk to get you a taxi, and you just have to wait here until it arrives, then you can go straight back to the Excelsior ...'

She hurried off, then darted back, as an afterthought. 'For God's sake, don't breathe a word to the boys. Their sister's honour and all that.'

She didn't thank me for coming with her.

I knew when I saw her disappearing into the hotel that I had no intention of going straight back to the Excelsior. I walked to the end of the little street, passing matronly prostitutes in shapeless fur coats, who whispered '*Komm, Süsser*' to potential trade. On the corner there was an 'informal' bar with sketches and signed caricatures covering the walls, and people standing up, singing. I hesitated for a moment, then went in, and as I did so the remarkable thought occurred to me that it was the first time I had done something on my own since the Motor deposited me at the steps of Russington Hall at the tender age of eight.

I stood close to the bar, and ordered a gin and french. Perhaps the sophistication of Berlin had rubbed off on me in the previous few days, because the barman didn't seem inclined to question my age. Not wanting to go and sit at a table alone, for fear of inviting unwanted company, I continued to lean against the bar and sip my drink. I didn't care for the taste very much, but its very bitterness made me feel old and worldly. I looked around at my fellow drinkers. They were a lively, cheerful crowd, with the men dressed in shapeless bohemian clothes and the women made up most unsubtly with white-powdered faces, magenta lips and lacquered hair.

The man on my left was just paying his bill in preparation for leaving. I noted with my photographer's eye that he was drawing out dollar notes from a crocodile-skin wallet with a golden fringe on it. Certainly he didn't look German. He had sandy hair and freckles and wore a shiny suit and strange boots.

He caught me staring at him and mistook my interest.

'Well, hullo there.'

'Hello.'

'You all alone?'

I wondered what Jack would have to say about this clumsy conversation opener. But we fell into a conversation anyway, for want of anyone else to talk to. He was called Deacon, and came from some place in the middle of America that I had never heard of, and whose name I immediately forgot. I imagined it as a vast empty space covered with waist-high cornstalks.

Growing up in such a place would certainly have accounted for Deacon's lack of sophistication. He was pleasant enough, and he was also rich, and bored, unable to think of any diversion except for spending his money. He said he was 'having a good time in Europe' but his appreciation of the Berliners or the bizarre political scene around them seemed limited.

It was odd sitting there quite alone and talking about myself to a stranger. Strangers had never been tolerated, except as a target for jokes and derision. I didn't find it difficult to think of things to say – years of dull dinner parties with the Old Faithfuls of Oxfordshire had given me a fund of small talk. The strangeness lay in not having my cousins around me, directing and shaping my thoughts. I felt exposed, and almost as characterless as Deacon himself.

Eventually Deacon tucked his wallet into a shiny pocket and said, 'Well now, better be gettin' along. Got a lot to do tomorrow.'

When I asked him precisely what he was going to do he became vague, but I had given him an obvious cue. 'Say, how about you and me meeting up, buying ourselves some entertainment?'

'Are you sure?' I looked at his bland, freckled face and concluded that he hadn't the least idea that I was only fifteen. 'All right,' I went on, deciding that if I was going to seek out Experience of my own, Deacon was at least a start. 'I could see you tomorrow evening.'

'That would be just great. And maybe I'll get a chance to meet that family of yours?'

'Maybe,' I said, extending my hand and giving it the brief shake that seemed more appropriate than a goodbye kiss. '. . . We'll see.'

'She's obviously not a virgin any more,' Frannie said to me the next morning, when I filed my report.

'Lucky thing . . .' I sighed.

'Even so, Kitty . . . with a *German*!'

'I shouldn't think it makes any difference when it comes down to . . . well, "it".'

Frannie lay back on her bed and let out a long sigh of pleasure. 'Now tell me again about the man that *you* met. Was he handsome?'

I thought about Deacon's large, freckled face. He had a gap between his front teeth, I remembered. 'Not really.'

'Oh Kitty! Honestly, you're so unromantic!'

I preferred to think of myself as cautious, and with this in mind, when I met Deacon later that evening, I took not only Frannie and Jack, but also Lexi and Hubertus. ('He's her *lover* now, you realise,' Frannie hissed as he arrived at the Excelsior.) Irving stayed behind to make up a four at bridge.

We sat on the roof terrace of the Café Josty, and superficially the evening passed pleasantly enough, but I was haunted by the fear that my true age would be revealed to Deacon. I had no reason to fear this, except the wish not to appear a fool.

Loyal Frannie would not have said anything, nor would Lexi who was in my debt, and was not a malicious person anyway. But then there was Jack. He looked as though he was in one of his trouble-making moods. A smirk played about the corner of his mouth, and he turned his dark eyes from my face to Deacon's and then back again, as though something was amusing him. Every so often he would start: 'Do you know, Deacon . . ?' and wait for me to glance up, then he would go on and make some pointedly neutral statement.

Our bizarre little party then made its way along the Kleiststrasse, passing a small, dingy café.

Frannie stopped and looked in through the window. 'Do let's go in here, it looks like fun. They're all having a sing-song!'

Inside the café there were a group of young people who looked like students, dressed in dirty, untidy clothes. The girls wore jaunty caps, and some of the men wore red armbands. On the scrubbed tables there were bowls of thin soup and plates of sausages.

'Do let's go in!' repeated Frannie. 'Hubertus, you can translate the words of the songs for us.'

Hubertus hesitated, then smiled slightly. 'This is a communist café. Those people are members of the Red Front, and the song they are singing is called "The Red Flag". It has been banned by the Reich.'

At the mention of communism, Deacon set his jaw. 'Reckon we should leave well along. How about you, Kitty?'

I didn't bother to reply, because Jack was already saying he wanted to go in, just to be difficult. I don't know how long we would have stood there on the pavement, arguing about it, had we not been distracted by an outburst of shouting at the end of the street. An open-topped car had been stopped, and while its engine was still running, two Brown Shirts were trying to pull the driver and another man from the car. The two blonde girls in the back seat were protesting loudly, and trying to pull their friends back into the car. The most alarming thing of all was that passers-by, rather than approaching to see what all the commotion was about, were hurrying on their way as if they had seen nothing.

The scene made no sense to us; it was only Hubertus who seemed to understand what was happening. He shook his head and looked sickened. Clinging to his arm, Lexi asked why the two men in the car were being arrested.

'They're not being arrested. Those men are Jewish, and the National Socialists don't think they should be allowed near Aryan women.'

'What if the women want to go out with them?' I asked.

'I'm afraid it doesn't make any difference.'

The two young Jews, smartly dressed and handsome, with black curly hair, had been pulled clear of the car and were being systematically kicked and punched in the abdomen. One of the Brown Shirts had a cosh and was trying to hit them over the head and neck. As they raised their arms to protect themselves, they exposed themselves to fresh blows to their bodies. The girls still sat in the back of the car, motionless, staring straight ahead.

'Surely we ought to do something?' I urged. 'Deacon . . .'

He flapped his arms uselessly, as though unsure where to put them. 'I think we should leave it to the authorities. They know what they're doing. Maybe those guys have done something wrong, for all we know they could be criminals, something . . .'

I looked at Hubertus. His expression was pained, but he too shook his head. 'Believe me, it's better not to get involved.'

There was no point in asking Jack, who would never have risked a beating if there was a way of avoiding it. Frannie, though, looked for a moment as though she would run down the street and attack the Brown Shirts with her own bare hands. Then she turned and followed the rest of us as we walked uselessly away, and her face was more sad than angry.

'The poor Jews,' she said. 'What have they done?'

'You're not really going to go out with that American again, are you?'

Jack had come into my room the next evening and caught me getting ready to go out with Deacon.

'Yes, why not?' I picked up my silver-backed brush (engraved with my initials, one of the few presents I ever received from my father, the late Reverend Conway) and started to work up a shine on my dull brown hair.

'He's a Nazi, that's why not.'

I ignored him, and went on brushing. Standing behind me, Jack took hold of a lock of my hair, looked at it thoughtfully then pulled it, hard. It hurt enough to make me wince, but I didn't give Jack the satisfaction of letting it show.

He looked over my shoulder, straight into the reflection of my face in the glass. Looking at me and yet not looking at me. 'You saw him when the Jews were being beaten up. He's the sort who'd like to see them all locked up in prison anyway.'

'I noticed you weren't exactly running to their aid.'

'That's not the point. It wouldn't have achieved anything if I had. It's what one believes about that sort of thing that's important.'

'Oh really?' I raised an eyebrow at his reflection. My voice sounded sharp in my own ears. 'I thought it was only the preservation of Jack Winstanley that was important.'

Jack didn't answer this accusation, but when I took my evening dress down from its hanger, he started to laugh.

'You're really going, aren't you?'

I muttered some remark about his nose being out of joint, because I preferred someone else's company. Jack laughed again.

'Why on earth should I care if you prefer a complete idiot like Deacon?'

Why indeed? I wondered. The fact remained that I wished terribly that Jack *did* care. If he'd asked me not to go, or suggested some alternative plan, I would have dropped Deacon like a shot. But he seemed content to leave me to my own devices.

Secretly I shared my cousin's opinion of my newfound beau, but I was young enough to be flattered and impressed by the interest he showed in me, and it made me feel madly old and sophisticated to have a grown man at my beck and call, ready to escort me about Berlin. So I was in a cheerfully defiant mood when I met Deacon in the lobby, having first checked that Nim was in the piano bar with the fat Hungarian countess and a selection of the Old Faithfuls. I told him I thought his suggestion of some dancing was a wonderful one.

We went to a club where the band were dressed in Bavarian costume and indulging in a lot of good-natured thigh-slapping and yelling. The dancers were yelling too, and skipping around the room with their hands on one another's hips. Deacon made a remark about it being something like square-dancing, but he and I were far too self-conscious to join in such an uninhibited display, so we waited at our table, sipping glasses of cold beer, until the band struck up a waltz.

Deacon pulled me very close. The way he touched me created a clumsiness that never existed in our schoolroom dance classes, and for a minute or two my feet could not remember what they were supposed to be doing. Then he kissed me, forcefully, on the mouth. I submitted willingly, not because I felt anything for Deacon but because I considered it essential that I chalk up the experience. I wanted to be able to say that I knew what it was like to be kissed.

Actually, it was quite enjoyable. Deacon had obviously kissed other girls before, back in that forgettable town in middle America. I allowed myself to relax and let him get on with it and soon pleasant sensations were running up and down my spine, making the back of my knees feel ticklish.

Frannie was very envious when I told her about it, and I spent the whole of the next day walking around feeling rather smug. Deacon – predictably enough – came back for more. I went dancing with him again the next night, feeling daring because Nim had spotted us in the lobby and I had been forced to tell a white lie about going in a party with my cousins. This time I found the kissing less exciting, and Deacon must have agreed with me. When he took me back to the Excelsior, promptly at eleven o'clock, he was not content to kiss me goodbye downstairs, but wanted to come up to my room with me.

I hesitated. I didn't particularly care for the idea of Deacon visiting my room, not least because there were three pairs of celanese knickers and a liberty bodice drying on the radiator. On the other hand, I wanted to know how men behaved when in that sort of situation, and I felt I owed it to myself and Frannie to find out.

We walked down the quiet, carpeted corridor in silence. The Suitable Topic of Conversation (Darling Beattie had told us that there was one for every occasion) eluded me. I was replaying the handing over of the room key in my mind, trying to remember if the desk clerk had given me a strange look or not. As I unlocked the door, Deacon was standing very close behind me, breathing on my neck, and as soon as we were in the room he had his arms round me and was kissing me all over my face. (So quickly that he surely wouldn't have had time to notice the underwear on the radiator?)

'Let's sit down,' I suggested, straightening my elbows to keep him at arm's length. 'We could order something from room service ...'

Deacon followed me to the sofa, but used it as a convenient platform from which to launch his next attack. His mouth was on my neck, biting me, and his hands roamed over my chest, which he was sure to realise soon was not voluptuous and womanly at all, but the scrawny chest of a fifteen-and-a-half-year-old ...

He put his mouth there and I could feel his teeth and the weight of his body was pressing on all the beer in my stomach, making me feel winded. I wasn't frightened, just annoyed that I couldn't move him and that he didn't seem to care that he was hurting me, and that I was therefore not enjoying myself. Worst of all to my fantasy-ridden adolescent mind (was this always the case? I wondered) he didn't speak to me throughout the proceedings, just emitted the occasional grunt.

I started to laugh. It was a well-established reflex; the strangeness and the ridiculous side of what was happening struck me forcibly and my sides started to shake. It was a painful business with thirteen and a half stone of corn-fed American on top of my ribs, and the sound I made was a strangled snorting.

Deacon tried to sit up. He lost his balance on the narrow sofa and rolled to the floor with a resounding crash and a yell as his elbow hit the table, scattering chocolates on the carpet.

'I'm sorry Deacon, I ...'

By now I was too weakened by laughter to speak. I couldn't even respond when he said in an offended tone, 'Well, it looks like I'd better leave you to get to bed,' but I did at least manage to walk to the door with him and wave him on his way down the corridor.

As I waited for the sound of the lift gates closing, the door opposite mine opened and Irving came out.

'Is everything all right?' he asked.

'Yes,' I said smiling. 'Why?'

'I heard one hell of a noise coming from your room just now. It sounded like someone in pain.'

Deacon, slain by laughter. 'You're imagining things, Irvie baby,' I said quickly.

I hoped he believed me. Irving and Jack were close, and more than anything I didn't want Jack to know.

I never saw Deacon again. He didn't telephone, and a few days later our visit to Berlin came to an end.

On the last day, I went into Frannie's room and found her scribbling away in one of her notebooks.

'The play?' I asked.

She shook her head. 'The play's finished. I'm writing a new story. It's about a group of young communists, who are being persecuted.'

On that last day, Frannie and I went with Nim to the Berlin Zoo in the Budapeststrasse. To our surprise, Nim professed that it was a place he had been meaning to visit as soon as the Games were over, and he escorted us there, carrying the cane and the blue cravat he had bought in Rome.

Frannie hardly spoke at all as we walked past the cages, and when we reached the flamingoes she leaned her arms on the railings and stood staring at them for a long time, in silence. Then she sighed.

I looked at her enquiringly.

'Those men with the banner,' she said at last. 'I've been thinking about them.'

She was referring to a group of brown-uniformed SA men we had passed on our way to the zoo. They had been carrying a banner which, with our growing grasp of German, we were able to translate:

'A TRUE GERMAN DOES NOT BUY IN A JEWISH SHOP'.

Frannie turned away from the flamingoes and looked at me, and her face and voice were alive with passion. 'Kitty, I just want all human beings to be treated equally, that's all I want! I just don't understand why they can't be.'

Then she looked at her father, as though she expected an answer, but he just shook his head.

I sensed then that the visit to Germany had been both revelation and disappointment to Frannie, and she confirmed this with the next thing she said.

'I'm not going to come back here, Kitty, unless everyone's made equal. Not until that happens.'

Three

Our return to Russington was a happy occasion.

Clem and Shoes had erected a home-made welcome banner, and hung it over the front door of the house. It was a mammoth effort in the style of the Bayeux tapestry, illustrated with scenes from our exploits abroad. We had sent home letters with full reports of all we had seen, and sure enough, there on the banner was Jack Lovelock winning the 1500 metres, and the elephants in the Berlin Zoo, and Lexi's new hat, a saxophone and a big bowl of chocolates (like all Winstanleys, they had an overwhelming interest in food). There too was the Führer with his black moustache, standing beneath a swastika in the Olympic stadium. I didn't fail to notice that he had a gun in his hand which he appeared to be firing.

'Why's Hitler doing that?' I asked Clem. 'He's not shooting someone, I hope?'

'It's a starter's pistol. He's starting the running race.'

'Oh, I see.' I was much relieved.

It was September when we returned. Summer had peaked and was fading fast. Thanks to the ministrations of the blind Tyler, the garden was in a colourful chaos as usual, with swollen peonies drooping their brown-tinged heads and roses dropping a profusion of petals in different shades. Chem and Shoes dragged us off to see their new tree-house and the latest arrivals in the chicken coop, with Flash wheezing along behind us. He had made a valiant attempt at running down the steps to greet us, but he was elderly now, and had arthritis which made him even more clumsy than he had been before. When Flash could keep up at all he stayed close to Jack, to whom – like me – he had a disproportionate attachment.

I looked back as we reached the pond and saw Nim and Darling Beattie standing on the steps together. She had her arm linked through his, and I wished I had my camera with me to record the moment. They looked content together, and that alone was enough to make me feel glad to be back. I also realised that whatever my own identity, and wherever it took me, Russington was my home.

Later that evening, I made time to go and visit Aunt Griz. Poor health kept her in her room much of the time, isolating her from the rest of the family, and I felt sorry for her. She had been desperate to go to Germany with us but Darling Beattie wouldn't hear of it, telling her that she would be a nuisance to the rest of us if she became unwell.

'Move over, Dearest,' Aunt Griz told the dog. 'Make room for Darling Kitty to sit here with us. She's going to tell us *all* about her lovely trip to Prussia.'

I narrated the same anecdotes to the old lady that I had detailed in my letters to my youngest cousins, adding one or two stories about the Berlin nightlife which I thought she might appreciate.

'... And you found some beaux to take you about?' she asked, fondling the head of her loyal little dog. 'That's good. It's important at your age to get to know young men, and learn how to have fun in their company, without compromising yourself. It saves one getting into trouble later on.'

She glanced at the photograph of the handsome young man, which always stood on her dresser, and went on: 'I went to Germany too, you know, when I was a little older than you. Would you like to see the pictures? In the second drawer of my bureau, darling, the brown book ...'

I carried them over to the bed and turned through the pages of blurred sepia photographs; men in boaters, girls in leg-o'-mutton sleeves.

'Archie – my brother – had just bought a camera. It was quite the fashion then. Of course, he didn't know how to use it very well ...' She giggled a little. '... Not at the beginning, anyway ... That's Flora and I in Baden ... Flora was my older sister, your darling Aunt's mother. I was the tearaway, of course, she had terrible trouble trying to keep me in line ...'

I followed Aunt Griz and her siblings through the progress of their Grand Tour, through Belgium and Germany to Switzerland, Austria and finally Venice, where they stayed with a very grand aristocratic family who had a *palazzo* on the Grand Canal.

'... Such a magical place!' sighed Aunt Griz. 'And in those days it was quite *crawling* with white Russians. Lovely, elegant, cultured people ... Look, in this one you can see Flora and me wearing the gifts that one Russian count gave us ...'

Looking very English, despite their surroundings, were the young Flora and Grizelda, swathed in long sable coats, with matching hats and muffs.

'You've no idea how much I loved that coat, darling. I wore it 'til it fell apart, didn't I, Dearest? It was the most wonderful garment in my entire wardrobe ...'

When I returned to my room, I opened my own wardrobe and looked again at the fur jacket Mireille had given me, stowed in a moth-proof cover until the winter months. As I stroked the inch of cuff that was visible, I thought first of Mireille, idly wondering where she had gone to, and then of Jack, remembering his sneering reaction to the gift.

My thoughts stayed with Jack. Ever since Mireille's visit, there had been a tension between us, and it had been worse than ever when we were in Berlin. He had been the first to sense Mireille's latent treachery; I had been the last to try to defend her, for which I had not apologised.

It was on my mind the next day, and I was conscious that I was half-avoiding him, or at least avoiding speaking to him. I finally snapped when I saw him through the drawing-room window, standing on the lawn and teasing Flash with a stick. The wretched dog was lumbering from side to side and wheezing horribly, trying to raise himself on to his hind legs to grasp the stick, which Jack held well out of reach.

I flung the window open and shouted at him.

'STOP IT! Just leave the poor dog alone, can't you? You know he's got a weak heart ... you're just tormenting him. It's typical of your selfishness ...'

Jack dropped the stick in front of Flash and stood there staring at me. I turned on my heel and stormed upstairs to my room, no longer trusting myself to behave rationally.

Moments later, Jack walked in without knocking. I had half expected him to come up, spoiling for a fight, or to pour scorn on my emotional outburst. After all, there was Flash at his side, wagging his tail and smiling his half-witted smile.

But he held out his hand and said, 'Come downstairs, I want to show you something.'

He led me through the kitchen and into the larder. There, on the shelf, was Cook's latest creation – a glistening trifle in a cut-glass dish. The cream on top was decorated with glacé cherries and crystallised flowers, silver dragées and sticks of green angelica which were particularly prized in the Winstanley household. Jack tipped the bowl towards us, and the creamy surface shook slightly.

'You go first,' he said.

'Oh, Jack, we really – '

'All right, I will.'

He reached past and removed a cherry. I took a crystallised violet and popped it into my mouth. Jack retaliated with a dragée. I took a second cherry ... We continued with a brisk rhythm until the surface of the trifle was almost bare of ornament. Only one piece of angelica remained.

'You have it,' said Jack. That was his way of apologising.

After I had eaten it, I turned away, licking my lips, but he caught hold of my sleeve and pulled me back. 'What about the cream?'

With the forefinger of his right hand he made a scooping motion and came away with a large blob of cream. He swallowed it with satisfaction, then grinned at me. Unable to resist, I followed suit, and soon the surface of Cook's precious trifle looked like a ploughed field.

Jack clutched his sides. 'Can't eat any more of the stuff ...' He scooped again, though, and flicked the pellet of cream at my face. I ducked, and it spattered on my shoulder and my hair, sending me shrieking to the bowl in retaliation. Soon we were both covered, and so were the walls of the larder, and the packets of table salt and suet and gravy browning that lined the shelves.

I was aware that we were behaving like children, but there seemed something symbolic in Jack's choice of pastime, as though this was his way of saying that the hatchet was buried and we were returning to the way things had been in the past.

The cream was all gone and we were staring at the hard yellow surface of Cook's custard.

I looked at Jack enquiringly.

He shook his head. 'No,' he said, 'I'm not touching *that*. I draw the line at rubber custard.'

After Berlin, politics moved to the top of the list of Winstanley passions, displacing animals, home-grown entertainments and other people's private lives. It was a natural subject for such lovers of argument, and there was no one they liked to involve in their debates more than Nim, who was cast in the role of opposition and devil's advocate.

It wasn't entirely inappropriate that he should be picked on in this way, since he had committed a *volte face* over his opinion of the barbarous Hun. Since witnessing the new regime in Germany, he expressed admiration for anything and everything German, and wrote frequent letters to the nincompoop at *The Times*, suggesting that the unruly hordes of Britain's unemployed should be conscripted into a movement resembling Hitler Youth. He explained his beliefs at length to Darling Beattie, who was most impressed and ended up believing everything that Nim said. ('He's brainwashed her,' was Frannie's verdict.) One letter was even published, and we cringed with shame when we read it.

Sir,
There is much to be learned from our German cousins' ability to organise themselves. What we should see in the followers of Hitler is a nation of decent folk who are freeing themselves from the pettiness of democratic politics ...

Frannie howled in despair when she read this ('The shame of having a fascist for a father') and rushed off to introduce a new theme to her young communist drama – the importance of democracy. With our new-found interest came a thirst for new information, and newspapers were much in demand. We hung around in the hallway, waiting to pounce on Nim's copy of *The Times* when it was delivered. We soon wanted a broader view however – after all, *The Times* was read by thousands of people exactly like Nim – and to that end pooled our pocket money and placed an order with Varsity News Ltd in Oxford for all that Fleet Street had to offer.

Gentle Frannie, with her inbuilt sense of fairness, was the most dogmatic of us all. She would cycle to the library and pester Miss Bean to order works from the Left Book Club. On her side of the bedroom, the wall was covered with home-made red flags, and pictures of the tortured faces of what Nim would call 'Russian Bolshies'. Her aim was to provoke her father, but he was becoming less and less provokable as he grew older, and when Frannie pulled out a copy of Beverly Nicols' controversial *Cry Havoc* at the breakfast table, he simply retaliated with Oswald Mosley's *Greater Britain*.

Our political discussions made talk of what we had seen in Berlin inevitable. It was very obvious to me that Lexi never made any contribution to the recollections. I longed to know the state of play with Count Hubertus von Russow, the man with whom she claimed to be in love, but she never mentioned him.

Darling Beattie knew nothing of her daughter's love affair, but she sensed that Lexi was listless and set about trying to pair her off with Suitable Young People. She made sure that her daughter's name was on the guest list of all her acquaintances' balls, dinner parties and country weekends. Poor Beattie – never had a mother's efforts so backfired. The results, at the end of all this socialising, were disastrous.

The trouble was simply that everyone fell in love with Lexi. And that included other people's husbands and fiancés. She was single-handedly responsible for three broken engagements that season, and Nim stamped about the house growling about having the telephone cut off after incessant calls from lovesick suitors.

Frannie and I pieced this information together through a combination of Lexi's amused accounts of her conquests, overheard telephone conversations and eavesdropping on gossip amongst Darling Beattie's friends. Finally we had the chance to witness Lexi's siren-like charm in action. Darling Beattie held a little dinner-dance at Russington, just before Christmas – '*for Alexandra*', it said on the invitations.

I had a new red velvet dress, and was being pestered by James Bleak-Wailer. The two things are linked in my memory, because James launched his attack (in his own peculiarly hesitant fashion) by complimenting me on the colour I had chosen.

'Red suits you,' he offered. This was followed by, 'Your hair looks nice.' I found this mode of conversation very irritating, because after the initial compliment, the onus for its development was thrown back on to me, and I could never think of anything to say to James. 'Thank you,' was about the best I could come up with, but this didn't put him off, because he spent the whole evening at my heels, asking me to dance. '*Dance with someone else!*' was the response I was continually having to bite back.

Finally, waltzing around in a trance, I spotted Jack over James's shoulder. He was standing in the doorway of the ballroom, waving a sprig of mistletoe in a menacing fashion. He caught my eye, pointed to the mistletoe and then nodded at James and me, grinning wickedly. I mumbled some excuse to James about 'the powder room' and fled upstairs, leaving him alone and partnerless at the centre of the dance-floor.

'Kitty!' Frannie emerged from the shadows on the first-floor landing, making me jump. 'Come in here, there's something absolutely *fascinating* going on!'

101

She dragged me by the wrist into Beattie's sitting room, at the front of the house, and pointed out of the window. From that height we had a good view of the terrace and the stone steps on to the lawn, and it was quite easy to make out the figures of Lexi and some unidentified man.

'If we open the window ...' Frannie instinctively lowered her voice to a whisper '... we might be able to hear what they're saying.'

'I doubt it.' I had a lightning flash of memory – Lexi going into the hotel with the gaudy neon sign above the door – and I had no wish to hear what Lexi had to say to this anonymous man who had his hair glossed back with brilliantine, making the outline of his head sleek and reptilian. Nevertheless, I was drawn to the window, and leaned on the sill next to Frannie, shivering in the sharp December air.

We were too high up to hear properly, but the tenor of the conversation could be guessed from stance and gesture. My cousin was behaving like the cheapest kind of flirt, clinging to the man's cuff, leaning on him as she laughed, letting him bend down and put his lighter to the cigarette while she held it in her lips. Her admirer (somebody's husband, though I can't now remember whose) seemed to appreciate her mood, and went as far as tracing the outline of her lips with his fingers, though she wouldn't allow him to kiss her.

'Goodness!' said Frannie. 'Why do you think she does it?'

I felt sure I knew why, and the more I thought about it, the less I could bear to see Lexi behaving so callously to hide her own unhappiness. A few days later I went to her room and caught her getting ready for yet another party. She was standing by the wardrobe in her underwear with her hair pinned into curls, cigarette in hand.

'Kitty, darling, just the person I wanted to see ... I need your advice.'

I assumed a helpful expression.

'What do you think .. ?' She pulled an evening gown from the wardrobe. 'The blue chiffon, or do you think I should wear my grey? Only everyone at this do is going to be frightfully sophisticated, silver lamé everywhere, that sort of thing ...'

I took an envelope from my pocket and held it out to her. 'I went down to the village today to collect the last of the films I took in Berlin. I thought you'd like this.'

Lexi took the photograph from me and sat down on the edge of the bed, staring at it. I sat down next to her.

'Hubertus,' she said.

The intonation of that one word was the nearest I was going to get to an admission that she was suffering. She said nothing else.

'What are you going to do about it?' I asked.

'What do you mean?'

'Well ... why don't you write to him, invite him to stay? Now Nim and Beattie are so pro-German, they're bound to approve of him, especially if he supports Hitler – '

Lexi dragged on her cigarette and blew out the smoke in one aggressive puff. 'Pride,' she said. 'Haven't you heard of it? Hubertus knows where I am. If he wants me, he can come and find me. If he doesn't, that's an end to it.'

Gerald came into our life at that time. Gerald, Lord Arboyne, to give him his correct title. It may even have been the same night that I gave Lexi the photograph of Hubertus; the night that she met him.

It was certainly around that time that Lexi's name was mentioned in connection with a particularly scandalous affair involving three people in one bedroom (which, knowing the more fastidious side to my cousin's nature, was almost certainly not true). And a week later, Gerald mysteriously appeared as a weekend guest at Russington, with the label of 'Lexi's friend', even though none of us had heard her mention him before.

The point about Gerald was that not only was he titled and disgustingly rich, but he was also safe. He was single and, moreover, far too gormless to become involved in any risqué goings-on.

His arrival at Russington provided us with a weekend of amusement. It wasn't that we didn't like Gerald, because he was amiable enough and made efforts to please. But he was simple and straightforward and therefore an easy target for our jokes.

They began when he was standing at the foot of the staircase with his luggage, waiting for the housekeeper to take him up to his room. There was a lot of luggage (oxhide, from Drews of Piccadilly) – as much for one weekend as I took to Berlin – because Gerald had a lot of clothes. We sneaked into his room later to check and found stiff shirt-fronts and rolled collars, black silk lace evening socks, an evening dress suit with white waistcoat and tie, a Norfolk jacket and plus-fours, hunting pink and riding boots, two lounge suits, an opera cloak and a greatcoat. There were several boxes of links and studs and even a pair of spats, though he didn't have the gall to wear them, having correctly deduced that ours was not that sort of household. He did, however, wear a monocle, and we all made a point of staring at it whenever he raised it to his eye.

His presence unattended in the hall (bar Flash, who was sniffing the oxhide cases in a provocative manner) gave us the perfect opportunity for a practical joke. Clem appeared on cue, wheeling Shoes in a rickety Bath chair which they had found in the attic; the former property of some ancient and infirm relative. Shoes had given herself a ghastly appearance by applying talcum powder to her cheeks and was swathed in one of Aunt Griz's white lace nightgowns.

'Hullo,' said Clem, extending a hand. 'I'm Clement, and this is Isolde.'

Shoes gave a spectral groan.

'Is she .. ?' ventured Gerald.

'She's been a cripple from birth. She'll never walk.' Shoes swivelled her eyes and groaned again. 'Or talk,' added Clem.

'My Gawd ... Alexandra never said ... I'm sorry, how dreadful for you all ... '

Gerald was led away, shaking his head and looking pale. He was no doubt thinking of the curse of congenital illness, which might have included insanity when he saw Aunt Griz wafting about singing to her dog. A dedicated actress, Shoes would have been happy to stay in the Bath chair all weekend, but Darling Beattie put her small, square foot down, and Shoes attended afternoon tea on both legs, in grubby jodhpurs and sweater. When Gerald saw her he turned very white, then very red.

A family with a sense of propriety and good taste would have stopped there, but our blood was up and we all wanted to have a turn at tormenting the outsider. Frannie and I put a ferret's skull in the biscuit barrel beside Gerald's bed, and a bird's nest in his deerstalker. Jack appended a skeletal hand ('borrowed' from the village doctor's surgery, I'm ashamed to say) from the schoolroom window and tapped at Gerald's window all night. Irving, with the straight face that he was famous for, told the unfortunate man that we breakfasted at half past six, and crept down to find him waiting politely in the dining room, long before dawn broke.

Lexi appeared irritated by all this tomfoolery, but made no attempts to stop us. In fact, she kept a cool distance from Lord Arboyne, behaving as though he were as much our guest as hers.

This disinterest seemed predictable enough, until Saturday evening when she came down to pre-dinner drinks wearing the present that Gerald had brought her. No less than a diamond and emerald collar, that looked perfect with her tawny blonde hair. And a matching bracelet.

Gerald might have been a fool, but he was a conventional one and would not have spent several hundreds of pounds on trinkets if the gifts were not part of the courtship ritual. I confronted Lexi with this suspicion when we walked upstairs together after dinner.

'What's he doing here?' I asked.

Lexi raised her eyebrow, making her expression deliberately blank. 'Doing here?'

'I mean, why did you ask him?'

'I didn't.' She laughed and began to pull at the diamond necklace, as if it was too tight. 'Mummy did. I met Gerald at a party, and when I mentioned to Mummy afterwards that we'd danced a lot together, she invited him down. She's keen for us to become an item of gossip ... you know, a peer of the realm and all that. Bags of loot.' She laughed and held the bracelet up under the light so that it sparkled. 'D'you think we'd like diamonds as much if they didn't cost the earth?' she mused.

'Don't you mind?' I persisted. 'Aunt Beattie asking him down here?'

'Mind? Why should I? Gerald's really quite amusing.'

I stared at Lexi sceptically, and she knew that she hadn't fooled me. For the remainder of the weekend she did her best to look amused, or at least, whenever she was under the stern eyes of Frannie or myself she did. She made quite a good job of it, and by the end of Sunday evening she and Gerald were behaving a little more like the conventional idea of a courting couple. Having seen Lexi with Hubertus, I felt sure that convention was where the relationship began and ended.

Gerald may have been stupid, but his upbringing ensured that he knew all the right things to do and wear and say. He also got on well with Nim. Politics had something to do with this – Gerald was as breathtakingly right-wing as only someone whose family have owned land since Norman times can be. Some of the statements he made had Frannie furrowing her brow and rushing upstairs to scribble righteously about the integrity of young communists.

About a week after Gerald's visit it was Christmas, and we forgot about Lexi's lovelife and devoted ourselves to the annual orgy of eating, drinking and merry-making. There was a tall fir tree in the sitting room (leaning like the tower of Pisa since, as well as decorating it, we were detailed to fix it in its pot) around which a confusing mound of presents was built like a multi-coloured cairn. The estate workers and sundry villagers would convene on Christmas Eve to sing carols and partake of Cook's dubious hot toddy ('Cooking sherry,' mouthed Jack during 'Good Christian Men Rejoice'). After the carols, the devout walked down to the village for midnight mass and the heathens attended to the all-important business of hanging eight stockings (Flash was temporarily elevated to human status) from the marble fireplace.

There was a sharp frost that year, and the lake was frozen. On Christmas morning, after yawning and giggling our way through Holy Communion, Irving, Jack, Frannie, Clem and I rooted out our skates and took them out to christen the ice. It was a small lake, and so crowded when we all stepped on to it that it creaked. It was decided that we would have to take it in turns, or our efforts would be more like musical statues.

Jack and I were sitting out on the edge of the lake when we saw Lexi strolling down the lawn arm-in-arm with none other than Gerald. Gerald was looking very pleased with himself, I noted.

'It's Lord My-Gawd!' said Jack. 'Look! What the hell's he doing here?'

I asked Lexi just that when Gerald was making the conventional Christmas greetings and shaking hands all round.

'He hasn't come to see me, he's come to see Nim,' she said innocently.

We were hardly going to be satisfied with this, since a stranger at Christmas lunch was unheard of. There would be more competition for the sixpences in the pudding and the rum butter, of which there was never enough to go round. The writing was on the wall when Lexi, with something not far from a simper, told Gerald that he could have her share. This amounted to nothing short of treachery.

Fran and I made a deputation to Lexi's room, and were rewarded with the sight of a black velvet ring-box on her dressing table, hiding in a pile of half-unwrapped handkerchiefs and bath salts. She wouldn't open it.

'It would be rather fun,' she teased, 'to be Lady Arboyne. Don't you think? Imagine being able to buy anything you wanted, in any shop ...'

'What about being in love?' Fran demanded fiercely.

'Oh Frannie ...' Lexi touched the box lightly with one finger. 'This has nothing to do with *love*.'

'Does that mean .. ?'

'All in good time. You'll find out soon enough.'

'Soon' was two days later. As avid newspaper readers we were unlikely to miss the announcement, on the Court and Social pages in *The Times* and *Telegraph*, 27 December 1936.

... The engagement is announced between Gerald Francis, only son of the Earl and Countess Arboyne of Dunmow House, Salop., and Alexandra Mary, elder daughter of Sir Ernest and Lady Winstanley of Russington Hall, Russington Without, Oxon.

Four

The wedding was to take place in the spring. At eighteen, Lexi was absurdly young to be a wife, but in consenting to the marriage Nim and Beattie clearly believed they were rescuing their daughter from a worse fate than premature adulthood.

With little more than three months to go before the ceremony, my aunt took on the air of a woman with a purpose.

'There are Preparations to Be Made,' she announced, and she and Lexi were promptly whisked away in Gerald's Lagonda; their destination London and The Trousseau.

A week later, Irving returned to St John's College, where he was reading engineering, and a week after that Jack went back to school to complete his final year. Frannie and I were left to malinger at Russington with Nim, Aunt Griz and the two youngest children. It goes without saying that we were most discontented with our lot. We had had a tantalising glimpse of the real world, only to be re-incarcerated in the fortress of childhood. Or so we saw it, as we wandered gloomily about the house, reading poetry and feeling sorry for ourselves. Lexi had stolen a march on us again, and in grand style.

We concluded finally that we would have to make the most of the resources available. Rural Oxfordshire must have *some* diversions to offer, other than the traditional country pursuits. 'There must be some Intellectuals around *somewhere*,' insisted Frannie.

Our search took us to Cottington, a village some five miles away, that was larger than Russington Without. There was a pub there called the Fox and Hounds, which was frequented in the evenings by the younger and more bohemian offspring of the Old Faithfuls and the county set in general. There was no question of us being driven there in the Motor, so our outings necessitated much advance planning, and required us to get changed at least an hour before we hoped to arrive at the pub.

'If only we both had bicycles,' lamented Frannie. 'You should have asked for one for Christmas, instead of boring old camera stuff.'

We found a second bicycle in the gardener's shed, but it had been abandoned because it only had one tyre. Frannie rejected a plan for us to take it in turns to cycle on her machine while the other ran alongside, so we were left with the interminably slow village bus (which dropped us in Cottington far too early), or a combination of walking and cadging lifts from whatever vehicles happened to be passing. One freezing cold February night we walked the whole five miles, singing a selection from *Hymns Ancient and Modern* and beating our arms against our chests to keep ourselves warm. I would happily have turned back, but Frannie was relentless in her pursuit of intellectual improvement.

We were younger than the rest of the 'young crowd' who drank at the Fox and Hounds, but we had travelled in Europe and were opinionated enough to keep pace, and so we were welcomed into the tight little clique. They were of a broader social mix than we were used to, not just local landowners but children of doctors and lawyers and even tenant farmers. In other words, people that Nim and Beattie wouldn't have approved of, which pleased Frannie. They seemed particularly interested in her political opinions, although her views were rather too extreme for most of the crowd.

One evening I was at the bar, buying myself a ginger beer, when James Bleak-Wailer and his sister came in. The three of us stayed chatting at the bar, and it was at least half an hour before I excused myself and walked back in the direction of the fire to see what Frannie was up to. I was reassured: she was being lionised by the others, sitting in the middle of the low wooden bench and talking with animation. Her eyes sparkled.

When I got a little closer, I could see that it was because she had had too much to drink. She had a glass of port in her hand, and the man next to her was taking it from her every few minutes and refilling it. He was small and weaselly, wearing a dark sweater and a raincoat.

'Come on!' he said to Fran. 'Do you really know the words of "The Red Flag"?'

'Of course,' replied my cousin, naïve to the last. 'I'll sing it to you if you like ...'

As she opened her mouth, I intercepted a look that passed between Weasel and a doctor's daughter in matching sweater and beret. It was the sort of look that signalled that they were both trying not to laugh, and Weasel winked at the girl over Frannie's shoulder.

'Fran, we have to go now,' I said desperately, interrupting the song.

Frannie stared up at me tipsily, furrowing her brow. 'But you said ... we said ... we were going to catch the bus back at ten o'clock. Or David'll drive us back.' She indicated Weasel and his port bottle.

'We're going now,' I said, and dragged my cousin to her feet.

She was angry with me, and turned on me once we were outside the door of the pub, and the bitter night air started to sober her up. 'What's the matter with you?' she protested. 'They were interested. They were interested in what I had to say.'

'Fran – they were *laughing* at you, don't you see? They were probably laughing at me too. Because of who we are.'

'But that doesn't matter. We're all the same, we believe in the same things ... '

Her voice tailed away, as self-doubt crept in.

I linked my arm through hers and started to pull her along the lane. 'No,' I said shaking my head. 'We're just the crazy girls from up at the Hall, that's all. People like that will never take us seriously – '

'But – '

'Not here, anyway. We'll have to go away first.'

'Like Lexi. Lucky thing.' Frannie sighed.

A few weeks after the episode at the Fox and Hounds, I received a phone call. I think it was probably the first phone call I'd ever had.

'Ah ... hullo. It's James here.'

'James?'

'James Peake-Taylor.'

'Oh.'

Only James Bleak-Wailer. For a moment I thought I might have a secret admirer.

'I haven't seen you or Francesca in the Fox and Hounds lately.'

James did not go on, leaving the conversational ball in my court, as usual.

'We've stopped going ... it got a bit boring, really. And Cottington's too far for us to walk.'

110

'Oh, I see ... I wondered if perhaps you'd like to come out with me.'

'If *I* would? Just me?'

'Well ...' James sounded slightly embarrassed. 'There's only really room for two of us in my car ... '

He had a car! 'Yes, I'd love to!'

Having transport at our disposal meant that James and I could make the twenty-mile trip into Oxford, which was the most sophisticated destination I could have hoped for in the circumstances. I felt quite excited as Frannie (who had generously decided not to be jealous) kept watch at the window while I dressed for the occasion in my red velvet dress, fur jacket and evening gloves. (Were three-quarter-length gloves the right thing to wear, I wondered? Would Lexi have worn three-quarter-length gloves? She was no longer there to ask.)

Nim came down the steps with me, shook hands with James, who replied with a polite, 'Good evening, Sir Ernest,' and helped me into James's Austin Seven. If Darling Beattie had been at home she would have fussed vaguely about the suitability of a girl not quite sixteen going out for dinner with a boy not much older, but Nim gave the enterprise his blessing, seemingly only concerned that I didn't choose a dish that would give me wind.

'Stay off the sprouts. Tend to catch up with one about two hours later. Good family, the Peake-Taylors, solid people. Shame he didn't ask your cousin, but then you are better looking than she is, so it's not surprising.'

We sped off into Oxford through Burford and Witney, exchanging few words on the way. James pretended to be concentrating on driving and I pretended to be concentrating on the road. Once we reached the restaurant, however, we both relaxed. He had chosen the Sorbonne, a traditional French establishment in the High Street, where we were the youngest diners by fifty years. The other tables were taken by dons and clerics, arguing stuffily about Spenser and obscurantism.

James pointed out in a whisper that one of them had forgotten to change out of his carpet slippers, which made both of us laugh very indiscreetly. I hadn't glimpsed a sense of humour in any of the Bleak-Wailers before, but then I hadn't really been looking for one, taking my cousins' word for it that they didn't possess one. Discovering it was a great relief, and I started to see James in a new light. What I had dismissed as feebleness was merely gentleness; an alien quality. His restrained approach to the courtship ritual was certainly a relief after Deacon. I decided that he was liberated by the

111

absence of the maverick Jack. As was I.

We ordered sole (easy to digest) and talked mainly about neutral subjects like the trip to the Olympics, and James's proposed study of history when he went up to the university that autumn. Then suddenly, half way through the *crème brûlée*, he looked at me very intently and said, 'You're very different to your cousins, you know. Nicer.'

I felt self-conscious and blushed, not because of the compliment but because for the second time in my life I was being singled out.

'They're nice too,' I said loyally. 'You just have to understand how they work.'

James looked unconvinced, so we didn't mention the Winstanleys again for the rest of the evening, which ended promptly at eleven o'clock, as Nim had ordered.

Frannie was lying in wait for me with her reading light on.

'Did he kiss you?' she demanded as I peeled off the gloves.

'Of course not!'

'Well, what was it like then?'

'Quite nice,' I conceded.

'And what about the Bleak-Wailer? Was he nice?'

'Quite.'

'Don't worry,' said Frannie darkly, switching off the light and rolling over. 'I won't tell Jack.'

Reports filtered through from London about the fabulous time Lexi was having, the money being spent and the wonderful silk organza bridesmaids' dresses that Frannie, Shoes and I were to have. But London life was a tantalising distance away and Frannie soon became restless again. She again went looking for trouble in the guise of intellectual stimulation.

She cycled back from the village one afternoon in a state of great excitement, waving a pamphlet.

'Look!' she shouted. 'A happening!'

When I took the pamphlet from her and read it, I was disappointed to discover that she was referring to an evening event hosted by Russington Women's Institute. It was a lecture to be held at the parish hall, entitled 'Our European Neighbours'.

'They're giving a talk about Europe!' said Frannie, her eyes shining with excitement. 'I'll be able to speak about the things I've read.'

'No you won't,' I said. 'A "talk" means that someone else speaks and you sit and listen.'

'Oh.'

Frannie attended the lecture anyway, with Miss Howland and myself in tow. When we arrived, the vicar's wife was already setting up the slide lantern, and testing it out with shots of what appeared to be her family holiday; two children eating an ice cream and the vicar with his trouser legs rolled up. Most of the seats were already filled with the good women of the village, holding their handbags on their laps in a self-important fashion. At the back of the room the tea urn was being cranked up, an ancient machine that groaned for the two hours it took to heat up.

The visitor speaker was some eminent lady travel-writer. The vicar stepped up on to the platform and made a welcoming speech.

'... And I for one am eagerly looking forward to hearing about the fascinating countries of Europe, and their people. So will you all be so good as to welcome Miss Adele Taylforth.'

That worthy spinster stepped on to the platform, fixed a pince-nez on to her nose and started to work her way through the slides, which seemed to depict chiefly the vineyards of France, the bull-rings of Spain ('What about the Civil War?' whispered Frannie) and the cuckoo-clock makers of Switzerland. The groaning of the tea urn and the whirring of the slide lantern made me feel drowsy, and after a few minutes I dozed off.

I woke as Miss Taylforth was delivering her closing speech, prompting her audience to let go of their handbags and applaud with polite enthusiasm. Beside me, Frannie was sitting on the very edge of the chair, her body tensed, her expression alert.

Miss Taylforth held up her hand for silence. 'I might just say, ladies, that there has not been time tonight for me to touch on the communist atrocities being committed in Spain, or indeed the evils perpetrated in Russia in the name of Marxism.'

Like a shot, Frannie was on her feet. Her freckled face coloured slightly, but she spoke out firmly and clearly.

'Perhaps your audience would like to hear about a greater evil? I'm referring to the evil of mass marches where every fist is raised and everyone chants in unison. Or what about the evil of the Jewish persecution, which we all so conveniently choose to ignore?'

With breathtakingly quick thinking, Miss Howland started to clap loudly, and I joined in, so that Frannie could no longer be heard clearly. To my surprise, several other members of the audience clapped too. The vicar leapt nimbly to the platform and said, 'I'm sure we'd all like to thank Miss Winstanley for her comments. Does anyone else have a question . . ?'

It wasn't much, but Frannie believed that she had introduced the just cause of the left into the consciousness of Russington and was satisfied. More than satisfied, in fact, when one of the people cheering her turned out to be the local funeral-and-flower-show reporter. He referred to the incident in his report in the *Windrush Gazette* and then telephoned to request an interview.

Frannie's hopes of setting the world to rights were dashed by Nim, who had been informed of his daughter's speech by some treacherous Old Faithful who had been lurking in the parish hall. He was furious, and even took the rare step of summoning her to his study to bark at her.

'He told me that my ideas were dangerous,' said Frannie afterwards. 'Of course I argued back, and he didn't like that very much. He said he didn't believe any daughter of his could possibly think those things, and that I would turn our family into a laughing stock. That's what you said, wasn't it, Kitty? The last time we went to Cottington.'

'This is different,' I reassured her. 'He's just saying it because he doesn't know what else to think.'

Nim did seem to be confused. I suspected that the confidence he gained from Mireille's attentions was duly shattered when the affair was discovered. He needed to cling hard to his old beliefs, but since Berlin the Huns were no longer the foe. The communists now filled that role, and the Jews, by association. Now that he had confronted Frannie, the two of them were forced to wear their beliefs on their sleeves. The alternative would have been to give in, and that was something a Winstanley never did.

The tension between Nim and his daughter was interrupted by the advent of March, which meant the wedding.

Fran and Shoes and I were transported to London, to begin a series of fittings for our dresses. Nim had rented a house in Orme Court for the duration of the nuptial hullaballoo, and the place was buzzing with activity and unsuppressed excitement. Parcels of wedding presents arrived by every post, and we had a wonderful time reading the cards from grand people we had never even heard of, and marvelling at the ugliness of some of the contents.

Lexi was there somewhere at the centre of it all, with a new, short hairstyle and lipstick worn every day as a matter of course – even at breakfast. A wide-eyed portrait of her appeared in a fashionable London magazine, and she seemed to waft around in an atmosphere of satin, lace and tissue paper as the all-important trousseau accumulated about her. Gerald popped up at intervals calling her 'darling' and sending round flowers and chocolates for the rest of us. ('Exactly how rich is he?' Frannie and I speculated greedily.)

Darling Beattie, stomping about the house with lists of menus, and remonstrating with florists on the telephone, seemed to think that her daughter's behaviour was all that was expected in a bride-to-be. But I was not convinced by Lexi's glassy-eyed serenity. She was playing the part all right, but she did not seem at ease with it, or with herself. It would have been highly inflammatory to say anything with everyone in such a state of excitement, so I just waited.

On the night before the wedding, when Nim and the boys and Aunt Griz had arrived and had somehow been squeezed into the house, Lexi came into my room. She was wearing a hairnet to protect her hair, and it made her look most peculiar, like Joan of Arc.

She looked at my camera equipment, laid out in preparation for the next day, and sighed. Sitting down on the edge of the bed, she lit a cigarette.

'Hubertus is in London.'

I put a hand on her shoulder. 'What are you going to do?'

'I don't know,' she said, but the expression on her face suggested that she did know.

I lay awake all night thinking about her dilemma, and by the time morning came I was stupefied with tiredness. I didn't mention what I knew to anyone, not even to Frannie as the two of us started to dress for the wedding. Frannie climbed straight into the delicate cream-coloured dress. I sat at the dressing table in my petticoat and waited.

Then Lexi came in, complete with lipstick. She was wearing a suit. 'Don't put it on,' she said, pointing to my bridesmaid's dress. 'Hubertus is downstairs.'

'*Hubertus?*' asked a dumbfounded Frannie. 'What on earth are you talking about? Lexi – '

She was already walking out of the room.

'*Lexi!*'

We followed her on to the landing. Sure enough, standing at the bottom of the stairs, his pale hair gleaming, was Hubertus von Russow.

'Oh my goodness!' Frannie's hand flew up to her mouth. 'They're going to elope!'

Nim and Beattie appeared on the landing. Beattie was in her wedding outfit, a corsage of orchids pinned to her bosom. She stared at her daughter.

'What's going on, darling? You should be getting ready for the church ...'

Her voice trailed away as Lexi hurried past her and down the stairs to where Hubertus was standing.

'Good God, it's that ruddy German!' stormed Nim. 'She's running off with him!'

'Which German? cried Beattie. 'Lexi, wait ..!' She rounded on her husband. 'You mean you knew about this person ..? Then it's all your fault! In heaven's name, why didn't you ..?'

'ALEXANDRA!' bellowed Nim. 'ALEXANDRA, COME HERE AT ONCE!'

He was running down the stairs, braces flying, but Lexi picked up the suitcase that was standing by the front door and simply walked out, to gasps of disbelief from the landing where the rest of us stood watching. Nim went out into the street in his bare feet and shouted himself hoarse, but it did no good. They had gone.

As is often the case in moments of high drama, my mind focused on small details and retained them at the forefront of my memory. I remember noticing how small Lexi's suitcase was. She's leaving the trousseau behind, I thought, so it must be true love. And I remember that Shoes kept her bridesmaid's dress on for the rest of the day anyway. She said it was hers, and therefore we couldn't deprive her of the chance to wear it, just once.

London society mourned on Darling Beattie's behalf, and sent her letters of sympathy when the terse little apology appeared in *The Times* Court Circular. I felt sorry for Gerald. He hadn't expected anything like this, but then he didn't really know anything about Lexi. I doubt she had even mentioned Hubertus.

Next to the notice in *The Times*, it was the ignominy of the unneeded wedding gifts that upset Beattie most.

'Oh dear, what are we going to do with them?' she wailed, waving her arms over the Aladdin's cave of booty that had accumulated in the dining room. Seeing the expressions that crossed our faces she added, 'They will all have to be returned, of course.'

'I'll tell you what,' said Jack suddenly. 'Why don't I do it? Take charge of returning them all, I mean.'

'Oh Jack, darling, you are an angel! *Would* you? Only it would be one less thing for me to worry about.'

116

The next morning, Jack came and found me in the breakfast room. He was carrying a pad of paper, a pencil, and a street map of London.

He put the paper down in front of me.

'Right, let's get down to business!'

'I take it this has something to do with returning the presents?'

'Precisely. You and I are going to work out the delivery route ... you'll find the names and addresses of the donors on that page. What we have to do is group them together according to their area, or their location within a certain area.'

'Not exactly difficult,' I said drily, scanning the list. 'They all live in Kensington, Mayfair or Belgravia.'

'Good. So, for example, to start with we have Mr and Mrs Henry Channing at 23 Eaton Square, the Dowager Lady Angus at number 45, then just round the corner in Elizabeth Street, Monsieur *et* Madame Richoux ...'

'It's awfully good of you,' I commented, as we scribbled away. 'Some of the presents are awfully big to lug around.'

'Oh, I'm not going to carry them! Come outside with me a minute, and I'll show you ...'

Tethered to the railings outside was a piebald pony, harnessed to a small delivery cart. On its side, in gold letters on blue, was written 'PICKERINGS BAKERIES – *Finest quality bread and cakes. Est. 1879*'.

'Jack, where on earth did that come from?'

'I borrowed it.'

'I hope you don't mean – '

'No, I didn't just take it. I'm going to pay for it – out of the profits.'

'What profits?' I asked, though I had already guessed.

Jack grinned. 'Why don't you come with me, and find out.'

We loaded up the cart with presents and climbed on to the driving seat, after Jack had first repulsed Clem's efforts to join us ('Sorry old boy, this trip's just for me and Kitty.').

We clopped along the edge of the path, which was ablaze with daffodils and crocuses, laughing at the frustration of the motorists who were stuck behind us. When we reached our first address in Belgravia, Jack handed me the reins and whipped a delivery boy's cap out of his pocket. 'Goes with the cart rental,' he told me. 'All right, watch this.' He rang the front-door bell, and the door was opened by a servant or housekeeper in uniform.

Jack tipped his cap. 'Good morning – J. W. Deliveries Limited. I'm returning a gift sent for the wedding of Miss Alexandra

Winstanley, which has unfortunately been cancelled.'

He proffered the parcel and the maid thanked him. Jack then scratched his head. 'I'm afraid there is a delivery charge – ten shillings.'

The maid looked doubtful, but took the parcel inside and duly returned with the money.

I was running through the number of guests on the wedding list and doing some mental arithmetic. Some of the guests lived in the country, and their gifts would be returned by post, but even so, that left a clear profit of around one-hundred pounds.

'It's immoral!' I protested, when Jack rejoined me on the cart. 'I've a good mind to tell Aunt Beattie when we get back and have you forced to give it all to charity!'

I didn't, though. We passed a florist in Belgrave Road and Jack ran in and bought me a huge bunch of yellow roses. I decided his venture was just free enterprise after all.

Two weeks later, after we had returned to the comforting familiarity of Russington, I received a letter from Lexi.

10th April, 1937.
Berlin
Darling Kitty and everyone,
Well, I've done it – I'm a German! A few days after you last saw me, I was in the poky basement of the German Embassy, renouncing my British citizenship and handing over my British passport in exchange for a German one. It's got a horrid swastika on the front – nowhere near as nice as the dear old British lion.

Of course to do this I first had to become Hubertus's wife – in another poky little room, a register office. We had a proper party when we got back to Berlin and Hubertus's uncle (his father's dead, poor lamb) stood up and made a sweet speech welcoming me to the family.

We have got a lovely house in the Grunewald – not grand but quite stylish. It's a very sociable place – H.'s friends drop in and out and I seem to be very busy entertaining them all the time. Such bliss to be in charge of one's own home, and sleep in as long as one likes.

You've no idea how sorry I am about the wedding, and disappointing you all, but I don't think it's a good idea to go into all that here. Please try to convince Mummy and Nim that everything is all right – *more* than all right, I am terribly happy, and could never have been happy like this with G. It wasn't all selfishness – I did a lot of it to please everyone else.

118

Hubertus and his friends are all very excited about a new movement they belong to, though to me it seems nothing more than an excuse to enjoy themselves and sit around talking politics at all times of the day and night . . .

I re-read the opening of the letter again. How typical of Lexi to gloss over her marriage to Hubertus, as though it was of secondary importance. I wasn't sure who she meant by 'Kitty and everyone', but with prompting from Frannie, took the letter down to the drawing room after dinner and showed it to Nim and Beattie.

'So you knew about this . . . Hubertus all along?' said Beattie accusingly when she had read it.

'Well yes . . . no.' I was flustered. 'What I mean is, I knew that they'd met, but I had no idea he was in London until he came to the house on the day of the . . . when Lexi left.'

I allowed myself a small white lie – my knowing Hubertus had arrived the night before couldn't have changed anything in the long run.

'It sounds as if you knew rather a lot to me,' said Nim heavily.

I didn't want the interview to turn into a trial for conspiracy. 'Look,' I said desperately. 'The point is that Hubertus is a very nice man, and his family is very well respected. Lexi's even a Countess now – '

'She's still a German, though. Can't change that.'

I was dumbstruck by Nim's hypocrisy, and said so. '. . . I thought you admired the way the Germans run their country.'

'One thing to admire their politics. Another to *marry* one!'

I didn't want to defend Lexi further – she was *their* daughter after all – so I left them with the letter in the hope that Darling Beattie would make a note of the address.

Up in my room, I felt overcome by a powerful new emotion. I was missing Lexi and her brisk pragmatism that was such a welcome foil to Frannie's sentimental optimism. None of us had ever been away from Russington for more than two months before, and now one of our number was gone and might not, as far as we could tell, ever come back.

Five

Frannie and I came out in the spring of 1938.

Nim and Beattie rented the house in Orme Court again, and Beattie came up to London with us to accompany Fran and me on what we considered to be a quite pointless ritual.

'This show of social inequality is completely against my political principles,' Frannie stated firmly (and not a little pompously) the night before we were to go to court, 'but I'm going to go through with it as a completion of my duties to my parents. After these duties have been fulfilled, I shall start to live the sort of life that my conscience demands.'

I knew that my cousin was nowhere near as confident as she sounded. Like me, she looked on this final passage into the adult world as the beginning of all sorts of uncertainties. And like me she was curious, even about the interior of Buckingham Palace.

Never one to pass up the chance of economy, Darling Beattie had hit upon the idea of remodelling our unused bridesmaids' dresses into court wear. Both Frannie and I had grown since the ill-fated wedding, and even though the dresses were altered by the skilful hands of Mrs Moira Soames of Farm Street, they were still punishingly tight across the chest. The ostrich feathers worn were never bought, but hired, and they had the sour smell of someone else's wardrobe interior. A hairdresser was engaged to come to the house and fix the feathers to the tops of our heads, a procedure which caused much hilarity. I think the hairdresser was glad to pack up her tongs and go.

'We look just like circus horses,' observed Frannie, as she viewed her complete person in a full-length mirror. I wriggled out of my three-quarter-length gloves, grabbed my camera and took a photo-graph of her as she stood there with her head on one side, capturing the amused and slightly quizzical expression on her face.

I was still clutching my camera in one hand when the time came for us to climb into the hired Daimler (the Motor was not to be exposed to the hazards of London traffic), and in the other, my stiff posy of white flowers.

Darling Beattie eyed the camera and frowned. 'Not very suitable, I wouldn't think, dear, to take that along ...' She looked out of the window at the queue of cars ahead of us, inching its way along the Mall, and sighed. 'By rights, of course, darling Lexi should be with us today, to be presented as a bride ... the Countess von Russow ...'

She said the name out loud, as though the sound of it comforted her. Once the scandal of the elopement had died away, Nim and Beattie had softened towards their wayward daughter. Her letters from Berlin had convinced them that she moved in the cream of German society, and eleven months after her marriage she had at least fulfilled one daughterly requirement by giving birth to a son, Paul.

When we arrived at the Palace we were herded into a brightly lit corridor that was already crowded with other debutantes and their musty-smelling ostrich feathers. A white-gloved flunkey politely removed my camera from my possession, assuring me that it would be returned when I left.

We shuffled our way down along the stretch of red carpet, rather as though we were queueing for a bus. Then someone tweaked at the trains that had been sewn on to the back of our former brides-maids' dresses and a voice from nowhere bawled, 'The Lady Winstanley, Miss Francesca Winstanley, Miss Katherine Conway.'

The King and Queen nodded, we curtsied twice (badly, in my case), and shuffled on. And that was it. We were Out.

Despite our outward cynicism, both Frannie and I quite enjoyed this peculiarly English rite of passage. We still liked dressing up, and the grandeur of the palace heightened our excitement at being on the brink of a new life which had limitless possibilities.

But the social season was a disappointment; every bit as boring as Lexi had said it was. Beattie stayed on in Orme Court and pored over the list of Suitable Young People to be invited to our coming-out dance. It was the same list she had used for Lexi, with some scribbled crossings-out and additions. In the meantime,

Frannie and I raced between fork luncheons, teas and cocktail parties, which were often all-girl affairs, and heart-stoppingly dull. Then there were the dances, several a night, at which the same faces appeared, as indistinguishable as the faces of the Friesians in Nim's prize dairy herd. Our redeeming hope as the season started was that the company of so many people of our own age would provide us with interesting encounters and stimulating discussions. It was a hope soon dashed. The conversation revolved around dances just attended, and dances about to be attended, with the occasional question about our favourite sporting pursuits. Politics may as well not have existd, and Frannie's concern for the persecution of the Jews was invariably laughed at or stone-walled. We were always being told by some fresh-faced youth that we had met the night/ week/dance before, and we never remembered them or their names. Darling Beattie was in despair.

The three months of the summer started to feel like a prison sentence for offenders in evening frocks − four of them to be precise, worn in strict rotation. Frannie rebelled sooner than I did. She invented flu or a cold, and finally a sprained ankle, which kept her incapacitated and in a bandage for three weeks, until her mother took her to Harley Street and she was found to have miraculously healed. After that she would simply be delivered at the dances, go in, munch her way through a plateful of food and walk out again, to spend the rest of the evening amusing herself at the pictures or sitting in a café reading the latest offering from the Left Book Club. I devoted my time to taking photographs of fellow debs, which I then sold to their mothers, and making friends with one or two of the more sympathetic and rebellious girls we'd met.

In the free time we had, which wasn't much, Frannie and I were plotting furiously. The lease on the London house expired in August, when Darling Beattie would put away her list and decamp to Russington. We were expected to follow her there, and spend an indefinite period of time accepting invitations from the friends we had made during the season until we were spotted by a Suitable Man and duly swallowed up by the matrimonial machine.

We would not go back to Russington, we decided. We were passable dancers, but apart from that we had none of the required talents for the social set, and the alternative was a dreary, intellectually barren incarceration in the Windrush valley. We would have liked to go to university, but we had never taken any exams.

'Er ... Mummy,' Frannie said tentatively one day. 'I think I'd quite like to stay here in London after you've gone home.'

'Why, dear? Don't tell me you've Met Someone!'

Frannie looked puzzled. 'No ... I just want to live here.'

My aunt was unfamiliar with the notion of anyone wanting to *live* in London, unless it was as someone's wife. However, we impressed on her that although we were officially Grown-Up now, we wouldn't be above running away if we were forced to go back to Russington. She knew us well enough to take the threat seriously, but was understandably anxious about two seventeen-year-olds living unchaperoned in London. In the end, a compromise was reached. We would be supervised by one of Nim's cousins, an elderly widow called Lady Reeve, and live as paying guests in her house in Carlyle Square.

We were more than satisfied with this compromise; in fact we were thrilled by it. Our accommodation was to be the three basement rooms of the house, which had their own bathroom, and more importantly, their own entrance from the street. Lady Reeve told us that her legs were bad, and that she never went down to the basement.

We eschewed the word 'basement' in favour of 'the flat' which sounded adult, modern and a touch risqué. We would get to know the *real* London, we decided idealistically, not just through parties (though we might go to one or two 'bring a bottle' affairs if we chose to) but by talking to people who lived and worked there, writers and artists and all-purpose Intellectuals. We weren't daunted by the fact that we had no idea where to find these people.

Our new life was not as idyllic or as easy as we had at first imagined it would be. For the first time in our lives there was no external regime imposed on us, and we found time hanging heavily on our hands. How to fill the day?

We visited cafés in the King's Road, frequented by an artistic crowd, and in Bloomsbury, but no one we met was very interested in us. London, we discovered, was a very big place and outside the narrow upper-class world we had been born into (through no fault of our own, as Frannie was continually pointing out) our importance was much diluted. We were just two fresh young faces amongst countless thousands.

Besides, the time spent in cafés could only be spun out so far. After one or two drinks, if nothing had happened, we would get restless, and our pose of sophistication would wear thin. We would wonder why the waiter was staring at us, and discuss leaving. We also made the discovery that many of these so-called bohemians were as boring as Nim and Beattie's Oxfordshire friends.

123

An inordinate amount of time was spent thinking about, and procuring, meals. We didn't know how to cook or keep house – no one had thought to teach us – and 'the flat' had no kitchen, yet three times a day, at least, our bodies demanded food. Occasionally Lady Reeve asked us to join her for the skimpy lunch prepared by her Irish cook/housekeeper, but we were too fearful of losing our independence to fraternise with the old lady very often.

Food cost money – another fact that astonished us at first. There was no estate farm to provide eggs and lettuces and lamb chops. We each had a small allowance from Nim, but we were very fond of visiting Heal's and buying interesting artefacts for our new home, and in the rush to acquire frosted-glass ice buckets and the latest gramophone player, we quite overlooked the need for budgeting. We ate cakes from the local bakery until we grew tired of them, then Frannie brought a calor-gas stove and fried eggs over it. Eventually we devised the plan of taking it in turns to go to the Chelsea farmers' market to buy 'sensible' food.

We had never lived in such a confined space before, and what had seemed 'cosy' at first began to seem oppressive after spending days on end with only each other for company. After a few weeks we were squabbling over every tiny thing.

One such quarrel had us not speaking for nearly a day. In the evening, we sat at opposite ends of the sitting room. I sorted mechanically through our collection of gramophone records, shooting poisonous looks at Frannie's unwashed frying pan, while she pretended to be engrossed in the latest copy of *Out of Bounds*, a subversive magazine for rebellious adolescents.

I knew that we were both thinking the same thing, and were on the verge of saying it, but neither could quite drum up the courage to vocalise such a negative thought. Fran, who had more courage than I, finally spoke.

'This isn't working, is it?' She put down her book.

'I know. I'm sorry, I – '

'It's not just you, it's . . . ' Frannie shrugged. ' . . . everything. Life isn't . . . I don't know, nothing about growing older is as easy as you think it's going to be.'

'It would help if we didn't spend so much time together. If we've been alone in the past, it's always because we wanted to be. And there were always the others to dilute things.'

Frannie smiled wistfully, and I knew she was thinking of Lexi, that unlikely peacemaker. 'Well, I'll try to be more tidy if you'll try to be more patient. And we shouldn't feel we're going to hurt each other's feelings if we want to go off and do things on our own.

124

Agreed?' She extended her hand to seal our pact.

'Wash the frying pan first.'

Gradually, inevitably, Fran and I went our separate ways. She sniffed out sympathetic political cells and committed herself to the cause of communism, while I got in touch with the friends I had made on the debutante circle, who now made up what was considered a rather fast young set.

Seeing less of one another meant that we could live together more happily. We still talked a lot, usually sitting up over a late-night drink of whatever could be found in the flat's haphazard larder: coffee, red wine, gin and bitters. Once, on a glorious night that embodied all we had imagined our new liberated life to be, Fran brought back two young men from a meeting she had been to. The four of us sat up until half past two and drank an entire bottle of vodka.

Jack Winstanley was also in London.

I don't know exactly when he arrived, since he didn't announce his plans to us. We heard of his move in one of Darling Beattie's dutiful weekly letters, which we always forgot to answer. He was not living in a flat with other young people, Beattie explained in a despairing tone, but *alone* in a *studio*.

Darling Beattie gave us the address and instructed us to go and see him, 'To make sure he's all right'. I was quite sure that Jack was all right and always would be, but I wanted to see him. What was more, I had a yen to go alone. I made sure that I mentioned the intended visit at a time when I knew Frannie was engrossed with other things.

'Oh yes,' she said vaguely, as she penned a letter of protest to one of the newspapers (more Nim's daughter than she would have liked to admit). 'You'll have to go without me this time, I'm afraid. Send Jack my best love and tell him I'll see him soon. Invite him over here, or something . . . '

Jack's studio was on the fourth floor of one of the Nash terraces overlooking Regent's Park. He had borrowed it from a friend who dabbled in sculpture, and the large, echoing room was filled with half-finished pieces of work draped in sheets. Every surface and the bare floorboards were covered in a fine film of plaster dust. The only sign of Jack's habitation was the open suitcase next to the narrow pallet bed in the corner. We sat on the edge of the bed to eat lunch – bread and cheese from a shared plate.

I was surprised, therefore, when Jack took me downstairs to show me his new car – a blue racing Bugatti.

'Jack .. ! It's beautiful! Is it really yours?' I stroked the gleaming bonnet and suspicions raced through my mind. 'How on earth did you pay for it?'

He gave me the familiar half smile. 'I invested the proceeds from returning Lexi's wedding presents. And I've done one or two other bits of business ... '

'You mean ... like the delivery business?'

'That sort of thing, yes. Buying and selling.'

He didn't elaborate, but held open the passenger door and distracted me with the promise of a spin. We drove into town and raced around Hyde Park Corner so fast that I screamed and clutched at his arm. I made him promise to drive back more slowly, and this gave us the opportunity to talk.

'It's rather strange, isn't it,' Jack said with a grin, 'us being out together like this.'

I had been thinking the same thing. We were two young adults, who just happened to be cousins, leading separate lives and who only needed to come together if they wished to. I became acutely aware that people in the street seeing us drive by would assume that we were a courting couple. Lovers, perhaps.

I didn't feel at ease with this new relationship, and the more I thought about it, the more I found it difficult to be alone with Jack. I *liked* being alone with Jack, but wanted the safety of Russington as a backdrop. It was dawning on me that perhaps I was in love with my own cousin, someone who knew me almost as well as I knew myself and who had been raised with me like a brother. The thought was too shocking and I pushed it firmly to the back of my mind. Nevertheless, I tended to invite him to the flat when I was confident that Frannie would be there, or to visit his studio only on social occasions. This wasn't easy, either, as I didn't care much for his friends. He only had time for the very rich, or those who could be useful to him, so they were a mixed crowd.

We had more success with my friends, who all liked and welcomed Jack. Particularly the girls, who regularly lost their hearts. I became acutely aware of the effect that his good looks and roguish charm had on the opposite sex, and was ruder and more critical of him than before. I tried telling myself that I was a disinterested party and it was my duty as a cousin to take him down a peg or two. And I became curious about Jack's own sexuality, since he always seemed indifferent to his conquests. He kept his distance, but he was happy to fall in with my crowd whenever there was a party in the offing. That autumn we went to so many – bottle parties, pyjama parties, baby parties, treasure hunts. We haunted the cabaret at the Café de Paris, and saw the New Year in at the Gargoyle Club, welcoming 1939 in a sea of balloons, funny hats and streamers. We saw no reason not to be optimistic about the next twelve months. After all, when it came down to it, Hitler and Mussolini were just a couple of foreign dictators, and we British had more sense.

So many parties. I made sure I went to them all, not because I was afraid of missing anything, but so that I wouldn't have time to think about the fact that I was growing bored.

Frannie had the edge over me when it came to spending time profitably. I envied her for experiencing life more intensely than I. But I was also aware that she was prone to being influenced by people she met.

The most notable example was Simon Gold. He was one of the young men that Frannie had brought home for our vodka-drinking session, and I returned one day from lunching with a friend to find him alone in our flat.

He leapt to his feet to introduce himself.

'Hello, I'm Simon. I take it you're Kitty? Fran has just gone to buy some food. She said to tell you she'd be back in a few minutes.'

I walked towards the bedroom to remove my hat and coat, but Simon said, 'Sit down, and let's talk.'

I wasn't used to this direct approach, and turned back to examine my cousin's friend more closely. He was short and thin, but strong-looking – 'wiry' was the obvious word to describe his build. His dark, curly hair sprang from his head with an energy of its own. He certainly wasn't handsome but he had mesmeric dark eyes, and his face had a mobile, watchable quality. I did as he said, and sat down.

He started to talk about Frannie. It was obvious that he was very fond of her.

'She's got so much courage,' he said proudly. 'She'd take on anyone in a fight, if she felt that the cause was right. Of course, her lack of education is against her, and she's been raised with some dangerous ideas ... d'you know, the other day, when we met a young girl who hadn't been able to find employment, Fran suggested that she might like to go and work at her parents' house, as a between maid!'

He laughed at this piece of snobbish idealism, and I saw clearly

127

that Simon was playing the role of crusader with a mission to rescue Frannie from the corruption of her class, and re-educate her. Frannie, for her part, appeared only too willing to be rescued.

I came to know Simon well during the early months of 1939, as he spent more and more time at our flat. Sometimes I would get up in the morning and find him asleep on the sofa, covered with a blanket that Fran had lovingly tucked round him. I wasn't sure of the extent of their relationship, but it was obvious to me that my cousin was in love, with Simon's ideals if nothing else.

Simon was a Jew, of Polish extraction, who had grown up in a drab street in Lewisham, where his father had a tailoring business. He was as committed to the cause of communism as it was possible to be.

'All Frannie's done is just deliberately pick the least suitable person she can find,' Jack commented sourly. 'I always thought it was Lexi who liked shocking people.'

There was predictable tension between Jack and Simon. Jack disdained fanatics, while Simon saw Jack as an embodiment of the militarism and fascism produced by the public-school system. Had he known Jack as we did, he would have realised that Jack was simply incapable of being partisan, and lived for himself alone.

I liked Simon, and to an extent I shared his feeling that all was not well in Europe, and in society as a whole. What I liked less was his complete influence over Fran, who was under the spell of his compelling personality. It worried me that she would stop thinking for herself, and end up in trouble. For some time now he had been taking her with him on marches to protest against the actions of the British Union of Fascists, and there had been violent scuffles with the blackshirts, who were armed with truncheons and knuckle-dusters.

Yet I, too, had allowed my thinking to be influenced by Simon, though to a much lesser extent. He had come into our lives at a time when I was in the grip of dissatisfaction with my own lifestyle. It was subliminal at first, but came to the surface more and more, as I found myself having to apologise to Frannie's new friend for my frivolous lifestyle. Simon was clever, and he knew that he didn't even need a direct attack to make me reconsider what I was doing. He just needled away at me with the chance remarks and comments he made in my presence, and when I turned to look at him, his glowing brown eyes would be on my face, enquiring, demanding.

I didn't like the fact that he thought me a lightweight, and it positively hurt me to know that Frannie must think the same thing. But finally my own boredom and restlessness had as much to do with my decision. I would dignify myself with labour, become a useful member of Britain's workforce. In short, I was going to look for a job.

Six

Ever since Nim had given me my first camera, I had been a keen photographer, and my interest and skill had grown over the years until I was more than proficient. And since I couldn't type, and the good Miss Howland's education had left me academically bereft, it was as a photographer that I planned to make my living.

I gathered together a portfolio of my better shots and took them around the picture departments of the major newspapers, but with no luck. I would have to fight tooth and claw to get an appointment, then sit ignored for hours while a busy pictures editor rushed to and fro past me as though I was part of the furniture. When they finally remembered to see me, the interviews were cursory and the conclusions discouraging. I was a talented amateur, but the subject matter of my photographs (they were, inevitably, pictures of Russington and family, with a few debutantes' portraits thrown in) was too limited to give an indication of my potential as a Fleet Street photographer. Besides, I was too young. And a girl, which meant I wouldn't be able to tolerate the jostling and discomfort that goes with capturing an elusive subject.

Surprisingly, I wasn't discouraged by all this. I *knew* that I was a good enough photographer; it was just a question of biding my time until I could convince the journalistic profession of this. Sitting around moping wasn't going to hasten this day, so I took positive steps. I wrote to Miss Howland, asking her to find the prints of shots I had taken of the athletes in action at the Olympic Games. Any free time was spent out and about in London with my camera, taking pictures of anything and everything I found. Simon took me with him to the East End, to a newly founded Welfare Clinic that he visited, and I trained my lens on the mothers and their babies, and the children playing in the street.

By the end of March, my patience was rewarded. Irving, who had heard of my ambitions, wrote from Oxford giving me the name of the uncle of one of his fellow undergraduates. This man, who rejoiced in the unlikely name of Harry Hoccleve, was the editor of a small but well thought-of illustrated periodical called *London Life*. They wouldn't be able to pay me very much, Irving wrote, but if they liked my work they would be prepared to consider me on a trial basis.

Harry Hoccleve was a small, square Yorkshireman with thinning red hair and a face that was neither good, nor bad-looking, but had absolutely no distinguishing features. He took an assortment of my best pictures from the envelope I had handed to him, spread them out on his desk and looked slowly from one to another.

'Hmmm . . .' was all he said, while I watched his face anxiously for signs of approval, outrage, anything. He chomped his teeth on the stem of his pipe and scratched at the elbows of his tweed jacket.

'Not bad,' he said. 'You have something there . . . a certain sensitivity, I suppose.' He pointed with the stem of his pipe to the expression on Frannie's face as she viewed herself in the mirror, dressed in her court finery.

'Does that mean . . ?'

'We'll give you a go. On a month's trial only, to start with.' Mr Hoccleve had looked up from the collection of pictures and was examining me instead, from my dashing hunter's hat and painstakingly set hair, to my lizard-skin court shoes and matching handbag. Did he realise the lengths I had gone to, I wondered, to appear older than I was?

'Of course, you're very young,' he observed. 'Younger than we normally use . . .'

'And I'm a girl?' I suggested.

'That too. However . . .'

I was put to work the following Monday, not as a dogsbody to the picture editor, as I had anticipated, but under the personal supervision of Harry Hoccleve himself.

'I think I ought to keep an eye on you myself,' he explained. 'Since you came under a personal recommendation.'

And keep an eye on me he did. Those nondescript, colourless eyes followed me around the premises constantly, seemingly neither approving nor disapproving, just looking. I had been given a small desk, squeezed up against an ancient, clanking radiator, but it was a relief to me that most of my time was spent away from the Holborn offices, scouting around London on the assignments that Harry Hoccleve personally picked for me.

I was earning a living as a photographer, and that brought its own satisfactions, but the work was not what I would have chosen. I wanted to work on news reports, taking pictures at rallies and demonstrations; pictures that would illustrate a political point. Instead I spent a lot of my time capturing the expressions on the faces of boring civic dignitaries as they were presented with long-service plaques, or photographing vegetation for the 'Nature in London' column. I came to know the lie of London's parks very well.

Some time, Harry Hoccleve was always promising, when I had worked for the magazine a little longer, I would be allowed to tackle more meaningful stories. If I was a good girl.

For a few months, life settled into a pleasant routine.

My job at least kept me busy and out of the flat for most of the day. The atmosphere there was calm and predictable. Simon was still in evidence and he and Frannie seemed to become increasingly engrossed in each other – if that was possible. But since Simon approved of my working for a living, and my (albeit futile) attempts to make my photographic contribution more significant, the earlier tension between us had eased. He had his uses, too. He was far more domesticated than either Frannie or I, and he took his turn with the shopping or cooking.

We kept meaning to return to Russington for a weekend, or for Easter, but there was always some reason to put it off. Meanwhile Darling Beattie's weekly letter continued to arrive, with codicils from Clem and Shoes. Occasionally we remembered to answer. Simon was never mentioned.

It was inevitable that our unconventional little applecart be upset in the end, though I'm sure thinking about this possibility was just another thing we didn't get around to. With the arrival of May, and the onset of the season, Darling Beattie announced that she would once more be renting a place in London for a few weeks, with the express purpose of spending some time with her children.

'For that, read "checking up on us",' I moaned to Jack, who had come round to the flat to issue an advance warning.

Darling Beattie had conveniently forgotten to mention her plans in her last letter to us, and had told Jack on the phone that he hoped it would be 'a nice surprise for the girls, don't you think?'

The problem as Jack and I saw it, after consuming a bottle of sherry together one evening, was not so much Simon, as Frannie. The obvious solution for the keeping of the peace was for Simon to lie low for a few weeks until Darling Beattie had gone away again. Simon could have no interest in meeting Frannie's Nazi-admiring mother, other than to have a heated political argument.

But Frannie not only refused to banish Simon from from the flat, she insisted on introducing him formally to Darling Beattie. Not to provoke, she insisted, but in the cause of honesty.

'After all,' she said, turning pink beneath her freckles as she always did when she knew everyone else disagreed with her, 'he's my best friend, and the person I spend most of my life in London with. He is my life in London ...' She blushed pinker at this dangerous statement. '... Why should I have to pretend otherwise?'

Jack, of course, did not stay around for the inevitable answer to that question. Frannie was holding a dinner party in Beattie's honour, but he refused to attend.

'Not for me, thank you very much. I prefer to stay out of rows that don't have anything to do with me.'

'And the ones that do,' Frannie reminded him crossly.

Not only was Simon to be present at the dinner, but he was to be responsible for *cooking* it. I tried in vain to persuade Frannie that it would be better to make her mother suffer our own culinary disasters.

'You are old-fashioned sometimes, Kitty, honestly! Why shouldn't a man do the cooking? All famous chefs are men.'

'Yes, but ...'

I tried, tactfully, to explain that far from being impressed by a man who cooked, her mother would be suspicious, or even appalled by the idea, but Frannie simply became more mulish.

'Look Kitty, if you don't want to come, go and join Jack. You and he are just as bad as each other sometimes! Just desert me, go on ... leave me to my fate.'

Wearily, I assured her that I would never do that.

On the surface, Frannie's little soirée went smoothly enough. Darling Beattie managed to find some nice things to say about the way we had arranged the flat, though she probably had to look hard.

'That vase is ... quite a pretty colour, isn't it dears ..? And the lampshade really is ... interesting.'

133

She was polite to Simon, but it was the rather vague politeness that my aunt and her class reserved for servants or inferior mortals. She showed him that she had noticed the absence of his jacket and tie by sympathising that it must get very hot in the kitchen, and beef stew was rather a hot dish to prepare, wasn't it? Simon in his turn cheerfully refused to treat my aunt as if she was anyone special, and addressed her as 'you' rather than 'Lady Winstanley'.

Frannie was satisfied that the supper had gone quite as well as could be expected. I knew otherwise. Sure enough, the next day I received a telephone summons from Beattie to join her for tea at Fortnum's. She did not ask me to bring Frannie.

'James Peake-Taylor was asking after you,' Beattie said innocently as she sat down on one of the Fountain Room's gilt chairs, and spread a pink napkin over her knee. 'Such a pleasant boy ... well, young man really, I suppose.'

'Mmm,' I said non-committally, twirling a silver cake fork.

'... And I'm sure he wouldn't approve of you doing this job you do – '

'You mean *you* don't approve of it,' I countered, trying to keep my voice level.

'Well, darling, you must appreciate that we worry. After all, you do meet some very rough types in journalism – '

'Then you'll be glad to know that the people I work with are all very pleasant and civilised.'

My aunt scrutinised me over a scone for signs of romantic attachment.

'If it's the money, dear, your uncle would be willing to raise your allowance a bit. Your father left a comfortable amount, well, for one child ...'

I shook my head. 'No thank you. I do it because I love photography. And you've got Nim to thank for that. He gave me the camera.'

Darling Beattie smiled her 'Don't-be-difficult-dear' smile.

'Since you're so responsible, perhaps you could talk some sense into your cousin. She does seem to be associating with some quite Unsuitable Types.'

'If it's Simon you're referring to, there's not a lot of point your worrying.'

Beattie sipped her tea thoughtfully. 'Yes, I expect you're right. Frannie does tend to go through these phases, and no doubt she'll grow out of this one and move on.'

'That wasn't quite what I meant.' I put down my fork so that my aunt would be sure I was serious. 'I meant there's no use your

134

worrying, because I'm quite sure there's no question of Fran giving Simon up.'

'Giving him up!' Her plump hand trembled against the Royal Doulton. 'You don't ... surely mean to say that she and that ... *person* are romantically involved!'

I shrugged.

Beattie thought for a moment, then smiled at me reassuringly. 'Still ... I shouldn't let it worry me, as you say. Since the whole thing is so preposterous. I simply shan't take it seriously. After all, there's no question of your uncle and me allowing ... I should simply put my foot down.'

I didn't relay this conversation to Frannie, and later had cause to wish that I had. She came into my room a few evenings later, and I knew before she opened her mouth that there was something she wanted to discuss with me. I patted the edge of the bed and she sat down, leaning back against my legs.

I waited. She sighed. 'I spoke to Mummy today ... ' She tugged at some loose threads on the counterpane, winding them round and round her fingers. 'About Simon.'

'I see. Was that a good idea?'

'No, but I had to do it.'

I put the book that I was reading on the night table and looked at Frannie's face, which wore a hurt expression.

'I think it was fairly obvious what she would say.'

'She was furious. You see ... I told her I was going to marry Simon.'

'Frannie!'

'Well, she provoked me! She was treating me like a child that doesn't know its own mind. And I *do* Kitty! I know that I can't be happy without Simon. I just know it. He's the only human being on this earth who really knows me ... '

She saw the look that crossed my face and said, 'Well, I know you know me too, Kitty, but ... well, it's as if Simon's inside me.'

'Let's get back to Aunt Beattie,' I suggested. My cousin's eulogies on Simon Gold's perfections invariably made me feel uncomfortable. 'I suppose she told you marriage was out of the question?'

'Worse than that – she's forbidden me to go on seeing him.'

'But you will?'

Frannie shook her head. 'That's the point. Simon won't be here anyway. He's been invited to join a group of people who are fighting Jewish persecution. He's leaving for Paris next week, for good.'

*　　　*　　　*

135

Frannie moped around for the next few days, but I was able to forget her problems during the hours that I was at work at the offices of *London Life*.

I was rapidly gaining experience at judging what made a good story, by keeping my ears open and listening to the ideas of the journalists around me, and by assessing over the weeks how our finished product stood up against those of our competitors.

'I shall have to watch you,' Harry Hoccleve said genially, when I told him yet again that he needed to devote more space to illustration. 'You're getting too ambitious by half.'

When I started to mumble an apology, he brushed it aside. 'No, no ... it's no bad thing to be ambitious. I like a young lass who's got her head straight on her shoulders, not stuffed with silly ideas.'

I was flattered by his praise, and inspired to try harder. I devoted my lunch hours, and any spare time I had between horticultural shows and mayoral lunches, to developing projects of my own. Then one evening I waited until most of the others had gone home, and the day's appointments were over, and knocked on the door of Harry Hoccleve's office.

'Mr Hoccleve ... '

'Ah, Kitty! Come in, come in. I was just thinking about you ... no need to look so worried, you haven't done anything wrong. Quite the opposite, really. I've been thinking about some of the ideas you came up with ... '

Encouraged, I opened the folder I was carrying and spread the contents out on the desk. There was a piece of card with a headline I had painstakingly prepared in my best copperplate handwriting: *London at Play*. The photographs that illustrated it were a selection that I had been building up over the weeks, the East End boys playing in the streets, riders in Hyde Park's Rotten Row, a game of dominoes in a pub, elderly gentlemen bowling in Kew.

I stepped back from the desk. 'They could be put together to form a feature,' I said, with more confidence than I felt. 'Or as a series. Either way, if you approve, I'll have to go out and get more material.'

Mr Hoccleve smiled. 'By God, you're a smart one, aren't you ..?' He sucked his pipe and looked at the photos again. 'A series, eh? Well, I'm not saying it wouldn't work, but ... '

I stepped forward again and started to shuffle the photographs back into their folder. Mr Hoccleve's hand came down on top of mine and trapped it there. 'Kitty ... ' He put his pipe down on the desk. His breathing was heavy, noisy.

I tried to pull my hand away, but he had a firm hold on it,

squeezing it and caressing it. The rhythmic movement made me feel sick.

'You and I could go out together and discuss your idea. I know a place where we could have supper.'

He looked up at my face, loosening his grasp. I pulled my hand away, and stuffed it pointedly into my glove.

'I'm afraid I'm going out, and anyway I don't think that would be a very good idea.' I was aware that my voice sounded cold, and I couldn't look at his face as I picked up the folder and tucked it under my arm. I didn't want him to see how angry I was. I wanted to keep my job.

'So . . . ' I kept my tone light. 'What would you like me to do with these? Shall I go out and start taking some more? You said – '

'I've changed my mind,' said Hoccleve gruffly. He fussed with his pipe to avoid eye contact. 'Tomorrow you can go and get some shots of the spring bulbs in St James's Park.'

I was owed several days' holiday by the magazine, and it suddenly seemed a good idea to take it. Mr Hoccleve's advances were incentive enough, but Frannie was also set on providing a diversion with her problems.

She had been wearing sackcloth and ashes and both Darling Beattie and I were assuming – for different reasons – that she had accepted the end of her affair with Simon.

I should have known that stubborn, brave, idealistic Frannie would never give in so easily. She was merely biding her time, and on the first day of my leave, when we were assured of some time alone together, she sat me down to tell me of her plans.

She was going to go and live in Paris with Simon.

'It'll be like Lexi's elopement, but better,' she told me calmly. 'For a start we'll have to do it in secret.'

I was shocked. Not at the idea of Frannie running off to live with her lover, but at the idea of her being gone, of living without her. There was no point my trying to talk her out of it though; for one thing she would have realised my efforts were self-interested. I thought of how she'd welcomed me to Russington when I first arrived and how she had always – with one exception – stuck up for me, and I resolved to help her with her scheme as much as I could.

Darling Beattie was still in London, and visiting frequently to ensure we were back on the path of righteousness and suitability. Any plan we made, therefore, had to be extra watertight. It turned

137

out that Frannie was still paying the occasional furtive visit to Simon's bedsit.

'That will have to stop,' I told her firmly. 'And he isn't to telephone the flat, not even to make travel arrangements. Beattie's got to stay convinced that you've given him up.'

Fran, with her melodramatic turn of mind, was all for bolting in the dead of night, with just a note of farewell pinned to her pillow. But however well I lied, I reminded her, Darling Beattie would still become suspicious very quickly, and have the police after them. No, what she needed was time in which to disappear, and for that she would have to have a legitimate reason for going to France, an alibi.

'We could produce a letter from one of your debutante friends, inviting you to spend some time in France. She'd fall for that.'

'But I don't have any debutante friends,' Frannie wailed. 'I was too busy skiving off, remember, or scaring them because I was a communist.'

We reached a compromise – the letter would come from one of *my* friends, inviting me and anyone else I wanted to bring. I would suggest that Frannie go as my guest to recover from the experience of having her heart broken. Frannie would go alone to France, and I would lie low for a while until I decided that it was safe enough to face the music. Fran knew I wanted to see (and photograph) Paris, and suggested I accompany her, but I felt the romantic adventure was hers and hers alone, and besides, it would be even harder to say goodbye if we had spent a sentimental last few days together.

'Victoria Station will be far enough,' I told her. 'I'll wave off your train, then you'll be on your own.'

Simon forged the letter from the South of France, filling it with dubious local colour ('. . . the bougainvillea is blooming all over the place') and I chose as his pen-name a friend whose family were unknown to Darling Beattie to minimise the risk of our cover being blown by a chance meeting in the corsetry department of Simpsons. Darling Beattie fell for the red herring without turning a hair and set about combing the stores for hideously suitable resort wear, which filled Simon with childish glee and made Fran and me feel very guilty.

The next problem was money. Frannie and Simon were going to need as much as we could scrape together to support them until Frannie found a job in Paris. Simon's work would be unpaid. Fran had been saving her allowance for weeks, but the resulting thirty pounds would not be nearly enough. I had some of my wages in the bank, and I donated all I could spare. Finally we hit upon a joint sacrifice. We had been given 'coming out' presents by a relative who was godmother to us both – two identical pearl necklaces. We would sell them to a jeweller and Frannie could take all the proceeds. She didn't much like the idea of me being without my pearls, but I insisted I would feel much better if neither of us kept our godmother's present.

Fran went on a shopping trip with her mother, to keep her out of the way, while I combed the streets of Chelsea to find a jeweller who would buy second-hand pearls. I finally came away with a hundred pounds for the pair, but was too ignorant to know whether this was a fair deal or not. The whole business took longer than I had expected, and I had to hurry into town to meet Jack, with five twenty-pound notes crammed into my purse.

I clung on to my handbag all the way through our lunch at the Café Royal, which drew some quizzical glances from Jack. But so preoccupied was I with avoiding theft that I forgot to be discreet when I pulled out my purse to pay for my share of the meal.

Jack looked sharply at the bundle of notes. 'What on earth are you doing with all that cash? Are you in some sort of trouble? Or have you just traded in journalism for crime?'

I tried to look casual but I was blushing, and I couldn't dream up a lie fast enough.

'It's not for me ... I'm lending it to a friend.'

'It's for Frannie, isn't it!' Jack declared triumphantly. 'I know she's been up to something lately.' His eyes shone with satisfaction at his own cleverness. 'She's pregnant, I'll bet.'

'No! It's not that. You mustn't think that – '

'It's something to do with her red friend, though, isn't it? She's running away with him! That has to be it, it's exactly her style. Come on, Kit, spill the beans.'

I did, but only because I could never fib convincingly to Jack, that master liar. I was then forced to beg him not to give Frannie away to Beattie. Jack still disliked Simon; for all I knew enough to welcome doing him a bad turn.

But Jack laughed and mocked my anxious expression. 'Oh ye of little faith! Listen, if there's one thing I do believe in, it's the freedom of the individual to do exactly as they please. If that's what Frannie wants, then good luck to her! Here – ' He pulled a couple of ten-pound notes out of his pocket and handed them to me with a wink. 'For the honeymoon.'

*　　　*　　　*

Simon Gold saw himself as my cousin's saviour. With this belief came the assumption that Frannie would be quite happy never to see her family again.

I knew only too well that this was far from the case. As the tickets were bought and the final arrangements made, her nerve began to fail her. She started to think not of the life that was to come, but of the old life that was left behind. Her political beliefs were new and urgent, but the ties to Russington had a life-blood of their own. She began to talk incessantly of the old days, the dreams we had, the games we played, even our few quarrels. The thought that she would never see Flash again appeared to distress her as much as anything, but then she would start talking as though she would not be gone long, and we would all be reunited soon. She was not ready to let go.

It was this thought that inspired my next action. I decided to alert Darling Beattie to what was going on. If Frannie was certain about her sacrifice then she would go with Simon anyway. But the old life deserved a chance to state its case too.

Telling Frannie I had some shopping of my own to do, I took a taxi to Orme Court. It was the day before Simon and Frannie were due to sail.

Darling Beattie was in the hall, buttoning her gloves and smoothing her skirt over her broad hips.

'Kitty! Well, this is a surprise, darling! ... Or was I expecting you?' My aunt was aware of her own tendency to vagueness.

'I need to talk to you about something.'

'Oh, dear, can it wait? I'm just off to the dentist to have that naughty tooth of mine seen to at last, and I can't really put it off.'

'It's really very important.'

'Well in that case, you'd better wait here until I get back. I shouldn't be much more than half an hour, and you can ask Mary to bring you some coffee.'

I sat on an uncomfortable chair in the morning room (all furniture in rented houses was uncomfortable, I decided) and allowed my coffee to grow quite cold. I was thinking about Lexi. She had run off with the man of her choice, and she was now happy. Perhaps the same thing would happen to Fran?

Sitting there alone, listening to the metallic ticking of the carriage clock on the fireplace, I was forced to a very disturbing conclusion. I was trying to stop Frannie from leaving because I didn't want her to go. I was selfishly terrified of the thought of life without her. In fact, as I thought about it now in that calm, silent house, nothing in my life so far had caused me so much pain.

'Mary!' I called out to the maid. 'Would you please tell Lady Winstanley that I couldn't wait any longer. Tell her not to worry, that the thing I wanted to tell her can wait.'

Handing my un-drunk coffee to the puzzled girl, I hurried out into the street and away from the house. Growing up at Russington, we had believed with all our hearts in the ideal of True Love. Now that my cousin had found hers, I was not going to stand in her way.

The next morning, Simon broke our agreement and telephoned me.

'Do you want me to pass on a message to Frannie?' I asked.

'Not exactly. I rather wanted to see you, actually.'

'Oh?' I felt instantly guilty. Did Simon fear that I was going to try to spoil things for them, as I so nearly had done.

'. . . And Fran too, of course.' He sounded uncharacteristically shy and cleared his throat. 'We won't be seeing each other for a while, and I thought it would be nice if the three of us spent the afternoon together.'

'Well, yes . . . won't it be a bit risky?'

'Meet me on the Heath, Hampstead Heath. Your aunt will never stray as far north as that.'

At two o'clock, Frannie and I travelled up to Hampstead on the Underground, and were met by Simon. He had a kite with him, which he carried on to the windblown heath. The three of us then spent hours struggling to untangle it and launch it into the sky. After several false starts we got it flying and ran in its wake, laughing and panting for breath.

'Come on, Kitty!' Simon shouted at me. 'You're not keeping up!'

The truth was that I was deliberately hanging back, allowing the pair of them to enjoy a few last, carefree moments. If anything convinced me that my cousin was in love with Simon, it was that afternoon. It was very plain in that open, uninhibited place that she loved him for his person, not just for his ideals, and that he was equally devoted to her. They played together like two puppies, using the constant reassurance of touch. When Frannie stumbled and fell, Simon was at her side instantly, picking her up and planting a kiss on the grazed elbow.

When it started to grow dark he took us to a little café with a hissing tea urn that steamed up the windows. We wolfed down dripping toast and wiped our fingers on our clothes, as there were no such refinements as napkins.

'I'm *so* hungry!' declared Frannie. 'This is the best food I've ever tasted!' Her eyes were bright and her cheeks flushed pink by the wind.

The two lovers were sitting opposite me. Simon's arm was draped round my cousin's shoulders. He smiled at me warmly.

'Come to Paris with us, Kitty!' he said. 'She should, shouldn't she, Fran?'

'Oh yes, you should! Think what fun we could have!'

'No.' I shook my head. 'Not this time. But I'll visit soon.'

I brushed their protestations firmly aside. Three – in this case – would most definitely be a crowd.

Seven

'Kitty, I'm not going.'

The day that we had plotted and planned for finally arrived, and I woke to find Frannie standing in the doorway of my bedroom like some Viyella-clad ghost.

I struggled for full consciousness. 'What do you mean . . . you're not going?'

'I can't leave.' In marked contrast to the day before, her face was pale and dead-looking, and I surmised that if she had slept at all, it was only after a considerable amount of weeping. 'I keep thinking about you, and Mum, and Nim, and all the others. What if I never see any of you again? Or Russington?'

I squeezed her hand. 'Don't be silly, of course you will. Paris isn't exactly the other side of the world.'

'But what if there's a war? Simon says Hitler's been planning one since February – '

'There won't be a war, silly! The British government would never let him get away with it. And anyway, if there is one, you'll just have to come back.'

Frannie sighed, and looked down at her chewed fingernails. 'It's not just that, though. The problem is . . . I love Simon but I love my family and my home too. It's just so *impossible* and unfair that I have to choose. What am I going to do, Kitty? I *can't* go!'

Her body was tense with anguish, and I sensed she was dangerously close to abandoning the journey. I chose my next words carefully. 'If you don't go . . . you'll never see Simon again.'

Fran promptly burst into tears, but I had given her the impetus she needed. She went into her own room and emerged wearing a grey flannel travelling suit with a plain white blouse.

'Do I look all right .. ?' She twirled for inspection. She had even applied some make-up to her chubby freckled face.

She saw my curious glance and asked anxiously, 'What do you think? I put on some eye-shadow so that my eyes would look less piggy.'

She was still worrying about her appearance when we climbed into the cab that was to take us to Victoria Station. 'Do you really think I look all right, Kitty? Only I'm not quite sure what one should wear to elope in. I wrote about it in my play, and I wasn't sure then, either. When Saint Anselm eloped with Saint Catarina, d'you remember?'

'I remember.'

'I think Lexi wore a suit, didn't she .. ?'

Frannie chattered nervously, but I was silent. There would be no one but me to witness her departure. Darling Beattie had been set on waving us off on our fictitious trip to the Continent, but we did our best to dissuade her. It would have meant my having to join Frannie on the train and disembark at Dover. But Jack, for once, proved his worth as a brother and offered to provide some convincing distraction. On the morning of our departure he telephoned his mother and told her he had succumbed to flu. Darling Beattie rushed to his bedside brandishing a thermometer, and by the time it revealed a normal temperature, we were already standing on the platform and loading Frannie's luggage on to the Continental Pullman.

No farewell speeches, we had promised each other. That would make it too final, as if we were never going to meet again. When the moment came, Frannie opened her mouth and started to try to tell me something, but I bundled her into the carriage, where Simon was already waiting. Arm in arm, they waved to me as the train pulled out.

'See you soon!' I shouted, and waved back.

It was only when the train was out of sight that I let the tears come.

Much as I missed Frannie and Simon, it was something of a relief to have the business of the elopement over, and to be able to attend to my own life, which had been left in a state of temporary disarray.

From Victoria Station, I took my own suitcase and boarded a train for Kent, where a fellow debutante called Louise had offered me sanctuary while I kept up the pretence of being in France. The weather was fine, summer was on the way, and I spent a very pleasant few days strolling through fields of hops and playing croquet with Louise and her brothers. I had to return to London sooner than I would have liked because of my job at *London Life*. I had already overrun the leave I had been granted, and Harry Hoccleve would not be amused.

The risk in returning was that my aunt would still be around for an unspecified period, and I had to avoid running into her at all costs. I lived like a fugitive, never leaving the flat except to go directly to work, and worse still, leaving the telephone unanswered when it rang. My social life was nonexistent.

But worst of all was the emptiness in the flat. Just the absence of another human being making the noises of everyday living, opening and closing doors, flushing the lavatory. I got into the habit of leaving the wireless on all evening, and would wake up in the morning to find it still on, talking to itself, talking me to sleep.

I felt painfully inadequate at living alone, and it made me more introspective than I was by nature. I found myself thinking not only about how familiar Frannie was, but also about how well she knew *me*, every detail about me, all my secrets. It was as though she had taken those secrets with her, leaving me naked and featureless. Am I so selfish, I wondered, that I have to have someone around who can talk about me? I even found myself missing Simon, who had been a fund of provocative discussion, and some good cooking.

And I longed to be with Jack. That would have allowed me to lapse back into the old familiar idiom again, lessening the pain. It was out of the question to turn to him for comfort, however. Too much risk of bumping into Darling Beattie.

At the magazine, there was inevitable tension between Harry Hoccleve and me. It seemed absurd that he should behave like a spurned lover, but he was definitely sulking. On the surface he was taking less interest in what I was doing, but I would catch him chomping on his pipe as he shot hurt looks in my direction. The assignments I was given continued to be mundane, and there was no mention of projects I wanted to initiate. It was as well for Hoccleve that I wasn't in combative mood, and kept my head down, although inside me a sense of frustration was growing.

After two weeks of pretending to be in France, I was unable to bear the isolation any longer. I phoned Jack for news.

He laughed at my desperation. 'Had enough of playing games, have we? That'll teach you to behave as though you're the heroine of some tupenny novelette.'

I laughed, too, acknowledging the accuracy of this description of myself. 'OK, you win, Jack. But I really don't want to go on playing any more. Living by myself in the flat is horrid, and if I'm not allowed to go out in the evening – '

'It's all right, you don't have to worry about that any more. To use the sort of language you would understand; the enemy agent's quit the field of battle. In other words, Mother went back to Russington. About three days ago.'

'Jack! Why on earth didn't you—'

'Sorry. Must have forgotten to tell you.'

When I returned to the flat that evening, I found a letter from Paris waiting for me. It contained a lot of predictable gush about the beauties of that city, mixed in with some very funny Fran-like observations about the habits of its citizens.

> ... honestly, Kitty, I don't think she was wearing any underwear *at all*, but I could hardly have asked Simon to take a look under the table and tell me what he thought ... he's away from the apartment a lot, working with Jews who have escaped from Germany. Some of them are wanted by the SS for nonexistent crimes, so we have to be very careful not to be seen with these people in public, though I sometimes think that Simon isn't careful enough. It's because he gets so angry about the things that have happened to them. Kitty, if you could hear some of the stories the refugees have to tell, you wouldn't doubt that we are trying to do the right thing. Not just their businesses being ruined and things like that, but far, far worse ...

The tone of the letter implied that Fran was finding the subterfuge of her new life exciting, and I wondered to what extent she understood its implications. But Paris was safe, and she was in no personal danger, so my concern was short-lived. I was more worried by the fact that she hadn't mentioned the subject of marriage, which Simon probably saw as bourgeois propaganda. If she had, it would have made my next task a great deal easier. I was about to come clean.

I took the train to Finstock, and telephoned Russington Hall from the station.

Shoes answered. 'But you're in France,' she said accusingly. 'Mum said.'

When I had convinced her that I was really in Oxfordshire, she said that she would ask Irving to collect me. By a stroke of luck he was home from college for the weekend to show off his new run-around, a Riley.

I smiled when I saw him at the wheel of the sensible, solid little car. I was thinking of Jack and his blue Bugatti, and how appropriate the vehicles were for the two very different brothers. We chatted comfortably on the way back, mainly about my photographic work. For a lot of my adolescence Irving – four years my senior – had been a distant figure. Now suddenly, we were two adults discoursing on an equal level, and it was a much more comfortable relationship than the one Jack and I found ourselves in. I told myself it was because Irving reminded me a bit of Frannie.

He avoided mentioning his younger sister, which I took to be a bad sign. As we drove in through the park gates he said, 'There's some sort of trouble, isn't there?'

I nodded.

'I thought so. It's not like you to turn up unannounced like this.' He smiled slightly, as he conferred what would once have been an insult on the lips of a Winstanley. 'You're far too sensible.'

The garden was enjoying its most fecund period, and the beds were the usual mêlée. Peonies, still in bud, vied for space with the rhubarb plants. Dandelion clocks popped up amongst the irises. As the car drew up, Clem came racing down the steps and flung himself into my arms, followed by Flash at a much slower pace. As I hugged them both, tears of relief sprang into my eyes. It was overwhelmingly good to be home.

I went on making a fuss of Clem, admiring the gaps in his teeth ('brilliant for whistling') to avoid giving Darling Beattie more than a brief kiss of acknowledgment. She was standing in the middle of the hall with Flash at her side, rather as she had been on the day I first arrived at Russington, aged eight. She may even have been wearing the same shapeless suit.

She waited until the children were out of earshot, then asked, 'Where's Frannie?'

'She's still in France,' I said truthfully.

But my aunt's face revealed that she already knew something of what had happened.

'I tried to telephone your friend's villa,' she said coldly. 'But the silly operator said the number didn't exist . . . did you perhaps give me the wrong one by mistake?'

She was giving me a chance to extricate myself, but I knew that my face had already gone pale. I started pulling at Flash's ears to avoid looking at her.

'I should warn you that your uncle is very angry indeed.'

I nodded, and went upstairs to the room that I no longer had to share.

After I had unpacked, and composed myself, I went downstairs with the letter that Frannie had left for her parents.

They were in the drawing room. Darling Beattie took the letter from me, thanked me politely and read it without a word. She handed it to Nim.

I was trying to remember the phrases Fran had chosen when she wrote it over two weeks ago.

Darling Mummy and Nim, I know you won't be very happy when you've read this, but I'm going to Paris to live with Simon Gold and help him with his work against the Nazis. For ever, as far as I know. I can't bear to hurt you like this, but I couldn't do it any other way. I hope you will want to visit us one day, or that we can come and visit you. Your loving daughter, Frannie.

Nim threw the letter into the grate and looked up at me, his eyes blazing.

'I hold you responsible for this!'

It was the first time he had ever shouted at me when I was on my own, and defenceless, and I just stared back at him, speechless. I had expected him to rant and rave, but at Simon, not me.

'You could have stopped this farce!' he was shouting, his face quite crimson. 'Did you not consider that you owed us the consideration of telling us what was happening? What you did was worse than running off with a bloody communist!'

I'd had time to gather my thoughts, and my own blood was up, staining my face almost as red as Nim's. 'She's *your* daughter!' I threw back at him, enjoying the liberating sensation of such outright defiance. 'Having to believe the same sorts of things that you always believed in made her unhappy! Didn't you consider it *your* duty to help her to find whatever it was that would make her happy?'

My sense of injustice was fuelled by the sight of a new photograph, in the place where Nim's used to stand, of the von Russows in a family group: Hubertus, Lexi and baby Paul.

'Has he married her, dear?' asked Beattie gently.

'No, but she and Simon – '

'You will kindly never mention Francesca's name in this house again.' Nim's voice had changed; it was polite, almost pleasant. 'We no longer have a daughter by that name.'

I stared at my uncle, then at Beattie, but she looked down at her hands. Blinded by tears of outrage, I stumbled towards the french windows and ran out on to the terrace. There was a sloping bank of grass along its edge where we used to lie, like a row of sardines on summer afternoons, seeing who could make the longest daisy chain. Lexi always won. Fran, naturally clumsy, would lose.

I flung myself down there now, and started ripping the daisies out of the turf, scattering them about me. After a few minutes Irving came out in his shirt-sleeves and lay down beside me.

'The parents took a hard line?' he asked.

I told him what they had said, and he waited patiently while I indulged in more tears. 'This means that Fran can't come back, whatever happens.'

'She may have to,' said Irving, rolling on to his back and looking up at the sky. 'They're saying at Oxford that there's going to be a war. People are even talking about joining up.'

'It's just talk,' I said and walked back into the house.

I was lying on my bed, loking at the place where Frannie's communist posters had been (predictably someone had already removed them) and thinking about the general unfairness of life, when there was a cautious tap at the door.

Aunt Griz came in, glancing over her shoulder to make sure that no one had seen her. I thought at once how much she had aged, the wafty chiffon and feathers she always wore were bedraggled, and her grey curls looked tired.

She put her dog down on my bed (the animal was wheezing loudly with the effects of age) and said, 'We thought you might like a pet to cuddle, didn't we, Dearest?'

As tactfully as I could I refused the loan of the dog, which I had always found a repulsive creature. Aunt Griz nodded, and swept the animal into her arms again, saying, 'You did the right thing, you know.'

It seemed that news of Frannie's exile had already filtered in her direction. It occurred to me that Aunt Griz, whom we happily dismissed as daft, was always there in the background and missed little, though she always chose to interpret events in her own way.

'You helped your cousin to be with the man she loved.' Aunt Griz tucked the dog under her arm and reached for the door handle. 'I believe that's something to be proud of.'

I did not feel very proud of myself in the weeks that followed, just lonely. I left Russington on Sunday evening and went back to London and work. Darling Beattie and Nim waved me off as if nothing had happened, and I found this shying away from perturbing emotions even more disturbing than I had when Nim's adultery was discovered. I would have preferred them weeping and shouting than pretending that Frannie did not exist.

Harry Hoccleve had progressed from wounded spite to disinterest and, as long as I handed in the pictures he wanted on time, he showed little inclination to police me as he once had. So in between photographing prize begonias and entries in the Royal Academy's summer exhibition, I raced around London doing the work I was interested in. Irving had suggested that I offer my services to other publications as a freelance, and I had some success at this. My long-term aim for my photography was to find enough takers to allow me to dispense with *London Life* altogether. As a freelance photographer I would find most of my work in London, but I wasn't sure I wanted to go on living there alone. Or I could travel. The latter option loomed larger and larger as the summer wore on.

In July, the British Union of Fascists staged a rally at the Olympia Stadium in Earl's Court. It represented a massive show of strength for the movement, and a very good photographic opportunity for people who, like me, were armed with press passes. I squeezed myself and all my equipment (including a flask of cold tea) into a seat in the press stand and trained my lenses on the speaker's podium.

Oswald Mosley was a natural subject (Frannie and I had secretly admitted to one another out of earshot of Simon that we thought him divinely handsome) and he spoke so well that I could almost have joined the rest of the audience in believing what he said. British fascists, apparently, were not a terrifying mob of dictators, merely a bunch of reasonable people who opposed the slow, obstructive processes of democratic politics and believed in leadership rather than committees. If they favoured an elite, it was an elite chosen by function rather than class, and therefore open to all ...

The speakers who came later were less good (extolling recovery of Britain's economic slump through management of the economy) and certainly less handsome. I took a long drink of iced tea, pulled my cotton sunhat down firmly to keep off the rays of the sun, and attached my most powerful telescopic lens. I decided I would do some random sampling of the audience to see if I could get a shot of someone newsworthy.

All the men looked the same, and the women were only distinguishable to me by what they were wearing. Ever fashion-conscious, I amused myself by training my camera on clothes that attracted my attention, and imagining the comments that Frannie and I would pass if she was with me. The latter was a mental tic that I couldn't quite get myself out of.

Now that, I told myself when I homed in on a blob of palest ivory, is what I call a damned fine hat! It had a generous brim and such a provocative line that it could only have been designed by a French milliner ...

The owner of the hat moved, revealing an exquisite profile. I recognised it at once. Something about the style of the hat had already forewarned me. Mireille de Vere.

I had somehow let myself imagine that she would leave England and never come back, but now I thought about it, that idea was ridiculous. Why shouldn't she visit the country, or even live in it? She had, I remembered, numerous mysterious 'friends' dotted all over the place, people she talked to on the telephone without wishing to be overheard.

Well there she was, as poised and beautiful and European-looking as ever. Still a hundred times more sophisticated than I would ever be. I stared at her through my lens with a sort of professional detachment and, without even thinking about it, squeezed the shutter and took the shot. I trained the lens on the people sitting next to her, to try to get a clue as to why she was there, but they were as anonymous as the rest of the crowd. Then I got up and left the stadium quickly, before she looked round.

I had quite liked Mireille, despite everything, and she in turn had been kind to me. But I balked at the idea of renewing our acquaintance. I didn't think that either of us would enjoy reviving the piece of the past that linked us together.

I thought it prudent not to mention Mireille's appearance to Jack when I next saw him. I found myself increasingly cautious about annoying him or provoking criticism. With Lexi and Frannie gone, I couldn't afford to alienate Jack too.

I found him in an infectiously cheerful mood. He met me at the door with a broad grin on his face, slapped me on the back, tweaked the tip of my nose and asked me to come in and tell him what I thought of his latest venture.

Arranged on the floor of his studio (which, incidentally, had not been swept since he moved into the place) were squares with captions printed on them, pieces of artwork and a few photographs. I looked at it from all angles, but it meant nothing to me.

'It's a magazine. A magazine that I'm founding, in point of fact. As a professional, what do you think of the potential layout?'

'Not much.' I knew tact would be wasted.

'That doesn't matter,' said Jack cheerfully. 'It doesn't have to be good. As long as it looks vaguely like a magazine. I thought I might call it *The Snark* for old times' sake. What do you think?'

'That rather depends what sort of magazine it's supposed to be.'

'A free sheet. Anyone can send in poems, letters, articles about all and sundry, articles written in Serbo-Croat for all I care. The bulk of the magazine will be classified advertisements, for people with things to buy and sell. Both will have to submit a fee to me, of course.'

'Oh, I see ... ' The light was beginning to dawn. 'In other words the magazine exists to provide revenue for J. Winstanley esquire.'

'Exactly.' Jack rubbed his hands then, to my surprise, flung one arm around me and hugged me to him, tight. I wondered what on earth he was up to. And whether he could feel my heart-beat rate through his chest wall.

'Now, darling Kitty ... how about you supplying, free of charge, an unusual picture for the cover of our first edition .. ?'

I pulled away from him and stepped quickly around to the other side of the 'layout' so that he wouldn't grab me again.

'I might ... if you tell me why you're doing all this. I don't believe it's just the profits. There must be easier ways to make money. In fact, after working on a magazine for six months, I *know* there are easier ways.'

Jack raised his long eyelashes to look at me, and his expression was entirely devoid of irony, which unnerved me. 'You may not know it, but editorship is a reserved occupation. And I am the editor of this magazine, which provides a public service. So when the time comes for us all to be called up and marched off to our deaths – '

'Jack!'

' – when that time comes, old Jacko will be getting off scot-free.'

'You're letting them scare you,' I said briskly. 'I didn't think you'd crack up so easily. It's just hysteria ... '

'Oh really?' Jack tossed a paintbrush up into the air and caught it with his left hand. 'Is that why Irvie Baby has put in to join the glamour boys in the RAF?'

'There isn't going to be a war,' I insisted, through clenched teeth.

And to prove that I had more nerve than Jack, I handed in my notice at *London Life*, booked a Pullman ticket to Berlin and wired the Countess von Russow to inform her that I was going to spend my summer holiday in Germany.

Eight

As the wheels of the train rumbled their way south through Germany, I reassured myself with Neville Chamberlain's words: *'There will be no war'*.

I wondered if the Germans could feel the same, as we passed scores of uniformed troops, and the tannoy system at every station inside the German border broadcast shrill propaganda about the evils perpetrated by the Polish nation.

I amused myself by imagining I was a foreign correspondent on a special assignment, sizing up everything I saw as a potential picture for the front cover of a newspaper. And it was easy to forget gloomy thoughts in my excitement at seeing Lexi again.

She was sitting on the platform as the train pulled in, one hand on the handle of a huge, Germanic pram, the other waving with all its might.

'You look exactly like what you are!' I laughed, after we had hugged one another.

'And what's that?'

'A happily married wife and mother, of course!'

She certainly looked much older than the reluctant bride who had picked up her suitcase and walked out of our lives. Her shining golden hair had been rolled into shoulder-length waves, and she wore a jaunty little felt hat that sloped over one eye. Her make-up was as immaculate as ever; her feet encased in the sheerest silk stockings and elegant high heels. Only Lexi could have contrived to look sexy and matronly at the same time.

'I'm glad you brought the baby,' I said, as she fussed over tucking in his blankets. 'That was a nice surprise. I was expecting you to leave him behind with the nanny.'

'Oh, I don't have one of those!' said Lexi airily. 'German wives are expected to throw themselves wholeheartedly into the role of *hausfrau*. Anyway ... ' She smiled at me. 'It may surprise you but I like looking after him myself.'

She extricated the body of the pram from its wheels and humped both into the back of a large battered sedan, then drove, at a pace that would have done justice to the old Lexi, back to the Grunewald.

As we passed through the centre of the city, I stared out of the window and tried to take in the fact that I was back in Berlin, the city Frannie had sworn she would never return to. It didn't seem to have changed much in the past three years. Still uniforms everywhere in various hideous colours, and more swastikas than ever, on every single flagpole. But these things no longer seemed to attract the attention they did once. The Berliners were going about their business as though they were well used to it all. The swaggering brown-shirted thugs and the doe-eyed Hitler-worshipping Valkyries, personnel of a regime which had once caused alarm, seemed to have a certain respectability now. Only a slight tightening of Lexi's lips as we passed them hinted at feelings that ran below the surface. The prospect of uncovering them sent a shiver of excitement down my spine.

It would be churlish to say that I was disappointed by Lexi's home, but I was somewhat surprised. Instead of a large, baronial home it was an unprepossessing villa, with apple trees in the garden and a picket fence separating it from the neighbours' land. The interior was brightly painted, and there were none of the lace tablecloths and gloomy pot-plants beloved by the German *hausfrau*, but the house still gave off the faintest whiff of impoverished gentility. The good pieces of furniture were battered and scratched, as were the frames around the family portraits, and Lexi managed the running of the household (including the cooking, to my amazement) with the sole help of an elderly Berliner called Ilse, who muttered to herself constantly as she shuffled from room to room.

Lexi seemed quite at peace in these less than glamorous surroundings, and it was quite impossible to imagine her as Lady Arboyne with several homes to choose from and nothing to think about except the next cocktail party. I was glad that things had turned out well for her, but felt a stab of resentment that things couldn't be this way for Frannie.

Most pleasing of all: the villa on the edge of the Grunewald was a happy place. There was a much-used gramophone in the middle of the sitting room, and the floorboards were scuffed where the carpet had been rolled back and Lexi, Hubertus and their friends had danced into the small hours. Lexi put on a record and poured herself a glass of wine, alternately sipping from it and singing along to the music while she prepared supper for us; sausages with potatoes, sauerkraut and apple sauce. I played on the carpet with young Paul and shortly Hubertus returned from work and joined in the game.

He greeted me with great enthusiasm, and was anxious to hear everything that was happening in England, particularly what they were saying about Hitler, and the chances of war. I gave him a copy of *The Times* that I had bought for the journey and he pored over it, devouring every word.

Ilse retired after she had put Paul to bed, and the three of us sat at a rickety table in the garden, eating our supper by the light of an oil lamp suspended in the tree above us. As the night wore on the air became heavy with the delicious scent of the pine trees in the Grunewald. Hubertus fetched a bottle of schnapps from the cellar and, as we relaxed over our drinks, I learned more about their circumstances.

Although of aristocratic birth, Hubertus's family were, in Lexi's words, 'quite stony broke'. Unlike their English equivalents, who could rely on the privilege of owning land, these families kept up their position with money earned from industry. The Great War, and the crippling inflation that followed, had bankrupted them along with everyone else. When we met Hubertus at the Olympics he had been a young man about town, impeccably educated and dressed ... but owning absolutely nothing. His much-diminished share of the family fortune had been just about enough to buy their home, but their day-to-day expenses had to be met by Lexi's small allowance, which Nim still sent out from England, and Hubertus's salary.

Hubertus, who had once advised us that there was nothing we could do for the victims of the Reich, was now working for the Reich himself. I learned this rather shocking piece of information to the comforting suburban hum of the neighbour's lawnmower as he cut grass while it was still light. He was working for the Foreign Ministry, he explained, as the mower droned to and fro and the birds twittered in the shadow, because the only other career as secure as the Civil Service was the law, and he had no training as a lawyer. Several of his friends were also in government service, and to hold these positions they first had to join the Party, after extensive investigations to ensure that they were in compliance with the Nuremberg Laws. In other words that they were of pure, Aryan blood.

'This is my Party badge,' said Hubertus, pointing to the eagle on his lapel. 'Not everyone is entitled to wear one of these, you know, Kitty.'

I looked more closely at that handsome face, searching his expression for the irony that I was sure I heard in his voice. But in the half light, I could not be sure of what I was seeing.

Guest or not, I felt I had to speak up, for Frannie's sake. 'But surely you can't believe in the policies of a regime which has done such atrocious – '

'Shhh, Kitty!' Lexi put her fingers to her lips and flung a glance in the direction of her neighbour, who had stopped mowing and was pruning a rose that strayed over the dividing fence. The message was clear: these were things which were not to be spoken of out loud.

The next few days passed in a tranquil fashion. I helped Lexi about the house as much as I could, especially with Paul, who was a delightful child. In the evening the three of us would stroll to a local café, or Hubertus's friends would drop round. The conversation was always kept to studiedly neutral topics, though on most evenings Lexi tuned in her wireless to listen to news on the BBC's Foreign Service.

I was anxious to do as much photography as possible, and during the day I would take the tram into the centre of the city and scout about for interesting illustrations of life under Hitler's Reich. Such pictures would be easy to sell when I returned to London, but at the time I wasn't thinking that far ahead. When I tried to conjure up an image of my future over the next months or years, I just came up with a blank.

Lexi accompanied me on these trips when she could take time off from her household duties (after struggling to run the flat in London, I could quite easily believe her when she complained that they took up more time than she would ever have dreamed possible). We strolled around the shops, or sat in cafés and drank the familiar strong black coffee.

Lexi asked questions about the family – although it was obvious that she felt very removed from the old world – and on my first morning as we were dawdling over our mid-morning refreshment and I was training my lens on some pigeons, she enquired casually,

'So how's good old Frannie? I haven't heard from her in such a long time ... what's she up to at the moment?'

I stared at her in shock for a moment and then I was struck by my own stupidity. I was assuming that she knew where Fran had gone and was preserving a tactful silence, but of course her main contact with England was the letters from Russington, and if Nim and Beattie were intent on pretending that their daughter no longer existed, then they would not have mentioned her.

I lowered my camera slowly, and my expression must have been explanation enough because Lexi nodded slowly, lit a cigarette and said, 'What's she done? You'd better tell me all of it.'

I told her the full story, including my near-sabotage of the elopement because I couldn't bear to lose Frannie, and the scene between me and Nim at Russington.

'Poor Kitty,' was the first thing Lexi said, stubbing out her cigarette with an angry movement. 'Always *in der Mitte* – in the middle. It's tough that they had to take it out on you, but they only did it because they were in pain, and you were the nearest whipping post ... or should I say horse-whipping post.'

We smiled as we remembered Nim's favourite form of corporal punishment.

'I'm glad Frannie went, but ...' Lexi sighed and looked down at Paul, sleeping peacefully in his ugly, Gothic pram. '... I don't know, Kitty, I'm scared too. Communism's illegal here, and the Party are putting it about that communists are almost as bad as the Jews.' She lowered her voice and glanced over her shoulder to make sure the waiter was out of earshot. 'They intend to drive them out by the same means.'

'Yes, but she's in Paris. It's very different there. There can't be many French who have sympathy with the Nazi regime.'

I lowered my voice too, instinctively.

'It may be different now, yes, but for how long? Things are changing so fast. There are things happening here that ...'

I hoped she would go on and explain about those mysterious undercurrents, but quite abruptly she decided that it was getting near Paul's lunchtime, and we ought to go home.

One day later during my stay, Ilse's husband Fritz, who acted as general handyman, came to the house to do some tidying up in the garden.

'Good afternoon, Herr Bauer.' Lexi greeted him in her best German.

'Heil Hitler!' The wizened little man thrust his thumb into his belt and flung out his left arm in a salute. Then he wheeled his barrow on to the lawn and set about picking up twigs.

Lexi was quite unperturbed by this behaviour, but I was appalled. I followed her into the sitting room and shut the door behind me so that we wouldn't be heard by the ubiquitous, shuffling Ilse.

'What on earth does an old man like that want with Nazism?' I asked. 'I can understand that someone of Hubertus's age might find some aspects of it appealing but . . . I would have thought men of his generation, who remember the Kaiser, would disapprove . . .'

Lexi smiled at me, and I knew she was thinking how much I had to learn. 'You remind me of myself, when I first arrived here. I used to think the same sort of things . . .'

She looked out of the window at Fritz, who was pulling up weeds from the herbaceous border. 'Herr Bauer sees Hitler as some sort of messiah. He's the son of a peasant, who fought for the Kaiser in the Great War, then returned from the war to find that there wasn't anything of Germany left. He slaved every hour that God gave to make a living, then the inflation in 1923 wiped out all his savings. They were absolutely worthless. He couldn't even afford furniture, let alone a house. Since then both he and Ilse have done odd jobs and scraped by as best they can, living in a shack that's no bigger than a dog kennel, working for Jewish businessmen who flout their money under his nose. His ambition was to own a pathetic little fruit and vegetable stall, but he never even managed that . . .'

I smiled at Lexi to show that I was beginning to understand, but I couldn't think of anything to say.

'Government and politicians were just ineffectual, faceless men who broke promises, as far as Herr Bauer was concerned. Then Hitler came along, a man who seemed ordinary and sincere like himself, and promised to make all that good again. The Party gave him a uniform and a role in life, other than clearing up after other people. Is it any wonder he gives Hitler his support? Think about it . . .'

I did, but the more I was confronted with the image of respectable, humble people like the Bauers saluting the Führer and singing 'Deutschland, Deutschland über alles', the more grotesque that image seemed. Herr Bauer didn't make the regime more acceptable. He was just being used.

A few evenings later, Hubertus announced that he would drive us out into the country for a drink. On the way out of the city, we stopped and picked up a friend of his from the ministry, a man

158

called Reinhard, and his pretty blonde wife, Hilde. With the five of us crammed into the old sedan, we drove passed the scenic splendours of the Tiergarten and out along small winding roads until we came to a country inn.

It was a warm August evening, and the patrons of the inn were seated under the trees in the beer garden. It was strange, in these pleasant surroundings, to accept as normal the presence of several stormtroopers in their Sam Browne belts and jackboots. The number of empty beer mugs on the table in front of them implied that they had been drinking for some time before we arrived, and every time one of them opened his mouth to make a remark, the others all laughed uproariously

I had my camera in my bag, and wanted to take a photograph of the uniforms dappled by light through the branches, golden heads and brass insignia flashing in the last of the day's sunshine. But Hubertus frowned at me and shook his head, so I concentrated on taking innocuous snaps of Lexi and Hilde, who looked the epitome of Hitler's robust yet feminine Aryan womanhood.

After half an hour or so, I was secretly becoming a little bored. Lexi and Hilde were gushing about the merits of their children and Hubertus and Reinhard were deep in conversation about people that they knew at work. I thought I was the only one who noticed three young Jews come in and sit down at a corner table. They kept themselves to themselves, ordering a beer each and talking quietly to one another.

The stormtroopers had noticed them too. They craned their necks to get a better look at them, and muttered obscenities which provoked more drunken laughter. The Jews ignored them, perhaps not daring even to look round, but the air was thick with tension.

Finally the stormtroopers pushed their chairs back from the wooden table and strolled not to the Jews' table but to ours.

'It's disgusting, isn't it,' said one of them, addressing Hubertus, 'that they allow those creatures in here?'

'Absolutely,' agreed Hubertus, his face betraying no emotion other than calm agreement.

'Breathing the same air as your beautiful, pure wives ...' The man leered down at the two blonde heads. Presumably I, with my dull brunette locks, was not worthy of a mention.

'... someone ought to report the landlord! Filthy Jew-lover!'

'Absolutely,' said Reinhard.

I felt hot all over by now, so hot that I thought I might burst into flames of indignation. Lexi must have seen the colour rise to my face, and my mouth half open to make some defence of the three young Jews, because quick as a whip her hand darted out under the table and squeezed my wrist hard: hard enough to hurt. I closed my mouth again, but treated the departing stormtroopers to my most baleful stare.

On the car journey back, I sat staring down at the marks of Lexi's fingernails on my wrist. I did not speak once, and declined to say goodbye to Reinhard and Hilde when they were dropped off. I was thinking of Fran in Paris, working to stop these people.

As Hubertus unlocked the door of the villa, and Lexi crept upstairs to check on Paul (watched over by Hitler's most devoted handmaiden, Ilse), I said, 'I think I had better leave Berlin.'

To my surprise, Hubertus smiled at me. 'Dear Kitty, I am so glad you have an active conscience.'

He ushered me into the sitting room and motioned for me to sit down on the sofa. Before he spoke, he checked that the doors and windows were firmly closed.

'There are a lot of informers about,' he said cheerfully. 'Some of them aren't even Party members, they just get a kick out of reporting things they hear and see ... '

It was only just dawning on me what Hubertus was about to say.

'Kitty ... ' He sat down opposite me with his arms resting on his knees. 'This country is full of people who have been brainwashed into thinking that the Jews are responsible for all the country's problems, and that the only effective panacea is National Socialism.'

'But you're a member yourself – '

'I know that I haven't been quite straight with you, but I had to be sure of the way you thought. And I wasn't sure whether I ought to involve you in all of ... ' His voice tailed off slightly and he examined his spotless fingernails. 'I'm putting Alexandra and Paul at risk as it is. And you're British ... '

I was bursting with a hundred questions, but Hubertus insisted that I let him speak first.

'I said there were people who believe Hitler can save Germany. But there are still some of us who can think for ourselves and who aren't taken in by the antics of that little Austrian ... '

Hubertus was squeezing and releasing his hands rhythmically, as though kneading some invisible dough.

'There's no room for any personal integrity under such a regime. But we ... the ever-growing number of people who think as I do ... are also aware that the Führer's mysterious charisma gives him

160

a deadly power, and that we can't just sit back and watch while he runs roughshod over the rest of Europe.'

'You mean ... you're a sort of resistance movement?'

Hubertus smiled. 'I don't think it's wise for us to use labels at this stage. Let's just say we're a group of people, many of us *adel* – from noble families – or officers in the regular army, who believe that we have the means to overthrow the current regime. I decided to work for the government, because it would give me a sort of disguise with useful privileges. At the Foreign Ministry we can arrange the issue of travel passes, and several of our number have already been to talk to sympathetic foreign governments to try to enlist support for our cause. Britain, the United States, Sweden ...'

'I feel a little foolish,' I confessed. 'I was beginning to think – '

'That I'd run off with an arch Nazi?' Lexi had come into the room after seeing Ilse to the front door. 'Come on, Kitty, I hope you know me better than that!'

'Well, I'm glad she thought so!' said Hubertus defiantly. 'It means I'm doing a good job of playing the model Party member.'

He stood up and poured drinks for all of us. I took mine gratefully and lapsed into silence as I tried to assimilate everything that had happened in the course of the evening.

'Sorry we had to carry out the little charade,' said Lexi. 'I wanted to tell you, but Hubie said to wait.'

'It's just so confusing. I'm going to have to think twice now before I believe anything anyone says.'

'That's good, Kitty, a very healthy attitude.' Hubertus slapped me on the shoulder. 'You know, the place is swarming with rumours, and not just about the likelihood of war. People say that Hitler chews the carpet during epileptic fits. They say that Goebbels is a Jew. The advice on the street is only believe what you see with your own eyes. I say don't even do that ...'

After I had said goodnight, I went upstairs and sat at the little table under the open window to record a summary of the day's events in my travel journal. A blackbird on the branch of the apple tree was still singing, enjoying the warm evening air. It was Saturday, 2nd September.

The next afternoon, while I was playing with Paul on the rug, Lexi showed in a visitor, a tall elegant lady with pale blonde hair piled up on top of her head.

'Kitty, this is Frau Drecker,' she said in English. 'She's the wife of Hubie's superior at the ministry.'

161

As she showed the woman to an armchair, Lexi was gesticulating wildly over the top of her head. What did the gestures mean? That she was one of us? That she was one of *them*? I gave the woman what I hoped was a non-committal smile, and continued my attempts to distract the baby.

'I've bought you one or two little things for your son,' said Frau Drecker, after Lexi had been into the kitchen to ask Ilse for coffee and cake. 'Some clothes that Heinrich has grown out of now. I thought you might find a use for them.'

She spoke in English, even though Lexi's German conversation was more than adequate.

Looking more flustered than I had ever seen her, Lexi thanked the woman and engrossed herself in examining the little garments she had been given (a charitable gesture that would have appalled Darling Beattie). The conversation flagged, and I felt bound to help out my cousin. Spying a rather striking golden cross pinned to the lapel of her frock, I said, 'That's a pretty brooch you're wearing, Frau Drecker.'

She gave me a pitying smile. 'The National Socialist's Mother's Cross. Given by the State in recognition of the service of child-bearing. The *baronen* – ' she stressed Lexi's title with a curling of the lip – ' the *baronen* is of course eligible for the bronze cross, but it seems she does not choose to wear it.'

It was starting to be obvious where our guest's sympathy lay, and the conversation sank to further depths of awkwardness. As we sipped our coffee, Frau Drecker turned her attention to me long enough to ask, 'You are visiting from England?'

I nodded.

Frau Drecker turned to Lexi and went on, ' . . . but of course, you are English too, my dear, aren't you?'

'No,' said Lexi firmly. 'I'm German.'

After she had gone, Lexi sank down into a chair and lit a cigarette with trembling fingers. 'I'm sure that woman's an informer! She was only here to check up on me.'

'I hope I didn't say anything wrong?' I asked.

Lexi waved her cigarette. 'Don't worry! The harder you try, the worse it looks, I'm sure. Anyway, I don't care; she's just a beastly old battleaxe anyway!'

This last remark was pure Winstanley and we both ended up laughing.

Our mood was further lightened that evening when some of Hubertus's co-conspirators (including Reinhard and Hilde) came round. The wives had been asked too, to convince nosy neighbours that it was a social visit, and we played the gramophone loudly while the men sat round in a circle and talked eagerly of their plans. One of their number was to be sent to London, for talks with Chamberlain; another to see the British Ambassador in Washington. Their schemes were gaining momentum, and growing more dangerous.

So engrossed had I become in the idea of overturning Hitler, I had almost forgotten the situation at home. But then Hubertus stood up and asked us to be quiet while he tuned the wireless in to the BBC.

... this morning the British Ambassador in Berlin handed the German Government a final note, stating that unless the British Government heard from them by 11 o'clock that they were prepared at once to withdraw their troops from Poland, a state of war would exist between us. I have to tell you that no such undertaking has been received, and that consequently this country is at war with Germany ...

Hubertus switched off the wireless and we sat in silence for a while. Then Lexi stood up and put a dance record on the gramophone, turning up the volume even louder than before. 'We might as well dance,' she said calmly, then kicked off her shoes and started to roll up the carpet.

And dance we did, more enthusiastically than we had ever danced before. Hubertus went down into the cellar for some bottles of wine and brandy, and the evening turned into a party. A last party.

It was later that Lexi broke away from the rest of us and walked out barefoot on to the dew-sodden lawn. I followed her. She went and stood beneath the apple tree, where the fruit was now ripe and ready to fall.

'Do you realise,' she asked me with a smile, 'that if I went home now, I'd be the enemy .. ?'

Nine

For the time being, it was I who was the enemy alien.

The following morning, Lexi and I tried to place a call to Russington, to reassure Nim and Beattie that we were all right.

'*I'm sorry, I cannot connect you.*' The international operator repeated those words over and over again. After our fourth failed attempt, it finally sank in. There was a war on.

'What are we going to do with you?' Lexi pondered. 'You'll have to think about getting back to England . . . if they'll let you out!'

But I had already made my decision. 'I want to stay.'

I repeated this to Hubertus, but he was not prepared to humour me. 'I'm sorry, but that isn't a possibility, Kitty. We can probably arrange to get you out of the country now, since you entered before war was declared, but if we leave it until later . . . it would be very difficult. You'll have to leave this week.'

'But Hubertus!' I pleaded. 'Don't you see what an opportunity this is for me! I'm Behind Enemy Lines! How many photographers does that happen to? If I can get a set of pictures together, it could make my entire career!'

Lexi took up my cause, and joined me in canvassing her husband. She had her own reasons for wanting me to prolong my stay. It would have been out of character for her to make any sentimental statement to the effect, but I knew that she was reluctant to let go of her last link with home and family. When, if ever, would she see any of us again? The thought was at the back of both our minds.

Hubertus finally capitulated, after consulting other members of the anti-government group. They suggested to him that it might be useful for me to make the journey at a later stage when communi-

164

cations with their foreign allies were even more risky. I could act as a sort of carrier pigeon.

'All right,' said Hubertus finally. 'But not for long. Only a few weeks. And I'm not at all happy about you going about taking pictures. It will attract too much attention. I want you to just put that camera away and start camouflaging yourself as good, ordinary little Berlin housewife!'

Acting the good Berlin housewife became less and less easy as the war set in. Lexi had accepted the role with sangfroid, but by German standards she wasn't up to much. With the arrival of food shortages and rationing, keeping the perfect home meant rising at the crack of dawn and standing in long queues all morning to secure the most paltry amount of food. Often the available sources were at far-flung corners of the city, and endless time, bus fares and shoe leather were wasted trying to garner a miserable portion of cabbage or cheese. If there was a rumour that smoked fish could be had at a certain market, the queues would arrive long before the food.

Our Winstanley temperament made us turn the business of shopping into a game at first, but we soon wearied of it. Besides, there were thousands of born *hausfrau* to compete with, and the German women were very good at imitating squirrels, egged on by Adolf Hitler. '*German women, your Leader and your country trust you*' smarmed the posters on every street corner.

In this very practical way, I was able to be of real help to Lexi during the autumn and winter months. With two of us to queue, we doubled our net result. And one or other of us always took Paul along too (carrying him in our arms; the pram was too much of a hindrance when it came to securing a good position in a queue). The sight of a beautiful blond baby was apt to make butchers turn patriotic and slip an extra ounce of meat into the parcel.

An extra pair of feet alone could not ease the difficulties that Lexi now faced. There was a shortage of money, as well as food. Lexi's allowance from Nim, wired regularly every month, stopped abruptly. She lamented the fact that she had never saved any of it for a rainy day, but had spent it on things for the house, and the baby (and on her own wardrobe, I suspected). That left us with Hubertus's salary alone, about twenty pounds a month. I pored over cookery books to find economical meals, feeling guilty about the additional burden I placed on the housekeeping budget. But Lexi insisted that she didn't want me to leave yet. 'I'm so glad

165

you're here,' she repeated over and over until it became a daily litany.

It was a cold autumn with sharp frosts and a thick crop of berries on every tree and bush, presaging an even colder winter to come. Both Lexi and I had lost weight on our cakeless, creamless diet and we both developed coughs, which we tried hard not to pass on to little Paul. But he was a robust child with a hearty appetite, and we did not worry about him unduly.

Until one morning in early December, when Lexi came into my bedroom and asked me if I would come and take a look at him.

'When I went into wake him up he was just lying there in his cot,' she explained. 'He's usually up and rattling the bars to get out.'

I looked down at Paul, who was lying with his eyes half closed. His face was flushed and he was breathing noisily.

'Call the doctor,' I said at once.

I sat and sponged the baby's forehead and hands while Lexi went to telephone Professor Meyer, the paediatrician who had taken care of Paul since his birth. She came back into the nursery a few minutes later, looking more rather than less worried.

'He says it's a chest infection; apparently there's one going around . . .'

'Well,' I demanded, 'when's he coming?'

'That's just it, he isn't . . . I don't know, Kitty, it was all so strange . . . he asked me if I had told anyone that I had phoned him. He seemed more bothered about that than about Paul . . . then he said he'd prescribe some medicine and leave it at the dispensary for me to collect. And not to worry, it would all be over in a day or two.'

We were both far more concerned with the health of her son than with Professor Meyer's behaviour, so I simply said, 'I'll go down to the dispensary now then, shall I?'

'No, I'd better do that. I have a feeling they'll ask for identity papers. You stay here and keep an eye on Paul. Keep sponging him with tepid water. And see if you can get him to drink something. If you have to leave the room for whatever reason, get Ilse to sit with him.'

Lexi returned with a bottle of foul-smelling pink medicine, and we struggled to get Paul to swallow it, without much success. We then took it in turns to sit by the cot and watch for signs of improvement.

At about four o'clock, Lexi called me upstairs again. She had always been one for making light of crises, and I knew just from the tremor in her voice as she shouted down the stairs that she was now seriously worried.

'He's getting worse, poor lamb,' she said, unable to take her eyes off the cot, where Paul was now struggling for breath. The rise and fall of his chest was clearly visible beneath the blankets and his hair was dark with perspiration.

'Perhaps I should take off some of his covers?' she asked, trying to keep her voice calm. 'Or we could bring the electric fan in here. Ilse says—'

'Call the doctor. Tell him Paul's worse, and insist that he comes over straight away.'

'Yes, you're right,' said Lexi, still staring into the cot. She seemed unable to tear herself away, terrified of what might happen when her eyes were averted.

'I'll telephone if you like.'

'No, no, I'll do it . . . '

She pleaded with Professor Meyer, who said that he would come this time ' . . . now that it has gone dark.' He was a small, elderly Jew, dressed in an immaculate dark suit with a gold watch chain. He muttered to himself in Yiddish as he examined the baby and took his temperature, then gave him an injection which Paul didn't even seem to notice, so listless had he become.

'Boil some water in the room,' he told us. 'If you make the air damp, he will breathe more easily.'

Ilse went off for kettles, and the three of us sat in a row of chairs in the nursery, watching the cot, and waiting. Now that he was with us, the doctor seemed in no hurry to end his vigil.

After an endless time, he took Paul's temperature again and pronounced that it had dropped slightly. 'He will be all right now, I think . . . '

He gathered his equipment into his bag, and we followed him out on to the landing. '*Baronen*,' he said in a low voice, so that Ilse wouldn't hear, 'I am so sorry that I did not come this morning. You must realise however that, under the Nuremberg Laws, it is illegal for me to practise medicine in this country.'

Lexi's hand flew to her mouth, as though it was the first time she had ever heard of discrimination against the Jews. 'Oh my God, Professor, I forgot, I'm so sorry . . . Only I thought, I was so worried about Paul . . . '

He smiled. 'I understand. And I know that I can trust you and your husband not to tell anyone I was here.'

'What about . . ?' I nodded in Ilse's direction.

'She worships Paul; that's all she's concerned about,' said Lexi confidently. 'She wouldn't have noticed if the doctor we called out had a forked tail and cloven feet!'

She offered Professor Meyer a fee for his services (cash of course) but he declined. 'All I want is for your son to get better.'

He did. The progress was slow at first, but at dawn on the third day after the doctor's visit he was sitting up and grinning when I came in to take over shifts from Lexi. After a week, even though it was still very cold, we decided that he was well enough to go out and about with us again.

'I know!' said Lexi, when we were returning from one of our interminable shopping trips, 'we should take Paul to see Professor Meyer, show him what a good recovery he's made. His clinic's only a short tram ride away from here.'

'Won't we be putting him at risk, visiting him in daylight?'

Lexi shook her head. 'It's a big apartment block – we could be visiting anyone.'

We found the building and puffed our way up five flights of stairs with Paul and our bags of shopping.

'I used to dread coming up here when I was at the end of my pregnancy,' Lexi told me, grinning at the memory. 'I had to stop on every landing.'

The frosted-glass panel on the clinic door still had PROFESSOR A. MEYER written on it, but no one answered when we rang on the bell.

'Perhaps he doesn't think it's safe to come here,' I suggested. 'He's probably at home.'

'But this is his home,' said Lexi, puzzled. 'He and his wife live in an apartment behind the surgery. That's how I got hold of him when Paul was ill, by ringing his home number.'

I put my bags of shopping down and tried the door. It was not locked. Instead of a receptionist's desk, chairs, cupboards and filing cabinets we found ... nothing. An empty room, save for a few unsealed wooden packing cases. The consulting room was also deserted, and hammering on the connecting door to the apartment provoked no reply.

'They're not there,' said a voice behind us. An elderly woman was standing there with a mop and bucket. 'The professor and his wife, they've gone away.'

'Have they left Berlin?' Lexi asked.

The woman looked at us suspiciously, but the sight of Paul must have persuaded her that we were no more than ex-patients. She came closer to us, and said in a whisper, 'I clean the place, so I know all the tenants. Professor and Frau Meyer, they were good people.'

As soon as she used the past tense, I knew only too well what she was going to say next.

'I came by one morning and Frau Meyer was packing all their things; books, china, clothes. Even the medical records. She said they were preparing to go away for a holiday, but not tell anyone, not even patients.'

'So where did they go?' demanded Lexi.

'Well they didn't ... not like that. Before they'd finished their packing, some men came round ... you know ...' The poor woman couldn't even name the SS, Himmler's shining blond knights, for fear of invoking them. 'They took them away. Both of them. In a van.' The stooped old woman brandished her mop. 'I told those men they'd done nothing; nothing except cure sick children, maybe even their own children, but they didn't listen.'

Lexi nodded her thanks to the woman and we set off down the stairs.

'That sort of thing shouldn't be allowed!' the old woman shouted after us as we walked down. 'They shouldn't allow it to happen.'

I barely heard her. I was thinking about Ilse, and wondering. When we got back to the house, I couldn't bring myself to look at her.

I suggested to Lexi that I ought to try to go back to England in time for Christmas, but the idea seemed to upset her, so I stayed. It was a strange time; the first time I had been away from the family and the familiar rituals, hanging up a stocking for Flash, fighting over the rum butter. But we spent a very cheerful few days, with a houseful of visitors. A neighbour presented Lexi with a live chicken which she promptly handed over to Ilse for killing and plucking, and Hubertus plundered the ever-dwindling supply of bottles in the cellar to make *glühwein*.

On Christmas Eve, Lexi and I sneaked into the dining room, where the wireless was kept, and tuned it in to the BBC in London. We had to press our heads so close to the speaker that our noses were almost touching: the minimum penalty for listening to foreign broadcasts was five years' imprisonment, the maximum, death.

'Tonight, on this very special celebration for Christmas all over the world, we bring you a service of lessons and carols ...'

The announcer's voice was so faint as to be almost indiscernible.

'Turn it up, turn it up!' said Lexi.

'Lexi – we can't!'

'Oh, to hell with it! Hitler can bloody well kill me if he likes, but he's not going to stop me listening to Christmas carols.'

We turned up the wireless a little, but sang so loudly through 'Hark the Herald' and 'Once in Royal David's City' that it couldn't really be heard anyway. I thought of the same carols being sung round the tree at Russington, and had to sing even louder to force back the tears.

After Christmas it snowed heavily, and we took time off from queueing for turnips to go tobogganning. One morning I was towing Paul along the street on his little sledge when I passed a tall, blonde woman in a fur coat. She smiled at me a little stiffly, and I automatically smiled back.

Then I froze in my tracks. The woman was Frau Drecker, exemplary mother and wife of a senior Party official. Not only had she recognised me as Lexi's English cousin, but I had been carrying my camera as well, though ironically only to take some innocent snaps of little Paul.

I ran along the street as fast as I could, not daring to stop or look at the people I was passing. Paul was bounced up and down on his sledge, laughing at first at the new game, then breaking into howls of protest when I showed no signs of slowing my pace. I left the sledge at the gate of the villa, tucked the bawling baby under one arm and raced into the house.

'What's the matter?' demanded Lexi. 'What's happened. Is it Paul?'

'She saw me!' I gasped, clutching the back of a chair to try to regain my breath.

'Who did?'

'That woman ... the one with the gold cross ... who brought you baby clothes ...'

'Frau Drecker! That Nazi cow ... Oh dear.' Lexi looked shaken, and fumbled for her cigarettes. 'Sit down. We'd better have a little think ...'

One cigarette later she said, 'It's pretty serious, I'll admit that. But you mustn't say anything to Hubertus.'

'I think we ought to, Lexi ...'

'No. He'll only panic. And she might not have recognised you, anyway. You were wearing a hat, and so was Paul. She might just have thought you were a fellow German mother.'

'I suppose so,' I said, but I didn't share her optimism. She hadn't seen the look on the woman's face.

As a Winstanley, Lexi was a great dreamer-up of schemes, and her proposition this time was that I would have to hide from visitors to the house, unless they were known to be 'one of us', and I was not to go out unless I was in disguise. She procured me a blonde wig from a friend of Hubertus who had been involved in amateur theatricals, and a pair of horn-rimmed glasses, whose lenses made the world tilt sideways. I would pad myself with a few cushions and leave the house looking like a plump, short-sighted blonde in a shapeless loden coat (it belonged to Hubertus). At first this was great fun, reminiscent of dressing-up sessions at Russington, but after a week it became very tedious and restricting, especially since we had to keep the disguise – and the robing ritual – out of sight of Ilse.

And even though we didn't tell Hubertus about Frau Drecker, he was getting worried. 'I really think I should arrange your journey home, Kitty,' he said when the snow was starting to turn to slush. 'Think how worried your family will be.'

'Just a little while longer,' pleaded Lexi.

I stayed, but made it a condition of my doing so that we tried to get a message to England, to assure everyone that I was all right, and would be back soon.

Hubertus set about finding the means to do this, but it wasn't easy, as the members of his movement were trying to avoid any activity that would draw attention to themselves. They were still meeting at our house, but their crusade had taken on a new urgency, and was no longer a rather enjoyable intellectual exercise to see how they could pit their wits against the devil, alias Adolf Hitler. There was a work to be done, and that work was becoming daily more dangerous.

One evening Hubertus came upstairs to speak to me after his friends had left.

'If you'd like to, you and Lexi can write a short letter to your family now. But don't say anything about where you are, or who you're with. Keep it to the minimum, and don't mention any names – don't even sign it.'

It turned out that a Jewish associate of the movement, called Werner, was going to be smuggled out of England to report to the British Foreign Office. He could take a letter as far as London.

I was overjoyed to be given this opportunity and spent several attempts trying to get the letter exactly right. The thought that my family would receive this reassurance made me easier in my own mind, and I tolerated the indignity of the wig (now that the weather

171

was growing warmer, it made my scalp itch) with better humour. I even ignored Hubertus's warning and started to take my camera about with me again, photographing the downtrodden citizens of Berlin.

When Hubertus called me into the dining room for a talk, I thought he was going to reprimand me for this professional indiscretion. But he looked more frightened than severe, and I noticed that his hand shook as he closed the door behind me. He switched on the wireless – loud German folk songs – so that nothing we said would be audible.

'I heard today . . .' His voice shook. '. . . Werner didn't make it, I'm afraid.'

'Oh.' I looked down at my hands.

'He was arrested before the train reached the border, and taken to one of the camps. Probably Dachau.'

'Oh no . . !'

We had known about the existence of concentration camps for several months, from military contacts of Hubertus.

'Excuse me a moment . . .' I ran past him and up to my room. Once I had closed the door behind me I paced the room, pressing my knuckles against my teeth. I was gripped with fear, terror even.

What am I doing here? I asked myself. I must have been mad, letting Lexi persuade me to stay on . . .

And how the hell was I ever going to get out? I should leave, but what if I were caught? What if I suffered the same fate as Werner . . ?

Lexi tapped at the door. 'Want some tea, Kitty? I'm just about to make some.'

She came in.

I stared at her angrily.

'What's the matter with you?' she demanded in her old, bossy tone. 'Come on – cheer up! Things aren't as bad as all that, not yet – '

'*I'm scared!*' I shouted. 'I know you Winstanleys are never frightened of anything, but I'm telling you, I'm bloody scared!'

Lexi banged the door shut and ran down the stairs. When I went down I found her in the kitchen peeling potatoes, stiff-jawed and white-faced.

'Do you want that tea?' she asked coldly.

'It's all right, I can do it myself.' I went to fetch the teapot from the shelf.

'I said *I'd* do it, didn't I?' She snatched the teapot from me and slammed it down on the table so hard that it broke. 'You're angry

172

with me for keeping you here in Berlin, aren't you? You think I've put you at risk just for my own ends?'

I shrugged.

Lexi turned back to the sink and said quietly, 'I've just found out that I'm pregnant again. That's one reason I wanted to keep you here with me ... and for your information, I *am* scared. I'm just as bloody scared as you are. But I don't want Paul seeing me that way.'

I put my arms around her. 'I'm sorry, Lexi.'

She hugged me. 'So am I.'

There was now no question that I would have to go as soon as possible, and in disguise. It was rumoured that Hitler was about to take the army into Holland, making travel on the continent even more difficult.

'Good job we've got the wig,' Lexi said firmly.

'No,' I insisted. 'Not the wig. It's uncomfortable.'

'Don't be difficult, Kitty, *please*!'

'I'm not being difficult. It's just too bloody obvious at close quarters, that's all. It's not you who's got to – '

'All right! All right! We'll dye your hair blonde ...' Hilde, Reinhard's wife, kept her blonde curls looking immaculate with the help of a peroxide rinse, and she lent us a bottle of the stuff. It took a generous amount, and a few attempts, to change the colour of my brown hair, and even then it was yellow rather than blonde.

'We'll plait it,' said Lexi confidently, 'and pin the plaits to the front of the head. That way you'll look like a real Sieghilde.'

Sieghilde was the name we had chosen for my false identity papers, which were really quite convincing once the photograph had been attached. Lexi and I were pleased with the result, but Hubertus just looked at it, nodded, and handed it back.

'What's the matter?' Lexi snapped at her husband. 'You don't think it's good enough, is that it?'

'No, it's not that ...' He sighed. 'It's Reinhard. He was arrested today. Outside the steps of the Ministry. He's been taken to Prinz Albrechtstrasse for questioning.'

'Oh, no ...' Lexi turned the pass over and over, her hand trembling slightly. 'Hubie, does Kitty *have* to go? Wouldn't it be safer to keep her here, in hiding, until the war's over?'

'Don't be stupid,' said Hubertus wearily. 'It's out of the question. The war could last at least another year!'

Lexi gritted her teeth. 'We'll just have to make sure we get the disguise right then, won't we?'

We kept the horn-rimmed glasses, and the loden coat, over a frumpy floral smock. The finishing touch was Lexi's Mother' Cross pinned to my lapel.

'There you are ... a good German wife and mother, going to visit her relatives in Saxony.'

My false identity papers would get me as far as the Swiss border, but then we had a problem. Hubertus's influence did not extend far enough to get me a German passport, so I would somehow have to bluff my way across the border. I did not dare admit – even to Lexi – the extent of my terror at this prospect.

After a tipsy, and a very painful farewell dinner at which we all feebly pretended to be cheerful, Hubertus and Lexi helped me into my disguise and drove me to the central station. I took my seat, arranged my shopping bag by my feet and (with a lot of squinting through the wretched horn-rimmed spectacles) opened the racy German novelette that Lexi had provided for Sieghilde to read. I didn't understand a word of it, but at least I remembered to hold the book the right way up in my efforts to look engrossed.

The other people in the carriage were all ordinary citizens (no SS, thank God) who probably had no interest in me at all, but like all people with a guilty conscience I was convinced that every one of them was staring at me, and I hardly dared look up from my book, turning the pages and moving my eyes so that they would believe I was reading about Matilde and her sinewy thighed Hans.

At Munich the moment I was dreading finally arrived. The guard came round to check the tickets. My hand trembled so much as I fumbled in my bag that I dropped the ticket under the feet of the man opposite me, and my glasses slid down my nose after it. The ticket collector fixed me with a stare, then held out his hand for my identity papers. I gave them to him without looking at his face, then cursed myself for being so obvious, and attempted a smile. My heart was thumping so loudly that I could hear it in my ears.

The guard glanced at the photograph, then back at my face. I smiled again feebly. There was no doubt that the picture matched the face, so perhaps something else was troubling him.

My hair. My hair's the wrong shade of yellow ...

Or perhaps he was suspicious because I just didn't look like a German peasant. Either way, I wasn't going to wait to find out. We were nearing the border now, and I was so nervous I could no longer control my shaking. I gathered up my belongings and, when the guard moved into the next compartment, I locked myself into the lavatory.

Sieghilde's shopping bag was a hindrance, I decided. But before I

174

could ditch it, there was one very important thing I had to do. I rummaged at the bottom, and pulled out the reels of film that I had hidden under some knitting. There was only one hiding place I could think of. I bundled the films, together with my string of pearls, inside the elastic of my knickers.

The train slowed down agonisingly as it shunted towards the Swiss border, and stopped altogether once we were at the checkpoint. Squinting through the small frosted pane of the lavatory window, I could see uniformed border guards (grey, which meant they were German) striding down the tracks and boarding the train. They were coming to check passports. I could hear their jackbooted feet striding down the corridor past me. My guts turned to water.

A hand tried the door, then said, '*Hallo! ist jemand drinnen?*'

I flushed the lavatory and switched on the taps in the washbasin. The boots moved on, but I knew I had run out of time. I took a deep breath, rushed out into the corridor and hurled myself from the top step of the carriage door, on to the track, where I landed on my face, twisting my ankle so painfully that I was only vaguely aware of a German voice shouting '*Hei!*' and a large body trying to intercept me.

I tried to raise myself to a crouching position, but my leg wouldn't work at all. Behind me there were footsteps crunching along the gravel of the track. I didn't look round, and I didn't even try to move away. It was useless. I had failed.

An arm reached down to pull me up and the rough serge of a uniform sleeve brushed my cheek. I opened my eyes. The uniform was blue, not grey. I fainted with relief.

The Swiss guards carried me into the station office, gave me a cup of hot chocolate and asked me a lot of questions, in French. I showed them my British passport, which had been in my coat pocket and not in Sieghilde's bag. Finally they seemed satisfied, and put me on a train to the northern coast of France, by way of Besançon, Dijon and – of course – Paris.

At another time I would have stopped there and tried to find Frannie, but now I didn't dare. It was terrible to pull out of the Gare du Nord knowing that she was so very close – probably only a few miles away – and yet she might as well have been in Alaska. I didn't even dare think about when we might meet again.

By the time I reached London I was so tired I was oblivious to the fact that I was finally in England again. My watch had been shattered in the leap from the train, so I didn't even know what time of day it was. I had no English currency, but a taxi driver saw my bandaged ankle and grazed face and took pity on me.

'You been away somewhere nice?' he asked me.

'You could say that.'

He proceeded to tell me exactly what he thought of Adolf Hitler and it was then that it struck me how far I was – not just in miles – from Berlin.

I asked to be dropped at the flat in Carlyle Square. I was too tired to go further than London, and the phone at Jack's studio went unanswered when I rang from the station.

Since I no longer had a key, I rang at Lady Reeve's door, and her Irish housekeeper answered. She paled when she saw me, and I assumed it was just my travel-stained appearance that had alarmed her.

'Sweet mother of Jesus ... !' She crossed herself. 'We were told you were dead, so we were!'

This turned out to be a slight exaggeration, but I learned over a welcome cup of tea that as my aunt and uncle had been unable to glean any information about my whereabouts, the worst was being assumed.

'Shall you phone them now ..? Only it'll be a terrible shock for them ...'

'No,' I said. 'I won't stay the night after all. I think I'll go straight home.'

My mind reasoned that having travelled this far, I might as well go on, but my body rebelled as I dragged it to Paddington station and bought a ticket for Finstock. It was evening by then – not that that made any difference to me – and the train was so full of troops that it was impossible to find a seat. One Tommy took pity on me when I began to sway a little and gave me his knapsack to sit on, on the corridor floor. Soon I was accepted as part of his little group, and the hipflask of grog was passed my way in a democratic fashion. The soldiers asked me where I had come from, but when I told them about that other, very different, train journey they just laughed. They didn't believe me. I made the mistake of insisting that it was true and I had photographs in my knickers to prove it. This proved that I was mad, and for the rest of the trip they kept a bemused distance from me.

There were never any taxis at Finstock during peace time, and I didn't even ask now. It was not only too late to phone Russington Hall, but it would be too much of a shock if I did, I reasoned. It would throw the house into uproar. I wanted to just slip back

176

quietly and go straight to bed. I hitched as far as Burford in the milk van, then caught a ride with a farmer as far as the outskirts of the village. I started to limp towards the park gates, moving pitifully slowly, until finally the village policeman took pity on me and drove me right up to the front steps of the Hall.

At the sound of a car drawing up, a light came on in the hall. The policeman had to help me up the steps and ring the bell for me – by now I was too weak to move. It was three o'clock in the morning.

Jack came to the door, almost as though he had been expecting me. He pulled me roughly towards him and hugged me. Then, just as abruptly, I was released, as he fingered a lock of my ugly bleached hair, and laughed. I thought I could detect lurking traces of gladness, and of relief, but he pretended to be merely amused.

'I knew we couldn't get rid of you that easily . . .'

THREE

War

One

When I first returned to Russington, I felt as though I never wanted to go away again.

The inhabitants of the Windrush valley grumbled incessantly about the imposition of the war on their tranquil way of life, but to me their existence seemed idyllic, blissful after some of the things I had seen. The proliferation of farms in the area meant that rations could be topped up with eggs, dairy products and vegetables and most landowners – Nim for one – turned a blind eye to the odd bit of illegal butchering. The fighting in Europe seemed far away, and when the subject did rear its head it was as a universal nuisance that was binding an already close community even closer together.

The pace of life at Russington Hall was slower now, and quieter with the house half empty. Irving was stationed at an RAF base in East Anglia, training for the 'wings' of a bomber pilot. Jack, still draft-dodging with his bogus editorship, flitted to and fro, spending a few weeks at Russington helping Nim with the estate, then disappearing to the clubs and theatres of the West End. No one, not even his father, ever questioned his movements. They knew Jack, so they knew better.

Nim and Beattie were anxious for news of Lexi, now that they could no longer write, and I told them the news about the expected baby, and as much as I could about her life in Berlin. They were thrilled with the pictures I had taken of Paul tobogganning, and added one to the growing collection in the drawing room. The photographs were the only things in that room that ever changed. The faded, stained carpet was still in place, the dusty furniture never moved. The idea of redecorating the place was unthinkable;

too vulgar and wasteful for words. Flash, now bedridden, had become another permanent fixture, always to be found in his basket by the brass fender. The only times he left it voluntarily were Jack's visits, when he would raise himself stiffly on to his legs and wag his tail in greeting. Poor misguided dog.

Those other misguided members of the household, Nim and Beattie, were silent on the subject of Nazism, and the German leader they had once professed to admire so much. They would never have been disloyal to their own country, but their attitude to the war was that it was all a big fuss over nothing that would die down once the world leaders saw the error of their ways and stopped being so childish. I told them that I had been through Paris on my way back from Germany. They did not mention Frannie.

By the time I had rested and recovered my equilibrium, it was summer, and there was too much to do to allow time for introspection. The estate farms were desperately short of workers, and it fell to Clem, Shoes and me to help with the livestock and, later, the harvesting. It was the source of some guilt at the time, but I enjoyed myself enormously. We would be up with the dawn, into old clothes and downstairs for a huge cooked breakfast. Then we would be handed a packed lunch each (the contents of the sandwiches were always extremely dubious – an improvement of Cook's skills was not part of the war effort) and would set off to wherever we were needed, bearing a huge hamper full of refreshments for the other workers. We travelled by horse and cart: petrol was too scarce for us to be lent an estate vehicle and Jack's Bugatti was hardly appropriate.

One of the best aspects of our new role was acceptance into the community. We worked alongside the youngsters from the village, and they made the startling discovery that we were as 'normal' as they were. I think we deliberately worked harder than anyone else, and it was worth it. At last we were freed from the stigma of being 'the children from the big house'. One or two of the girls were my age and became friends. They expressed surprise at my willingness to talk about make-up and hairstyles and gossip from village dances.

'We thought you'd want to talk about ... well, you know, politics and the like.'

'No,' I said, examining the rubberised ham in my sandwich, 'I don't want to talk about politics.'

One girl who took a particular liking to me was Pattie, daughter of Jeb Harman, Nim's dairyman. 'Pretty Pattie', we used to call her, because she had a lovely rosy complexion and thick-lashed brown eyes like those of the cows in my uncle's herd. Pattie attached herself to my side like a limpet, but was extremely reticent when it came to striking up a conversation.

One hot June day, when the two of us were scything grass in one of the meadows, she asked me shyly, 'Did you really go to Buckingham Palace and see the King and Queen, like the girls say you did?'

'Yes,' I said, taking a swipe at a thick clump of grass, 'I did.'

'Oh.' Pattie looked taken aback at this piece of information. 'I thought they was pulling my leg.'

'It was when I was a debutante. You know, you're presented at court with the other debutantes, that sort of thing.'

I was aware how stupid this sounded as the two of us stood there in our overalls, slashing grass at the same pace, equals. I felt profoundly glad that that period of my life was over and I could turn my back on 'Society' but I didn't know how to explain this to Pattie.

Alas, she seemed excited and impressed by this piece of information. 'Do you think you could . . ? Would you mind telling me a bit about it? Like what they looked like an' all . . . their majesties? Were they, like . . . regal?'

I hadn't expected to have a diehard royalist on my hands. As we scythed away, I explained the presentation ceremony as disparagingly as I could, playing down its more dramatic elements, suggesting that our monarchs were no more interesting than Mr and Mrs Bantry who ran the village pub.

'Goodness!' Pattie sighed. 'You're so lucky, Kitty! I wish I could be like you!'

This was exactly what I had hoped to avoid. I opened my mouth to make some nonchalant dismissal of this idea, but before I got anywhere Jack appeared on the horizon, waving his arms and bounding towards us. Pattie blushed and returned her attention to her scythe.

'Hullo, pretty Pattie!' shouted Jack, who was no respecter of shyness. She responded to his wink by looking away, and he slapped her on the shoulder, exclaiming, 'All right, play hard to get, see if I care!'

'Jack, don't tease . . ! What do you want, anyway? We're supposed to try and get this finished by tea-time . . .'

'A word in your ear, Kitty . . .' He led me away from Pattie, and I prayed fervently that she didn't think we were talking about her.

'Sit down . . .' He pointed to the grassy bank of a tributary that ran into the Windrush. Beyond the stream and the weeping willows that shaded it was a field of ripening corn, glowing beneath a cloudless June sky. The only sound was the breeze rippling through the willows and the rhythmic slicing of Pattie's blade.

'I've just been listening to the news,' Jack said. His tone of voice was entirely serious, a rarity that filled me with dread. 'The Germans have just entered Paris.'

'Oh no ...' I lay back on the grass and let the fact sink in. I feared for Lexi and Hubertus playing dangerous games in their own city, but a city occupied by a foreign power was even more dangerous.

I clenched my fists to try to stop myself from trembling. 'And Simon ... if they get caught ...'

'Hold on a minute ...' Jack squeezed my hand. 'We don't even know for sure that she's still in Paris. How long has it been now, since she left?'

'Over a year.'

'Exactly. She could be anywhere. Thousands of people have fled from Paris, so maybe they had the sense to get out in time.'

Jack didn't speak with much confidence, and I knew we were thinking the same thing.

'Not Simon. He'd see it as running away. And he'd persuade Frannie that she ought to stay to the bitter end.'

'And she'd believe him.'

'She'd *want* to. You know how she is, Jack ...'

'Look ...' Jack touched the palm of my outstretched hand, lightly this time. 'I know how you feel about Frannie. I reckon you and I are the only people who want to actually do something about the situation. So I'll go up to London again and squeeze my contacts, see if I can get some help in finding out where Fran is.'

'Oh Jack ... could you?'

He touched his forehead in a mock salute. 'Just leave it to your Uncle Jacko.'

After several sleepless nights, worrying about Frannie, when the girls deputed Pattie to ask me along to the village hop the following week, I accepted readily. A little frivolity would distract me, I decided.

It was as well that I didn't allow Pattie's interest in me to make me big-headed, because during that week it became clear what lay behind the interest.

Or who. She had fallen for Jack Winstanley, and in a big way. The day after he left for London to make enquiries about Frannie, she missed him in the fields and asked me, haltingly, where he had

184

gone. As we munched on our sandwiches at lunchtime, she found some excuse to bring him into the conversation again.

And so it went on; her constantly prodding me into mentions of Jack, which would swiftly be followed by questions about him. Like many a poor stooge before me, I was merely being cultivated for my useful proximity to the love object. I have to confess that sometimes I would lead Pattie on, say his name just to see her blush, or lead her into thinking I was about to make some great revelation about his secret life, which then turned out to be completely trivial. But like all those who are completely smitten, she hoarded every tiny nugget of information. And I quite enjoyed having a chance to talk about him and see him as a flesh-and-blood man, and not just the other half of my consciousness, the perennial thorn in my side.

Darling Beattie took all my dancing frocks out of mothballs, but I turned my back on them in favour of a simple floral print and a strand of pearls that Lexi had given me in Berlin, my own having been sold for Frannie's dowry. How I missed her then as I dressed myself for a night out! And yet I was looking forward to the village dance more than any debutante ball, which made me feel horribly guilty. I must be a callous and hard-hearted person, I told myself, to be cavorting all night long while my poor cousin was suffering God knew what hardship, or had even been...

My morbid thoughts were brushed aside by the arrival of Pattie who had come to call for me, even though the hall was miles out of her way, quite the opposite direction in fact.

'That's very sweet of you,' I had said when she offered, biting back a giggle. I knew she wanted a chance to sniff around Jack's home, or perhaps even to accidentally bump into him.

'Is ... anyone else coming?' she asked wistfully as I grabbed my bag and stole and set off down the stairs.

'Just us. Shoes is still a bit too young and everyone else is away.' I was drawing out the agony.

'So Jack .. ?'

'In London.'

But Jack, devil that he was, proved me wrong and turned up at the village hall halfway through the dance when the cherry-flavoured punch had run out and prospects for the evening were looking a little drab. James Bleak-Wailer (in his new guise as a second lieutenant) was the nearest thing to excitement I had found, and that was not very near.

As soon as Jack came in, hey presto!, Pattie was at my side and sticking like glue. He strolled over to where we were, chatting to some servicemen, and her hand trembled on her cup of lemonade.

He had not had time to dress and this would have set anyone else at a disadvantage next to all the military uniforms. But Jack wore his expensive shirt-collar open, revealing a 'V' of suntanned chest, and his sweater was slung casually around the shoulders of his blazer. He didn't even have to try.

He took me straight on to the dancefloor, which was a ruse for him to tell me about Frannie, but poor Pattie didn't know that and stared forlornly into her lemonade.

'Bit like schoolroom days, isn't it?' he asked, as we did a competent waltz. 'You, me, old James there ...'

'Jack! Tell me! What happened in London ..?'

'Nothing to report yet, I'm afraid. I gave all the details to a sympathetic party who's heading for France ... on business, of course, but it could be months before she can get any information back.'

'She?'

'No one you need to know about ...'

He was looking over my shoulder, in need of distraction. 'I say, pretty Pattie's looking fairly tasty tonight – '

'Jack!'

'I don't know why you're sounding surprised. Girl's been making eyes at me for weeks, and you know it ... why don't you go and have a chat to the worthy James ..?'

Jack let go of me abruptly and walked over to Pattie, who lit up like a beacon. I watched them dance, and felt my old curiosity about Jack's sexuality. He had never mentioned any girl except as an attractive object (or otherwise), and although they fell for him in scores he remained unmoved and rarely went to the trouble of taking them out. He had never had a steady girlfriend, that any of us knew about. Frannie had once confided that she thought he might be homosexual. The problem with that theory was that he didn't seem much interested in men either. Only in himself.

I danced with a few of the squaddies, then James monopolised me for the rest of the evening, and ended up walking me home, since everyone else had paired off or disappeared. In the absence of street-lighting, the village was a haven for canoodling couples, and we almost had to pick our way over them to get from one side of the green to the other. As my eyes became accustomed to the dark I started to recognise people by what they were wearing. One white blob could only be Pattie Harman's white dress. Its owner was semi-prone on the grass and making feeble efforts to push a pair of hands from under her skirt, while a mouth engaged hers in a furious kiss. The sight of a signet ring glinting on one of the roving

186

hands was all the confirmation I needed – not that it would have taken many guesses. A curious mixture of arousal, jealousy and displeasure washed over me, making me grasp James's arm tighter than before. He took this as encouragement and awkwardly slipped his arm around my shoulders.

'It's late,' I said, and pushed him away.

Pattie steered clear of me the next day, but there was no mistaking the lovesick look in her eyes. It didn't seem to matter to her that Jack, who was working with us until his next disappearance, barely acknowledged her existence.

He came and sat with me to eat his lunch, on a bench outside the sheep pens. This posed a problem for Pattie, who didn't have the gall to come and sit there with us. She hovered somewhere within worshipping radius of her idol, staring at him as if bewitched when he was looking the other way, but averting her eyes quickly if he moved his head.

'Hey, Pattie!' Jack said suddenly, his mouth full of sandwich. 'There's a Bette Davis picture on in Oxford tomorrow; *Dark Victory*. D'you fancy seeing it?'

He finally deigned to turn and look her in the eye.

'Oh ... ' Pattie had not expected to be singled out so publicly (was Jack doing it on purpose to embarrass her, I wondered?) and turned bright crimson. The other girls whistled and clapped. 'Yes, yes, that would be nice ... I'll have to check with Dad.'

Mr Harman must have given his blessing, because for the rest of the day Pattie scythed her grass in a blissful daze, like some character from a Thomas Hardy novel. I felt mildly irritated. Jack ignored her again.

The following evening, when Jack and I returned, filthy, from the fields, Darling Beattie met us in the hall. She was wearing a straw hat and gardening gloves and carrying a glass of vintage champagne from Nim's un-rationed supply in the cellars.

'There was a telephone call for you, Jack darling. I wrote down the name. One of your London friends, I should think ... '

'Jolly good, Mother ... ' He planted a grubby kiss on her cheek and went off to phone from the morning room, while I declined a game of Snakes and Ladders with Clem and ascended the staircase in search of a shallow bath; wartime regulations stipulating no more than five inches of water to be used.

When I came down again, Jack was in the hall, washed and scrubbed and wearing black tie.

'That's a little formal for the Oxford Odeon, isn't it?' I asked.

'Oh . . . ' he waved his white silk scarf airily. 'I'm not going to the cinema after all.'

'So where are you taking her?'

'Her?'

'Pattie. Your date. Remember?'

'Oh, *God*!' He clapped a hand to his forehead. '*Her*! Oh yes . . . I'd forgotten about that. You see, I'm going up to London.'

'London .. ! Jack .. ! '

By now he was through the front door and heading down the steps to where the Bugatti was parked.

'Jack! You're supposed to be taking Pattie Harman out! She's expecting you. You can't just − '

'Yes, well, I'm sorry about that . . .' He vaulted over the door and into the passenger seat. 'But a friend of mine in London needs my services. Got a couple of rather good-looking WAAFs lined up, apparently, who are expecting to be taken up to the Rainbow Club. Now I'm sorry, Kitty, but I've got to go . . . '

He turned the key in the ignition.

'Aren't you even going to phone her?'

'Sorry − haven't got time.'

'You know what you are, Jack Winstanley!' I shouted above the roar of the engine. 'You're a real bastard!'

This observation was rewarded with a blown kiss and a toot of the horn. I ignored it, stomping my way to the telephone, to do Jack's dirty work for him.

As the winter set in, life fell into a cosy rhythm. I continued to work on the estate, increasingly helping Nim with its management. With the darker evenings, I socialised less with the villagers I worked with, though the closeness of the community persisted. Pattie Harman dated and eventually became engaged to the local butcher, having apparently forgotten her attachment to Jack. He meanwhile continued to descend on Russington, though less now than in the summer, and broke the heart of a different village girl every time.

They were quiet months. At Russington, with fewer staff, Nim and Beattie worked together as a team, and seemed more of a couple than they had ever been before. Beattie put on another stone, despite rationing, and Nim's hair started to grey. After the blackouts had been erected we spent the long winter evenings sitting round the drawing-room fire listening to sentimental love ballads on the wireless: Vera Lynn singing servicemen's requests for 'Sincerely Yours' or 'I'll Keep the Love Lights Burning'.

War had brought a kind of peace to the house, a calm atmosphere that had never existed before. Nim had even given up writing to *The Times* for the duration, and he didn't bark at Clem and Shoes in the way that he had done when we were young. But I never stopped being aware of the missing faces, and for me the place was no longer complete, perhaps never would be again. Fears for Lexi were voiced by all of us; we hadn't even received word that her second child had been born safely. My fears for Frannie were shared with Jack alone, or occasionally with Irving when he returned on leave from his base. Jack's friend had been unable to send any news other than that Simon and Frannie were still in Paris, which was bad news.

But despite their silence, I knew that Nim and Beattie could never put Frannie from their hearts. My aunt went up to our old, shared room regularly to tidy and rearrange Frannie's things. I walked in on her once and found her gazing sorrowfully at a desiccated sheep's skull from Fran's old 'collection'. She thrust it aside and pretended to be looking for something.

And Nim tuned in to all the bulletins from the continent, pacing restlessly while they were on. I didn't often stray into his study, but on one occasion when I was looking for the farm account book, I saw a half-finished letter on his desk, addressed to Sir Jolyon Ricketts, an old school friend now in the War Office. It asked if he had any means of gleaning news about British nationals in the occupied French capital.

The knowledge that I was having a 'good' war heightened my discontent. I contemplated joining the forces myself. Donning a uniform would have made me feel more useful, even though the work I did on the estate was important, as Nim and even Jack grudgingly pointed out.

Jack came home for New Year. No one else seemed much surprised by his presence, but I felt it was a portent. There had to be a reason for his passing up the sybaritic parties the capital had to offer.

I was right. He came to me on the evening of 2 January and announced that he was leaving the country, for France.

'You don't mean you're joining up at last?' I asked with some incredulity.

He laughed. 'Me – go and fight? Don't be silly! I'm going to make money, of course.'

'Doing what?'

'A little bit of supply and demand. People still in Paris are starving, and the entrepreneurial few who undertake to provide them with what they need are raking in all the wealth of the city. I thought I'd give it a try.'

I let this information sink in for a few minutes. He didn't need to explain that what he was planning to do was illegal, and dangerous, in occupied France. His leaving the country, leaving Russington ... leaving me, was a terrible blow, the worst I could have suffered at that time, short of still worse news from France. But I didn't even attempt to dissuade him; it would have been futile.

'Will you look for Frannie?' I asked.

'I'll do my best.'

'Promise?'

'All right, I promise'.

'When are you leaving?'

'Tomorrow – early. But I don't want you to tell the others until after I've gone. No scenes, all right?'

No scenes. I muttered that to myself when I got up the next morning to see him off, dressing myself with cold, fumbling fingers. I walked to the park gates with him, but then he wouldn't let me go any further. He didn't kiss me, just squeezed my shoulder and looked into my eyes for a second.

'Wait!' I shouted after him. 'Wait, there's something I've forgotten!'

He stood patiently with his knapsack slung over his shoulder while I groped around in my pocket for the scissors I had brought with me. I couldn't grip them with my gloves on, and my fingers were so cold without that I couldn't cut very well. With a rare show of patience, Jack bent his head for me while I snipped off one of the dark, shining locks that curled over the collar of his greatcoat. Then he was really gone. I watched him walk down the lane towards the rising sun, his jaunty, Chaplinesque figure growing smaller and smaller, and eventually disappearing. For ever ... I told myself, he's gone for ever. But my numb senses wouldn't take it in.

I trudged up the frosty driveway and into the house. Somewhere in the background a bath was running, and I could hear Shoes whistling the mournful strains of 'I Vow to Thee My Country'. In my room, I put the lock of Jack's hair to my lips. It smelled of him; of clean clothes and shaving cream. I put it away in a manilla envelope in the drawer of my desk. Later, when I took it out, it smelt of nothing except the envelope it was in.

There was a faint tap at my door, and Aunt Griz came in, leaning heavily on her stick.

Go away, you crazy old woman . . .

I wasn't in the mood for the vagaries of an infirm, elderly lady, one who lived increasingly in her room, away from the rest of the family.

'I was watching from the window,' she said. 'Jack's gone for good, I suppose. You must be heartbroken.'

I looked at her sullenly, challenging her to explain herself. She smiled at me and said, 'Don't make the mistake of thinking you're the only one who knows what it is to feel pain. You don't have it all to yourself, you know . . .' Using her stick, she lowered herself on to the edge of my bed. 'I wonder if you've ever seen a certain daguerreotype that I keep in my room?'

She knew very well that I had. I nodded anyway.

'That's dearest Dan. Daniel Crossley. He was my brother's fencing master. And I . . . well, you know how young gals are!'

She laughed a cracked little laugh. 'What a man! He was as handsome and as graceful as . . . well, never mind. I knew I'd never feel that way about another one, I told them so; Papa, Flora, Archie. They listened . . . oh yes, they listened. And then they decided for me. There was no question of me becoming Mrs Dan Crossley. Flora had already married her title, you would have thought that would satisfy them, but . . . we were going to marry anyway, you see, but they made sure we couldn't. They sent him away from the house, no references of course, but Papa found him a family who were willing to take him on. In Canada . . .'

Aunt Griz looked down at her liver-spotted hands, twisted an imaginary engagement ring.

'Couldn't you have gone with him?'

'Oh, I was going to. Eloping was quite commonplace then. But Archie wrote and told him I was married to someone else, so he stopped sending the letters. And when I asked, finally, Archie said he'd heard Dan had married a Canadian girl – '

'You mean, they *lied* about it . . . that's terrible . . . it's criminal.'

'Oh, they did it for me, darling, they did it for me. To save me from a bad match. They had my best interests at heart, the family. They protected me. Gave me a home when I ended up a spinster. Protected me from the world . . . I lived with Flora, and then when she died I was handed on to Darling Beattie . . .'

'Just like a bloody parcel!'

'Oh no, dear, you mustn't think that! It was good of her to take me on.'

'And Daniel?'

'He died at the age of sixty-four. He never had married. And the

191

pain never went away. That's what I wanted to warn you about, really.'

I looked at Aunt Griz; for the first time in my life I really looked at her and saw more than just the eccentric old aunt of my youth. The world, and that part of the world that was Russington, was a changed place.

Two

The remainder of 1941 passed in a blur.

I waited for news from Jack, but none came. Not a thing. I knew that communications would be difficult, if not impossible, but this didn't prevent me from feeling an overwhelming, irrational anger towards him. He had dumped me here in Russington, a place forsaken even by the war, a place where nothing ever happened. And where, after the desertion of my four eldest cousins (that didn't apply to Irving, really, since he was serving king and country), I was having to shoulder more than my fair share of family responsibility.

I didn't resent this; it seemed quite fair after the years my aunt and uncle had put into raising me that I should try to do something for them. I spent hours discussing the estate with Nim and the running of the house with Darling Beattie, I helped care for the nearly bedridden Aunt Griz, and all of this I did as cheerfully as I could. 'You won't go off and leave us too, will you, Kitty?' my aunt said over and over again, until I abandoned all thoughts of getting a job elsewhere. I had a job; my job was paying back the Winstanley family.

Frannie was still not mentioned, and Jack mentioned little. Nim and Beattie didn't seem to worry about him in the way they did about their other children. His trip to Nazi-occupied France was treated as something of a jaunt. 'You know how Jack is, dear,' was the attitude permanently adopted by his mother. She probably thought he would be able to charm his way out of trouble.

The only other member of the household who seemed to miss him as I did was Flash. He was so affected by Jack's absence that he pined away and died. The others said it was from old age; I knew better.

As much as I missed Jack, the feeling receded to a dull ache, and I thought about him less as time went by. The human heart has its own ways of saving us from Flash's fate, I would tell myself. Then I would think of Aunt Griz and Dan Crossley, and shudder. The daily problem became one of keeping boredom and introspection at bay. I filled every spare moment with work of one kind or another.

And I started to spend more time with Shoes, who was now fifteen and better company than anyone else around. I found her personality an intriguing mixture of her two elder sisters. She had some of Frannie's sentimentality and love of the melodramatic, but she also had Lexi's blithe pragmatism. And she was very funny in her own right. The two of us did part-time work at the local WVS canteen, serving up food to the troops at the basic training camp near Burford. Shoes made it her business to know *everything* about the other women we worked with, and she would fill me in in stage whispers as we scrubbed counters.

'You see Muriel there,' she said to me one day, pointing to a pretty young matron in a flowered apron. 'Well, she's P-R-E-G-N-A-N-T. Only she doesn't dare tell her mother-in-law because the doctor says she's three months gone, and her husband only came home on leave two months ago ...'

Muriel glanced in our direction and Shoes instantly started to whistle, a habit she had never given up. 'Her mother says she should go and get a second opinion from another doctor, but Muriel said to hell with it, she's just going to hope the baby's late, or if it's on time say it's premature. She said her husband was so stupid he'd never know the difference.'

I tried to keep a straight face, but the corners of my mouth twitched. Taking this as encouragement, Shoes went on, 'Mrs Southern's got an even worse problem ... she's the fat, old one over there ... her husband's been invalided out of the navy, and it turns out the reason is a *prostate* problem. The woman she was talking to didn't know what that was, so she told her it was a problem with his "winkle". Imagine calling it something like that? ... Anyway, she's worried that he won't be able to do it any more. Isn't that disgusting! That people of their age do it at all, I mean!'

'*Shoes!*' I shushed her, and turned my attention to scouring the tea-urns.

'Well, well, look at this ...' said my cousin. The door had

opened and someone had come in, but I kept my back turned, not wanting to provoke yet more indiscreet revelations.

'*He's* certainly no new recruit .. !'

'Good afternoon, Miss Winstanley,' said a faintly amused male voice. Whoever it was obviously knew Shoes, but that was no surprise. She was a terrible flirt.

'. . . And Miss Conway.'

I turned round. A handsome officer stood on the other side of the counter, smiling at me. It was only when he removed his forage cap that I realised it was James Bleak-Wailer. I never could get out of the habit of corrupting his surname.

He saluted, a rather corny thing to do, but I overlooked it. I was just so glad to see someone, *anyone* remotely connected with civilised life, with life before the war.

'Fancy going out for a drink tonight?' he asked.

Shoes nodded vigorously. James laughed.

'I think he meant me . . . ' I pushed the girl off in the direction of the dirty urns. When she was out of ear-shot I said, 'It's good to see you, James. You don't know how good.'

He blushed, busying himself with adjusting his cap. 'So, what's it to be, then? A drink and then some dancing? There's a hop on at Oxford Town Hall tonight. A new swing band. Fancy it?'

Shoes was glancing in our direction, so I just nodded and said, 'Pick me up at eight.'

'What are you being so secretive about?' she demanded crossly when James had gone. 'It's a bit silly, if you ask me.'

She was right. I was creating secrecy where none existed, so desperate was I for a bit of intrigue. And this really was desperation, I thought, laughing at myself, turning to a Bleak-Wailer for Experience.

Nevertheless, I felt quite breathless when I came to get dressed and couldn't find a thing I wanted to wear. I went into Lexi's old room and thumbed through her jettisoned collection of pre-war dresses, some of which were very glamorous by Winstanley standards. They hung there in plastic covers and mothballs, giving off a faint breath of perfume, just like the old dresses in Beattie's wardrobe. I tried the grey one she had worn to the Christmas dance in 1936, but I could scarcely get it over my shoulders, so narrow was the cut. In the end I picked one from her trousseau, a frothy pink organza dance dress which must have been a generous fit. At any rate, it had never been worn, still smelling of the paper it had been wrapped in. I found a bottle of her scent in the dressing-table drawer and dabbed some on my neck, behind my knees and between my breasts, which were more than hinted at by the neckline of the dress.

I rather enjoyed going out in Lexi's dress, smelling of her. It was as if she was with me, or had given me some of her confidence, her sexiness. I fluttered my eyelashes at James all evening which must have confused him a great deal after the way I behaved when we had last met.

The dance was in the main Council Chamber in Oxford Town Hall, a few yards away from Christchurch's domineering Tom Tower. We danced beneath bedraggled balloons, on a parquet floor which normally only felt the stout brogues of Oxford's city councillors, and was now scarred with dozens of fresh marks from high-heeled dancing pumps. There were the usual ubiquitous servicemen, mixed in with a few wan-faced students back for the Michaelmas term. They, like me, had been left behind by the war.

Dressed as Lexi I felt silly, flirtatious. I drank too much of the foreign 'fizz' that James procured with the aid of a well-directed five-pound note. Worse still, I touched James constantly, and encouraged him to touch me too. We danced cheek to cheek, thigh to thigh, until the excitement was no longer feigned.

I had imagined that all men were wont to seize the moment, but James seemed disconcerted by me (or by Lexi) and started asking a lot of boring, standard questions about my work on the estate. Then he asked in turn about each of my cousins. Irving's experiences were obviously something he felt at home with, but he went rather quiet when I told him the latest about Lexi and Frannie. Jack's venture provoked outright hostility.

'But that sort of things puts innocent people in danger,' he said. 'Surely you don't approve?'

'Of course not!' I retorted, then launched into a rather drunken defence of all Jack's actions.

James said nothing, just nodded, as though this was exactly what he would have expected to hear. 'I've always wondered ... '

'What?' I demanded.

'Oh ... nothing. Let's go and get another drink, shall we?'

We left the dance soon after that, and wandered slowly up to Magdalen Bridge, hand in hand. When James kissed me, I felt an unexpected thrill of pleasure. I kissed him back, fervently.

I had enjoyed my night out with James Peake-Taylor, but the next morning I got up and went about my work and didn't think about him at all, not until he telephoned me several days later.

'I was rather hoping you'd phone me,' he said.

'Oh ... why?'

'Well ... never mind. I'm ringing to ask you out to dinner.'

'How nice. Where are we going?'

'Well, I thought you might like to come here, actually, and have dinner with my family.'

'Oh.' I couldn't keep the disappointment out of my voice. 'I'd hoped we could go out ...' I stopped myself just in time from saying 'somewhere more interesting'. '... and do some more dancing.'

I was in the mood for more mindless hedonism, with James or anyone else who came along. The Bleak-Wailers' house, which I hadn't set foot in since I was a child, was not the destination I had in mind.

'... Do say you'll come, Kitty,' James was saying. 'Mother and Father are so longing to meet you again.'

This was prompting enough for me to behave as myself that evening, and not Lexi. I wore a sober frock and high-heeled shoes and gave James only the chastest of hello kisses when he tried to corner me in the hall.

Dinner was, as I had expected, a dreary affair. We sat in the underheated drawing room and sipped watered-down sherry, while Mrs Bleak-Wailer bleated on about how to make coupons go further. Sarah Bleak-Wailer, that other victim of our schoolroom dances, sat unravelling a tea-cosy that she was going to knit up into a balaclava for some poor serviceman. When I suggested flippantly that it would be easier for him just to wear the tea-cosy, she smiled nervously.

Sarah and I were left alone for a few minutes while Mrs Bleak-Wailer went to supervise the meal, her husband went to find the sherry decanter (and presumably tip a bit more water into it to eke it out further) and James went to bring in some logs.

'I say,' said Sarah, laying down the tea-cosy/balaclava and looking animated for the first time. 'I'm so glad about you and James.'

'What ..? What about me and James?'

'Well ... that you've got together after all this time. I know he's always thought a lot of you.'

'But we haven't,' I said, draining my sherry glass with a rush of irritation.

'Oh, it's just that he said ... well, never mind.' She picked up her knitting again.

Dinner was pig's liver, which I hated. ('I do hope you like pig's liver,' Mrs Bleak-Wailer gushed. 'It makes such an economical meal!')

I transferred my lump of economical liver into my lap, wrapped it in my handkerchief and slipped it into my bag, to take home for Aunt Griz's dog. After then dining frugally on onions, gravy and watered-down claret, I was feeling like a nun and in no mood for James's advances, which came inevitably when he drove me home. Before I had a chance to get out of the car he grabbed me and aimed his lips at my neck. I pushed him away, annoyed.

James shook his head slowly, straightening his uniform cuffs. 'I just don't understand you, Kitty, I thought – '

'Oh, I know what you thought ... and what's the saying? One swallow doesn't make a summer!'

The puzzled expression on James's face stayed with me as I went upstairs and undressed. I ignored Shoes's whispered entreaties to tell her all about it, bundling her back to her room and sitting down on the edge of my bed to reflect on why I had led on poor James. I had been badly in need of distraction, but any distraction in male form would have sufficed, it didn't have to be James. That was what one did in wartime, wasn't it? Reeled from one brief, meaningless encounter to another in the name of a good time. I actually liked James quite a lot, which was probably why he wasn't the man for the job.

He phoned (predictably) the next day, but I asked Shoes to tell him I was out. When I finally decided that a decent interval had passed and returned his call, I was told he had returned to his regiment.

The early months of 1942 brought new excitement. American GIs arrived in Oxfordshire, not just the ordinary kind, but *black* ones too. It was the first time most of the inhabitants of our sleepy, slow-moving community had ever laid eyes on a coloured person. Their curiosity overcame their initial reserve, and they discovered that the negroes, particularly those from the Southern states, were more courteous and charming than many white GIs. Any hostility they encountered came from those same white GIs, and Southern whites in particular.

Shoes and Clem were both fascinated by the Americans, and became camp followers, often returning from their forays to the village with oranges, chocolate and chewing gum. Shoes was a talented mimic, and quickly learned to distinguish between, and imitate, the accents from the various states. Her favourite was a

Southern white-trash drawl, though she could do a passable New York twang, thanks to an amiable GI from Brooklyn called Mickey Israeloff. Darling Beattie, who had long since lost interest in disciplining her youngest children, allowed Shoes to invite her favourites up to the house for tea and crumpets.

The occasion was a great success, with the GIs speechless with admiration for 'the old place', and Darling Beattie was charmed by the way they all called her 'ma'am'. (Nim stayed locked in his study; he still avoided foreiɡ ɴers if at all possible, and had a great contempt for 'damned Yankees; too cowardly to get their hands dirty before now'.) My aunt then delegated to me the job of keeping Clem and Shoes out of trouble – an impossible task.

Despite their reputation for debauchery (one which Shoes was anxious to see proved), the Yanks brought a lot of fun and life into our war-weary lives. Their dances or 'hops' were the liveliest we had seen yet, and no man in the village was worth a thing unless he had learned to jive in American style. In the midst of all the fun and frivolity, and my attempts to chaperone my young cousins, James Bleak-Wailer returned on leave, his last before going overseas, and renewed his assault on my virtue. He suffered in comparison with the Americans – quite unfairly, in retrospect – seeming more conventional and conservative and tweedy than ever before. I never refused to go out with him; he was going off to fight for king and country after all, with the shortened life expectancy that implied, but I was careful to limit any physical intimacy this time. Like the true stiff-upper-lipped Englishman he was, he appeared not to notice, being grateful merely for my company.

One mild spring evening we drove over to our old haunt, the Fox and Hounds at Cottington. We took Shoes with us, along with Mickey Israeloff, who was 'dating' her. I wasn't happy when I first learned about him, but Mickey treated her with the greatest respect. Whether this was out of reverence for English womanhood, or terror of Nim and his shotgun, I couldn't be sure, but his affections were limited to hand-holding and orangeade-buying. And of course Mickey always called me 'ma'am'.

The Fox and Hounds had been discovered by the GIs, and there was quite a crowd of them in there, drinking scotch in preference to our warm beer, and flashing their full wallets around, which the local men pretended not to notice.

'I can't help thinking these Americans are a bit ...' began James as he sipped the froth off his bitter.

'A bit what?' I demanded.

'I don't know ...' He looked around him. Shoes was frowning in his direction, but at least he had waited until Mickey was at the bar, out of earshot. '... A bit much, I suppose.'

I laughed. 'Why, Lieutenant Peake-Taylor, I do believe I detect a bit of professional jealousy. Or are you jealous of their brash charm?'

'Well, I – '

'Seriously though, what's wrong with them? They cheer everyone up, and they've never caused any trouble ...'

As I spoke, I noticed heads turning towards the door. I craned my neck to see what they were looking at. Four black GIs had just come into the pub.

They took their turn queueing at the bar, waiting far longer to be served than they needed to, for fear of seeming pushy. Their attempts to act inconspicuously were almost painful to watch.

'Hey, you!' shouted a white GI, as the first one ordered his drink. 'You're not allowed in here!'

'That's right!' said his friend, pushing the negro roughly backwards. 'Can't you see decent white folk are trying to have a drink without dirt like you getting in their way? You blind, or something?'

'Leave them alone. They're staying.' The landlord's wife, Mrs Fraser, a small wiry Scots lady with a no-nonsense air, spoke up from behind the bar.

The white GIs ignored her (she was so tiny, they probably hardly saw her) and continued pushing the negroes back towards the door. Mrs Fraser reached below the bar for her twelve-bore rifle which she laid down on the counter in front of her.

'I'm afraid we don't observe the colour bar in here, sir. Now will you leave these gentlemen alone.'

I was already tensing myself in readiness and, sure enough, a second later the first punch flew. Within a minute all we could see was an indistinct mass of khaki as the negroes tried to defend themselves. One of them threw a hard right hook at the innocent Mickey, returning from the bar with his glasses of orangeade. Shoes screamed.

'I say ... now that's enough!'

James was on his feet, and pushing his way towards the scrum. He grabbed the two white offenders by their collars and pulled them, protesting, towards the door, with the aid of the indomitable Mrs Fraser. There was a spontaneous round of applause from the other customers, which made James blush. And Shoes let go of Mickey's hand long enough to throw her arms round his neck, which turned him even redder.

James became something of a hero after the incident at the Fox and Hounds that night. I grudgingly allowed him to rise in my estimation. He had a certain quiet strength, which accounted for his persistence where I was concerned. But our relationship continued in the same circular way – me feeling pleased to see him, and acting warmly towards him, he becoming encouraged and making fresh advances, then me brushing them aside.

The coloured GIs also reinforced their position as local favourites. Even so, a subliminal prejudice remained on the subject of inter-racial love affairs, so I was surprised to see one of Nim's farmworkers, an Irish landgirl called Molly, walking out with a six-foot negro called Justice.

Shoes was the fount of all village gossip, so I asked her about it.

'Oh, they're engaged,' she informed me blithely.

'Aren't her family a bit ... concerned about that?'

'Not after what Clem told Molly.'

I recognised that gleeful Winstanley smirk. 'And what *did* Clem tell Molly?' I enquired.

'He told her that the black Americans have had their skin specially darkened for camouflage on night missions. And when they get back to America, they give them a special injection and they turn white again.'

'She didn't .. !'

'She did! She believed him!'

I made a valiant effort not to laugh. 'I'll tan the hide off that boy when I get my hands on him ...'

I went off in search of my twelve-year-old cousin, but when I found him he already had a powerful diversionary tactic at his disposal.

'Mum told me to give you this.' He thrust an envelope into my hand. 'Letter from Jack.'

Three

As I was toying with my scrambled eggs the following morning, Nim stumped into the breakfast room.

'Meant to tell you, Kitty, fence at the bottom of Sturley meadow needs fixing. Get Jim on to it, will you? Sooner, rather than later ...'

He picked up his copy of *The Times* from the sideboard and said, 'By the way ... there's some bloody man to see you, apparently. Your aunt told him to wait in the hall.'

He was waiting for me, in full uniform.

'James ..!' My mind had been so preoccupied with other things that I had almost forgotten his existence.

James interpreted the cause of my surprise as the early hour of his visit. 'Sorry to call round now, but I had no choice – I'm on my way to the station. We're off.'

'Off?'

'The regiment sails for India tonight. We'll be stationed in Delhi for a while then after that ... well, we could be sent off anywhere in the Far East.'

'You must be glad,' I said, rather lamely. 'I mean, to be doing some real soldiering at last.'

James nodded. 'Look, can we go somewhere private and talk? There are one or two things I want to say to you.'

I led the way out into the garden, and we strolled down the lawn towards the lake. The golden willow had just come into leaf. I broke off a trailing frond and examined it, remembering how Frannie and I had made a secret den under the tree.

I must have looked just like the posters one saw of the wistful soldier's sweetheart saying a tender farewell to her love. In reality my thoughts were far removed from James's departure. He put his hand on my shoulder.

'Kitty . . . ' He cleared his throat. 'I'm hopeless at this sort of thing . . . it must be obvious to you how I feel about you. And I wondered if you would be prepared to tell me how you feel about me . . . '

At that precise moment, what I felt was an impatient desire to hear out his speech, peck him on the cheek and pack him off to the front.

'Well . . . ' I looked at his handsome, serious face. 'I think an awful lot of you, you know that. I mean, you've been an important friend during this last couple of years, but – '

'Only, I wondered whether . . . now I'm going away, if we could think of ourselves as – well, sort of engaged.'

' "*Sort of*" engaged?' I challenged. 'What's wrong with the real thing?'

'Nothing, nothing . . . but since I'm going away . . . we have to be realistic about the future. I know there's no point thinking about a wedding or anything. I just wanted you to have it in your mind, so that if I come back safe and sound – ' He gave a nervous laugh, that sounded like a bark. 'With all my bits, as it were, then we could take it from there. If . . . if that's what you want, of course. But do say if I'm rushing you.'

He looked eagerly into my face, and I felt a sudden flood of compassion for this young man standing there, joking about death. He wanted something to take with him, something only I could give. I thought of all the desertions; Lexi, Frannie, Jack . . . then I put myself in James's position, and realised how much I would want to be able to take something with me. It wouldn't do any harm, I reasoned, for him to have that hope to sustain him. And then when . . . if he came back, I could tell him the truth then, when he had the whole of the rest of his life before him.

This scheme made me feel rather patriotic and proud of myself. I was doing something unselfish, for the war effort. I grinned at my suitor in a very unromantic fashion. 'Yes. All right.'

'You will?' James looked stunned. 'Oh . . . I'm so glad, Kitty.' He kissed me gently on the cheek. 'I hope you won't think I'm calculating or anything, but I brought you this.'

He took a velvet ring box out of his breast pocket and handed it to me with the dewy-eyed solemnity of the hero in a romantic matinée. Inside, on a bed of white satin, was a single diamond solitaire in a star-shaped setting.

My thanks were entirely sincere, and I was gratified that he had chosen something so pretty. But although I slipped the ring on to show him how it looked, it was only for a moment, before I returned it to its pristine white satin cushion. I was going down to one of the farms, I told him, and I didn't want to risk losing or dirtying it while I was working.

'You don't want your diamond solitaire covered in manure, or slurry, do you?' I joked.

I would keep the ring with me, but it would never be worn. And there wouldn't be a wedding.

James made me promise to write, but I knew in reality that this was going to be difficult, now that I had plans to go abroad myself. I said nothing about it, but as we walked up the lawn together hand in hand, fiancé style, I could feel Jack's letter crackling in my pocket.

As soon as I had sent James on his way (perusading him that ours was a private agreement, and there was no need to go and alert my uncle and aunt to the happy turn of events) I took it out and re-read it. Jack had given it to a friend who had smuggled himself back from France on a fishing boat. He had then been so afraid of trusting the precious document to the Royal Mail, he waited until he was going to be in our part of Oxfordshire and delivered it by hand. Consequently the news it contained was rather late.

29 March 1942
Kitty!..

How typical of Jack that peremptory opening was; demanding immediate attention!

...Not Sunday-best handwriting, I'm afraid, but you'll have to put up with it, on account of the fact that I'm sitting in the back of a truck, rattling my way through the lanes of Normandy in bone-breaking style. The driver swears he knows the way to the market in Lisieux, but I'm not convinced. My only travelling companions are a dozen over-fed geese, but at least they won't try and read what I'm writing here.

Kitty, old girl, the news is not good, I'm afraid. Though I suppose it could be worse. So try and brace yourself. It's about Frannie's husband (yes, she and Simon entered the time-honoured bourgeois estate of marriage).

He's dead, Kitty. He was arrested by the Gestapo, and the evidence all points pretty unanimously to the same conclusion, i.e. that he was executed.

As for Fran, she's in hiding in Paris. I managed to find her, after a lot of inconvenience to yours truly, which she didn't seem to appreciate. She's in a bit of a state, understandably, a lot of the time refusing to accept that Simon is dead. I tried to persuade her to come down here to the country with me, but as we suspected, the stubborn little cow won't budge. She insists in putting herself on the line by helping sundry Jews, dissidents and resistance members to outwit the Nazis. Very dangerous stuff, and certainly not for me. I couldn't wait to get out of Paris.

I don't see what else we can do. I tried everything I could think of to get Fran up to Normandy. You have my word on that, whatever that's worth. She talked about you a lot, but obviously there's nothing *you* can do.

You'd better tell the old folks that I'm fine, not to worry. I'm rather enjoying myself and I think I'll stay on here. The locals are just getting over their suspicion of this eccentric young Englishman, so business is starting to pick up. The more time I give it, the greater the rewards I can reap. I'm an agricultural produce distribution expert. The less polite term is a black marketeer.

For obvious reasons, I can't post this letter, so it may be a while before it reaches Russington. Give my love to the old place. And take care of yourself, until we meet again.

Your cousin, Jack.

I carried the letter around with me all that day, in the same pocket as the ring box. About once every hour I took it out and read it, examining every squiggle and crossing out until I knew it off by heart.

'... Obviously there's nothing *you* can do ...'

Well, I thought differently. If anything, I could move about in Paris with more ease than he had done. He seemed to have forgotten that I had once worked as a journalist. A certain number of vetted foreign correspondents were allowed into the occupied French capital, and allowed to work as long as they toed the line. I could think of no reason why an editor would want to send me, a twenty-one-year old with poor French and no knowledge of the city, but I was prepared to try. For Frannie's sake I was going to do more than just try.

When I got back from the fields, I went straight up into my room and stripped off my boilersuit. I took the ring box out of the pocket, and put it away at the back of a drawer.

Then, dressed in my bathrobe, I lugged my suitcase down off the top of the wardrobe where it had been collecting dust since I returned from Berlin. I laid it on the bed and started to throw clothes into its gaping jaws in a haphazard fashion.

When I looked up from my task, Darling Beattie was standing in the doorway, watching me.

'Goodness me, darling, you're in a hurry! Are you going away somewhere? Not for long, I hope ...'

I paused in mid stride, with a pile of underwear in my hand. 'I'm going to Paris.'

I had intended to say that I had to spend a few days in London, and then slip off from there without any fuss. But as soon as I saw my aunt's face, so anxious not to lose her last henchwoman, her mainstay, I knew I had to challenge her. I owed it to Fran.

'I'm going to try to help Frannie. Simon – her husband – has been killed.'

I made sure I looked her directly in the eye when I said this.

Darling Beattie turned pale. 'Oh no ... oh no – that poor boy!'

For a moment she looked as though she was going to say more, that she *needed* to say more. But instead she just muttered, '... Will you excuse me, dear ..?'

She turned to go, but I wasn't going to let her get away with it that easily. Not without provoking some sort of overt maternal response. I realised now how long I had been wanting to do just that.

I grabbed an old blue gingham dress from the back of the wardrobe and thrust it under my aunt's nose. 'Do you remember this?' I demanded.

'Yes, dear, it's one of your old summer frocks. You must have been about – '

'NO! It's not *my* dress!' I pushed it so close that the faded cotton was touching her face. 'It's Frannie's dress! Frannie! Your daughter! The daughter you gave birth to! The daughter you and Nim love – '

'No ...' she said faintly, pushing the frock away from her as though it was burning her skin. 'No, don't. Please ...'

She turned and hurried from the room, but not before I saw the tears that started into her eyes. And I was glad. Glad that I had proved she still cared.

It was three years since I had spent any time in London, and I found the capital city a grey shadow of its former self. There were no Bright Young Things racing around Hyde Park Corner in sports cars, but that was probably just as well. The atmosphere in the place suited my own rather bleak and self-denying mood.

I parked myself, unannounced, on Lady Reeve's doorstep, only to be told apologetically that the 'flat' had been lent to some Polish émigrés. Even the spare room was occupied; one of her many great-nephews had taken up residence as a sort of token male talisman in the face of German air-attacks. It was his job to tell the elderly women precisely when to hide under the dining-room table.

Most of my old London friends had left the city, either to serve in the forces or retreat to the relative safety of their country homes. Those who had stayed were living in more cramped conditions than before, and the most anyone could offer me was a sofa to sleep on. In the end I found myself a room in a boarding house in Blooms-bury. The other residents were Londoners who had been bombed out of their homes, escaping with their lives but no possessions. In some cases not all the family were lucky enough to survive, and some of the women had already been widowed by the war. I felt inadequate in the face of such suffering, and although my fellow guests were quite prepared to welcome yet another stranger with all her possessions in a suitcase, I tended to keep myself to myself.

I spent the first morning at the boarding house using the landlady's telephone to ring newspaper editors and beg for a hearing. This approach proved futile, so I took myself, and my 'Behind The Lines' photographs from Berlin, to Fleet Street and tried approaching them personally. They were impressed by the photographs, but clearly none of them believed that I had taken them myself, and anyway, they were too busy trying to keep pace with the war correspondents they had to recruit any more. Especially not for Paris.

'Everyone wants to go to Paris,' I was told. 'Now, if it was Damascus, or Cairo ...'

In the end, loath as I was, I took the only option that was left to me. I went to see Harry Hoccleve.

'So ...' he said, chomping on his pipe, and looking me up and down in his old, all-seeing way. 'Our little photo-journalist is back, is she? What have you been up to, then?'

I showed him the Berlin pictures.

'They're good ... very good. And you say you want to go to Paris?'

I nodded, hardly daring to breathe lest some expression on my face, some unintentional gesture made him decide to refuse me.

'I'd really like you to do some shots of London for me first. I want some pictures of bomb damage, and you're good at that sort of thing. And then ... well, I'll think about the other thing.'

I opened my mouth to argue, but decided it was useless. 'All right,' I said, smiling pleasantly, 'I'll get the shots you want.'

Having worked for Hoccleve before gave me a head start. I knew exactly the sort of thing he liked. And I asked around at the boarding house for some likely bomb sites, which they knew only too well. The next morning was spent stumbling about in the rubble of the City (laddering a precious pair of American nylons and breaking the heel off my shoe in the process) trying to turn unrelieved decimation into an interesting set of photographs. I found a cat that had just given birth to its litter under a fallen girder, an old man clutching the remains of his wife's best tea-set, children playing a game of hide and seek. They all made obvious and predictable pictures, but it would have taken time to do something more original, and I was haunted all the time by a sense of urgency, rushing to get the job done and get on to Paris...

In the afternoon I raced back to the *London Life* offices and spent an hour cursing and swearing in the darkroom over light intensities that refused to come right. Finally, at five o'clock, I dropped the pictures on to Hoccleve's desk and waited for his verdict.

He examined each one with irritating slowness, grinding his teeth to and fro on the stem of his pipe.

'Hmmm ... you've done better, we both know that. But they're not bad. I'll run them in the next issue with a caption like "Life among the Ruins" or something like that. Right, next, I'd like you to – '

'*Please!*' I begged. 'I've got to have that press pass now! I'm desperate ... I'll do anything you like, Mr Hoccleve – '

'Anything, eh? That's strong talk, my girl! I tell you what ...' He shrugged on his Harris tweed jacket and stuffed his tobacco pouch into the pocket. 'Why don't we go and talk about it over a drink, eh?'

'All right,' I agreed. As if I had any choice in the matter. We walked together down to the Strand, me with my camera round my neck, until we came to a bar that had been much frequented by journalists before the war. With its cellar windows boarded over, it looked as if it was closed, but a sign propped up against the sandbags declared 'BUSINESS AS USUAL'.

There was no wine or gin available (Hoccleve raised his eyebrows when I requested the latter) and I didn't want to drink beer, so I made do with a glass of port, which I didn't care for very much. Forcing back the medicinal liquid was in keeping with the self-sacrificial tone of my whole enterprise, and it helped me to remember that I wasn't doing this for myself.

'So,' said Hoccleve, lighting up his abominable pipe with his usual deliberate slowness, 'what have you been up to then, these past three years? I must say, I was hardly expecting you to show up on my doorstep again.'

I told him about Germany, and about Russington and managing the estate.

'It's all right for girls like you, isn't it?' he observed. There was no mistaking the resentment in his voice.

'Girls like me?' I took a swallow of the offensive port.

'Brought up in the lap of luxury, coming out into society, playing at doing a real job ...'

I was longing to contradict him, to tell him that there was nothing very amusing about the hours I'd spent slogging round London photographing prize begonias. But the whole point of this expedition was about humouring him, so I bit my tongue.

'Yes ...' he went on, with that philosophising tone that the self-pitying adopt, '... and when a war comes along, all you have to do is run back home to Daddy and sit tight, living off the fat of the land until it's safe to come out and go to parties again, while others go off and get themselves killed for the country that you lot think you own ...'

He ran out of breath at the end of this vitriolic outpouring, wheezing slightly. Then interpreting my silence as a sign that I had been offended, he patted my hand, then forgot to remove his own. I looked down at the ginger hairs sprouting from his knuckles, then looked away quickly.

'Aye, it's different up in Barnsley, I can tell you! My brothers have gone straight from the pits into the ruddy trenches. It's t' devil to know which is worse ...'

He lapsed, sentimentally, into broad Yorkshire.

'Did you not think of going to fight yourself?' I asked.

'I wanted to. But they wouldn't have me. Not with my chest.'

'Oh.'

We lapsed into small talk, which was predictably strained. In the end I was quite relieved when he said, 'You'll let me take you home, then?'

When we reached the boarding house, the subject of Paris had been avoided, deliberately on Hoccleve's part. He stopped me on the doorstep and cleared his throat, no doubt to make some sort of pompous speech, but I interrupted him.

'Come up to my room.'

He stared at me for a second. Then he followed me up the stairs without a word. One or two of the other boarders passed us, but they obviously thought nothing of me taking a middle-aged man

209

upstairs with me, even one in civilian dress. They had seen it all before.

The room contained nothing but the bed and washbasin, my suitcase and a bottle of gin that the landlady had bought me through her connections. I went straight over to it and took a large gulp. Hoccleve was standing behind me. When I turned round, he bent and kissed me, wetly, clumsily, on the mouth. I found the taste of his pipe tobacco quite repellent, enough to make me gag. I stepped backwards. It's the war, I kept saying over and over, people have to do certain things in wartime.

Hoccleve came towards me again. Before he touched me I closed my eyes for a second while I conjured up Simon Gold's intense, dark eyes dulled by death, a bullet hole between them And that was if he was lucky. Being shot, rather than some other method.

'Are you all right, lass?' Hoccleve asked.

I opened my eyes again. 'Look ... if I sleep with you, will you give me that press pass?'

'So you're that desperate ...'

He was lighting his pipe, and I thought he was going to let me off, give me the pass anyway. Until he turned round and looked at me, with that same intense, greedy look he used to wear in the past, in the magazine offices when he watched me ...

'All right, then. You'd better get undressed, hadn't you? And properly. I want to see all of you.'

I gripped the neck of the gin bottle tightly. 'First, you've got to promise that you'll give it to me. *Promise* ...'

He nodded, but I didn't trust him.

'If you don't ... I'll do something terrible to you!'

Since he had no idea what was at stake, he must have assumed that I was drunk.

'I'd put that bottle down if I were you, you've had enough. Come here ...'

He unbuttoned my blouse and pulled the straps of my petticoat down, kissing and biting me, leaving a trail of tobacco-stained saliva on my skin. I allowed his weight to topple me backwards on to the bed, only too anxious to get the business over with. As he fumbled with his trousers, then jostled around awkwardly on top of me, I wished the first time had been with James, whom I didn't love, or even with Deacon ... strange, it was the first time I had thought about him in years ...

I let my thoughts wander, and was only vaguely aware of Hoccleve saying, 'It's all right, lass, I'm taking precautions. You don't have to worry about getting pregnant.' I found if I concentrated on Frannie, and the pain she was going through, it wasn't so bad, in fact I got a perverse pleasure out of the act, knowing that I was giving something of myself for someone I loved.

It was when he rolled off me and went to urinate in the washbasin, as if it no longer mattered what intimate acts he performed in front of me, that I couldn't stand any more. I wrapped my dressing gown over my damp, smeared petticoat and ran out of the room. The bathroom door was locked, so I went into the little makeshift kitchen that was used by the residents for making tea and coffee. I leaned over the sink and gave way to a wonderfully indulgent fit of sobbing. One of the homeless bomb victims came and put her arm around me, patting me gently.

'That's all right, love, you have a good cry ...'

She didn't ask me what was troubling me, there didn't seem any need. 'It's that bloody Adolf Hitler, that's what it is. Look what he's done to us all ...'

Four

Lying in my rented room the following morning, feeling soiled and hungover, I was no longer sure that Harry Hoccleve intended to keep his side of the bargain, or even whether I cared. I was certainly not prepared to go to the offices of *London Life* to collect the press pass. Fortunately Hoccleve had the sensitivity to realise this, and had it sent round to the boarding house, together with a passage on the night sailing to Dieppe and a cheque for the previous day's work, made out as an international money order. A short note, typed by his secretary, said that as far as the German authorities were concerned I was working for a Swedish publication, since the Swedes enjoyed neutral status in the French capital. There was no message.

Paris was not as gloomy, or as cowed as I had imagined it would be. In many ways it appeared a more cheerful place to be than London. The buildings that had closed all their shutters and drawn their blinds when the German troops arrived on 14 June were open again. There were crowds on the streets, going about their business, and restaurants and cafés appeared to be doing a good trade, even if it was serving the invaders. As for the German troops, the novelty of the place was still fresh enough for them to behave like tourists. They were carrying cameras to take snapshots of the sights, and handing out chocolate bars to any children they saw.

Although I carried my own camera about with me from the start, I had very little time to exercise my journalistic talents. I had my work cut out. In the face of my supposed uselessness, Jack had not seen fit to say exactly where Frannie was. I had to set about the near-impossible task of finding her hiding place in a city that I knew nothing about, where I was supposed to be, of all the unlikely things, a Swede. The guards at the port and on the train had been happy just to check the press pass, but I knew that if at any time suspicion fell on me, I might be asked to produce a Swedish passport that I did not possess.

In the light of this problem, the Embassy seemed as good a place to patronise as any, especially since the British Embassy was boarded up and being used as a furniture store. The vice-consul I spoke to assured me he would treat my enquiry with discretion, but that the Swedish legation's neutral status prevented it from partaking in a search for an outlawed British citizen. He was sure I would understand. However, he did give me the address of a few places where I might find 'sympathetic' accommodation.

'... and stay around here a little, Miss Conway. Some of our own journalists might be able to help you with your ... problem.'

After a lot of trudging, I found lodgings in the 16th *arondisse-ment*. My landlady was a young wife who had obviously been very well-heeled before the war. She now lived in isolation in her large apartment, with only her maid and two young children. I didn't enquire what had happened to her husband, whose picture was displayed so prominently in the sitting room. She didn't try to find out anything about my own circumstances, so I felt I owed her the same courtesy.

After I had unpacked my belongings, taken a hot bath and changed out of my travel-stained clothes, Madame Monnier asked me if I would like to take a little light supper with her. I was sorely tempted, as I was by the other option of sinking into the high, old-fashioned feather bed and falling asleep. But I had to decline them both. Paris was out there, and in it, somewhere, my cousin Frannie. I had to start looking straight away.

I went back to the Swedish Embassy and sat in the lobby, reading a magazine. People came and went constantly, using the place as a meeting point, discussing their day's work, what they hoped to achieve tomorrow. I heard some American accents, and also some English and French. I hoped I looked both conspicuous and available because, for the first time in my life, I wanted to be lured into conversation by strange men. However, nature's perverse laws dictate that when you desire such a situation, it doesn't happen. I received the occasional polite smile, but everyone who passed me must have assumed I was there to meet someone else.

'Can I help you?' said a voice in my ear, finally. I turned round to find an immensely tall, gangling young man looking down at me with a kindly expression. He had straw-coloured hair and round spectacles rather like those I had worn in my disguise as Sieghilde. Remembering this made me break into a smile.

'That's better ...' he said, with an American accent, 'you were starting to look a little worried there, for a moment.'

'To tell you the truth, I am. I've just arrived, and I don't know a soul'.

'Well you do now.' He extended his hand and shook mine in a grip so firm it made me wince. 'Charles Olsen. Charlie, to you.'

'Kitty Conway.'

'Here, Kitty, let me get you a drink from the bar, then you can tell me all about why you're in Paris. You're English, right?'

I didn't tell him all about it. I was aware of the need to be cautious. Instead I concentrated on trying to find out all about Charlie.

'I've been here since the beginning of the war,' he said proudly. 'There's not many correspondents here who can say that. I'm from Minnesota, but my father's family are Swedish and I'm entitled to a Swedish passport. My stories go from here direct to Stockholm, then my Uncle Jens cables them out to the *Washington Post*. Pretty neat set-up, huh?'

'So ...' I considered the best way to phrase my next question. 'So you've had a chance to get to know Paris pretty well?'

Charlie grinned. 'Modesty aside ... I reckon I know what's going on here better than any of these piss-ass professionals ...' He indicated a group of older journalists who were helping themselves from the bar. 'They waste most of their time hanging around here and moaning about their expenses. Whereas old Olsen here ... but you don't want to know about all that kind of stuff. Have another drink, why don't you ..?'

I declined the drink, and assured him that I did want to know, very much. I have to confess I fluttered my eyelashes *à la* Lexi, and tried hard to look like an English *ingénue*, so that he wouldn't treat me with suspicion.

'Tell you what then, why don't you and I meet up tomorrow? I could show you around a little.'

I gave him a smile that was pure relief. At last I could leave and head for that big feather bed.

When I met Charlie the following morning, he took me straight off to have breakfast on the pavement outside a small café near the Ile St Louis.

'I always come here,' he told me. 'Jean-Marie, the patron, is a friend of mine. He's ... all right. If you see what I mean?'

214

I gave him a brief nod, to show that I understood, then took my courage in both hands. After Jean-Marie had left two bowls of steaming *café au lait* on the table and gone back into the café, I said, 'I'm glad you asked me here today. There's something I need to ask your advice about.'

I told him about Frannie and her situation, not laying it on too thick about the communism, as I wasn't certain yet where Charlie's sympathies lay. As I was talking, he shook his head occasionally, and sighed.

'We hear a lot of stories like that. Life has some normality on the surface . . . but any one of us could wake up tomorrow morning and find that our next-door neighbour has just disappeared. The SS usually work at night. They come . . . they take someone away . . . and it's "Sorry boys: no questions asked" . . . '

'Do you think there's any chance of me finding where Frannie is?'

Charlie stared down into his cup of coffee. 'I don't know, it's difficult. I mean, if you mess around in that sort of stuff, you're really putting your ass on the line . . . '

'Yes, I suppose you're right. Oh well . . . ' I smiled at Charlie, but the disappointment I felt must have shown in my face, because he gave my hand a friendly squeeze and said, 'Look, Kitty, I'll ask around for you, see if I come up with anything. OK?'

'OK.'

'And in the meantime, you keep your nose clean. We don't want any suspicion falling on you, and believe me, we're all being watched, even when we think we're OK.'

I relaxed after that, sufficiently to accept Charlie's invitation to go out on the town that night and 'have some fun'. Wartime friendships blossomed at a hothouse rate, I decided. Charlie and I had been forced to acknowledge that we were prepared to trust each other, and it felt good. I felt at ease in his company.

We visited some of the more lively bars, ate Chateaubriand steak at Ciros in the rue Daunou and danced at the Niger club in the rue de la Fidelité, where the *patronne* was a splendid African woman who had had her skin artificially whitened. In all these places, there were high-ranking Nazi officials, usually with pretty French girls on their arms.

'It's best just to ignore them,' Charlie advised. 'Try to pretend to yourself that they're not around. If you want to go to the fun places in Paris, you have to swallow your principles a little.'

Every time I saw those uniforms, those heads of gleaming fair hair, I saw Simon's face before me. Sometimes he had been shot, sometimes strangled.

'I'd really rather just walk around in the fresh air,' I told Charlie. We went up the Champs Elysées, passing beautifully dressed women who I was assured, despite my incredulity, were prostitutes.

'The brothels are thriving,' Charlie told me. 'They do even better business than the restaurants these days.'

'And do you ever visit them?' I enquired.

He blushed. 'I'd like to, I don't deny that. But it's too risky. They're crawling with Gestapo, and you can never be sure exactly who the girls are working for. Pity . . . '

The biggest congregation of *filles de joie* was outside a club called the Cercle Européen. Charlie curled his lips as we walked by.

'That place looks very grand,' I commented.

'It's just a sumptuous rubbish bin! Every collaborator and black marketeer in Paris is a member. Now that's one place I would *not* go into. You've got to draw the line somewhere.'

I stared in through the doorway to the bright lights beyond, thinking of Jack.

'Hey . . . c'mon dreamy! What do you want to do now? Eat caviar at Petrossian's? Have a night cap at the Café de Paris . . ? '

'You're really having fun here, aren't you?' I asked. 'Living in Paris like this, the safe existence of the naturalised Swedish *Washington Post* correspondent . . ! '

Charlie looked a little guilty. 'I hate to admit it, but yes I am. I'm having a lot of fun.'

During the next few days, I wasted a lot of time.

Charlie assured me regularly that he was doing all he could to help me, but that I mustn't be impatient.

So, adopting an air of false patience, I wandered around Paris, taking photographs and staring in shop windows. Around every corner there were antique shops selling off people's heirlooms at laughable prices, a sacrifice made to make ends meet in an impossible economy. No fresh food was available in the city, except at restaurants frequented by the Nazis. My own money was rapidly running out, and I practised the art of sitting for several hours over one cup of coffee, learnt in our days pursuing the intelligentsia in London. Establishments like Hermès, Cartier and Boucheron all managed to maintain their standards, and I would sigh over their window displays as we had once sighed over Mireille de Vere's Beautiful Things.

Mireille de Vere . . . I forgot my own troubles long enough to wonder about her fate. Where was she living out the war, and with whom ..? I had last seen her in London, but perhaps by now she was back in safe, neutral little Switzerland.

This speculation led naturally to thoughts of Russington. It came to me suddenly that since I had been in Paris I hadn't thought once about James, the man I was supposed to be marrying. No doubt Nim and Beattie would be commenting on a growing pile of unanswered letters on the hall table. (Or perhaps that little hoyden, Shoes, had spirited them away and steamed them open?) There was little point regretting my promise to write to James. The only atlernative had been to disclose my intended trip to France, and he would very likely have tried to stop me going.

Company came in the guise of Madame Monnier, whose English was quite good, and who was clearly lonely. She was always pressing me to eat with her and her children, Fabienne and Claudine, who attached themselves to me like two handmaidens whenever I was in the apartment. Her hospitality presented something of a dilemma. The price of meals was not included in my rent, and no one in Paris could easily afford to feed another adult. On the other hand if I continually refused, she seemed offended. I tried the compromise of buying food when I could and contributing it to the household's resources. Madame Monnier liked to talk of Paris in the old days, but offered no information about the absence of her husband, who was obviously much missed.

Then there was Charlie, whom I came to like more and more despite (or was it because of?) his happy-go-lucky attitude to Nazi domination. Our friendship could not have flourished if he had entertained any romantic ideas about me, but fortunately he had a sweetheart back in Minnesota. The idea of a little wartime flirtation didn't seem to occur to the straightforward Charlie, and in view of my recent experiences, I was profoundly glad of his attitude.

One morning he appeared on the doorstep at Madame Monnier's and announced that he was taking me out to breakfast. Charlie was usually so laconic that I detected straight away that he was suppressing excitement.

'What's happened ... have you found out something?'

'Wait ..!'

He wouldn't say a word until he had taken me to the safety of Jean-Marie's back room, and we were alone with our coffee and croissants.

'I think I've found someone who can help you.'

A meeting was arranged.

It was not to take place during daylight hours, and not at a place chosen by us, nor were we told whom we were meeting. Charlie only had an address, scribbled down on a piece of paper, and I stared at it in a sort of trance while we sat outside Jean-Marie's café until the appointed hour, drinking a thermos of coffee he had left us to keep us awake. When it was empty, and the church clock on the Ile St Louis struck two, we set off.

It was an address on the left bank, in the Italian quarter, and after two hours of staring at the piece of paper, neither of us was likely to forget it. We had set fire to the paper it was written on with a match; once more according to our instructions.

We found ourselves at the bottom of basement steps in a narrow street of tenements.

'There's no one here ...' said Charlie, peering through a grimy window.

'Perhaps we got the wrong address?' I suggested flippantly, but he frowned at me. It was only after we had hammered on the door several times that a single light was switched on, and the door was unlocked.

I'm not quite sure what I had expected. Not someone's home, because of the danger of us being followed. What we found was a factory storeroom of some kind, stacked high with bolts of material. It was fiendishly dusty, and I was sneezing so hard, that it was difficult to get a proper look at our host. If that was the correct way of describing him.

He was small and very undernourished, with thinning, oily black hair and dark shadows under his eyes. From his facial bone structure and his accent, I guessed he was East European; Hungarian or Rumanian. All his movements betrayed that he was extremely nervous, and from the way he kept glancing at us I guessed that he expected us to be, too. I was far too busy trying to control the streaming from my eyes and nose, caused by the dust and the lack of air.

Our interviewee gestured for us to sit on some upturned bolts of serge, and started to roll himself a pathetically frugal cigarette.

'This place used to belong to a Jewish tailor,' he said. There was no need to enquire about the man's fate. The expression in those sunken eyes said it all.

'So you want to see Frances Gold?' he asked, looking at me.

'Francesca,' I corrected him. 'Frannie.'

'Good – just checking ...' He took a photograph from his pocket and showed it to me. It was of a young woman about Frannie's age, who had a very slight resemblance.

'This is the girl you mean, isn't it?' He was testing me, and it was just as well that I had looked at Frannie's face nearly every day of my life, and knew it better than I knew my own.

'No. That isn't her.'

'Describe her.'

This was easy. 'She's an inch shorter than I am, quite plump, freckles on her face, mousy hair, a few shades lighter than mine ... Her eyes are greyish and they're quite small ...'

I smiled as I remembered the grief this deficient feature used to cause Frannie, her Piggy Eyes...

'You find this amusing?' demanded the man, in a low, furious voice. He dropped his cigarette on the floor between us, and ground it with his toe. 'People like you are happy to wander round this city behaving like bloody tourists, while there are human beings in hiding here, trapped like rats in a sewer, with no money, no food, afraid to stay but unable to go – '

'What about Frannie?' I asked, interrupting his invective. It seemed pointless to try to explain what had made me smile. 'Is she all right? Can I see her?'

He nodded.

'When?'

'I will tell you, soon.'

'But how – '

'I will let you know. That's all.' He stood up.

I became frightened, seeing a tenuous link with Fran slipping away. I opened my mouth to remonstrate with him, to plead, but Charlie pulled me to my feet.

'Come on, Joan of Arc, let's get out of here.'

I was forced into more waiting, and this time it was even harder to distract myself with the trivial pursuits of the foreign visitor. I had no more money to spend, except on the essentials of existence, and I was weary of trudging around looking at things. Charlie was tired of being nagged for news, so I resorted to passing my time with the Monnier children, playing endless games of noughts and crosses and solitaire. Their pastimes were far more sedate than the ones the Winstanleys had indulged in, but there wasn't enough room in the apartment for me to teach them Hunting the Snark.

One day I returned there after a walk in the Tuileries and found the man we had met in the tailor's basement. He was obviously waiting for me, but he looked very much at home, listening to one of the girls read from her favourite book of stories.

219

I stood there looking at him, not removing my jacket or hat, so that he would understand that I expected an explanation.

'I followed you,' he said.

'You were checking up on me.'

He shrugged. 'I wanted to be sure the place you were staying was safe.' He glanced towards the kitchen, where Hélène was making coffee. 'It's all right. Hélène Monnier is safe, as far as we are concerned. Her husband was arrested for helping Jews.'

He smiled for the first time, and I knew then that I had passed some sort of test. This was confirmed when he told me his name: Mikhail.

'Could you dress yourself up a little?' Mikhail asked me. 'Say ... to look like a prostitute?'

I burst out laughing with sheer amazement, but Mikhail's face was quite serious. 'Frannie is hiding on the top floor of a notorious brothel.'

'Is that safe? Surely so many German officers – '

'Precisely. It's the best sort of place there is. We're calling their bluff. Besides, when the Nazis visit these places they have one thing only on their mind. Why would they want to go and look in the attic?'

Mikhail accepted a cup of the coffee that Madame Monnier brought in, adding more milk and drinking it down greedily. It made me shudder to see a grown man so hungry. Then he told me to dress myself up and meet him at nine in the rue de Provence.

I hadn't brought any smart clothes, but I did have my precious fur jacket, taking up space at the expense of more sensible items. I had told myself that I might need it if the evenings were chilly, but the real reason was that I couldn't bear to be parted from it.

Hélène Monnier exclaimed over the beauty of the fur, stroking it and burying her face in it then, quite carried away with the spirit of the occasion, she went into her bedroom and found me a smart toque with a veil, and some spindle-heeled shoes. Then she and the girls helped plaster my face with foundation, rouge and lipstick until, in my own eyes, anyway, I looked quite unrecognisable.

'*Comme tu es belle!*' exclaimed little Fabienne, clapping her hands with pleasure.

I teetered my way to the rue de Provence, cursing the uncomfortable shoes and the fur, which was making me sweat profusely on such a warm summer evening. The 'disguise' must have been effective, as several men slowed down as they passed me and gave me knowing looks, some of them in Nazi uniform. I thought I was being propositioned when one of them took my arm, but it turned out to be Mikhail, dressed as a 'client'. His thin body looked pathetically frail under a greatcoat with a Persian-lamb collar, and his face was half obscured by a homburg that didn't really fit him. He told me to walk up the street ahead of him, to the notorious number One Two Two, and he walked behind as if he were following me. We went up the steps and into the house in this fashion, and the maid at the door didn't seem to think there was anything amiss. Not only was I doing a good job of looking like a prostitute, but I also looked like one of the inmates of the One Two Two.

The house was grand, almost palatial, with heavy chandeliers, beautiful oil paintings on the walls, and thick carpets muffling the noise. The silence made me feel nervous, but I knew instinctively that I must look as though I knew what I was doing. I started to walk straight up the wide staircase, then up again, with Mikhail on my heels. I could tell from his wheezing that I was going too fast for him, but I didn't dare slow down.

Suddenly, on the third landing, Mikhail grabbed me and pushed me against the wall, forcing his face against mine in a kiss. It was not a pleasant experience – his breath tasted sour – but I tried to act as though I meant it, putting my hands up to the back of his neck to display my newly painted talons. I heard a silky, swishing sound as a woman walked past us. Then, finally, Mikhail let me go.

'That was the madam,' he said, calmly. Then, 'It's all right, she couldn't see your face.'

On the fourth floor, Mikhail took a key out of his pocket and unlocked what looked like a cupboard door. Beyond the door was a steep staircase, uncarpeted this time. Mikhail motioned for me to remove my spiky shoes, and we began to climb.

I felt a great rush of emotion as I went up, slowly so as not to make a noise. I felt excitement at what I had achieved and an unexpected dread at the nearness of the encounter. My childhood at Russington had prepared me only too well for dressing-up games, and I threw myself into the art of disguise with gusto. But this was no longer a game. I felt ill at ease with my appearance; grotesque.

At the top of the staircase was a narrow corridor under sloping eaves, with two rooms, one on either side. Mikhail put his hand on my back and pushed me gently into the room on the left.

And there, sitting on the bare floorboards, pale, thin and heavily pregnant, was my beloved Frannie.

Five

'I'm going to have a baby,' said Frannie. 'Isn't it wonderful?'

Her voice was thin and, as she clung hard to my hand, her knuckles were a translucent grey. She expressed no amazement at my being there in Paris, probably she was tired.

Of course, the pregnancy wasn't wonderful at all; it was the worst thing that could possibly have happened, but I just looked up from the hand that was squeezing mine, and smiled, and nodded and wondered what on earth I was going to do. I had put so much of my energy into finding Frannie that I hadn't really stopped to consider what I would do once I found her.

Now it was more obvious than ever that I must try to get her away from Paris; if not to England then at least to the unoccupied zone in the south.

'Fran ...' I put my shoes down and crouched on the bare floorboards next to her. 'I'm here to try to help you get away, somewhere safe ...'

She stared at me with that familiar, stubborn look of old. I decided to cheat and try appealing to her maternal instincts.

'It would be better for the baby,' I went on, 'living in the country, in the fresh air, where there's plenty for you both to eat — '

'No.'

'But Frannie—'

'I can't leave Paris, Kitty. I have to be here, in case Simon comes back, and comes looking for me. He'll need me.'

'But Frannie ...'

Mikhail caught my eye and shook his head, indicating that I shouldn't pursue the subject of Simon's death. I took him on one side and asked, 'Can't she come back with me, to the apartment in the *seizième*? If what you said about her is true, then I'm sure Hélène Monnier would understand.'

But once again Mikhail was shaking his head. 'It's too dangerous. As a foreign journalist, you're at risk of surveillance. We can't risk you leading the Gestapo to Frannie, that's why we went through our little charade tonight. She and Simon were both helping others escape the regime, don't forget. She was luckier than him last time, but she's still wanted on criminal charges. It's too dangerous even for her to go out in daylight ...'

Hence the squalor. There were no cooking facilities, and rotting kitchen waste was piled up in a bin in the corner. There was no bathroom either, not even a sink, and it was impossible to ignore the stench coming from the covered chamber pot next to the bin. Every time I breathed in that odour, my stomach rose, and if it hadn't been for the incongruous make-up I was wearing, I'm sure I would have been as white as Fran herself. Mikhail had already explained that opening a window was out of the question; too obvious a sign of habitation. There was nothing I could do then but leave her there in that foetid attic, promising to come back as soon as it was safe to do so. As we said our goodbyes, I could hear a faint ripple of laughter from downstairs, from the affluent luxury of the bordello that seemed even more grotesque now than the surroundings Fran had to exist in.

We didn't leave as we had arrived. Mikhail led me out through a door at the opposite end of the passage and down a fire escape into the yard behind number One Two Two.

'Why didn't we come in this way?' I demanded. 'Instead of putting us through this ridiculous game of fancy dress?'

Inside my fur jacket there was sweat trickling down my back, and the whole costume was making my skin crawl, so that I couldn't wait to rip it off.

'Because it wasn't completely dark when we arrived, and someone might have seen us ...' He looked into my eyes, and smiled slightly. 'But also I wanted to see how well you managed with the game of disguises. Another little test, if you like.'

I was sick of being tested. I felt as though I was crawling through a maze on my hands and knees, unable to come out in the open and declare my need for help, encountering a fresh obstacle with every corner I turned.

The latest one was lack of money. Frannie and I would need it to get ourselves to the Vichy zone, and to support ourselves once we were there. And how long would it have to be for? When, if ever, would I return to England? It was no wonder that I didn't have time to think of James, dear, dependable James, far removed from these ever-present, daily anxieties.

But first, I had the task of persuading Frannie to leave. I considered trying to find Jack, and enlisting his help in removing Frannie forcibly. But such a venture would be difficult enough even with her co-operation. Meanwhile, as I battled with the problem, I was running out of cash to use on a daily basis. Charlie Olsen helped. He realised that I didn't like to accept money, and sought out black-market food for me instead.

One day he met me at Jean-Marie's café, grinning broadly as though he had just done something clever. He motioned for me to sit down, then handed me a bulky parcel wrapped in newspaper. Inside was butter (almost impossible to find in the shops) and some lean beef steak. He then fumbled in his pockets as though searching for cigarettes, and brought out two brown eggs, which I popped into my handbag.

I took this booty back to the apartment, and Hélène and I spread it on a newspaper on the kitchen table and sat drooling over it. Much as we would have liked to, we could not eat it ourselves, though I did offer the eggs to the children. We were trying to decide on the best way to get it to Frannie.

In the end, Hélène turned the butter and beef into a rich stew, with some onions and carrots grown by a friend in a tiny balcony garden. She seasoned it with bay, black pepper and cloves and the whole apartment was full of the most mouth-watering aroma. It seemed to drift under the door and down the stairs, filling the whole block, the whole street even, with the smell of cooking.

'This will get the neighbours talking!' exclaimed Hélène. She gave the girls a little taste each, then let them wipe the pan clean with their bread. The rest of the stew she poured into a screw-topped jar, for me to take to Frannie.

Mikhail arranged for me to visit the bordello after dark, entering by the fire escape. To my irritation, he wouldn't let me go and see Fran alone, but insisted on accompanying me, as though he was afraid of what I might say to her.

He waited, smoking his hand-rolled cigarettes, while Frannie dutifully munched her way through Hélène's stew, now a little cold and congealed. We both waited, and we both stood there, helpless, while Frannie staggered into the other room and vomited it all into the waste bucket that stood in the corner.

'It was too rich for her.' This was Mikhail's comment. He stubbed out yet another cigarette on the bare floorboards. 'You should never have given her that.'

'Well why didn't you tell me that before she ate it?' I snapped. The tension in that terrible, airless place was making me edgy.

'I thought she should at least be able to enjoy the sensation of eating it.'

I was desperate. After helping Frannie back to her sleeping place of cushions and blankets (there was no bed; it would have been too risky to bring one up) I wiped her face with my handkerchief and renewed my efforts.

'Fran, wouldn't it be better if you came with me for a little rest, in the country? You could look on it as a holiday, just for a little while, then you could come back to Paris ...'

She wasn't listening to me. 'Sorry about the stew, Kitty. I suppose it must be the baby. It's made me sick a lot.'

There was no bitterness in her voice, or self-pity. I looked at her face. It would have been reasonable to expect her eyes to be dulled or clouded, but they were as bright as ever. She was still committed to her cause, the one that had led her to Simon in the first place. In contrast with the thinness of the rest of her body, her pregnant belly looked disproportionately large and swollen. I felt a sudden rush of hatred for the child she was carrying, a parasite sucking the life out of her.

'Have you asked her?' said Mikhail, addressing Fran.

She looked at him for a second, then at me, placing her hand on my arm. 'Kitty ... we need your help with something. With ... helping other people in trouble. Will you do it?'

'That depends what it is,' I replied stiffly, though I could already imagine the sort of thing she was going to ask. I was angry with her for wanting to use me to help others while she refused to accept my help for herself.

'Frannie tells me you're a good photographer,' said Mikhail, stopping his pacing long enough to roll another cigarette.

'I'm a photographer, yes.'

He offered the cigarette to me, and without really wanting it, I accepted. The smell of the smoke helped keep the other awful odours at bay.

'We need you to take some photographs for us. For passports.'

I puffed on the sour-tasting tobacco. 'Forged passports?'

'Yes.'

'Well, I could certainly take the pictures. There's no problem

225

with that; I've got all my stuff with me. But how on earth are you going to develop them?'

'We thought you could do that, too, Kitty. You're awfully good at that sort of thing. You saw Mr Munson do it in the village, remember?'

Frannie smiled at me eagerly, as though we were at Russington and she was proposing some sort of parlour game. I made a strenuous effort to quash my irritation, reminding myself what she had suffered, what she was suffering ...

'It's just not as simple as that. I know how it's done, sure, but you need special equipment, special chemicals. I don't have those things.'

'You're a journalist,' said Mikhail smoothly. 'Use your contacts. Dress yourself up a bit before you ask them. You must know how to do that.'

I threw the remainder of the cigarette on to the floor with an angry movement.

'Please, Kitty!' pleaded Frannie. She put her hand on my arm again but I moved away and started walking around the room. 'Please ... if we could just get a few more people to safety, then I'd be prepared to think about leaving Paris myself.'

I stood still and looked at her, then at Mikhail. His face was impassive. I could hardly believe Frannie would suggest such a *volte face*, just to be sure of using me. On the other hand, I knew that deviousness was as alien to her as it was second nature to Jack. The fact she was prepared to make such a concession proved only how important this venture was to her.

'All right then,' I said. 'Yes. I'll try.'

Mikhail and Frannie both smiled at this, even though my spoken assent was a mere formality. We all knew I had no choice.

'Silver nitrate,' I said to Charlie as we strolled around the Invalides together. 'And a strong overhead light, and some light-sensitive paper ... Oh God, there are so many things I'm going to need.'

'Don't worry, I'll get you as much as I can.' He thrust his hands deep into his pockets. 'It's not going to be easy, you know.'

'I know, and I'm grateful, Charlie, I really am.' I linked my arm through his. 'I don't know; I keep on asking you for things, and it makes me feel guilty. What have I ever done for you?'

He laughed. 'Well, you've made my life a whole lot more interesting, that's for sure!'

A couple of days later I made another night visit to Frannie's attic prison, armed with some old baking dishes of Hélène's and various bottles of fluid. The time, as usual, had been designated by Mikhail, and he was there waiting for me, along with a young woman who was introduced as Eva.

She was to be the subject of my photographic experiments, and I was to try to make her look as Aryan as I could. This was explained by Mikhail; Eva herself did not speak once during the entire evening. Her eyes darted around the room constantly, as though she expected someone to come in. Her sallow features were unmistakably Jewish but her hair had been bleached with peroxide, just as mine had when I was disguised as Sieghilde. The result was less good, since Eva's original colour was darker than mine. My own straw-coloured locks had been toned down with a brunette rinse when I returned to Russington.

I pinned a white sheet against the wall and Eva posed in front of it while Mikhail covered the small skylight window to hide the light of the flash. Then I knelt on the floor and had a stab at developing the pictures. In another corner, Mikhail was working by candle-light, putting the finishing touches to Eva's 'passport', copying the size and style of print from a real example on to paper stolen from the Ministry of the Interior.

I only had a simple anglepoise light to work with, and there was no focusing mechanism for adjusting the distance between the negative and the paper, and therefore the size of the finished print, which had to be precisely one and a half inches square. I drew the square of the correct size on to the paper and, cursing under my breath, tried a series of acrobatics with the lamp to get the negative in the right place. With the airlessness of the room, and my exertions, and the unbearable tension of knowing a life hung on the success of my efforts, my whole body was soon running with sweat. I enlisted Frannie's help in holding the negative while I directed the light beam, but her hands trembled and I was afraid the image would be blurred.

Peering hard at my watch so as to be accurate, I waited for two minutes, then immersed the paper into a baking tray of silver nitrate solution. Frannie squatted next to me, not daring to speak. The image of Eva's face, framed by a one and a half inch square, slowly drifted into view.

Mikhail put down his pen and ink and came to have a look. 'It's too dark,' he said. 'She looks like a rabbi's wife. You'll have to do another one.'

I gritted my teeth and tried again, giving the exposure three minutes this time. The initial result was certainly better; Eva looked distinctly fair-haired by now, and her cheek bones weren't so prominent.

'I'm worried about the fixer,' I admitted, as I washed the print with some of Frannie's precious supply of clean water. 'The proper stuff contains a special sort of acid, but we couldn't get that, so I'm having to make do with a solution of vinegar.'

I let the print dry, and we waited an anxious ten minutes to see if the image would fade away altogether, or stay in place. It stayed.

'Good,' said Mikhail. He didn't seem to think it necessary to thank me, or praise my efforts. The precious photograph was snatched from my hand, and he immediately set about cutting it out and gluing it on to Eva's passport.

Then he did a strange thing. He lifted up Eva's skirt, and her petticoat, and yanked roughly at the elastic on the waistband of her knickers.

'Your pubic hair's still black,' he said dispassionately. 'You must dye it blonde. If they're suspicious, that's the first place they'll look.'

Mikhail's diligence paid off. When I visited the attic of the brothel three days later, bringing eggs and milk and a little brandy from Charlie, Frannie announced triumphantly that Eva's attempted escape had been a success. She was staying at a farm in Provence.

'So now will you come with me, Fran?' I asked, as I whisked up raw egg and milk with a fork. 'Please. You said you'd consider it.'

Frannie's eyes were very bright, a sign which I had learned to recognise. It meant that the cause was still claiming her commitment.

'Soon. But first we need another photograph. Mikhail's in trouble. They found out about the stolen passport paper. We need to make a passport for *him* now.'

I seemed to spend so much of my time shut away in darkness that I was starting to feel strange, uneasy, when I was out of doors. I stopped for an indulgent *demi-tasse* of coffee at a pavement café on the Champs Elysées, savouring every sip of my 'treat'. I was existing on hand-outs from Charlie and the last of Hoccleve's guilt-induced expense allowance.

The bright light hurt my eyes, and I had to put on my sunglasses. This at least allowed me to take a good look at the other customers without seeming too obvious. Everyone seemed to be part of a group or a couple except for the occupant of the next table. He was an SS officer, barely older than myself, and yet he had been decorated with Himmler's Iron Cross, the highest honour he could achieve. As I speculated about how he had earned it, I found I could not stop looking at him. He had one of those faces which is instantly attractive, with clear, well-spaced features and limpid grey eyes. I wished I had my camera and could take a picture of him as he sat staring into his glass of schnapps. He looked lonely.

I averted my gaze quickly when he looked up, but it was too late. He had seen me staring at him. He walked over to my table, clicked the heels of his shiny boots and gave a little bow.

'*Vous êtes française, madame?*'

I shook my head. '*Suède.*'

'Ah ...'

He pointed at the other chair and I nodded. 'Will you let me buy you a drink?' he asked in faultless English. 'Or perhaps something to eat?'

My stomach was growling with hunger but I shook my head, nervous of accepting anything from him.

'My name is Kurt von Himpel. And yours?'

'Er ... Ingrid,' I said, with a lack of originality that would have shocked my cousins. 'Ingrid Olsen.'

'And where is your home?'

I invented a story, using Charlie's Swedish-American back-ground and giving myself a job with the International Red Cross. Kurt did not seem disposed to doubt any of it, or to ask more questions, for the time being. Instead he told me about his home, in Prussia, and an upbringing very like that of my cousin-in-law, Hubertus. I opened my mouth to say, 'My cousin lives in Berlin,' then thought better of it. I had no idea what sort of trouble Lexi and Hubertus might be in now.

'Can we walk somewhere?' asked Kurt, putting down some money for the bill.

I hesitated. Falling into conversation with a German was one thing, but strolling around the city like some SS moll was another.

'Please. I just want to walk with someone, that's all. It's so difficult when one is in a strange city, and knows no one ...'

I couldn't resist those sad eyes of his. We walked through the Tuileries together, beneath an avenue of chestnuts whose foliage we both admired in a rather formal way. At first it felt strange walking beside a Nazi officer, but after a while I managed to ignore the uniform and treat him as though he were Jack, or even Clem. He was nearly two years younger than me; just nineteen years old.

We passed some children sailing their boats in the shallow pond, and a strange expression crossed Kurt's face, one I could not decipher. We watched them for a while, and when one of them capsized his toy yacht and started to cry, he rushed forward to help him set it afloat again.

'You like children?' I asked, curious. There was a special gentleness in the way he had dealt with the child. He was too young to be a father himself, but perhaps he had practice with younger siblings.

Kurt turned and walked away from the pond. He would not look at my face, and for several moments he would not speak either. Finally he said, 'I was in the *Einsatzkommande*. Do you know what that is, Ingrid?'

I shook my head.

'It is the extermination squad.'

I didn't want him to go on; but he did. He had to, it seemed.

'They told us we were going to get our revenge on the Russians. I thought perhaps I would be one of those soldiers liberating Latvia with flowers stuck in their caps . . .'

We had come to a flowerbed, full of wilting rose bushes. We stopped and both stared at those fading flowers, to avoid looking at one another.

'They told me I had been given a very great honour. My job would be to shoot the Jews. Some of us shot, the others buried. You were lucky if you got to shoot. Those people . . . those people . . .'
He covered his eyes, as if he could see them still.

'Don't, Kurt . . .' I said gently.

'I must. Everyone should know. They should know that those people were brave. They made it a point of pride to stand up straight as we pointed the rifles. One man stepped forward and said to me, "My son, God is watching what you do, and he forgives you."'

He was fondling the cross on his breast. 'I did well at the job. I didn't know you could be good at killing people, but they told me I was, that I had done well. They moved me on. This time it was my job to shoot the children. Just the children . . .'

I felt an unbearable suffocating sensation in my chest, but could say nothing. I touched his arm, gently. 'Kurt . . .'

'I had a . . . a nervous breakdown, I think that is the English expression. They gave me the Iron Cross and sent me here, to be an administrator.'

He looked at me at last. 'I'm sorry,' he said, suddenly formal again.

230

I was sorry too. And more fervently than ever I wished that the war could end and we could both be spared; Kurt and I.

Talking to me had given Kurt some sort of release, and it was predictable that he should seek me out again. He asked me to meet him at the café the next day. At first I refused, feeling that it was incompatible with my position to consort with a member of the SS death squad. But he looked so sad when I refused that I changed my mind. Inside the grey uniform he was a person, just like me, and he had suffered more than I had at the hands of Adolf Hitler. Besides, I reasoned, being escorted around the city by a German officer would give me protection, a sort of false cover.

When we next met, Kurt shyly handed me a present, a box of chocolates. In the hope of ending up with something more nourishing, I told him that I didn't much care for chocolate. The next time he bought me a pot of *foie gras*. I swallowed my pride then, for Frannie's sake, and told him that foreign correspondents didn't receive much in the way of allowances, and I saw few square meals. I was growing thinner, so it was really only a white lie. Kurt didn't make any comment on this state of affairs, just nodded gravely and turned up the next day with an enormous basket containing butter, eggs, fruit and a chicken.

I dutifully passed on some of my spoils to Hélène (allowing her to assume they came from Charlie, whom I still saw occasionally) and helped her to prepare some chicken soup for Frannie. I took it over to the attic of the brothel on the night that had been designated for making Mikhail's passport.

He took the soup from me and sniffed it suspiciously. 'Is this pigeon?'

I knew that in their desperation, the residents of Paris had taken to shooting or snaring the pigeons on their rooftops. I could have lied, but Mikhail's manner, as ever, goaded me.

'No, it's chicken.'

'*Chicken*! Where the hell did you find chicken in Paris, without selling yourself for it?'

'A friend gave it to me – '

'That American, I suppose?'

'No, a German.'

The look on Mikhail's face was so outraged that I was tempted to smile. I was enjoying goading him.

'Not a Jew, surely? Anyone in our positions couldn't afford to give away – '

'No, a member of the SS, actually. He's called Kurt, and he's very sweet. And don't worry, he doesn't know what I've done with the food.'

Even in his rage, Mikhail remembered that he mustn't raise his voice. 'You've been *collaborating*!' he hissed. 'Do you realise how many people you're betraying just by speaking to a Nazi, let alone befriending one? Do you know what those animals *do* . . . ?'

'Yes,' I said calmly. 'They shoot people. They shoot children. That's what Kurt had to do; to shoot children.'

I looked Mikhail straight in the eyes. He raised his hand and was about to hit me across the side of the face when Frannie flung herself between us and pushed him away. '*Don't*!' she shouted, forgetting to whisper. 'Leave her alone! Kitty knows what she's doing. I trust her.'

'I'm surprised at you,' said Mikhail, with contempt. 'After all that *you* have suffered! How could you even contemplate – '

'Because you have to love good more than you hate evil,' said Frannie quietly. She sank down on to the floor again as though all her energy had been used up in that one outburst. 'Otherwise there's no point in our even being alive.'

Six

Mikhail finally calmed down enough to eat some of the chicken soup, and when my own mood of defiance faded, I attempted to persuade him that not only was Kurt harmless, but that he might also be able to help in some way in the future. Mikhail declined to discuss the subject further, asking me if I would get on with the business of preparing his passport photograph.

I set out the makeshift darkroom, but before I started, I said to Mikhail, 'This time there's a condition attached to my work.'

He looked at me with more contempt than suspicion. 'What now?'

'I want you to make a passport for Frannie too.'

He shrugged and started to roll one of his foul-smelling cigarettes. 'I'd like to, but it's not possible. I'm leaving as soon as I can, and I can't get any more of the paper. It's too difficult.'

'You've got to try,' I said firmly. 'Otherwise, no photograph.'

Mikhail threw his freshly lit cigarette to the floor and ground it out. 'All right, I'll try. But you'd have more luck if you asked your German.'

I ignored this and got on with the business of developing the photographs I had taken on an earlier occasion. I did one of Frannie, too, for use in the not-too-distant future. While I worked, Mikhail paced around me, continually lighting cigarettes and then extinguishing them when they were only half-smoked.

When I was finished I pocketed the picture of Frannie and handed Mikhail his. Without a word to me, he sat down and glued it into place in the 'passport' he had already prepared.

'When will you go?' I asked.

'A couple of days, maybe. As soon as I can arrange transport.'

He looked up at me and smiled. I realised this was the nearest thing to thanks I was going to get.

The next day I resolved to put the perennial problem of escape behind me and enjoy myself for a short time. I had a drink with Charlie in the bar of the Swedish Embassy, and then he took me for lunch at the Berkeley. Afterwards I met Kurt and we went for a stroll along the Faubourg St Honoré and took tea at a street café peopled with Nazi officers and their female auxiliary staff, who were known as *Blitzmadchen* or *souris grises* because of their drab grey uniforms.

I was in a pleasantly hedonistic mood when I returned to the apartment in the *seizième*, humming to myself as I walked up the four flights of stone steps, and swinging my handbag by its strap.

'Hélène!' I called, as I unlocked the door. 'Hélène, you'll never guess what I saw in a shop this afternoon. Only the most perfect – '

I stopped dead in my tracks. The apartment had been decimated. Furniture was tipped over, food was smeared on the walls, china was broken. The photograph of Monsieur Monnier, which had had pride of place, had been thrown to the floor and smashed. Hélène was sitting in the middle of the chaos, crying, with the two little girls clinging to her, ashen-faced.

I flung my bag and Kurt's food parcels to the floor and ran over to them.

'Hélène . . ! In God's name . . . what's happened?'

Hélène pushed her hair back from her forehead and tried to compose herself. 'The Gestapo were here.'

'Here . . ?' I looked around the room, confused. 'What did they want?'

Hélène shook her head and looked down again. 'I . . . I don't know.'

She couldn't look me in the face. We both knew, though neither dared voice it, that they might have been looking for me. Had I been too gullible in trusting Kurt, too swayed by his resemblance to Hubertus? No, it was impossible . . . He could not have faked the suffering in his self-revelation.

'It's all right, Hélène,' I said quietly. 'I'll go. Charlie can help me find somewhere else. I'll just put this food in the kitchen, then I'll pack my things.'

'Wait!' said Hélène. She pushed the children aside and came after me. 'Wait, Kitty . . . there's something else . . .'

I put the joint of ham I was holding on top of the fridge, and waited.

'Mikhail Kublik has been arrested.'

It took a few seconds for this information to sink in. So it must have been Mikhail who had betrayed me, no doubt under torture. And if they could make him tell them where *I* was, then...

With a strangled cry, I ran past Hélène, out of the apartment and down the stairs that I had just sauntered up, singing.

It was still broad daylight when I reached 122, rue de Provence, but I raced straight up the front steps and into the brothel, pushing aside several astonished prostitutes who were gossiping on the landing in their negligées. In seconds I was on the top floor, at the door which led to the attic stairway. If the door is still locked, I said over and over to myself on my way up there, then everything's still all right. Still all right...

The door had been broken off its hinges with a crowbar. I walked slowly up the last flight of steps. The smell was more overpowering than ever, and I discovered that the waste pail had been overturned. There were scuff marks on the floorboards, as though there had been a struggle. In the middle of the room, looking bizarrely misplaced, was an old Mason & Pearson hairbrush that I recognised from the shared room at Russington, and a none too clean handkerchief. Apart from that, there was no sigh. Frannie had gone.

I knew that Kurt lived in a luxurious apartment in the Avenue Foch, commandeered from a white Russian princess, but I didn't know the address. I knew there was a brasserie near there that he frequented; he had taken me there once or twice, so I went and sat in there on the off-chance he would come. I couldn't think of anything else to do.

I had to have something stronger than coffee so, stretching my exhausted budget, I ordered a pastis and a jug of water and spun it out for two hours. Finally I saw Kurt, walking past the window with his arm around a very pretty, well-dressed girl whom I was now able to recognise as one of Paris's more prosperous class of courtesan.

The first emotion I experienced, despite my desperate predicament, was absurd, misplaced jealousy. I must have flattered myself that he was a little sweet on me. However, this passed in a second, as soon as he walked past the brasserie and continued up the avenue, and I knew I must attract his attention at once. I tapped on the window and called his name.

'Kurt!'

He reddened a little, then slipped a bank note into the hand of the girl, after a short whispered conference which left her looking very disgruntled.

'Kurt ... ' I sighed as he strode into the brasserie looking exactly as Himmler would have liked him to look; tall, fair and glamorous, his Iron Cross glinting in the lamplight. 'Thank God I found you. I need your help ... '

He just nodded and went to the bar to fetch me another drink. When I reached out to take it from him, I found my hands were shaking violently.

'You have a problem, Ingrid?' he enquired.

While I had sat drinking my pastis, waiting for two interminable hours, I at least had plenty of time to consider my strategy, so I knew exactly what to say to Kurt. I stuck to my story about being Ingrid Olsen, but I confessed that my prime reason for being in Paris was to find out what had happened to my English cousin, who had made an unwise and unfortunate marriage (I did a little fibbing about my own attitude to Fran's politics) to a communist. I was aware of the patent absurdity of the tale, particularly given my own very English accent. Kurt pretended to believe every word, politely collaborating in the game of bluff.

'You say we have arrested her?' He used the 'we' very coolly, I thought, but then he was accustomed to being linked to far worse atrocities.

'I don't know for certain. But the door of ... her apartment ... had been broken down, and there was no sign of her, no note.'

'It sounds very much that way,' said Kurt, shaking his head sadly. 'I am very sorry, Ingrid.'

'Can you help?'

He looked me in the eye and asked me a quite unexpected question. 'Is she innocent?'

'Yes,' I said. It didn't feel like a lie. No one had a more innocent heart than Frannie, and she hadn't hurt anyone. 'And she's pregnant.'

Fran had not been seen by a doctor during her pregnancy, but from my limited experience I had been able to deduce that the baby would be born very soon.

'I will ask about her,' Kurt promised. 'But more than that I cannot do. If they suspect me ... ' He drew a finger across his throat and I nodded.

'... And thank you, Kurt.'

He retreated into his formal mode again. 'That is all right. You are my friend. We must all help our friends.'

I spent the night on Charlie's sofa, and met Kurt for lunch the next day at the brasserie, after he had had time to make a few enquiries.

'Did you find out anything?' I asked, as soon as he had sat down.

'Yes.' He was frowning. 'Why did you not tell me that the Gestapo also went to your apartment?'

So that was it. He must have confirmed, then, that I was Kitty Conway.

'I ... I'm sorry, Kurt. I suppose I didn't want you to know.'

'You must leave Paris,' he said. 'Straight away. They might arrest you, or at least question you. You do not want to be questioned.'

I understood from his tone of voice that it would not just be a matter of personal preference.

'But what about Fran? I can't just – '

'You cannot help her. Not now.'

I stared at him. 'You mean ...?'

He shook his head. 'She is not dead, no. She is in a detention centre, here in Paris, but soon she may be moved somewhere else. I don't know where. But I do know that if you are arrested, you cannot help her.'

I couldn't argue with this, nor did I want to put Kurt at any more personal risk than was necessary. He gave me an address where I could write to him safely, and told me he would let me know as soon as he found out more about Fran. Then I went back to collect my things from the ransacked apartment, stopping off to bid goodbye to Charlie Olsen, who gave me all the francs he could spare.

My last stop was Zazoste's Basque restaurant, where Kurt very solemnly treated me to a farewell supper. He presented me with a flask of cognac for the journey, and took me to the Gare Montparnasse, where I caught a train for Normandy.

Jack had not given me his address; the idea had probably not even occurred to him. But I still had his letter, stuffed into the pocket of my fur jacket for safe-keeping. I took it out and re-read it on the train, though I still knew it by heart even now. The only name he mentioned was the market town of Lisieux, but it was only a small town, and there couldn't have been many British black marketeers in the district. If he was still there, I was sure I would find him.

It was late when we arrived at Lisieux, so I took a room for the night at the local auberge, raising provincial eyebrows with my transparently schoolgirlish French accent. The next morning I sat in the main square and enjoyed a leisurely breakfast of croissants dipped in milky coffee. Now that the decision had been made for me, it was a great relief to be out of Paris. A couple of Nazis drove past in an official vehicle, but they were smoking and telling jokes, and didn't exactly represent a sinister presence. Not when the phlegmatic pink-cheeked Norman farmers were going about their business as though they had never heard of Hitler. Where was the war?, one might well have asked.

By nine o'clock, the square was bustling as the market got underway. The stalls that had been erected at first light were spread with their wares; fruit and vegetables mainly. No doubt it was a meagre display compared with pre-war days, but after the privations of Paris it was like an Aladdin's cave. Everyone looked well-fed.

After a couple of hours, I spotted Jack. He was haggling with the proprietor of a dairy-produce stall. It was his voice that I recognised, since his face was obscured beneath a shapeless felt hat. He wore the same baggy cotton trousers and jacket that all the other farmers wore, and on his feet was a pair of wooden clogs.

He had his back to me, and just as I reached him, he handed some money to the stall-holder and moved on. I was forced to follow him through the crowd, and this made me feel suddenly shy.

'Jack.'

His face betrayed a flicker of surprise as he turned round, then it was gone.

'Well, well, well ...' He continued with the task of stuffing his parcels into the large pockets of his jacket. Then he pushed up the brim of his hat to see me better. 'You look terrible.'

I was suddenly very tired, and angry with the coolness that greeted my arrival. And I was overwhelmed by my sheer luck. Had it not been market day, I would have had to wait days for a chance of sighting him. 'I found Frannie,' I said.

'And?'

We were blocking the main thoroughfare between stalls, and a group of farmers' wives pushed past us, jostling me with their baskets.

'Look,' said Jack, taking me by the elbow and leading me out of harm's way. 'You'd better tell me about it later. I'll get you home first.'

We collected my luggage from the auberge and set off on foot, leaving the town behind us and heading into country lanes.

'How far are we going?' I asked Jack.

'About eight or nine miles.'

'Do we have to walk all the way?'

'Sometimes. Sometimes someone will stop and offer a lift.'

'Like the man with the geese,' I said, remembering his letter.

'Precisely. Like the man with the geese.'

After a while I began to enjoy the walk, letting the steady clack-clack of Jack's clogs give me my rhythm. We didn't talk, but every few hundred yards we would silently hand over my suitcase and take our turn at carrying it. The pale blue sky was lightly scattered with white clouds, and the lanes were densely green with fresh hazel and hawthorn leaves, and scented with mallow and camomile.

Eventually the smells changed, and it became obvious that we were at last approaching a village. I could smell and hear chickens, and wet hay, and cooking.

'Welcome to Notre-Dame des Anges,' said Jack.

We passed the church, and the village cemetery, and finally came to a large rectangular cottage, with its shutters closed to keep out the sun. The small fenced plot at the front had roses and hollyhocks, and at the back there was a kitchen garden with rows of cabbages, and blackcurrant bushes.

'Is this your house?' I asked.

Jack shook his head. 'Whole houses to rent are like gold-dust. I have two rooms here. And I pay good money for them, too.'

He led me up the garden path and presented me to his landlady, introducing me as '*ma cousine*'. Madame Loty was an elderly lady with a face like one of the hens who ran around the kitchen garden. Her thin hair was dragged into a centre parting, smoothed with water and coiled on her head like a snail shell. Monsieur Loty was playing dominoes. He looked up, squinted at us with his one good eye (the other was made of glass) and returned to his game.

'D'you think they believe we're cousins?' I asked, as Jack led me upstairs to his rooms.

'Why on earth shouldn't they?' he replied blandly.

'Oh, never mind . . .'

Jack's rooms were in the attic, beneath sloping roofs decorated with strings of Madame Loty's fat, shiny onions. In one room there was a cherry-wood bed with a feather-stuffed eiderdown and starched curtains at the windows. The other had a red-tiled floor and a small fireplace for burning wood. There was a lumpy horse-hair sofa that would have to serve as a spare bed. The whole place had a clean smell of furniture wax and washing soda, tinged with the scent of onions.

'I take all my meals here, at an extra charge,' Jack explained. 'If they're going to feed you, too, you'll have to help me with the work, earn some extra cash.'

'What will I have to do?'

Jack grinned. 'Don't worry, it's bloody easy.' He looked out of the window, and gave a sigh of satisfaction. 'The land of milk and honey, that's what this place is, Kitty.'

We went downstairs and ate supper with the Lotys. It was the biggest meal I had consumed in months. Pickled pork and endives, potatoes, bread and baked custard, all liberally smothered with butter and cream and washed down with calvados. I concentrated on the food, while Jack bantered with our hosts in the local *patois*, telling jokes that made Madame Loty giggle and blush like a girl.

After supper Jack and I sat upstairs and drank more calvados, while I told him everything that had happened in Paris. He listened without committing himself to any show of shock, admiration or horror. All he said was, 'You did the right thing, coming here.'

I was to have Jack's bed for the night, while he had the sofa. It was wonderfully comfortable among the plump pillows, but for a long time I couldn't sleep. I listened to every sound he made, and some small part of me responded to those sounds with the purest joy, joy at having him back. But I thought about him downstairs with the Lotys, who were eating out of his hand. They were attracted to him, charmed by him. He would give himself to such people – or rather lend himself for as long as it suited his purpose – but he still eluded me.

I was woken up the next morning by the sound of Jack's wooden clogs clacking on the tile floor. He came into the bedroom carrying a cup of coffee and a roll, which he handed to me over the bedclothes.

'Breakfast in bed – aren't you lucky? Actually, I thought it would save time, because I'm in a hurry to get going. I'm afraid you slept through Madame Loty's fry-up.'

I dressed in a plain cotton dress and sandals, and followed Jack out of the house. The sun had only just risen and it felt strange to be up at that hour, particularly with Jack, who had never been noted for his early rising.

'There are two stages to this job,' Jack explained as we set off out of the village. 'Collection, and distribution. We're going to be collecting this morning. Just watch me for a while, then you can have a go on your own.'

We stopped at a farm, and after chatting with the farmer's wife for a while, Jack came away with some bacon and a pound of butter, which he duly paid her for. On to another farm, and this time another half-pound of butter and half a dozen eggs. At the next place it was some home-made preserve, and still more butter, all of which was stored away in pockets sewn into the inside of his jacket.

'Butter,' said Jack. 'They always want butter, remember that.'

Wherever we were, he didn't just march in and ask for food. There was a ritual to go through, a few minutes' small-talk, an exercise of his charm, perhaps the acceptance of a cup of coffee or something to eat.

We walked an awful lot. Across meadows, through brambles and gorse. Jack's thirst for that glowing yellow butter was like a prospector's quest for gold. He didn't seem to tire. I did.

Around midday we arrived at a large, ramshackle farm. Jack hung back at the gate. 'Your turn now,' he said. 'Go in and ask them if they can spare any eggs.'

I found two women in the farmyard; one thin, middle-aged and pinched-looking, the younger one heavily built and rather plain.

'Ah ... *excusez-moi, mesdames ...*'

My French accent must have sounded strange to their ears. I asked as best I could if they had any eggs, but was just met with a peremptory shake of the head. The older one went back to wringing out clothes with a mangle, and the younger one stared at me like some dumb animal.

It was only when she saw Jack leaning on the farmyard gate that her face showed any sign of animation at all. She even blushed. The older woman called to him and they fell into conversation, the gist of which was that of course they had some eggs – for Monsieur Jacques. She went into the house to fetch them and Jack told me to wait for her there, in the yard.

His task accomplished, he strolled over to talk to the young girl, who was idling in the most unsubtle fashion against the side of the barn. I could hear them talking and whispering behind me, and although I couldn't decipher the girl's accent, I recognised the tone of voice only too well.

The farmer's wife was still in the kitchen. She called out, irritated, 'Elise! Elise! *Viens-ici!*'

I couldn't resist the temptation to turn round and see what effect this had. Elise was disposed to ignore the summons, and no wonder, since Jack was leaning over her and whispering something in her ear. As he did so, his hand moved up and rested very lightly on her right breast. She giggled and turned red.

I turned back quickly, feeling my own face flush as though someone had slapped me. Then the woman was handing me the eggs with a curt nod, Jack was at my side and we were on our way again.

Misinterpreting my silence as we trudged up a steep hill to the next place, Jack said, 'Don't take it too much to heart, Kit. It took a while for me, too, but they accept you in the end . . .'

'. . . Now this place belongs to Fernand. The biggest cattle merchant in the district. He's got masses of food to spare, but he's a difficult bugger. Perhaps I should handle this one. Wait here . . .'

He approached the large, red-faced man on the steps of the house, and I stood looking around me, once more surplus to requirements. I could hear children's voices, and after a while managed to locate them. There was a deep ditch running along the perimeter of the courtyard, with a stream flowing through it. Two boys were wading in the stream.

I thought at first they were playing some arcane local game, but then I realised the noises were cries of distress. I hurried towards them, and Jack and Fernand ran up behind me.

The boys had a puppy, who had wriggled free and had been swept away by the fast-moving waters of the stream. The creature had been caught up, temporarily, in a knot of branches, but they couldn't reach him.

I took off my sandals and waded in up to my thighs. The force of the water was unexpected, knocking me sideways. I struggled for my balance, grabbing at an overhanging tree.

'Don't be so bloody sentimental!' Jack shouted. 'You'll hurt yourself!'

I ignored him and went in deeper, almost up to my chin. I grabbed the puppy, which was only just alive, and staggered back to the bank. One of the boys took it from me and dried it with his sweater.

Monsieur Fernand was staring at me, and I felt self-conscious, a little foolish even, standing there in my dripping dress. But he was nodding, with mixed approval and respect. He took off his own jacket and handed it to me, then gestured that I should go into the house. Jack followed, looking amused.

'Change of plan,' he whispered, as Fernand fetched me brandy, and a blanket. 'You've obviously impressed him. *You* ask him. Ask him if he's got a duck.'

242

I waited until our host had come back.

'Monsieur Fernand, I wonder ...' I began in my best French. '...
I've heard that your ducks are very good.'

He nodded.

'Shall I be able to buy one ... perhaps ..?'

He fetched me one, and a good big one at that. Jack, delighted,
decided we had collected enough that day, and we took our
purchases back to Madame Loty's house, with me shivering most
of the way in my damp dress. Once upstairs, Jack took out several
letters from 'clients', noted their requests and scribbled something
on to a list. Then he divided the food into several bundles, wrapped
each one in waxed paper, and then brown paper and string. While
he was addressing them to various places in Paris, I scribbled a
quick note to Kurt, telling him where I was, and asking him to get in
touch with any news of Frannie.

The 'distribution' stage of the operation meant walking three
miles to the local post office and queueing up at the counter to
register the packages.

'Not foodstuffs, are they?' asked the clerk.

'Of course not!' Jack winked at her. 'Just some duck, some
butter, some – '

'Shhh!' the woman reprimanded him. 'I'm not supposed to know
that!'

'It's a game,' explained Jack. 'Everyone knows what I'm really
doing. Most of the parcels leaving this place contain food. As long
as the Germans stay away, it's OK.'

I was exhausted by the time we returned, too tired even for
Madame Loty's apple tart and cream. I was just excusing myself to
go upstairs when there was a knock on the door.

'C'est Monsieur Fernand!' exclaimed Madame Loty.

He was obviously not a regular visitor, looking pathetically
self-conscious in his Sunday-best suit and hat. He was carrying a
large parcel wrapped in newspaper.

'I came to see how mademoiselle was after her experience,' he
explained. 'I've brought her a present.'

He couldn't quite bring himself to look me in the face, but just
handed over the parcel and left. Inside it was a large side of beef,
fresh and beautifully marbled. The Lotys exclaimed with admiration.

'Clever girl!' said Jack, taking it from me. 'I can get nearly a
thousand francs for this ...' Without waiting for any response
from me, he went on, 'So that's settled then. From now on you can
deal with Fernand.'

I turned on my heel and walked out of the room.

Jack followed me up the stairs to the attic and, quite without warning, flung his arms around me and kissed me on the lips. He held me like that for a little longer than was necessary.

'You did wonderfully today, Kit. I'm glad you're here.'

'Why?' I pulled away. 'Because I'm an asset to the business?'

'Of course.' He gave me his strange, half smile. I could never interpret his moods, his thoughts when he looked like that. And now, alone with him in our garret, I felt an overwhelming urge to find out, to talk to him properly.

'Jack . . . '

'You can have the bed again tonight if you like. I'm going out.'

He grabbed his jacket and was gone.

I went to bed, but I couldn't sleep. At midnight, there came a noise so faint that it might only have been sixth sense that drove me to the little window. I pulled back the curtains and the full, yellow harvest moon stared back at me, blank-faced.

Jack was at the bottom of the garden, and there was someone with him, a girl. I was pretty certain that it was Elise, the farm-girl, but I didn't want to look any more. I climbed into the cherry-wood bed and lay on my back, looking at the ceiling, waiting.

Jack was not gone very long. I heard his clogs on the stairs, then moving around on the tiles. He sat down in front of the fire, lifted a loose hearth stone and pulled out a tin. Inside it were hundred-franc notes, seemingly an endless number of them. Jack examined them. I couldn't see the expression on his face, but I could imagine it. He counted them, and wrote down the total. He counted them again. Then again, more slowly, and again . . .

Finally he fell asleep, holding his profits lovingly in his arms.

Seven

I stayed in Notre-Dame des Anges as summer turned to autumn, and the leaves in the narrow lanes that we tramped daily turned from green to russet, bronze and cardinal red. The days ended earlier and earlier for Monsieur and Madame Loty, who retired to bed as soon as it was dark. Jack and I would build pine-cone fires in our sitting room, and bake apples in the blaze.

After a few weeks, I wrote again to Kurt and begged him to tell me what had happened. He replied by return. Frannie was no longer being held in Paris, but he was having trouble discovering her whereabouts. I would have to stay where I was, and try to be patient. He signed himself, with great formality, '*Your obedient servant, Kurt von Himpel*'. Jack laughed at this, but his overall reaction to the letter was cynical.

'How do you know you can trust this Nazi?' he wanted to know.

'Because I know, that's all. I trust my own judgement.'

'Well you're a fool, then. You're always too quick to give people the benefit of the doubt. There could be a knock at the door any minute, and the storm-troopers will be there to carry you off. You should think about hiding somewhere else.'

'If I did that,' I replied coolly, 'you wouldn't have anyone to get lumps of beef from old Fernand.'

'So you're going to stay, is that what you're saying?'

'Yes.'

'Good.'

So I followed Kurt's advice. Being patient wasn't easy, but I enjoyed staying on in the village with Jack. People came to know me and accept me, as he had predicted, and I became familiar with

245

the faces I saw every day. In that respect it was not unlike the experience of working on the estate in Russington. There was the counter clerk at the local post office, an awkward spinster who had a giant crush on Jack. There were the evacuee boys from Paris, who ran wild about the place, creating a scandal by stealing fruit from the villagers' gardens. And there was another escapee from Paris, renting lodgings as we were. He was a poet who called himself 'Zazou' and wore his hair long. He would sit for hours on the riverbank, muttering to himself, an eccentricity which was excused by the villagers on the grounds of his poetic calling. I found the veneration with which they treated him quite touching. Jack found the whole business a huge joke, and would walk along the riverbank with Zazou, teaching him to recite classics of English poetry.

'He's not a real poet, of course,' he would say, laughing. 'I've yet to hear or see a single thing he's written.' He added in the sinister tone he liked to use to scare me, 'And he's half Jewish.'

It isn't easy for me to admit to enjoying my work as a black marketeer, but I did. Jack's obsession with seeking butter, with seeking liquid gold, quickly infected me. As the winter months approached, it became even more rare a commodity, and we had to walk further and further afield to find it.

I seemed to enter countless kitchens, full of the smell of pickling meat and hot cooking fat, and have the same conversation over and over, which ran thus:

'Do you have any butter . . . ?'

'Do you hear that . . ? She's asking for butter.'

'Butter! Where do you think we're going to get butter in the middle of winter? Our cows are in calf and they're not giving milk. We could give you a rabbit.'

'You wouldn't even have just half a pound . . ?'

As the supply dwindled, so the demand increased. Jack spent longer and longer dealing with the 'orders' he received from Paris. The postman brought more and more letters, from customers we didn't even know, asking for meat, lard, cream, pâté, fresh eggs, and butter, always butter. They all wanted butter . . .

We ran out of packaging, and had to enclose letters in our parcels requesting that the customers send us string, wrapping paper, cardboard boxes. Meanwhile the profits in Jack's tin box built up, as the postman delivered money orders with the requests for food. I calculated that we were making at least thirty thousand francs a month. It was never formally alluded to, but we both accepted that some of the money was mine. It had been my idea that we keep our own ducks and geese in Madame Loty's garden, and fatten them with the scraps from her generous table. I also hit on the idea of diluting the cream with a little water, to make it go further. I was becoming quite a business woman.

Meanwhile, Jack and I were united in our obsession. We walked six, then ten, then twelve miles a day, carrying twelve, sixteen, twenty pounds of food in our concealed inner pockets. Our sheer physical exhaustion, and the long hours we worked, helped to deflate the tension of living together in two rooms, with a forced physical closeness that is often only experienced with a spouse. Nevertheless, the tension was there, beneath the surface of all we did. I longed to break it by talking, by telling Jack about my engagement to James, and losing my virginity to Harry Hoccleve, just to ensure reaching Paris.

But when he wasn't sleeping, or counting his profits, he would go out alone. Sometimes he went to amuse himself with Zazou, but more frequently he went and dissipated his own tension with the simple-minded Elise, who had the unlikely role of his mistress. Unlikely because the village was full of far prettier, and far more coquettish girls. I knew this because the affair was a source of village gossip; not because Jack confided in me. As far as I knew, Jack had not confided in anyone since the day he was born.

Some weeks after Kurt's letter had arrived, Jack and I were on one of our regular visits to Monsieur Fernand, the cattle merchant. In the summer we had gone there once a week, perhaps, but the hardships of the winter seemed to send us up there almost every day, asking if he had anything for us. If it hadn't been for his painfully suppressed infatuation with me, he probably wouldn't have tolerated it.

That day was a Sunday, and we left the Lotys preparing themselves for mass; Madame Loty in a desiccated black straw hat with a veil, and Monsieur Loty, forced to abandon his beloved dominoes for at least an hour, in a necktie. The sound of the creaking harmonium followed us as we left the village and walked up the hill. It was a bitter, frosty January morning, and most of our energies went into bracing ourselves against the cold. Usually, during this time of relative energy and freshness at the beginning of the day, Jack cracked little jokes at the expense of his customers, or told tall stories about Zazou, but this morning he was silent. Once upon a time I might have preoccupied myself with trying to work out what he might be thinking, but I knew better now. I thought

247

instead of how cold my fingers were, and how Fernand would give me a lovely hot cup of *café calva* to warm them on. Or perhaps a steaming bowl of soup . . .

Fernand was not a churchgoer, so we visited him regularly on Sunday mornings, and he was expecting us. He welcomed us, in his own reserved fashion, and sat us in front of the fire with cups of sweet black coffee fortified with calvados. Jack gulped his down and said to me – in English so that Fernand wouldn't understand – 'I'm just popping down to the Dinon place to see if they've got eggs. Get what you can out of the old goat and wait for me here until I get back.'

I felt a flash of irritation. The Dinon place was the farm owned by Elise's mother, and he always preferred to visit it on his own, thinking of any old excuse to get me out of the way.

Fernand watched him go through the window, narrowing his eyes and nodding shrewdly as he saw Jack turn right at the bottom of the drive, on to the narrow track that led to the Dinon farm. He brought me more coffee and fussed over tucking a rug round my knees, then gave me a rare smile.

'It's the girl,' he said, in that thick accent that I now understood without difficulty. 'He goes up there to see the girl.'

He sneered as he spoke of her, and at the same time fussed with my rug again, indicating that in his opinion I was altogether of a superior breed of womankind.

'But surely she'll be at mass?' I said, trying to keep my tone casual.

He laughed derisively. 'Oh no, not that one! Not that Elise. She's made a bargain with her mother, you see. She looks after the farm while her mother goes to matins, and goes to the evening service instead. That way she gets to be alone on the farm all morning, *and* slip out in the evening as well, the crafty little vixen. Her poor mother thinks her daughter is devoted to worshipping the Almighty, that's all!'

This was quite an outburst for the taciturn Fernand, and he was too gentlemanly to go on. And since he was also too shy to make banal small talk with me, we sat there in awkward silence until Jack returned, while I tried to assimilate this latest piece of information.

'You're in a sulk,' Jack observed, as we left Fernand's place in silence, as we had arrived. He started to whistle. I ignored him. My coat was weighed down with an enormous leg of lamb that Fernand had given me, and Jack's bulged with eggs, butter and cream. Since there was not much business to be done on a Sunday lunchtime, we set off back to Notre-Dame des Anges.

248

'Look!' said Jack suddenly. 'Do you see what I see?'

I took no notice.

He was pointing at something, and grabbed my elbow to try to make me look too. I pulled my arm away roughly, but the object of his attention was already in my field of vision. It was an open-topped jeep with two men in it. Inevitably they turned out to be Nazi storm-troopers in peaked caps, jackboots and pistol-belts.

'Oh good!' said Jack as they slowed to a halt in front of us. 'This should be fun!'

I had resigned myself to this happening at some time. The more 'business' we handled, the greater the risk of being caught by the Germans. And here we were, not only without identification papers, but carrying enough black-market goods to ensure imprisonment.

'Open your coat!' The senior officer addressed me.

I saw no point in not doing so promptly. The outline of the leg of lamb was not exactly going to be mistaken for a pocket hand-kerchief.

'What's that?' he asked, pointing at the lamb.

Out of the corner of my eye, I could see a facetious reply forming on Jack's lips. 'It's ... my lunch,' I said quickly. 'I'm taking this home to cook for my lunch.'

I stumbled over my French, but the officer appeared to think I was merely half-witted. He snatched the lamb from my pocket, sniffed at it, then hurled it into the ditch. I ground my teeth at his wastefulness. If he had kept it to eat himself it wouldn't have been so bad.

Jack looked at the piece of meat in the muddy ditch, and laughed in the man's face. That was the sort of person he was, but I also sensed that he was trying to transfer their attention from me to him. My French wasn't good enough to stand up to close questioning.

'And I suppose you have half a cow in your coat?' sneered the German.

'Why should I have anything in *my* coat?'

This seemed to me to be a rather dangerous line of reasoning. I stared fixedly at my shoes, afraid even to breathe out.

' ... Well, as it happens I've got three pounds of butter, a dozen duck eggs, a pint of cream and some bacon. Care to have a look?'

I didn't dare to look up, but I heard the officer give a short, impatient laugh and tell the driver to start up the engine. He had dismissed Jack as an idiot who wanted to waste his time.

'You shouldn't have done that!' I said as the jeep drove away. 'You shouldn't have taunted them like that!'

My legs were shaking so much that I could hardly put one foot in front of the other.

'It worked, didn't it? I called their bluff.'

'This time, perhaps. But what happens next time?'

Jack grinned. 'Next time I'll think of something else.'

'Next time you'll push them too far.'

I thought of this incident again several days later when I was returning to the village by the same route, wondering how long we could go on living like this, on the point of being arrested. I wasn't even sure what we wanted all the money for.

I was in a particularly bad mood on that evening. It had been raining all day, a sort of icy drizzle peculiar to the region, and my clothes were damp, chilling me to the bone. Jack had been to the post office and on his instructions I had made the journey up to Fernand's place alone. It had been a wasted trip: Fernand was attending to a sick cow and had nothing for me.

My simmering frustration was compounded when I returned to the Lotys' house. I squelched into the back garden to check on our precious collection of fowl, only to find that one of the ducks was missing. There were no scattered feathers or signs of a struggle so I decided that the culprit was a human being rather than a fox.

'One of the ducks has been stolen,' I said to Jack, as I dragged myself up the stairs to the attic.

'Oh.'

He was kneeling on the floor, wrapping a large parcel, and didn't look up.

I went to warm myself in front of the fire. 'What's that?' I asked. 'What are you wrapping?'

He didn't seem to hear me, so I reached out and lifted a corner of the brown paper. It was my fur jacket, the one that Mireille had given me.

'That's ... *Jack*! What on earth are you doing?'

'The women in Paris want clothes,' he said calmly, knotting a length of string that had been used five, ten, maybe twenty times before.

'But that's *mine*!' I was so angry I could scarcely string a sentence together. 'It was in the cupboard, with my things. You had no right ..!'

'We could get two thousand francs for this thing,' he told me cheerfully. He pulled the string tight, then calmly held it up to me so that I would hold my finger on the knot, as I usually did.

That was the last straw. I knocked the half-wrapped parcel on to the floor, shouting, 'What do you want the bloody money for anyway? We don't *need* any more money. It's just greed – '

'And you've no need to hang on to something *that* woman gave you.' His voice was suddenly cold.

'Oh, I see! That's what all this is about, is it? You don't like the coat because Mireille de Vere gave it to me! Well how bloody childish can you get!'

Jack ignored this, and continued talking in the same cold, reasonable tone. '. . . But then you always were a little turncoat, weren't you? I suppose it comes of being a Conway rather than a Winstanley like the rest of us . . .' He smiled at me suddenly. 'Still, I suppose it's not your fault, is it . . ?'

The implied indulgence enraged me. I picked up the rusty scissors he was using and flung them at him. They hit a glancing blow to his temple, breaking the skin slightly.

We stared at one another, and it was hard to know who was the more shocked. Then Jack stood up.

'Keep the jacket if you like. But I doubt you'll want to wear it now.'

He picked up his overcoat and clogs and pushed past me.

'Where are you going?'

'Out.'

I decided to follow Jack.

It was a stupid thing to do, and I'm still not quite sure why I did it. Perhaps I wanted to get his attention, or perhaps I just didn't want to be alone up in the attic, with the wrapping paper and balls of string, and the wretched fur jacket.

It was dark, and the village street was deserted and silent except for the church bell, which tolled to mark the end of the evening mass. Zazou was there, siting on the riverbank as usual. He was scribbling in a notebook, though how he could see to write was anyone's guess. All I could see of him was the lighted end of his cigarette, a miniature ember in the darkness.

'He went that way,' said Zazou, pointing towards the church. Then he returned to his scribbling.

The last of the evening worshippers had not long left, and the doors of the church were still open. I looked up the lane past the church but there was no one in sight. The one bar in the village (run on an informal basis from the back of the *boulangerie*) was closed. Zazou could only have meant that Jack had gone into the church.

Perhaps he had a conscience after all and had gone to pray for forgiveness ...

Elise was in the church, too, and the two of them were far from praying. I remembered what Fernand had said about the girl's sudden fondness for attending evensong. So she stayed behind afterwards to meet Jack.

In the light of the last, guttering candle I could see that she was buttoning her blouse. Jack had his back turned towards me, but it looked as though he was making some sort of adjustment to his own clothing. Then he walked towards the holy-water stoup and scooped some up, to drink it. This gesture alarmed Elise, because she crossed herself. I was calm enough to think it somewhat foolish after the profanity she had just committed.

I walked back slowly to the house. Poor Madame Loty had had supper on the table for ages, and I registered the surprised expression on her face as I walked straight past her and up the stairs. I sat on the bare tiles and stared into the embers of the fire. The half-wrapped fur jacket was still where I had flung it, but I couldn't bring myself to move it.

I heard Jack come in and exchange a few words with Madame Loty. Then there was the dull thundering noise of his clogs on the stairs.

'You're not still sitting here moping are you, Kit..? Come down and have something to eat. It's ready ...'

I looked up at his face. 'You went to see Elise.'

He nodded.

'Doesn't it bother you?' The words came tumbling out in a painful flood. 'Doing something so disgusting ... using someone for sex ...'

'Is there anything so wrong with that? She enjoys it, you know.'

I flinched, and turned away.

'We all have these animal urges, you know. Even you, I suspect ... though you're far too virtuous to ever let a man touch you, of course ... not without a wedding ring, anyway.'

I stood up and stumbled into the bedroom, tears stinging in my eyes. Jack came after me.

'Go away ...' I sobbed, stumbling my way to the bed. The room was pitch-dark.

I could feel him behind me as I groped on the night table for the matches. I lit one and dropped it, my hands were shaking so.

'Kitty ...'

'... Just trying to light the lamp ...' I muttered. He was trying to take the matches from my hand. '... It's *all right*! I can do it ...'

252

His arms were already around me, pinning me against his chest. I squeezed the matchbox in my fist, trying to keep hold of a sense of reality.

'You think I don't care about you, don't you ... *don't you*? Look at me, Kitty ...'

I turned round, still clenching the matchbox. He kissed me, and it was wonderful, as wonderful ... no, more wonderful than it had been in my fits of useless dreaming.

'Jack ... Jack, I've got to tell you something ...'

'What?' I was about to express in some jumbled way that I was in love with him and always had been. But I couldn't. I just couldn't. My fingers slowly released their grip on the matchbox. It fell to the floor. We went downstairs and had supper.

The next morning, on waking, I went to retrieve my fur coat from the sitting-room floor. It had gone. Jack had decided to post it anyway.

Eight

As the winter wore to a close, Jack continued to flaunt himself in front of the occupying troops. The Germans in our corner of Normandy were making their presence felt more and more. Notre-Dame des Anges was a sleepy enough place, but one or two of the neighbouring villages had taken it into their heads to exercise some resistance. There were rumours of fires being started deliberately, home-made bombs being planted in German vehicles.

Jack sat in the village bar night after night, listening to these stories, and reported to me with great glee that he had tried to get the stolid inhabitants of Notre-Dame des Anges to stage their own act of resistance. Would he give them a hand if they were to plan it?, I asked and received the reply that of course he wasn't fool enough to get involved in all that underground business.

Given that Jack was always so keen to save his own skin, it seemed contradictory to indulge openly in an illegal practice such as black marketeering, virtually begging the Germans to arrest him. I could only conclude that he did it for a short-term thrill, or to induce a sense of danger that he had forsaken when he decided not to join the forces.

No mention was ever made of the night of my outburst, or the uncousinly way in which he had kissed me, but it was there in both our minds from time to time. That brief incident had gone some way to defusing the tension between us; as if we had both made some statement of acceptance of our situation, but now we had to be guarded, and more distant with one another, to prevent anything like it happening again. We became more like business partners than ever. But I felt that I had to watch over him the whole time, to try to keep him out of trouble, like some guardian angel. When he went off on an errand alone, I wondered if he would ever get back. I began to feel afraid of leaving Normandy, just for that reason, and yet I couldn't resign myself to sitting out the rest of the war here, playing conscience to my wayward cousin. When I had the energy left over, I fretted about Frannie.

I tried to ensure that Jack and I went out together as often as possible. One such occasion was an evening in March, when we took our latest consignment of produce to the post office to send it off to Paris. We were returning to the village at dusk, empty-handed after despatching the parcels, when once again we spotted a Gestapo car approaching.

Quick as a flash, Jack bent down and removed the thick woollen socks he wore inside his clogs. He screwed them up into balls, and stuffed them into the pockets inside his coat.

'Jack! what the hell . . ? '

His muffler was next, and the cotton kerchief he wore knotted around his neck. The result was that the contours of the long coat bulged as though the pockets were stuffed with the usual con-traband.

The grim-faced officer in the back of the car put up his hand, indicating that we were to stop. I did so, but Jack continued to walk past, flapping the sides of his coat. The German jumped from the car and grabbed him by the collar of his coat. With his other hand he twisted Jack's right arm back behind his body, forcing him to stop. He shouted a command to the driver, who came over and started to go through Jack's pockets.

The driver pulled out a woollen sock and held it up to his superior officer with a puzzled expression. Jack laughed out loud.

The German knew better than to continue with a game that was designed to humiliate him. Cursing under his breath, he pushed Jack away and jumped back into the jeep. Jack waved his sock at them as they roared away.

I was too tired to reprimand him this time, and said nothing as we walked back to the village with Jack whistling 'Onward Christian Soldiers' in my ear. I had become like a machine lately, thinking of nothing but eggs, butter and cream, packing parcels in my sleep. But I reflected inwardly that Jack's time was running out. He wouldn't be able to get away with it much longer.

They came the next day.

'*Mademoiselle!*'

255

I heard Madame Loty calling to me up the stairs. She sounded distressed. I hurried down to the kitchen. Through the open door to the parlour, which was only used for funerals, I caught a glimpse of the familiar grey broadcloth. Two Nazi officers stood in front of the fireplace.

'Do they want Jack?' I whispered. 'Where is he?'

'He's with the chickens. But it's not him they want to see, Mademoiselle. They asked for you.'

I went into the parlour with my heart pounding. I attempted a smile. The two men smiled back, and bowed. They had already removed their caps, to reveal short, smooth blonde hair. Both were young.

'Miss Olsen?'

They were using the name I had given to Kurt. I nodded and smiled again in a rather guarded way.

'We have a letter for you, from Kurt von Himpel. We were passing through Lisieux on official business, and he asked if we would deliver it to you.'

One of them handed me a letter and bowed again. He seemed to be waiting for something.

'Thank you ...' I said. 'Would you ... will you have some coffee?'

They declined, and I was relieved, not only to have spared Madame Loty the scandal of having Nazis entertained in her front parlour, but also to be able to get them out of the house before Jack came in and caused trouble. I asked them to convey my best wishes to Kurt, and went upstairs to read my letter.

My dear friend Ingrid,

It is now a long time since we have met, and I miss our walks and the sympathy you gave me.

As your devoted friend, it gives me pain to write to you and tell you of your cousin's continuing internment. She has been brought back to Paris for questioning, but I am now able to tell you that it is likely Francesca Gold will be sent to one of the resettlement camps. You know of these places, I think. I am reluctant in saying this to you, but it is sometimes possible for people to be released, with the correct papers.

You asked in your letter what has happened to her child. There is nothing in the records about a child of hers, and you must believe me when I say it is better if the baby did not survive. You know that I have seen what happens.

Soon I will return to Germany myself. I will see what can be done, though it is dangerous. In case your other friends have influence, I can

256

tell you that the Kommandant in charge of her case is a man called Liedke. He has recently returned to the house in Berlin, that he shares with his mistress. All of the SS knows of this Swiss woman: she is called Mireille de Vere...

I felt quite faint and for a few minutes didn't even read the rest of the letter. Was it so surprising, that Mireille should be in Berlin? I had seen her at a fascist rally in London, which was a strong indicator of her own sympathies. And once war broke out, was it so surprising that she should make her residence in Germany? It was just the sheer coincidence that almost knocked the breath from my body. Here was a chance, a final chance, to try to help Frannie. I had no choice but to take it.

I told Jack that I was going to try to go back to Berlin, but I didn't mention Mireille.

'You're a bloody idiot,' he said angrily. 'We don't even know that Lexi's still there. No good could possibly come of going back there. And that's assuming you get over the border. You're the one who's going to end up in trouble!'

'Maybe. But I have to try.'

For the next few days I went about in a state of fatalistic calm. I was sad to be leaving Notre-Dame des Anges. I decided to compile my own memento of the place, using my camera. I took a picture of the Lotys' cottage, and the bar frequented by the village elders, and the church. I took a picture of Zazou reciting poetry to the ducks on the village green. And I took a picture of Jack standing on the steps of the cottage with Madame Loty in her Sunday best. He had his arm round her and her embarrassment was making him grin. He had a spotted kerchief knotted round his neck, and his dark hair flopped over his eyes. That was how I wanted to remember him.

On the day that I was due to leave, Jack disappeared for the morning, supposedly on a job. A true Winstanley, he wanted no scene. I went for a last walk around the village, prolonging my departure. Finally I had to leave, in order to catch my train from Lisieux.

'Has Jack come back yet?' I asked Madame Loty, when I had collected my luggage (lighter now without the fur jacket).

'Oh yes, he came in, but he has gone out again.'

I had missed him. I expected no more, but my heart sank like a stone.

'He left this for you.'

She handed me an envelope stuffed with money; nearly a

hundred thousand francs. The scrap of paper wrapped around it said simply, 'Goodbye, darling Kit.'

I knew this time that I would never see him again.

I went to Paris first.

I was just in time to catch Charlie Olsen; who was returning to Minnesota. He seemed dispirited, dejected even.

'You can only go on so long in looking-glass land,' he said to me as we sat drinking absinthe at the Select. 'I mean with everything so upside down. You accept it all at first; it's like you're on the outside looking in, waiting to see who's going to win, the good guys or the bad guys. And then suddenly you can't take any more of the perverted morality of it all ...'

Like Jack, Charlie was sceptical about my plan to return to Berlin, but once again he agreed to try to help me. I stayed with him for a couple of days while we worked out the details. I still had, in my file of personal papers, Sieghilde's German identity card. Charlie, who wore spectacles himself, went and bought a pair of wire frames, then we set about dyeing my hair blonde again. We didn't dare go into a hair salon and ask for peroxide, so I had to use a powerful household bleach that made my scalp sting. It was a long and painful process that had to be repeated several times, but the end result was quite good.

Charlie arranged for a Swedish Embassy car to take me to the Swiss border. From there I was Sieghilde, and I was on my own. I said goodbye to Charlie with more bravado than I felt. I had no idea what I would find when I got to Berlin, and since the bombings it seemed quite likely that Lexi would have taken the children and gone to the country.

My reaction when the car dropped me at Basle Station was to vomit into a litter bin. All of me balked at climbing aboard that night train through Switzerland, remembering that other journey when I had clutched my German novelette and felt paralysed with terror. But this time it was easier: I was gradually hardening. A sleepy border guard glanced at my pass, and I managed to match his disinterested expression. I was dozing when the train finally pulled into the central station in Berlin.

For several minutes I just wandered about outside the station, trying to get my bearings. I had visited the city twice before, and it had been a different place on each occasion. But now it was unrecognisable. The German army were still omnipresent, like jumping, heel-clicking marionettes, but the grand buildings that had created the back-drop to the endless marching were gone. The Potsdamerplatz, the Opera House and the Memorial Church had all been razed by bombs, as had the Café Josty's roof-terrace, where I had danced the night away with Deacon in 1936. The pleasure boats on the Havel had been left to rot. And worst of all, amongst the ruins, the once-gay Berliners were scavenging in the rubble, looking for food.

I saw no sign of a bus or tram in those crushed, half-deserted streets, so I walked to the Grunewald. The von Russow house was still standing, though it looked a little dilapidated, with blistered paint and shutters hanging off their hinges. There was someone in the overgrown garden; a thin woman in an apron, hanging washing on a makeshift line. As she turned, her stringy hair clung against the nape of her neck.

'Excuse me, madam,' I said, in German.

The woman turned to face me, and I saw at once that it was Lexi. I had known this the instant I saw her, I just hadn't been able to admit it to myself.

She stared at me for a fraction of a second, then dropped the washing on the muddy ground and ran towards me with a sharp cry of disbelief.

She flung her arms round me and hugged me hard. Her body felt light and frail against my own, fattened for months on the rich diet of Normandy.

'God, I'm glad to see you,' she said, wiping her eyes quickly. 'I need you to give me a hand with all this dreadful housework.'

'What happened to Ilse?' I asked, as we stood at the sink scrubbing the handful of vegetables that were to be our lunch. Four-year-old Paul, dressed in distinctly dirty overalls, was pushing a train around on the kitchen floor, while baby Alexander screamed to be removed from his high-chair.

'Ignore him . . .' said Lexi, nodding in the direction of the baby. 'He has no consideration. He can see his poor old mother's trying to manage on her own . . . we had to get rid of Ilse and Fritz. It was becoming impossible for Hubertus to talk with friends here, we were having to be so careful all the time. Now at least we know there's no one listening when we're in our own home . . . Be careful that you scrub those greens thoroughly, Kitty, the city's crawling with typhoid.'

'And what about Hubertus's . . . job?' I asked.

'He's still at the Ministry, but as for the other thing . . . I don't

259

know . . .'

I saw the fearful expression in her eyes, but she just shrugged quickly and went on. 'A resistance group calling themselves the Rote Kapelle have just been arrested for conspiracy. Their work was linked to what Hubertus and his friends are doing. They've all been condemned to death for high treason.'

It was the nearest Lexi would come to admitting she was frightened.

'And what about the Jews? We heard in France that they'd been made to wear a yellow star on their clothes, but I didn't see anyone wearing one when I was walking here.'

'We call them the submarines,' said Lexi, smiling. 'Because they've all gone underground.'

Her tone was brisk, uncaring even. It was only when we were discussing the food shortages over supper that I discovered that the whole family was going short in order to help the Jews. Lexi and her friends went about every week, collecting spare food coupons for the 'submarines'.

I was woken that night by a massive air-raid. The only other time I had heard sirens in the night was in the boarding house in Bloomsbury, and when I first woke up I thought I was in London. London, Berlin . . . was there any difference any more, I wondered? In both places the bombs did not inspire fear so much as the will to survive. And the civilians struggling to survive in both cities were equally the victims of Hitler's war.

I was struck forcibly by this thought and lay awake on my bed for some time, pondering the pointlessness of it all. Like Charlie Olsen, I was falling prey to a sort of moral exhaustion. The more atrocities one heard of, the harder it was to respond to them with a proportionate sense of horror. I had always been blessed with a straightforward optimism, and the Christian teaching I had been exposed to in my church-going years at Russington had provided me with a fairly solid conviction as to the ultimate triumph of good over evil. Good, of course, meaning all things British.

But it had turned out that there were no such things as black and white, just a grey mass that we were all clinging to in our own different ways. And it occurred to me that we Winstanleys (I counted myself as one of them for this purpose) were involved in things which would be considered criminal and unethical by our enemies. What Charlie saw as a place beyond the looking glass, I just saw as a blur. I think at that moment I would have been quite happy to just lie there and wait for a bomb to drop.

'Kitty! Kitty, come down here!'

I became aware of Lexi calling me from the bottom of the stairs. I thought she wanted me to go down into the cellar with her, but instead she led me out into the garden to watch the raid, after first handing me a huge steel helmet that almost covered my eyes.

It was a moonless night and we couldn't see the planes, but we could hear and see the bombs as they fell. They were phosphorous bombs which glowed green as they exploded, emptying themselves down the shattered walls of the city, and along the streets in rivers of unquenchable flame, seeping down cellar steps.

'Isn't Irving a bomber pilot?' asked Lexi.

I nodded.

We both spontaneously burst into shouting. 'Hey Irv! Irvie baby!' we yelled up at the glowing, green sky, making a bizarre spectacle in our nightgowns and tin helmets. 'We're down here..!'

I couldn't afford to waste any time in trying to reach Mireille, but at first I was reluctant to discuss the matter with Lexi, who had problems enough trying to maintain sanity in her beleaguered household. So I told her I was going to take some pictures of the bomb damage and set out by myself to try to find where she was living.

This wasn't as random a task as one might have expected. I already knew from my last visit to Berlin that high-ranking SS officials favoured the exclusive suburb of Dahlem, on the western edge of the city. And as if to protect Hitler's chosen, the anti-aircraft guns were sited there in Domane Dahlem, pointing their blunt noses at the sky. Two young men wearing the red lapels of the anti-aircraft regiment were covering them with tarpaulins; they clearly weren't expecting a raid that morning.

Dahlem was exactly the sort of place that Mireille would live, I reflected as I wandered its wide streets. The luxurious villas were virtually hidden behind high walls, their driveways barricaded with iron gates. Several of the larger houses were guarded by uniformed soldiers. I smiled at one of them as I passed, the sort of smile that indicates you are not in a hurry, and willing to pass a little time in idle chat.

He looked up at me from his copy of the *Wermachtsbericht*, the daily war bulletin, and gave me a non-committal smile in return. The message was clear: I was young, female and reasonably attractive, he was bored and therefore not averse to striking up a conversation.

'It's a lovely house, isn't it?' I asked in the most convincing

German I could muster. 'It must be the one belonging to Komman-dant Liedke. What a great man he is – '

'No,' said the soldier, lowering his paper and shaking his head. 'You're wrong. Herr Liedke's house is that one, there.'

He pointed to a similar residence several doors down the street. 'You know Herr Liedke?' he asked, looking sceptically at my shabby coat and laddered nylons.

'He's a friend, yes.'

The guard shrugged and returned to the *Wermachtsbericht*. I approached Liedke's villa as nonchalantly as I could.

Quite unexpectedly, the tall iron gates opened with a clang, making me jump. A black Mercedes limousine slid out. I thought I could see a woman sitting in the back seat, but it was difficult to tell because the windows of the car were of dark, smoked glass. The gates clanged shut again.

I found a button connected to some sort of electric bell, and a mouthpiece to speak into. I rang the bell. Nothing happened. 'Hello!' I said into the mouthpiece.

There was a crackling over the intercom system and a voice said, 'Ja?'

'Hello!'

There was no further response. I continued to press the bell and rattle at the gates, but this time no one answered me.

Two heads are better than one, so I decided I would ask Lexi's advice on the matter of penetrating Mireille's villa.

But when I returned to the Grunewald, she had other matters on her mind. A thin, anxious woman was standing at the gate to the house, as though she was waiting for something, or someone. She had dyed blonde hair, like mine, with a line of black at the roots.

In the sitting room, Lexi was engaged in some sort of urgent discussion with a young man I hadn't met before.

'Kitty, this is Dieter ...' She added quickly, 'It's all right, Dieter, she's quite safe.'

I sat down on the sofa and picked up the tail end of the conversation, which seemed to involve Dieter trying to persuade Lexi to do some favour. I was instantly struck by her demeanour. I had never seen my cool, phlegmatic cousin looking so anguished or distressed.

'She could pass as an Aryan,' Dieter was saying. 'She could help you with your work about the house.'

'I *can't*, Dieter! If it were just Hubertus and I ... but I have to think of the children. It's just too dangerous for them if I were caught.'

'You'd better go and tell her your decison, then. She's waiting.'

Lexi nodded, and got slowly to her feet. She gripped the arms of her chair as she stood up, and I could see that the decision had caused her terrible pain, physical pain.

It turned out that the woman was a Jewess, who had fled from her apartment that morning when the Gestapo arrived. She and her husband wanted to shelter in Lexi's cellar. By refusing, Lexi was almost sentencing them to death: they had nowhere else to go. This thought must have been so overwhelming that when the woman asked quietly, 'What is your decision, *Gnädige Frau?*', she offered a compromise. She told the woman that she and her husband could stay for two nights, but no longer. After that time, they would have to find somewhere else. Their thanks, for those two pitiful days of grace, were more than Lexi could bear. She went upstairs to her room and would speak to no one for several hours.

During those two days, we took what food we could spare down to the cellar, but saw and heard nothing else from our guests. They must have been making superhuman efforts to be quiet, for our sakes. They left in the night, with no fuss, folding up the camp bed we had put there, and leaving the bedclothes in a neat pile on top of it.

That same night the Zoo in the Budapeststrasse received a hail of bombs, asphyxiating the flamingoes that we had admired in the summer of 1936. The noises sent the lions mad, and they had to be shot.

Nine

I returned on a daily basis to the villa in Dahlem, but had no luck in gaining admittance. There was simply no answer when I rang on the doorbell. The process became tedious and dispiriting, but I knew I had to persevere.

Late one afternoon, I was trundling over there on the rickety old 'M' bus, when the driver pulled over to the side of the road.

'*Alle aussteigen* – everyone off please.'

It was such a familiar cry by now that no one questioned it and, sure enough, there was the high-pitched whine of the air-raid siren and the distant booming of the anti-aircraft guns.

'God knows what they think there is left to hit,' grumbled one old man, as we all scurried to the nearest shelter. 'If they want targets, they'll have to start bringing them with them.'

I glanced up at the sky, wondering, as I always did, whether Irving was up there somewhere. There seemed no reason to believe he was any less safe up there than the rest of us down here on the ground: myself, Lexi, Jack, Frannie . . . if she was still alive.

Before I reached the bottom of the shelter steps there was a massive explosion, which sent me tumbling into the lap of a woman sitting on one of the narrow benches. She sat upright with her back pressed firmly against the wall and her capacious handbag – hallmark of the true German *hausfrau* – taking pride of place on her lap. On her head was a felt pork-pie hat, Bavarian style, its feather now coated with white dust.

Apologising as briefly as I could, for I was anxious not to expose my shaky German, I dusted myself off a bit and sat down beside her. The whole of the concrete dug-out rocked with the next explosion, making my companion close her eyes and mutter in annoyance, as though the whole affair were being conducted by a noisy group of workmen drilling holes in the road with no thought for public convenience.

When it had gone quiet again, she said comfortably, 'Well, we may be here another hour yet. And I'm supposed to be giving my Fritzi his tea.' She took a ball of grubby knitting wool from her handbag and started to crochet. 'A tray cloth, for my daughter-in-law,' she told me. 'They've just got married.'

I nodded, and since I could hardly sit in silence for another hour, I asked, 'Do you live near here?'

'Why yes, I live in Dahlem,' she replied, laying down her needles for a moment until the next series of tremors had passed. 'My husband, Fritzi, is inspector of sanitation for the entire city.'

'He must be a very busy man.'

'Too busy, at the moment, God bless him. What sanitation do we have left, I ask myself ..? And this wretched typhoid! It'll be cholera next, you mark my words!'

In full flow, her German was rather too rapid for me to understand, but I just nodded at the words I recognised and guessed at the rest. She was obviously disposed to chat, and I knew I had to take any opportunity that presented itself.

'If you live in Dahlem, then you must know Herr Kommandant Liedke?' I made the enquiry as casual as I could, and added, 'A dear friend of my family.' In as much as Mireille was related to me through marriage, this was probably true.

'Why of course I know the Kommandant, who doesn't? Such an eminent man ... Well, when I say I know him, I know *of* him. Not that they're there at the moment, of course.'

'Oh really?' My disappointment was genuine enough. 'I was hoping to visit them.'

Our conversation was interrupted by more whines and crashes outside, even nearer this time. The sanitation inspector's wife brushed the dust off her crocheting, which was dirt-coloured anyway. 'Oh, those Britishers!' she exclaimed, before continuing as though nothing, bar death, would impede the progress of her precious tray cloth. ' ... Yes, he and the young lady have gone away for a while, to his hunting lodge in the Black Forest. To escape all this bombing, one presumes.'

'What is she like? The Kommandant's lady friend.'

'Ah ... ' A smile came over the woman's face. '*Wie schöne, wie elegante!*'

I was sure now that I was right, and that the woman in question was indeed Mireille de Vere.

'A holiday in the Black Forest, how lovely! And how long did you say they would be away? I must make sure I visit as soon as they are back.'

The woman shrugged. 'A few weeks ... who knows? How long will this madness last .. ?'

The madness was over, for the time being at least. The all-clear sounded and we emerged, dusty and blinking, into an unrecognisable street. It was time for my companion and me to say goodbye.

'*Heil Hitler*!' she said, a trifle wearily.

'*Heil Hitler, meine Dame*,' I replied.

In automatic response, gripping her large handbag with one hand, she saluted. Was it really possible, I asked myself, as I watched her go, that eight years ago we had found it amusing when people shot their left arms out, like so many clockwork soldiers?

Mireille had left the city, and there was nothing I could do about it. Even I was not prepared to go looking for her, not this time. I resigned myself to waiting for her to return, which she surely must if her paramour was such an important official.

In the meantime I concentrated my efforts on helping Lexi and Hubertus in their daily struggle for a sane existence. Sympathetic though they were to Frannie's plight, they had to think of their own family first, and the problems of raising two little boys in a war-torn city.

Though she said nothing about it, Lexi continued to pass on some of her food coupons to the 'submarines', and with another adult in the house there simply wasn't enough to eat. Those tedious mornings spent queueing in the market at the outbreak of the war seemed like times of plenty now.

'I could try to get a job,' I suggested. 'Then at least we'd be able to buy more on the black market.'

'Too dangerous,' said Lexi firmly. 'You're an enemy alien, remember? Hubertus tells me off for even letting you go out of the house.'

'Then perhaps I should at least find somewhere else to stay. I don't want to put you and the boys at more risk ...'

'I need you here with me,' said Lexi, equally firmly. 'Hubertus can't avoid being drafted for ever, you know, and he reckons he's just about at the end of his run of luck. He'll probably end up being sent to the Russian front, and then where would I be without you? I'd never manage.'

I felt quite sure that Lexi was resourceful enough to manage in any circumstances, but I said nothing, instead continuing with the daily round of scraping meals together. It was amazing how time-consuming it could all be now, putting tea leaves to dry on the radiator so that they could be used a second or third time, trying to find ways of making vegetable stews taste interesting, forcing the boys to drink the juice of crushed raw onions, the only source of vitamin C that we could find.

For the rest of the summer the bombs continued to fall, mutilating, suffocating and burning the inhabitants of Berlin. For some reason this destruction became part of a landscape, and less hard to bear than irritating, minor inconveniences. We ran out of toilet paper, and had to use newspaper instead, on which page after page was chequered with black crosses, each one recording the death of a soldier.

'I bet you never dreamed you'd end up wiping your behind on dead Germans,' Lexi said to me with a wicked grin. Turning down the Jewish 'submarines' had been a low point for her, her helplessness affecting her strongly, but since then she had remained cheerful, never losing sight of her irreverent sense of humour. And yet in so many ways she had changed. Who would have imagined the languid, ravishingly beautiful debutante scrubbing clothes in a solution of carbolic until her hands turned red and raw, humping bags of coal through the streets, even sitting up with her children all night when they were sick?

I was thinking about this after a particularly disturbing raid, during which shrapnel splinters had rained down on our roof all night.

'Such a nuisance!' Lexi had commented over breakfast. 'I've just been out to take a look, and we've lost at least half a dozen tiles. Still, we won't be able to get anyone in to fix it, so I'll just have to get up there myself.'

'Don't you ever feel bitter?' I asked, as I helped her prop the ladder up against the side of the house.

Lexi removed a handful of nails from her mouth, so that she could answer. 'Nope. Not really. Pass the hammer, Kit.'

'... I mean, here we are, I'm twenty-two and you're still only twenty-four... I thought we'd be spending these years living, really living, not just existing. They're supposed to be the best years of our lives, after all.'

'If you really want to know...' said Lexi, twisting on the rung of the ladder so that she could face me. 'I feel more alive now than I ever have. I know it sounds dreadful, with so many people suffering

'... Look, Kitty, I have to confess that before the war, I behaved in a certain way on purpose. I mean, I wanted people to see me as an enigma, but inside I was just a blank.'

I nodded, to show that I knew what she meant.

'I think about when we were growing up a lot,' she went on, 'and all the time we were at Russington, it was as though I was somehow being prepared for something, in training for something really big, something that would make me feel like a whole person. And this is it. I mean, this must be it.'

I remembered a conversation I had had with Charlie Olsen when I first arrived in Paris, and asked, 'So are you happy? Is that what you're saying?'

'I worry a lot,' said Lexi, taking a nail and driving it into the edge of the roof felt with great care. 'About Hubertus and the boys mainly. And I do want the whole business to end, yes. If only for proper lavatory paper ... But when I'm not worrying ... yes, I suppose I'm happy, in a way.'

There was a sort of happiness to be found amid the deprivation of war, I was discovering that. It was the happiness brought by tiny things. Seeing the looks on the faces of the boys when Hubertus brought home some sour cherry jam for a treat. Finding potatoes growing underneath some rubble. And talking to the Berliners we met while we scavenged for food amongst what used to be houses. Walls were blown in, blown out, and sometimes – much to the delight of Paul and Alexander – the front of a house would be blown off completely, exposing the contents. They looked like large versions of the dolls' house we had in the schoolroom in Russington Hall.

Lexi and I became attached to one fellow scavenger in particular, an elderly man. He would be out there every day, combing the very same streets that we walked through with the pram. At first this seemed a coincidence, but it gradually became clear that he was lonely, and the little chats he had with us were his only form of human contact.

The most notable thing about this bent little old man, with his brown, weatherbeaten face, was that he spoke no German at all. He would nod, and smile, and raise his battered trilby, but shook his head when we addressed him in German. We tried French, and English, but again came the polite shake of the head.

Then Lexi hit on the brilliant scheme of trying Latin. We had so loved the subject in our schoolroom days, refusing to treat it as a dead language and perversely insisting on Latin conversation classes, with Miss Howland's encouragement. Our skills were a bit rusty by now, but we could remember simple nouns like 'house', 'soldier', 'war', and verbs like 'raze', 'burn' and 'attack', even if our declensions were a little inaccurate.

'Good job our unseens were all about battles and warfare,' observed Lexi. 'Though it would be handy to know the Latin for "potato".'

Mainly we were pleased that our idea worked. The old man seemed to recognise the words we were using and replied in kind, though I suspect his vocabulary was based on the Bible rather than Kennedy's *Latin Primer*. It turned out that he was a Latvian refugee, terrified to speak in his native tongue lest he be discovered and deported. Once it would have amazed me that Berlin was preferable to where he had been before, but not now.

One day I was alone on a scavenging trip and, after straying beyond our usual haunts, decided to take a bus home. This was less because of the distance involved than because the bombing removed familiar landmarks and made it impossible to keep a sense of direction. The bus drivers seemed to know where they were going.

I was staring out of the window at the rows of frontless houses when I spotted a familiar figure walking along what was left of the pavement. My heart missed a beat. Could it really be ..?

'Stop!' I shouted to the driver. 'Stop! I have to get off!'

I jumped from the still-moving bus and raced down the street after her. I had slowed down, but was still breathless when I reached her.

'Mireille! It's me ... d'you remember? Kitty Conway. From England ...'

She looked up at me from beneath the brim of her hat. It was artificial straw, but a hat nonetheless, and veiled at that.

'Why yes ...' She looked shocked, but managed a smile. 'My dear Kitty! Of course I remember.'

Her English was more heavily accented than I remembered. 'And what brings you to Berlin – of all places?'

The enquiry, though polite, was guarded, and she continued to walk fast as though she wanted to get away.

'It's a long story ... can we go somewhere and talk?'

'I really don't know, Kitty ...' She frowned. 'I'm very busy.'

She was ahead of me now, acting as if the conversation was finished. I grabbed at the sleeve of her coat. 'Please.'

She seemed to change her mind quite abruptly. 'All right,' she said, smiling. 'Why not? We'll go back to my house for some coffee and cake. I asked the car to pick me up on this next corner, so we'll just wait here ... ah, here it is!'

We climbed into the back seat of the black Mercedes and the driver, who wore SS uniform, took us back through the bomb-scarred streets to Dahlem.

'I do hope you understand why I was being so cautious, Kitty,' Mireille said in that lovely, musical voice of hers. 'Only you don't know who you can trust these days, do you?'

The gates of the villa opened and the car slid inside. I nodded. I was going to point out that it was surely different with one's family, but decided that this would be a little tactless given the circumstances in which she had left Russington eight years earlier.

A maid appeared in the hallway and took our coats, and Mireille's hat. I stared, as she removed it. Underneath the elegant little straw she was wearing her red-gold hair in thick plaits twisted round her head, the favoured style of the *Nazisse*, the devoted female Nazi. That heavy coil of hair looked grotesque on top of her delicate, fine-featured face.

'I've just been to the hairdresser.' She smoothed her plaits. 'It's so very difficult to find a good one these days ... '

She was staring at my own two-toned locks, which Lexi had tried to make more acceptable with a coloured rinse.

'Let me show you around a little, then we'll go and have that coffee.'

I was treated to a full-blown guided tour of that hideous house, which from the inside was not at all the sort of residence that one would imagine Mireille choosing. The big, gloomy rooms had metal-studded doors, a profusion of modern lamps and over-varnished nineteenth-century oils in bright gold frames. The strangest thing of all was that Mireille seemed so proud of the ghastly place, so proud that it made me feel uncomfortable. Behaving like a suburban *hausfrau* didn't suit her, and she didn't seem comfortable in the role either, glancing at me nervously to see how I reacted to everything she showed me.

Most eery of all was the hovering presence of her SS lover, never mentioned, but there wherever you looked. A pair of shiny black boots in the hall. A man's gloves on a table. Mireille showed me the bedroom, smoothing the pink satin bedspread with one hand and asking me what I thought of it. But I was transfixed by the sight of two robes hanging from the back of the door, a fine cambric negligée clinging thinly to a man's paisley dressing gown. I longed to find out about her relationship with this man, but I felt inhibited about mentioning him in casual conversation, knowing what I was going to have to ask.

Mireille had picked up a pair of burgundy leather slippers and was stroking them as if they were pets. She arranged them neatly at one side of the bed, the side where *he* slept, presumably.

'Have I shown you the dressing room?' she asked in the same bright, chatty tone she had employed throughout the tour. '... I *must* show you the dressing room ...'

I went in there after her, trying to ignore the suits and dress uniforms, concentrating on the Beautiful Things I had once coveted so much; the silk blouses and cashmere suits, the puppy-soft vicuna ...

Someone had been buying her furs; I could see at once that her collection had expanded. For some reason I didn't want to look at them, let alone touch them as I was invited to.

Mireille caressed the sleeve of a sable. '... Of course, you share my weakness for fur, don't you, Kitty? I remember that. I gave you a fur jacket didn't I? When Beattie ...'

Her voice trailed away.

'It still gets a lot of wear,' I told her, which seemed a most satisfactory interpretation of the truth. It very likely did, by whoever Jack had sold it to.

'Let's go and have that coffee ....'

We sat in the drawing room underneath an oil painting of hunting dogs tearing a hare to pieces. The smell of the coffee almost made me faint: it was the real thing. Lexi and I had to dilute a couple of beans with several pints of water, and that was only for a very special treat. There were shortbread biscuits with the coffee. I ate three and sneaked two into my bag to take home for the boys.

Mireille probably saw me do this, but she made no comment. After all, the entire population of the city was near starvation, why shouldn't I be? She sipped her coffee slowly, waiting for me to speak.

'I wanted to talk to you about Frannie,' I said, staring at the clouds of scented steam that drifted from the pot.

Mireille poured me another cup. 'Go on ...'

'She was living in Paris and got into some trouble ... she was arrested by ... by the secret police.'

'What sort of trouble did she get into?'

'She was married to a Jewish activist.'

'I see ...' Mireille's hand shook and she put the coffee pot down hard on the tray. For a moment she seemed to have forgotten my presence. I cleared my throat.

She smiled. 'So why do you think I could help?'

'Your friend ... Herr Liedke ... was in charge of her case.'

'I see . . . ' She hesitated slightly. 'And you think that I could talk to him about this?'

Why was she being so wary? Why couldn't she just say, yes, she'd do what she could to help? As if she could read my thoughts, Mireille went on. 'Of course something must be done . . . poor dear Frannie . . . you must leave it with me, and I'll try to arrange something. We are family, after all.'

'I'll come back tomorrow then?'

'Not tomorrow; it's too soon. Next week, perhaps.'

Another week . . . But I forced myself to smile, and thank her warmly. Mireille showed me out herself. There was a room off the hall that I hadn't been shown round on the tour. Its metal-studded door was ajar, and I automatically glanced through. Some sort of trophy room, I thought. I looked again, quickly, as Mireille was drawing back the bolts on the front door and fetching my coat.

They were not trophies at all, those shapes that were mounted on the wall. I was so horrified I could not speak when Mireille bade me goodbye. I kissed her, silently, and she stood on the doorstep waving. With her other hand she smoothed her coil of plaits self-consciously.

That was all I could think of on the way back to the Grunewald. That stark, ghastly contrast. Mireille the *hausfrau* with her golden plaits. And the bizarre instruments of torture on that wall in her home: the whips, the manacles and the chains.

I unlocked the front door to the sound of the children screeching. They were in the sitting room, fighting over a tin fire engine. Lexi didn't seem to notice them. She was motionless on the sofa, staring out into the garden.

'Hubertus has been arrested,' she said.

'Oh no . . . '

I went towards her, but she turned her back on me and buried her head.

'Lexi . . . don't cry.'

'I'm not crying!' She flung me a hard, despairing look. 'What use are tears?'

I stumbled from the room. Later I was unable to remember going upstairs or climbing on to my bed. But I must have done, for I found myself staring at the square of the window pane. It was dusk.

How long have I lain here? I can't remember . . .

Something has happened . . .

I thought, for some reason, of Frannie and Simon.

No, not that, something else, something just as bad. Hubertus ...

When I went downstairs, I found Lexi more composed. I went to the cupboard under the stairs where the emergency supply of plum brandy was kept, and poured us each a glass.

'You'd better tell me what happened.'

'What I know ...' Lexi sighed. 'I was out in the middle of the town with the boys ... there seemed to be a lot of troops around the place, more than usual. And they weren't just marching about aimlessly the way they usually do, they were going into buildings as if they were looking for someone ... I just stood and watched them with all the other passers-by, never dreaming ...'

I pushed the brandy glass into her hand, and she drank some. 'Paul ...' She turned to the two little boys. 'Will you take Alexander upstairs and show him his building bricks? You know how he loves you to do that.'

'But Mama – '

'Just do as I say, Paul.'

When the children were out of earshot, she went on. '... Then I saw that the government buildings in the Wilhelmstrasse had been cordoned-off. People watching were starting to whisper about an attempt on Hitler's life ... I went straight back home and switched on the wireless. They interrupted the music with an announcement saying that a plot to overthrow the Führer had been successfully foiled. A bomb had been planted, but the Führer had only sustained a few scratches. Then they read out a list of people who had been arrested ...' Lexi's voice trembled. 'I recognised the first few of them, and that's when I knew ... and then I heard the announcer say it, as if he was reading a cricket score. Baron Hubertus von Russow.'

'Surely there's some way we can find out what's happened? He may just have been questioned.'

'A friend of Dieter's, a lawyer, is going to look into it for me. Dieter said he might be able to help me.'

At five-thirty the phone rang, and I answered it. 'Dieter, it's you! Thank goodness. We've been going crazy here waiting to find out what's happened to – '

Lexi was waving her arms wildly, mouthing something to me. 'Tapped ..! The phone's T-A-P-P-E-D ...'

I immediately assumed a non-committal voice. 'You want to speak to Lexi? She's here ...'

'The cases are being "progressed" at the Gestapo H.Q. in Prinz Albrechtstrasse,' Lexi said slowly, when she had hung up the receiver. 'He says if I go down there I might be able to find out something.' She didn't sound very hopeful.

I insisted on going with her, so we left the boys at a neighbour's house and set off straightaway. Lexi was dressed in her best coat and hat, and wearing lipstick for the first time in months.

'Might as well put one's best foot forward, as Mummy used to say . . .'

She was unnaturally cheerful all the way to that grim, grey building. Only when we reached the top of the steps did she falter slightly. She put her hand on my sleeve to hold me back.

'Do you remember what we were talking about the other day? Well the answer is, I *was* happy, before this happened.'

Ten

The Gestapo building in Prinz Albrechtstrasse was silent and deathly cold. Along its dimly lit corridors, the faintest gleam of arc-lights filtered from beneath padlocked doors. At its centre, a huge, echoing lift shaft descended into the cellars.

'Go home, Kitty,' said Lexi, as soon as we were inside. It was the first time I had ever seen her really scared. 'I don't think I want them asking questions about you, too.'

'There isn't a lot of point worrying about that now – '

'Go, Kitty, please. Go home and take care of the boys. I think it's better if I do this alone.'

I hated leaving her there, but I could see that she was right. Questions would be asked about me, and that might only make things worse for Hubertus. I bathed the boys and put them to bed, then sat waiting in the twilight.

It seemed as though most of the past four years had been spent like that – waiting.

'*What did you do in the war, Mummy?*' – '*I waited, dear.*'

The ticking of the clock over the fireplace began to infuriate me. I buried it under a cushion. To fill the silence, I switched on the wireless.

I recognised the voice that was speaking, and it turned my flesh cold. It was Adolf Hitler himself, affirming his intention to continue with his task.

'I will continue with my work, since Providence has spared me ...'

I switched the dial to 'off', preferring the silence. It was dark now. I tried to calculate what time Lexi might be back. Did they have a time for closing the building? Probably not. And they kept you waiting for hours in these places, just to demoralise you ...

I dozed off, and woke again when I heard the front-door key turn in the lock. It was one o'clock.

'Lexi?'

For a moment I forgot everything in my sheer relief at seeing her. It had crossed my mind that she, too, would be arrested as a sympathiser.

Then I looked at her face, and I knew that things had not gone well.

'Make some coffee,' she said quietly. 'Then I'll tell you about it.'

I brewed up a precious couple of beans to make a thin, pale brown liquid. I still had Mireille's shortbread biscuits in my handbag, and I fetched those too.

'Where on earth did you get these from?' Lexi asked. She stared at the biscuits as though she had never seen such extravagance before.

'I'll tell you later. First, I think you ought to talk. Otherwise you'll never sleep.'

Lexi nodded slowly. Her face was grey and puffy. 'They called him Herr Kriminalrat, the man I had to go and see ... rather appropriate, don't you think? "Criminal Rat". I kept saying it over and over again to keep my mind off things ...'

Lexi's eyes were wandering around the room as she spoke, unable to focus on anything. 'How dare they,' she said suddenly. 'How *dare* they do that to other human beings?'

I stroked her hand, hoping she wouldn't feel my own trembling. 'Come on, Lexi,' I cajoled. 'Start at the beginning.'

'... They have numbers, all those rooms. They told me to go to room 453. The windows were all boarded-up and it was so stuffy ... no air in there at all ... And those lights, the arc-lights. They fix them to the ceiling and shine them in your face so that you can't think straight. I told them to turn them off. Not asked, told. But they didn't. The Criminal Rat was horrid, of course. Shaved hair and piggy blue eyes. And horrible blubbery lips. He asked me to give my name. Then he said, "You're English, aren't you?"'

'"No", I said. "I'm German. A German citizen." I kept saying that over and over. It was the lights, that's what they do to you ... Then I thought, Come on, pull yourself together, what's he going to think? So I told him, very politely, that he'd made a mistake. That Hubertus and I weren't interested in politics, and never had been. He listened to everything I said, smiling at me on the other side of the lights. "That was a very nice speech, Baronen von Russow," he said. "Very charming. Now let's consider the facts."'

'He reached into a drawer and took out a file with Hubertus's name on it. Everything was in there, Kitty, everything. The names of all our friends: Dieter, Reinhard, Hilde … when they came to our house for meetings. All compiled by informers, I suppose.'

'The Bauers?' I asked.

Lexi nodded slowly. 'It would have to be. Only they would know some of the things that we did. It was all there in minute detail. Transcripts of all our phone calls. He even quoted some of the things Hubertus had said about the Führer, word for word. You were in there too, Kitty … your visit at the beginning of the war, anyway. I don't think they know about now. The fact that Paul was attended by Professor Meyer. It even mentioned Hubertus giving someone a lift to the Jewish hospital once, years ago …'

'What did they say … would happen to Hubertus?'

'His case would be "looked into", but that doesn't mean anything. Then the Criminal Rat started asking me questions. I asked for a glass of water and he said, "Of course", as if he was a waiter in a restaurant, but they didn't bring it. He asked questions about Hubie's job, and his family. I knew they were doing it to check my answers against his, and I knew that if I gave the wrong answer it would prove he was lying, but there was nothing I could do about it.'

Lexi stared down at the uneaten biscuit on her plate. 'I don't mind telling you, Kitty, I was frightened. I was really frightened.'

'Come on,' I said gently. 'I think you ought to try to get some sleep.'

I helped her take off her coat, which she was still wearing. As I pulled the sleeves away from her arms, I saw marks, red weals, on her wrists. A horrible thought hit me for the first time, turning me cold from the inside out.

'Lexi …' I whispered. 'What else did they do to you?'

But she wouldn't say.

Lexi was placed under 'house arrest', which meant that she was not to leave the central Berlin area.

The house was almost certainly being watched, too, which created problems for me. The knowledge that I was already on the Gestapo files was frightening; and we could not afford to give them any further ammunition to use against Hubertus. I would have to become a 'submarine' myself, and cease to exist. Any excursions from the house would have to be made after dark, and even that was unadvisable.

I made an exception for my return visit to Mireille's villa, leaving the house a little before midnight. Somehow the fact that I was visiting the home of a fully paid-up member of the SS made me feel safer. There had been another onslaught of bombings that week, so the streets were deserted.

I distracted myself during the walk to Dahlem by wondering how I was to get past the gates. I could see myself standing there pressing on the bell, ignored or unheard, perhaps even intercepted by a guard.

As it turned out, I was saved from any of these possibilities. Just as I turned into the street where Mireille lived, I was passed by the black Mercedes limousine. The gates of the villa were open to admit it, and I ran in after it.

The driver held open the passenger door, and Mireille stepped out. She was alone, dressed in a full-length evening gown and fur stole. Diamonds sparkled at her throat and in her hair.

I felt a surge of anger. Mireille had been out at some function, dancing the night away with the leaders of the Reich, possibly even with the Führer himself, while ...

'Mireille ..!' I called after her as she ran up the front steps. 'Mireille, wait ...'

'Kitty! What are you doing here?' She was annoyed, glancing round to make sure the driver hadn't seen me.

'I'm sorry, this was the only time I could come.'

'You'd better come in. But you can't stay long. It's ... not convenient.'

I took this to mean that Liedke was expected. We went into the ugly sitting room and Mireille poured us each a glass of schnapps. She alternated sipping hers with rubbing face cream on her neck and shoulders, from a small pot she had taken from her evening bag.

'You should never let your skin get too dry,' she said firmly. 'Especially not at my age.'

I speculated about how old she was, but it was impossible to tell. Forty possibly. She looked no older now than she had when she first made her appearance at Russington Hall.

'Did you manage to find out anything?' I asked, emptying my own glass in one gulp.

'Not yet, no.'

'Mireille, please, Frannie's life is at stake!' So was Hubertus's now, but regrettably I didn't feel I could plead for him too, not yet.

278

'You must be able to do something to help, you could ask – '

'Listen to me!' Mireille stood up abruptly and walked over to the shiny, too-new grand piano next to the window. She sat down at the keyboard and played one chord, in a minor key.

'Kitty, my dear, you must understand that nothing is as simple as it appears from the outside.'

I recognised that gently elusive tone she had used on us when we were children and annoyed her with our games, our questions. 'There are many things to be considered here ... such things aren't just asked ...'

'Not even for Frannie?'

Outside, the gates opened with a loud clang, admitting another car. A headlamp beam swung across the window, making Mireille's diamond clips sparkle with brilliant light, illuminating her startled expression.

'You'll have to go, Kitty! Quick!'

I went towards the front door.

'No! For God's sake, not that way!'

I was bundled through the kitchen and found myself standing in the back garden, just as the front door had slammed. I went round to the front of the house. I could hear their voices. Mireille's and a man's.

I was reluctant to leave with my business so unsatisfactorily resolved, but was there any point in waiting for a second hearing at this late hour? I hovered uncertainly by the side wall of the house, waiting to see if its occupants were about to go upstairs. It was just possible to discern the glow of a lighted room through the blackout.

A second light was switched on downstairs. By its position I calculated that it was in the little room off the hall, the room whose walls were decorated with instruments of torture. I heard Liedke's voice and knew he was in that room. The actual words were indiscernible, but he made a short, barking sound as if he was giving a command.

My curiosity about what went on in that room was overwhelming. If I crouched beside the window, with my nose level with the sill, I could just see in, through an inch-deep gap below the blind. Mireille was leaning on the back of a chair. I could see a section of Liedke's body, from the neck down. He wore a black SS uniform with silver facings. The tunic was covered with ostentatious medals for valour; silver swords, golden oak leaves decorated with precious stones. Months of over-eating while the rest of Berlin starved had made him stout, and the silver buttons were strained.

I watched with fascination as his plump hands fastened a pair of iron cuffs around Mireille's slender wrists, chafing on her diamond bracelets. The action must have excited him, for his hands trembled. He moved over to the wall where his instruments were displayed and when he returned he was holding a cat o' nine tails. He trailed it over the naked flesh exposed by the back of Mireille's gown. Then he brought it down hard, with a stinging blow.

Her head was bent, and I could see the expression on her face. It was resigned, passive. The submissive little *hausfrau*. That was what shocked me most of all. That and the way she stood so very, very still.

I sank down on to the grass, unwilling to see more. I don't know how long I sat there, perhaps ten minutes, perhaps an hour. I was jolted back into reality by the downstairs lights being switched off. Seconds later, a light appeared in the bedroom window. I stood up, stretching my stiff limbs, thinking about the long walk home. But first I had to overcome the obstacle of the front gates, which were now firmly locked. There were just enough footholds for me to scramble up one side and down the other, a task made harder by the constant need to avoid being seen.

I had just reached the pavement, and crossed on to the other side of the street, when I heard the scraping of a key in a lock. Squinting through the darkness, I saw a figure on the other side of the gate I had just climbed. The gates were unpadlocked, opened to let out the cloaked figure, then locked again from the other side.

The escapee was a woman, a slender woman carrying a parcel in her arms. She darted off down the street, keeping to the shadows cast by the high villa walls.

'Mireille!' I called. 'Mireille ... stop! Where are you going?'

I tried to go after her, but she had already vanished into the night.

For the next four days I had other concerns.

For four days, confined to the house, afraid to leave the telephone, Lexi waited for news of her husband. She was like a caged animal, trapped and impotent. Most of Hubertus's friends had also been arrested, and those who hadn't were afraid, or unable, to help.

And like a caged animal, she lashed out at anyone and everyone who came near her. Her sons' childish antics irritated or enraged her, and I was berated for causing trouble, worsening Hubertus's chances, placing them all in danger with my stupid schemes.

There was no point my reminding Lexi that it was she who had asked me to stay, on both of my visits to Berlin, and that I had risked myself for her. Her irrational anger was born out of fear, and the terrible tension that hung over that household. And I knew better than to urge her not to think the worst. Instead I concentrated on keeping the boys out of her way as much as possible, and on ensuring that meals appeared on the table three times a day. The latter was a trial in itself, as we were very short of food. I couldn't go out for more, and Lexi wouldn't.

On the fourth day of this nerve-torturing existence, the telephone rang. It rang three times, then stopped, before Lexi could answer. This small event seemed like a sign, and for the rest of the day we sat silently in the sitting room, just waiting. The ticking of the clock grew louder and louder until it completely dominated my consciousness and I was relying on its rhythm for my breathing.

Tick ... TOCK ... tick ... TOCK ...

When the phone rang again, I jumped out of my skin. Lexi answered. She didn't say anything, she just listened. I was too cowardly to look up, to watch her reaction. I heard her replace the receiver, then she ran past me and out of the room. I heard her bedroom door slam and lock. Then she started screaming: just screaming and screaming and screaming.

For a long time she wouldn't unlock her door, and when she did, she was unable to relate the contents of that phone call. It was several days before I learnt that Hubertus has been tried by the *sondergericht*, the summary court, and sentenced to death. There was no possibility of appeal. The sentence was carried out straightaway. Hubertus made a speech to his SS interrogators, which was recorded in his file. He quoted the New Testament – 'He died that we might be forgiven'. He and his fellow conspirators were dying to absolve the sins of the Nazis, he said. Then he was hung from a meat hook. They filmed him while he was dying.

I went out of the house when I heard this, ignoring the fact that it was daylight and I was supposed to be hidden. I wandered the shattered streets, just staring, unable to think or feel. I met our little Latvian and he walked beside me, respecting my silence. There had been a very heavy raid the night before, resulting in record loss of life. Near the remains of one decimated house we came across a charred corpse, blown right out of its bed. It lay there in the tattered remnants of striped pyjamas, spread-eagled on the road, staring sightlessly at the sky.

The old Latvian looked down at the corpse, and he smiled.

'*In paradisum*,' he said, in Latin.

The look on his face was one of envy.

*   *   *

281

If I ever reached breaking point during the war, it was on that terrible day when I heard the news of Hubertus's death. All my frustration and rage against Hitler's regime boiled to the surface and spilled over. I paced the house until darkness had fallen, then slipped out and almost ran to Dahlem, ignoring the air-raid-warning sirens and the muffled explosions. This time, I was not going to take no for an answer.

I ran to Liedke's villa and rattled on the gates, pressed frantically on the bell, shouted into the intercom; anything to get myself heard and admitted. After a few minutes the front door opened and Mireille herself walked down the drive to unlock the gates, ghostly in an ivory satin peignoir. She didn't seem surprised that I should be there, howling the place down like that. She just gave me a little nod and led me into the house.

She put a finger to her lips as we went in. 'He's upstairs.'

I shuddered at the thought of Liedke up there in the pink satin bed. I had still not set eyes on his face but I could picture his body, stout in its pyjamas. Perhaps he had a selection of his 'toys' up there with him, and I had interrupted his ritual humiliation of Mireille.

We went into the kitchen at the back of the house, and Mireille lit a single candle.

'If I'm gone for long, he'll come down looking for me. You'll have to be quick.'

I opened my mouth to begin my tirade, but she said suddenly, 'I know about Lexi's husband. I'm very sorry.'

'Are you?' I asked bitterly. 'Look, what exactly is going on here, Mireille?'

'Nothing. Nothing's "going on", it's just I – '

'I asked you a favour, a favour that could possibly mean saving the life of a member of your family. That's if you're really who you say you are. I'm beginning to wonder if you really are Beattie's cousin after all, or whether you're just some sort of con-woman who goes around wheedling her way into other people's families ...'

I said all this so fast that I rapidly ran out of breath.

'I am Beattie Winstanley's cousin.' Mireille spoke calmly.

'Then why on earth are you acting like this? Avoiding the issue. Putting me off. Sneaking around town in the middle of the night. I'm sure there are certain proprieties to be observed when you're an SS moll, but I don't believe you couldn't have done *something*, asked some questions, found things out ...'

I picked up the candle and held it up squarely between us, so that I could see her face better. 'So come on now, what's the answer?'

I was remembering the Truth Game at Russington, and so was she. She had been asked about a certain phone call she had made, and had lied about it. It seemed the most obvious thing in the world to recall the refrain from that uncompromising game.

'Tell the Truth now, Mireille.'

She sighed, and hung her hed. '*Ich bin Jude* – I am Jewish.'

She lifted her face, and the candle's glow lit up an age-old mixture of fear and defiance. 'My mother – the one who married into your Aunt Beattie's family – was born a Polish Jewess. The rest of the family emigrated to America, changed their name from Verowska to de Vere. They helped raise me, paid for my education, gave me a place in society. But Mama was widowed young and went back to live in Europe, in Switzerland for a while, then with her sister in Vilna. She went back to her old ways, speaking Yiddish ...'

'And you pretended not to be Jewish?'

'With the war coming, it seemed the best thing to do. I even joined the fascist movement.' She laughed. 'I thought it would stop people asking questions about me. I went to Munich and was introduced by friends to high-ranking officials in the National Socialist Party. I was invited to Berlin, and I stayed here after the war broke out ...' The expression on her face grew sombre again. '... Then Hitler introduced the Nuremberg Laws and I was trapped. I have two Jewish grandparents, I am officially a Jew. What could I do, but go on pretending?'

I was staring at her dumbly, my head swimming after this extraordinary confession. Clues from the past came together in my mind like the pieces of a puzzle. There were a thousand things I wanted to ask her.

'But Mireille – '

There were footsteps on the landing, a heavy tread.

Mireille blew out the candle.

'You'll have to go now. Meet me tomorrow night, at about one, on the corner at the end of the street. I'll be able to explain more then. Oh, and Kitty – '

She darted after me to the back door. 'Bring as many cigarettes as you can lay your hands on.'

'I want to go home,' said Lexi the following day. 'I just want to take the boys and get out of this place.'

For a long time she had barely spoken at all. Now she was harping constantly on one theme – returning to Russington.

'You know it's not possible to go back to England,' I reminded her as gently as I could. 'You're a German citizen with a German passport.'

'I could smuggle myself in.' Lexi was wearing her most stubborn expression. 'You managed to get in here and out again. Twice.'

'But I didn't have two children with me, have you thought of that?'

'I'm sure they'd let us in. And if they didn't, then Nim would know someone important in the War Office. He'd sort it out.'

It was a sign of Lexi's desperation that she, usually so pragmatic, should romanticise the power and influence of an eccentric country squire. Or perhaps she had just forgotten what he was like. It was five years since she had set eyes on any of her family other than myself. And Russington itself, once a place we couldn't wait to escape from, had turned into a symbol of peace and sanctuary.

'And while Nim was trying to "sort it out", you'd let them clap you in jail, like they did with the Mosleys? What would happen to Paul and Alexander then?'

I was playing devil's advocate, since no one could have understood better than I why Lexi felt the need to put Berlin behind her. I was simply worried about her being strong enough to endure the journey home, with all its potential difficulties. Her courage had been undermined by Hubertus's dreadful end.

'You're not going out *again*?' she said when she saw me getting ready to go to my meeting with Mireille.

I nodded, dreading what she was going to say next.

'Oh, Kitty, please don't! Please don't go out and leave me here on my own, tonight, you know how I hate it ... '

She was holding my sleeve, using all her strength to stop me leaving the room. 'When I'm in bed ... I hear things ... '

I tugged my arm away. 'I have to go, Lexi, I'm sorry. Just this once. I won't go again, I promise.'

Hating myself for leaving Lexi to her nightmares, I set off on the now all-too-familiar trek to Dahlem. On the way I passed the bombed-out house where we had seen the burnt corpse. It had been taken away, but someone had left a makeshift wooden cross to mark the spot. Probably the old Latvian man.

Mireille was waiting for me, dressed in trousers and a cloak. (Had I ever seen her wearing trousers before? – surely not.) We didn't speak as we walked, except for Mireille asking me if I had brought any cigarettes. I had managed to find a few in the house, in a packet that had belonged to Hubertus. I had taken them without asking, but I was sure that Lexi would want as few reminders as possible. They had been bought before the war, anyway, and were undoubtedly stale.

We walked for miles and miles, right to the edge of the city, which was now a wasteland. An old warehouse was still standing, its windows all blown in. Mireille led me down some steps into the basement, where the water tanks and yards and yards of heating and ventilation pipes were housed.

She switched on a torch that she had in her bundle. 'Mama?'

The beam fell on a huddled figure, an old woman. She wore a man's boots, grotesque at the end of her stick-like ankles. Hunched round her shoulders was a fur coat, which I recognised as one of Mireille's cast-offs.

'This is my mother,' she said simply. Then she pointed to me and launched into an explanation in Polish, her voice low and gutteral. Her mother nodded.

We sat down on the floor beside her and Mireille unwrapped her parcel, which contained bread, meat, cake and matches, and several dozen cigarettes. I added mine to this substantial pile.

'Is she really going to smoke all those?' I asked, looking at the tiny old woman.

'She doesn't smoke them,' said Mireille, without the merest trace of irony. 'She lights them and watches them burn. It's a way of passing the time.'

Mireille's mother turned her attention to the food, tearing at it greedily in a way that was embarrassing to watch. Mireille lit one of the cigarettes and proceeded to smoke it. 'It's easier for us to talk here.'

'Go on . . .'.

'When Poland was invaded in 1939, Mama and I both thought it would be safer if she came to me in Germany. And with a third of the population now dead or in camps, well . . . ' She shrugged and took a puff of her cigarette. 'She's been in hiding since 1942, since the Jews were forced underground. So now you see why I couldn't be seen to go to the authorities about Frannie. I had to protect Mama. For the last few months, anyone asking favours for Jews has had their own family history investigated by the *Rassen-forschungsamt*, the Race Investigations Office. In the end they would have found I was half-Jewish and it would have made it impossible for me to go on helping Mama.'

She made no mention of the deportation that would surely have befallen her.

'What about Liedke?' I asked, unable to contain my curiosity. 'Surely living with someone like that – '

'It's the perfect cover. And I'm lucky, I'm blonde, the way he likes them.' She put her hand up to touch her ugly plait.

'But Mireille . . . the other night, when I was leaving the house, I looked through the window . . . I saw him beating you.'

She nodded, quite calm. 'He's a sadist, it's well known. But he never goes too far, and I think it's a small price to pay for the protection his position gives me.'

As she lifted her cigarette to her mouth, I saw the red weals on her wrist.

' . . . Besides, what I have to put up with is nothing next to the suffering thousands are going through every day. Why should I complain? As long as he thinks I like it . . . I'm safe.'

I shuddered.

'About Frannie . . . ' She went on. 'I can't plead her case, but I do know the right official forms that would release her. I can forge Liedke's signature. It's just a question of stealing the bits of paper.'

She looked dispassionately at her mother, who was cramming a piece of cake into her mouth, crumbs squeezing through her gnarled fingers. '*Po malu, Mama, po malu.*'

A tiny glimmer of hope flared inside me, but died as quickly. 'But you couldn't do that. If you were caught – '

'If I'm caught, I'll be shot.'

Mireille took an exquisite lace handkerchief from her pocket and gently wiped her mother's hands. She lit a second cigarette and handed it to the old woman, who held it upright, staring in fascination at the glowing amber tip. Her lips worked rhythmically as she repeated something over and over to herself in Polish, some sort of song or verse.

Mireille turned back to look at me. 'I'll do it. If you want me to take the risk. But it has to be your decision.'

Eleven

'Are you all right, Kitty?' Lexi asked as we sat down to our meagre breakfast the next morning.

I nodded, and she did not pursue the matter even though I must have looked far from all right. Lexi had enough to preoccupy her, picking up the fragments of her shattered life and maintaining a stoic front for the sake of the boys. They were too young to understand her grief and were confused by her alternate bouts of snapping or ignoring them and her tearful embraces, loving and punishing them all at once. And of course Lexi had even less money now than she had before Hubertus was arrested.

I mumbled some excuse and left the breakfast table. The sitting room was empty and silent, except for that eternally ticking clock. In a fit of impatience I picked it up and hurled it to the floor, before flinging myself down on the sofa.

How was one supposed to solve such a dilemma? What perversity had inspired Mireille to do such a thing; to put me in a position where I had to choose one life over the other? If I accepted the papers for Frannie, I was putting Mireille at risk of her own life. But if I refused Mireille's offer on those grounds, I was condemning my beloved Frannie to the same fate.

Voices from the past, from Russington, came back to me then. They were saying *Choose good, brave Frannie over selfish, vain Mireille*. But for the past few years I had been plunged into a world where the straightforward duality of good and evil no longer existed. Frannie had turned her back on her family and her home. Mireille was prepared to risk her own neck to shield her ageing, helpless mother.

287

I ripped a sheet of paper from an old magazine on the table, and found one of little Paul's coloured crayons. I started to scribble; drawing a schematic diagram of all the protagonists in this dilemma with arrows indicating the links between each. Next I tried rearranging the diagram into an equation that would fit, one in which no one would lose. I stared at the diagram until my head ached, finally screwing it up and throwing it in the direction of the broken clock.

There had to be *some* way...

Mireille had told me to phone the villa at six o'clock, when she would be at home and waiting for my call. Since Lexi's phone was still tapped, I was not to ask for her by name, but as 'the lady of the house'. And I was simply to say, yes, I accepted her offer, or no, I refused it.

'Is ... the lady of the house there, please?' I said when a woman who was not Mireille answered.

'She is not here.'

I had not been prepared for this possibility. Mireille had given me her assurance that she would be there, waiting.

'Are you sure?' I persisted. 'Madame is expecting my call.'

There was a strange sound on the end of the line, a stifled gasp. 'No ...' The maid almost whispered. 'No ... she cannot ...'

The receiver was hung up abruptly.

I recalled what Mireille had said to me the previous day. '*Unless anything happens, I'll be there ...*' Something was wrong, that much was plain.

I broke my promise to Lexi and left the house, before it was dark. The maid's voice had frightened me, and I negotiated the mounds of rubble that had once been streets as rapidly as I could without drawing attention to myself. After taking several wrong turnings, I came to the warehouse where Mireille's mother had been concealed.

It was empty. The cast-off fur coat lay in a rumpled heap on the ground. The pathetic pile of cigarettes, arranged neatly in rows, had been crushed by a heavy boot.

I ran all the way to Dahlem and flung myself against the iron gates, gasping for breath. The Mercedes was gone, and most of the windows were shuttered. I pressed the bell and rattled the gates.

'Hello ..! Mireille, are you in there ..? Let me in ..!'

There was no response.

'YOU'VE GOT TO LET ME IN!' I screamed at the top of my voice.

Eventually the maid appeared on the front porch. She stared at me for a second, then walked down the drive to unlock the gates and let me in. She was crying and frightened.

'Where is she?' I demanded. 'Where's Mireille?'

The girl shook her head and wouldn't speak to me.

'I'm her friend,' I said gently. 'Don't you remember? I came to see her here once before.'

The girl nodded, and gestured for me to follow her up the carved wooden staircase. We went into the bedroom. Mireille was lying there on the pink satin coverlet. Her lovely red-blonde hair had been released from its plait and was fanned out around her face in waves.

I knew at once that she was dead. There was no mistaking the waxy pallor, the rigid stillness. I walked slowly to the bed and looked at her face. Her mouth sagged slightly to one side. There was a bullet wound in her left temple, black with coagulated blood and surrounded with powder burns.

The maid stood at the end of the bed, sobbing into her handkerchief.

'Who did it?' I asked. 'Who shot her?'

She went to the chest of drawers and took out a small ivory-handled pistol, wrapped in a lace handkerchief. She handed the gun to me for inspection, then mimed holding a gun to her own head and pulling the trigger.

'She shot herself?'

The girl nodded.

I shook my head slowly and turned back to look at Mireille's body. I was numb, and with something much more disturbing than mere shock. What sort of strange game had my life been caught up in? I had been asked to decide which life to save and now both lives were over – in Frannie's case as good as over. I didn't even know what I had phoned Mireille to tell her. I hadn't been able to reach a decision, and now I didn't need to.

The maid had fetched a sheet, and was hovering with it, indicating that it was time for me to say my last goodbye and go. There was an arrangement of white carnations on the dresser; I took one and laid it across Mireille's hands. Then I unfastened the little gold and pearl brooch that was holding my scarf in place, and pinned it on Mireille's nightgown, just above her heart. The maid pulled up the sheet, covering the face.

Once this ritual had been performed, she relaxed a little. 'You must go now,' she said firmly, and led me down to the hall.

At the foot of the stairs we both glanced upwards, in the direction of the bedroom.

'Are you Kitty?'

'I'm Kitty, yes.'

The maid reached inside her overall and took out an envelope. 'Earlier ... before she ... she said if Kitty comes, give her this ...'

I was reaching for the envelope, but she held on to it. 'Please ...' she said, frightened again. 'Please, in God's name, you must promise me *never* to say that I gave this to you, or they'll shoot me, too ...'

The envelope contained no letter, no note of farewell, no explanation. Just the papers for the release of F. Gold.

It was time for me to leave Lexi and the boys.

This time there was no decision to be made, no choice. I had to take the papers to Paris, it was as simple as that. Lexi understood and didn't complain, but this made my defection all the more painful. At the actual farewell, I was stiff and unemotional. I was getting too used to this, saying goodbye to my flesh and blood without knowing if I would ever set eyes on them again. Paul and Alexander cried; Lexi and I remained stubbornly dry-eyed.

Once more I was to travel as Sieghilde, but this time I was too weary to feel afraid. The brown uniforms of the SA were becoming a rarer and rarer sight, a sign that the military tide was turning. Besides, the train headed for Lucerne and Besançon was so crowded that no one was in a position to pay any attention to a frumpy Nazi spinster in wire-rimmed glasses and wearing a woollen hat to cover the two inches of dark roots on her scalp.

In fact the journey was quite a jolly one, definitely the most enjoyable I had made during the war. The train was full of troops who were being transferred from the Russian front in readiness for a rumoured Allied invasion. They were the last recruits of the war; boys little older than Clem. I sat with them on the floor in the corridor, sharing their bottle of peasant kirsch and playing a card game calls *skat*. The border guards assumed I was some sort of camp-follower and didn't even ask for my papers.

The train arrived in Paris early in the morning, and I went straight to the detention centre in St Denis. The doors didn't open until nine o'clock, so I sat on the steps and ate my way through three almond croissants. There was still food to be had in the shops of Paris – at a price – and I still had my share of the black-marketeering profits; hundreds of francs in grubby notes stowed away in my washbag.

I couldn't quell a slight tremor of excitement when the doors were finally opened and I was shown into a waiting room outside the superintendent's office. There was a real possibility of seeing Frannie, and soon.

'These papers have come from Kommandant Liedke, in Berlin.' I addressed the man in French, hoping this would enhance my neutral role. 'I am a friend of his. He asked me to deliver them to you personally.'

The superintendent took the envelope from me with a faint smile. He had thin, mousy hair scraped back from his forehead, and aquiline features.

'I see . . . ' He held the form up to the window and scrutinised the signature. 'I'm afraid somebody is going to be very disappointed.' He didn't look at me as he spoke. 'And you have had a wasted journey, *mademoiselle*. The detainee in question was moved several weeks ago, to a work camp . . . in Germany.'

'Are you sure it's the same F. Gold? Can't you at least – ?'

With the same faint smile he threw the form on to the floor and spat on it, to show his contempt for the forgery. The interview was over.

I dragged my heavy heart around the city for hours, unaware of the passing of time, of the people on the streets or the sights around me. Finally, when it was starting to grow dark, the problem of a bed for the night forced its way into my consciousness.

Charlie Olsen had left Paris and returned to the United States. I thought of Kurt. He would help, if he could. I walked to the brasserie where he and I used to meet and sat there for two hours. Eventually a group of German soldiers came in, among them one or two I recognised. I went over and asked them if they knew where I might find Kurt von Himpel.

Curious eyes took in my bedraggled appearance. 'Kurt's gone,' they told me. 'He's been posted back to Berlin.'

The only other place I could think of was Hélène Monnier's apartment in the *seizième*. The chances of her still being there seemed small; after her experiences the last time I was in Paris she was talking about taking the children away to the countryside somewhere. Even so, I lumped my suitcase all the way to the Place de Triomphe and up the four flights of stone steps in her apartment block. If the worst came to the worst, I would just sleep here, on the landing.

But Hélène was there. I heard a rattling sound as she put the chain across the door and opened it a crack to say, 'Who's there?'

'It's me, Hélène ... Kitty Conway.'

'Kitty ..?'

The door was flung open and Hélène stood staring at me, first with disbelief, then with joy.

'Kitty! I was hoping so much you would come back, but I never thought ... oh, I can hardly believe it!'

Quietly, so as not to wake the girls, Hélène brewed a celebratory pot of coffee and we sat talking. I told her as unemotionally as I could about the atrocities of Berlin. She took my hand in hers and held it while I allowed myself the indulgence of crying a little over Hubertus and Mireille.

'... And I was thinking I would never see *you* again, but then when the message arrived for you, I wondered – '

'Message? What message?'

Hélène looked surprised, then puzzled. 'I thought you must have known about it. Did you not leave this address as a contact point? That's strange ... '

'What happened?'

'A man came to the door with a message for you. He – '

My heart leapt. 'Who was it?'

'He wouldn't tell me. He just said he was delivering the message on someone else's behalf. He said that if you ever came to Paris again, I was to tell you to go to a place called Notre-Dame des Anges, where someone would be waiting for you ... '

Jack. It had to be Jack, didn't it?

I allowed myself the merest whisper of hope as I trudged my weary way to the Gare Montparnasse and caught yet another train, to Lisieux.

From there, there was no way to reach Notre-Dame des Anges except by walking. I knew the road so well I could have made the journey in my sleep, which was just as well since I hardly had the energy to put one foot in front of the other. A farmer took pity on me and gave me a lift for the last few miles, riding in the back of his truck with the pigs.

The village hadn't changed, except for the absence of Zazou's black-clad figure on the riverbank. I felt I should be changing into my work clothes and clogs and tramping up the lane to see if

Fernand had any butter.

Madame Loty shed a few discreet tears when she saw me standing on the doorstep, wiping them away with the corner of her apron. Even Monsieur Loty left his domino game and came to pat me on the shoulder.

'We knew you would come back, didn't we, Henri?' said Madame as she bustled about making me a black coffee laced with calvados. 'But we told him not to worry, we'd get in touch with you somehow ...'

'Am I supposed to meet someone here, is that it?' I asked.

Madame Loty shook her head, smiling. 'Not meet someone – there is someone already here, waiting for you to come.'

I smiled back at her 'You mean ..?'

She took the steaming coffee cup out of my hands. 'Go up to the attic and look.'

I ran up the stairs. There was no sound coming from the attic rooms. 'Jack ..?' I opened the door of our sitting room. It was deserted, the grate raked out and dusted. I went into the bedroom.

There was a Moses basket on the cherry-wood bed. As soon as I saw it, I understood. Two tiny, flailing fists were just visible over the rim of the basket. I lifted up the precious bundle and held it close. It was Frannie's baby.

Madame Loty showed me the note that had been pinned to the baby's vest.

'Her name is Beatrice. Take her home to Russington.'

Beatrice. So Frannie had named her for Darling Beattie. That was her way of apologising. I couldn't stop looking at her. She had a shock of dark hair like Simon, but the little snub nose and the worried look around the eyes were pure Frannie. I stroked her cheek with one finger as I carried her downstairs.

'So where's Jack?' I asked Madame Loty, confused.

She turned away from me and started chopping up a cabbage with quick, angry movements. 'They took him away, those Gestapo. He was just selling a little butter and meat, where's the harm in that? Loty and I asked. They said it was punishable with imprisonment, or if he didn't cooperate ...'

I clutched the baby to me, unable to move or speak.

'... They wanted him to name people in the area who'd sold him the food. He wouldn't. He was shouting and cursing at them when they took him away. "I'll never tell you anything, you bastards," he said to them, didn't he Loty?' There was pride mingled with the pain in her voice.

I knew better than she did that Jack wouldn't let principle get in the way of saving his own skin. But it wasn't beyond the bounds of possibility that he would defy the Gestapo out of sheer bloody-mindedness.

'How did Jack know about the baby?' I asked. 'And how on earth did he manage to send her here?'

But Madame Loty couldn't answer my questions. 'I don't know any more than you do. It happened after Jack had been taken to Paris by the Gestapo. Loty and I just had a letter saying that there would be a parcel arriving for us at Lisieux station on a certain day. She was there in the station-master's office waiting for us, the poor little mite ...'

Frannie had been in Paris, and her baby was probably born there. Jack had been taken there too. There was some connection there somewhere, but I had to admit that I didn't know what it was. I'd told Jack about my lodgings with Hélène Monnier; he must have tracked down the address.

I took baby Beatrice with me to Paris and set about arranging my last journey of the war. I made my way to the International Red Cross building, where a kind Swedish lady arranged a passage on a boat from Dieppe. As an afterthought I asked her if she could find out what had happened to a British prisoner called Jack Winstanley. She promised to try, but told me as gently as she could not to hope for a miracle.

Little Beatrice's introduction to Russington Hall was an echo of my own, some fifteen years earlier.

I phoned from Finstock station and asked if someone could collect me. The Motor was sent; the same Motor that I had ridden in when I was eight years old, and in the same condition. I didn't recognise the middle-aged man who was waiting for me outside the station entrance, not until he removed his cap and said, 'Hello, Miss, welcome back.' It was Tony, our childhood idol, invalided out of the infantry.

The garden was as chaotic as ever; worse if that was possible, since the death of the blind Tyler. At least he had managed to mow the lawns. Now the grass stood knee-high.

'It's a bit of a mess, isn't it?' said Tony apologetically. 'Only they've got barely any staff at all now. Her ladyship even has to do her own cooking.'

Tony left me at the steps and took the Motor back to the stables.

I walked alone into the hall, and stood looking up the stairs, as I had done that first time. There was no Flash to greet me, but I could hear the familiar sound of voices raised in argument; Clem and Shoes I supposed.

My aunt appeared on the landing and immediately hurried down the stairs to embrace me..

'Kitty, darling ..! Oh, thank God ... Poor darling girl, what's happened to you ..? You're as thin as a bean-pole.' She wiped the tears from her cheeks and made an effort to be brisk, practical. 'We'd better take you into the kitchen and find you something to eat ...'

She saw the Moses basket at my feet.

'Your granddaughter,' I said simply. 'Beatrice.'

Darling Beattie examined the sleeping face, and I knew that, like me, she had seen the resemblance to her daughter. She scooped the baby up into her arms and held her close, murmuring to her.

'Ernest!' she called, in the direction of the drawing room. 'Ernest, look who's here!'

Nim appeared; a greying, tired-looking Nim. My aunt handed the baby to him.

He held her at arm's length, frowning. Then suddenly there were tears running down his cheeks and I knew that Frannie had been forgiven at last.

Part
FOUR

Aftermath

One

'A lot of people were very angry with you, you know.'

I was sitting on the bed in Shoes's room, as she smoked an illicit cigarette. She stood by the open window, blowing the smoke outside, and every so often she would try to disperse the lingering clouds by flapping her arms, making her ponytail flap to and fro wildly.

The smoking was all part of the seventeen-year-old's attempt at sophistication, as was the padding she brazenly stuffed into her brassière. The war had made her tougher, older than Frannie and I ever were at her age. I was amazed by the way she talked about men. She had long since progressed from Mickey, the innocent GI, and was spending her evenings in the company of a thirty-year-old motor mechanic, with whom she confided she went 'nearly all the way' ... 'but don't you *dare* breathe a word to Mum, Kitty. She thinks I go out to WVS meetings.'

'Why were they angry?' Falsely casual, I let my gaze wander round the room at the pin-up pictures of Clark Gable, Montgomery Clift and Laurence Olivier. ('My ideal man. Isn't he absolutely scrummy?') As if I didn't know.

'Because you just went off like that, to London, and then went abroad without saying anything, for months and months and months ...'

'Eleven months,' I told her. Two months in Paris, then seven months in Normandy, then another two in Berlin. I was amazed when I added it all up. Was it really that long? Now that I was back in England, the whole period seemed telescoped into the very briefest moment. This was reality now, the brown-tinged roses dropping their petals all over the paths as the summer of 1943 came to an end.

'I couldn't exactly pick up a phone and say how I was,' I explained. 'Most of the time I couldn't even write a letter.'

As I spoke I was examining the truth of this statement. Charlie Olsen could have got a message through to London without much difficulty, or perhaps one of Jack's mysterious contacts. The truth was that I hadn't really tried. Because reassuring the family at home hadn't seemed important enough. And because, perhaps, they had turned their backs on Frannie, so I felt that it served them right.

'I stuck up for you, though, Kitty ...' More puffing and flapping of smoke in the direction of the window. 'I told them whatever it was was probably an emergency, and that you had no choice but to go and do it. I said you were being selfless, not selfish.'

I smiled at her. ' Thanks, Shoes.'

She liked to be known as Isolde now, in keeping with her new sophistication, but I was allowed the privilege of using her old nickname. The mechanic, I learned, called her 'Izzy', which she disliked.

'If you ask me, the thing that made them crossest was you not telling them you'd got engaged to James Bleak-Wailer.' *Puff puff, flap flap.* 'Mrs Bleak-Wailer blabbed about it after you'd gone, and Mum's nose was out of joint because she didn't know about it first. Then James and his whole family were on to us every five minutes wanting to know where on earth you'd got to. They must have thought we'd sold you to the White Slave traders.'

I laughed as I imagined the scandalised conversations going on in the Peake-Taylors' drawing room, over the watered-down sherry.

'Poor old James ... fancy being engaged to someone who doesn't exist!'

Shoes stubbed out her cigarette on the windowsill and tossed it into the flower bed below. She groped underneath the bed for her handbag, and popped a peppermint into her mouth. ' ... D'you think Mum wonders why I'm always eating mint imperials?' She offered me one before they were put back in her bag, then, pushing the sweet into her cheek, she asked, 'What about you and James, then? Have you gone all the way together?'

'I'm not sure if James is that type of man.' I hedged. I had no desire to discuss my relationship with my absent fiancé. I had no convenient response to questions that I couldn't answer to myself. I hadn't even got round to taking the engagement ring out yet, and putting it on my finger where everyone now expected it to be.

I changed the subject. 'If you and this ... this mechanic—'

'Billy.'

'If you and this Billy go nearly all the way, what happens when he ... well, when he comes across the padding in your bra?' I added quickly, 'You don't have to answer that if you don't want to. It is a bit personal ... '

''Sall right.' Shoes slurped on her mint, 'It's quite simple really. I wait till the last minute, then before things really get going, I make some excuse to slip into the little girls' room, then I just whip it out.'

'Doesn't he ... well, doesn't he notice the difference?'

'Are you kidding?' Shoes heightened her scorn with one of her fluent American accents. 'He's only a bloody man after all, isn't he?'

There were several letters from James awaiting my arrival at Russington. The sight of them was enough to made me feel guilty. They started off in the sort of tone one would expect from a man newly-engaged to a girl he claims to have admired all his life. Then, as he heard nothing from me, they became impatient and finally despairing.

Interspersed with his reproaches and concerned enquiries after my well-being were lengthy accounts of his daily life as an administrator in a big military unit in New Delhi. The fact that he was safe and sound behind some desk, not slogging it out in the jungle, irritated me beyond belief. He was in no immediate danger at all, which took the edge off our affair for me. I had assumed that a fiancé abroad in the forces meant danger, the front line, a threat to life and limb. How typical of James to be working in an office, doing nothing more dangerous than flirting with the wives of superior officers at cocktail parties or buffet luncheons!

To say I wanted James conveniently killed off would have been stating the case too strongly, quite apart from the fact that such thoughts made me feel rotten and wicked to the very core of my soul. But I had to admit to myself that I had accepted his proposal in the belief that it would never develop into marriage, that something would happen between now and consummation which would erase that very possibility. And the most obvious scenario was the noble war hero, taking a bullet in his chest just as he is about to return and claim his bride.

With a self-pitying sigh, I picked up my pen and prepared to do my duty.

30th August 1943
Russington Hall
My dear James,

A thousand apologies! You must have been so worried – I am sorry. By now you will have received a letter from your parents, explaining something of what has happened to me during the past months.

I just felt I had to do something to try to help Frannie. You do understand, don't you James? Now I have to face the fact that I largely failed, which is very hard for all of us. She is being held in an internment camp and there is no foreseeable way of obtaining her release until the war's over.

I say 'largely' failed - there was one very positive outcome. Frannie had given birth to a daughter in Paris, who was rescued by her friends and brought back by me to Russington. I will tell you more about that when we next meet.

Your descriptions of life in New Delhi are very interesting. How on earth do you cope with that heat? I don't think I could. I particularly enjoyed the account of the party at the governor's house. Did your friend Rupert go on and win the polo match, or did you lose your bet? Rupert and his fiancée sound very nice; I'm glad you've made some good friends out there. I can't help feeling that life in Oxfordshire is going to seem very dull after the hectic social whirl you've been used to in India.

By the way, I would have said yellow, rather than blue, for the upholstery in your drawing room.

I've been back a few weeks now, and I'm more or less getting used to the idea of being here, though it was strange at first. The family are quite well, though not quite as well as one would like. It's the same for everyone, four years of war has tired us out. My Aunt Beattie manages wonderfully, considering she's down to almost no domestic help at all, and now has a baby to supervise as well. My uncle's managing to keep the estate ticking over – but only just. I think the whole thing has become a big worry to him, though he's not the sort of person who would ever say so. I think that once the war is over he'll decide to sell off some of his land. Aunt Grizelda is rather poorly these days, and can't really walk, but we push her into the garden in her wheelchair, which she seems to enjoy. Isolde has finished her education now and is putting all her efforts into being the local vamp, but Clem is about to go back for a new term. The whole school has been evacuated to a former convent on the South Downs. Apparently last term the little horrors discovered a cache of nuns' undergarments, which must have provided them with enough smutty dormitory talk to last weeks!

In these past few days I've been giving a lot of thought to the question

302

of what I do next. The prospect of staying here at Russington, doing nothing, fills me with gloom. I really want to go back to London and see if I can get my photographic career off the ground, but there is an unseen moral pressure for me to stay here at the moment, as though running off again so soon would be letting the side down terribly. So here I am, for the duration, and I shall just have to find something useful to do with my time. Whenever I get the chance, I give Beattie a hand with the baby; little Bea as she is known. It's my way of trying to make amends. I can't quite shake off the mantle of the black sheep, as though by going to Paris after Frannie I took things into my own hands when I had no right to. Of course, nothing is ever said.

I stopped myself at that point. I was straying on to philosophical ground that I would rather stay off. I took the black velvet ring box from the bureau and laid it, open, on the desk in front of me. I did not put the ring on my finger, but used it as a sort of talisman to inspire me to the right fiancée-like ending.

I picked up my pen and crossed out the last two sentences.

... I look forward to hearing from you again soon. You are much in my thoughts.

Love, as ever, Kitty.

A few weeks after I had written this letter, Irving's plane was shot down over the Channel.

The news was good, however. He had managed to bail out and was later picked up in the sea. The doctors treating him expected him to make a full recovery from his injuries; chiefly burns. In October he was transferred from the military hospital near his unit to a nursing home in Kent, and we were told that he would be home with us in time for Christmas.

Darling Beattie was delighted. Here, at last, was a situation that she could feel at ease with, not one that would cause her social embarrassment like the exploits of some of her offspring. No, here was her eldest son, a dashing RAF pilot wounded while gallantly serving king and country, returning to his childhood home a hero. And what was more, he was bringing a *girlfriend* with him to meet his family.

'She's called Margaret,' Darling Beattie announced with a serene smile. 'We know nothing about her people, of course, but I trust Irving's taste implicitly.'

Had we been in possession of a fatted calf, no doubt we would have killed it. As it was, we were reduced to scratching a cele-

303

bratory meal together with whatever odds and ends we could find. The domestic arrangements at Russington were in a sorry state. For the first time in her life, Darling Beattie was in charge of her own kitchens. They had always been a little untidy in Cook's heyday, now they were positively sordid.

Apart from spending time in a makeshift darkroom, developing my war pictures, I had not yet found myself profitable employment, so I was appointed to the role of Beattie's handmaiden. The afternoon of 21 December, the day before Irving's return, found us in the kitchen together losing our tempers over the preparations for the meal. The kitchen waste was heaped up in buckets beside the back door and the estate cats were prowling round them, looking for scraps.

My aunt was poring over a book of 'Favourite Wartime Recipes'.

'I thought we would make some sort of a meat loaf ... ' She spoke without conviction. 'It says here that it will allow us to use all sorts of ingredients that we already have. Is that the best plan, d'you think dear?'

I shrugged. 'I suppose so.'

Beattie tied on an apron to cover her clothes; a lilac tweed skirt and a shapeless cardigan of Nim's with leather elbow patches, both already smeared with dubious stains. She rummaged in the fridge and brought out a plate with some week-old bacon stiffening on it and a couple of hard-boiled eggs that were grey at the edges.

'These can go in ... and I'll just put this scrag end that Mr Kingley gave me through the mincer ... Cook always said it was easy to do ... '

While she fumbled with the package from the butcher, the joint of beef slid from its greasy wrapping paper and fell on to the floor, which after scant attention from the one remaining maid was coated with crumbs and dust and dog hair. Flash's replacement (an aggressive border collie called Ripper) was the first on the scene, his tail wagging chaotically with disbelief. Beattie calmly removed the meat from his jaws, wiped it down with a cloth and crammed it into the mincer.

'Since we've got plenty of eggs, I thought we could do a lemon meringue pie ... what d'you think darling? Do you know how to make a lemon meringue pie?'

I shook my head.

'Oh well ... I'm sure we shall muddle through. Perhaps you would go down to the cellar and find us something to drink with dinner tomorrow. Ernest said he'd do it, only I know if I leave it to him he'll be mean about it ... '

I obliged her in this task, selecting a couple of bottles each of a dry white and a very respectable '29 claret, along with a bottle of vintage Heidseck. The food will be a disaster, I thought, so we might as well have something decent to wash it down with.

Back in the kitchen, Beattie was throwing herbs indiscriminately into her meat mixture; sage, marjoram and cat-mint.

'Do you want me to do something about vegetables?' I ventured. 'We've got heaps of potatoes. I could make a dish we used to eat in Normandy, *pommes dauphinoises,* you just slice up the potatoes very, very finely—'

'No thank you dear. I don't think that would be suitable, do you? Not French food. It's not as if we've met this girl before ...'

Little Bea, ensconced in her high chair, crowed loudly and flung her bread and butter on to the floor.

'... And that's enough of that, you wicked thing!' My aunt bent down stiffly to retrieve the food before Ripper got there. 'There'll be none of this sort of nonsense when your mummy comes back to take care of you!'

Beattie's attitude to Frannie's plight amazed and irked me. She behaved as though her daughter was just a naughty schoolgirl who had been caught in the act and was, for the time being, receiving due punishment, one that would all be forgotten when the war was over. Similarly Lexi's bereavement, though lamented, had been greeted as no more than was to be expected if one married a German. Now well into middle-age, Beattie had become complacent. She made no attempts to trim down her stout figure and her clothes were defiantly shabby. The dancing frocks in her wardrobe had been moved up to the attic to allow Shoes some much-needed wardrobe space, and the memory of the doe-eyed debutante had been laid to rest for ever.

My uncle was altogether a more complex creature.

He had been a figure of fun in our childhood, reduced to size with the ridiculous 'Nimbleshanks' epithet, but I realised now more than ever how little we understood him. He had always been something of a mystery man, despite his bluff, squire-of-the-shires pose. That was why my cousins had reacted with such outrage when they discovered his affair with Mireille de Vere. It proved to them that they knew nothing about their own father.

Little Bea's arrival seemed to please Nim, but he was still quiet and withdrawn, slow to air his reactionary opinions. He drank more then he used to, but this seemed to subdue rather than rouse him.

He spent a lot of time in his cinema, and I went to join him sometimes, just as I had when I was a little girl. One evening, some weeks after my return, he asked me to go up there after dinner.

'Got something I'd like you to see ... ' He brandished a reel of film.

I asked what it was but he seemed not to hear me, lighting up one of his Havana cigars and pouring me an over-generous glass of malt. 'Have some of this. Better not drink too much of the stuff though, or you'll get tight. Can't stand it when women get tight.'

With this admonition, he switched on the projector and we settled back to watch. It was a newsreel film with a German soundtrack; its subject was a work-camp for Jews who had been transferred there from a Polish ghetto.

One had to admire it as a clever propaganda exercise. A delegation from the International Red Cross was visiting the inmates, there were posters on the walls advertising cultural events which one could be sure did not take place. The Jews were shown pursuing their artistic leanings; painting and sculpting, playing in an orchestra. They were all given sardines for supper. A little Jewish boy was captured in close-up saying, 'Thank you, Uncle,' to the SS officer who handed them out.

Nim puffed on his cigar in silence, and I gulped down my whisky, trying to quell my rising nausea. When the reel flickered to its end, we sat there in the darkness.

'I wanted to know how things are for Francesca. Seems these places are not so bad after all, eh?'

He waited for me to comment. I did not.

'They're not really like that, are they?' he asked quietly.

'I shouldn't think so.'

He gave a long sigh. I wondered then whether I should tell him about Mireille's death, but decided he had already suffered enough.

'You were the only one I ever loved.'

Aunt Griz was addressing her photograph of the fabled Daniel Crossley. 'And I only loved once ... Have another choccie, Dearest.'

She stuffed a caramel into the jaws of her decrepit lap dog, which wheezed and slobbered its appreciation.

'Aunt Griz, about dinner tonight ... '

I had called in to see her about her part in the celebrations for Irving's return. After a mild stroke that had left her partially paralysed on her left side, she was confined to bed for much of the day, and had her meals taken up on a tray. The room had that sick old lady smell; a smell of eucalyptus lozenges and disinfectant and unwashed hair. Aunt Griz didn't like to trouble the overworked maid with her small requirements, so her underthings had been rinsed out in the basin and left to dry on the radiator.

'Clem and I could come up and fetch you,' I told her, 'We could carry you into the dining room. Or perhaps we could find you a wheelchair from somewhere?'

'It's all right, dear, I think I'll just have a tray up here, like I usually do. Less bother.'

'But Aunt Griz, you can't miss out on all the fun—'

'Well I would like to see dearest Irving, I must say, but ... ' Her frail body trembled slightly. 'But Darling Beattie wouldn't be happy, I don't think. And I shouldn't want to be an embarrassment.'

'But that's nonsense, Aunt Griz—'

'I don't always get to the bathroom on time these days, you know.'

I sighed. 'All right. I'll ask Irving to come up and see you immediately after dinner – how's that?'

I was sorry about Aunt Griz's banishment, and felt uneasy throughout the whole affair. Irving appeared to be very well, there was plenty of colour in his face, and he walked only with the slightest limp. He seemed determined to make light of the whole business of being wounded, telling tales of squadron life throughout dinner, in a bluff, joky way, and using a lot of jargon that none of us understood. There were nods and smiles from his girlfriend Margaret, who was in the WAAF – but even then I decided she was bluffing: she couldn't possibly have appreciated the finer details of such tedious locker room talk.

The conversation was not flowing freely enough to detract attention from the food, which was predictably awful. The ration-book meatloaf was grey and smelt funny and the lemon meringue pie had collapsed into a runny heap. And all washed down with the best Nim's cellar had to offer. God knows what Margaret must have thought of us. She, like Irving, seemed adept at putting on a cheerful face. She was not, as it turned out, the scion of some well-connected family, but a very ordinary bottle-blonde who filled out her blue-grey uniform in all the right places and had a distinct South London twang.

Darling Beattie did a reasonable job of hiding her disappointment, but her chatter about Margaret's father's newsagent's shop in Cheam was so feeble as to be patronising.

'Oh well,' she said to me as we went into the kitchen to scrape the leftovers into the pig bin. 'She's rather common, but then that's what one has come to expect, in wartime ... '

I reserved judgement. Margaret seemed pleasant enough to me, but it was Irving I was concerned about. I tapped on the door of his room that night after we had all retired to bed.

He was sitting up in his pyjamas and dressing gown, listening to Mozart's clarinet concerto on the gramophone. 'Margaret doesn't go for this sort of stuff much,' he said. 'She'd rather listen to a bit of swingtime. Still, can't complain. She's a great girl really.'

'Yes, she seems very nice.'

'I'm lucky to have her, I really am.'

'So... how are you, Irving?'

'Pretty good, pretty good, you know? Now that I've got all this stuff behind me ... Here ... ' He scraped the needle across the record. 'Let's have that slow movement again, shall we?'

'And you've got over ... what happened?'

'Like I said, Kitty, I'm bloody lucky! I got away with nothing compared with some of the poor blighters you see in a military hospital. Covered in burns, some of them paralysed. Just a scratch, that's all I've had.'

He was fiddling with the record sleeve to avoid looking into my eyes, but I had already seen what lurked behind the cheery smile.

'It's not really all right, is it?' I asked gently, taking his hand.

He pulled away from me, and turning towards the wall, started to sob.

'Bugger you, Kitty! It's impossible to hide things from you, it always was. Those bloody photographer's eyes of yours ..!' He wiped his nose with the back of his hand. 'Everything's not all right, OK, but there's nothing you can bloody do about it!'

'Suppose you tell me—'

'Just get out of here, please. Go on – get out!'

But he stopped me as I reached the door. 'Wait Kitty ... ' He blew his nose, 'Sorry to be such a pig. I might as well tell you. You see, since it happened, I can't ... the doctors say there's nothing wrong, but I can't function. I'm not a man any more.'

Before I had another chance to talk to Irving about his problem, he and Margaret went off to visit some friends, and thereafter he was only at Russington for the occasional weekend. Perhaps he was avoiding the place. I continued to worry about him intermittently well into the new year. I wanted to help, but I did not want to interfere. It seemed possible, too, that the best cure was the passage of time, so I kept my counsel on the subject.

Meanwhile, the months slipped by quickly. I was working for Nim on the estate again; this time handling the accounts which were predictably in a mess. It was not a job that I was qualified to do, but as far as I could tell one only had to apply some common sense, and have the ability to add up correctly. In my spare time I catalogued and sorted all my photographs into a professional portfolio, and I spent time out and about with Shoes.

She continued with her efforts to shock me, which she obviously enjoyed. She also made a good job of it on occasion, despite the life I had led over the past two years.

'D'you know what some GIs said to me one night?' she asked, as we were sitting drinking in the village pub. 'They said "Would you like to see some real action?" I said I would, and it turned out they meant an orgy, sex with lots of different people, all in one room.'

'Shoes! What on earth did you do?'

'I said no thank you very much; I was only interested if it was just me and the men, no other girls. I told them I didn't like to share the limelight. And they said that was a pity because for someone who was just a kid, I had a great pair of—'

'*Shoes*!'

'Well, I couldn't help it if they had dirty minds, could I? It wasn't my idea!'

'And would you have done it if there were only men?'

She gave me a wicked, sidelong look. 'Might have.'

Despite this sort of silliness, I found Shoes's company very relaxing. There was none of the claustrophobia, the demanding closeness of my relationship with my older cousins, yet she had been witness to most of our childhood schemes and pranks and we spoke the same language. Darling Beattie liked us to do things together; she thought I was a good influence on Shoes.

This was no doubt true, since my life had become so dull and static. I continued to write to James once a week and receive long letters in return, full of plans for our future. I did it because it was the simplest thing to do. I should have broken away and started a new life for myself, but I simply didn't have the energy. My energy had been used up and my initiative drained in chasing my cousins around Europe. Darling Beattie pressed me occasionally about my wedding plans, but I told her that I wouldn't consider making plans until the war had ended, and she had to accept that this was sensible. Sensible – that was me in those days.

I was jolted out of this passivity by James's return on leave in the early summer of 1944. It was a brilliant, clear June morning when he called round to see me, claiming to be too impatient to wait until the evening.

As I dressed myself up a bit in a pretty floral print and pearls, I could feel nothing but a sense of dread. This was crazy, I told myself; if nothing else I liked James very much, I enjoyed talking to him. I should be happy at the prospect of seeing him.

But there was something else on my mind. A letter had arrived that morning from Paris. On the envelope was the stamp of the International Red Cross. I knew what it was about but, as I started to rip open the envelope, James had arrived and I had been forced to bundle it into my bureau. The thought of it gnawed at me every minute it went unopened.

James and I strolled around the garden as we had done on the day he first proposed to me. We were being watched discreetly, I felt sure, by Darling Beattie who was ensconced somewhere near the drawing-room windows. And less discreetly by Shoes, who waved frantically from her bedroom window, illicit Craven 'A' in hand, gesticulating that I ought to kiss James.

I did, and then I drew back.

'You look as though you've got something to say.' James drew his brows together. He was thinner, tanned a dark brown, and looked and behaved like a man much older than the one who had asked me to wait for him. 'Is it something about the wedding?'

'Yes ... ' I hesitated.

'I notice you're not wearing the ring I gave you.'

'It went to the jewellers, to be cleaned,' I lied. 'I haven't got round to putting it on again yet.'

'So what did you want to say?'

I had been about to tell him about my time in Normandy, about how it had made me admit to myself that I was hopelessly in love with my cousin, someone who had been raised with me like a brother, that in fact I was some sort of monster and he ought to be repelled by me ...

Of course I didn't. 'It wasn't anything important,' I said lamely, pulling some dead heads off a peony bush. 'I was just wondering what sort of a ceremony you wanted.'

I was thinking about the letter in the bureau. I couldn't stop thinking about it. 'Excuse me a moment, James ... '

I ran back into the house.

The letter was in the top of the bureau, next to the ring-box and the manilla envelope that contained Jack's hair. I took out all three things and carried them over to the bed.

The letter was from the kind Swedish lady who had helped little Bea and me get back to England. My hands were shaking so much that I could hardly hold the paper still and the words danced before my eyes.

> ... Sorry I have been so long in replying to your enquiry ... finally met with some answers ... sorry to say it is bad news ... your cousin, Jack Winstanley ... arrested and served with a death sentence ...

I had tried to prepare myself, but nothing could save me from the shock of those words. It felt as if someone had struck me a blow on the chest with a heavy plank of wood, inflicting the deepest pain in the region of the heart.

I opened the buff envelope and took out the lock of dark, curling hair, handling it with the utmost care so that no single precious strand would be lost. I stroked it gently against my cheek, enjoying the silky feel. Then I put it away just as carefully, and folded up the envelope. My tears splashed on to it, making a dark, wet stain.

The ring in the velvet box felt cool and untouched. I took it from its cushion of satin and put it on my left hand, a gesture fitting to the sealing of my fate.

Two

Darling Beattie interpreted my donning of the ring as a positive sign and, wreathed in smiles, invited James to stay on for a 'modest' lunch. Making a titanic effort, I managed to smile my way through wizened ham and tinned peaches with evaporated milk. I wanted the other members of the family to enjoy the occasion before I told them the news I had received in my letter.

All of me balked at carrying out that task. I wanted to keep Jack's death to myself for a while, to allow myself briefly to indulge in the loss of a lover before grief became a family affair and Jack went back to being 'just' a cousin. But I had a responsibility to share what I knew; it would have been morally wrong for me to keep the news to myself.

I took James to one side after lunch and quietly explained what had happened. He nodded, told me to 'keep my spirits up' and promised to be in touch. I was aware both of how little he understood, and how I felt I needed him to help me piece my life together somehow.

Nim read the letter first.

He said, 'The bloody, stupid fool!' and disappeared into his study, where he sat scarcely moving from his desk for two whole days.

Beattie was simply disbelieving. She frowned at the letter, as though such an unworthy document had no business finding its way into her drawing room.

'We only have their word for it,' she told me. 'This good woman is ... well, foreign after all. She may have misunderstood the situation.'

Shoes flung herself on her bed and cried copiously, repeating Jack's name over and over again through her sobs. I was grateful to her; she was giving voice to some of the grief that I felt but could not express.

James telephoned me a respectable forty-eight hours later.

'How are you feeling?'

An unanswerable question: I ignored it.

'I thought you might like to come away with me.'

'Come away?'

'Yes. I thought we might go away somewhere for a couple of days before my leave ends. To London, perhaps.'

'James, I don't know ... listen, let me—'

'Only I thought it would be a a good idea. I thought you might want to get away from home for a bit.'

He was right, I did. 'All right.' I was aware that I sounded cautious. 'Let's go to London. Where will we stay?'

'Why don't you leave that to me? I'll fix something up. With friends or something.'

We went the following weekend, for two days. I packed my best clothes for the occasion, but performed the task like a robot, with the blank resignation of the bereaved. Darling Beattie waved us off with her blessing. She knew James's family and, as far as she was concerned, that meant that he would be observing all the proprieties.

James's car had been sold so we took the train up to Paddington, which left us with the immediate problem of disposing of our luggage.

'I think we should take a cab straight to our hotel,' said James, bracing himself to lift both suitcases.

'Hotel?'

He coloured slightly. 'It seemed the simplest thing. You don't mind?'

Mind? I turned the word over and over as we trundled through the streets of Mayfair in the taxi, trying to rouse myself from the torpor of grief. I could hardly mind since my whole attitude to our engagement had been that of the lamb to the slaughter. But I had not prepared myself mentally for any extremes of closeness, and my experience with Hoccleve had left me a little afraid.

We were booked at the Savoy, which was still struggling to maintain standards in its bomb-torn corner of London. During the taxi-ride, James exclaimed and tutted over the Luftwaffe's destruction of London but I was unimpressed after witnessing what Irving and his colleagues had done to Berlin.

I thought James might give an alias to the desk clerk; Mr and Mrs Smith, or even Mr and Mrs Taylor, but he gave our real names and we both signed the register. I was clutching my vanity case nervously as we followed the bell-hop up to the third floor, but I needn't have done. He unlocked two different doors.

'I thought adjoining rooms would be best,' said James, as I admired the bouquet of hot-house lilies left by the management. 'I thought you would like to have some space to yourself.'

Relief made me magnanimous. 'There was really no need, I wouldn't have minded ... one room.'

He blushed. I squeezed his hand and stood on tiptoe to kiss his cheek. 'But thank you anyway. It was a nice thought.'

'What would you like to do now? Shall I see if they can do champagne?'

I kissed him again, feeling suddenly carefree and infected by the spirit of the occasion. 'I'll tell you the first thing I'm going to do ... have a long, hot bath. There's never enough hot water at Russington, and the bathrooms are all so damned cold!'

My extended soak in scented, bubbly water (with a glass of champagne that James had left discreetly outside the bathroom door) marked the begining of a very pleasant day. We had a light lunch in the hotel dining room, the best that the Savoy could muster on its dwindling supplies, and then went to do some shopping. James took me to Swan and Edgar and, since he was flush with unspent army pay, insisted on buying me a new hat, black felt with a drooping pheasant feather, some pretty evening shoes and a silk scarf. What I really needed was a new dressing gown and some underwear, but I didn't like to involve him in a visit to the lingerie department, despite the triumphant amusement it would have afforded Shoes.

After that we stopped for some tea and just wandered around, looking at things, pointing out places we knew. I was enjoying myself so much that I had all but forgotten the pain of the past few days. It came back to me when we walked down Jermyn Street and passed a certain shop window.

'Oh look!' I exclaimed, and then stopped, just as James looked round to see what had caught my attention. I had been about to say, 'Jack has his shirts made here'. Then I remembered, and it was like being hit in back of the head with a stone. I pressed my face against the cool of the shop window, pretending to be looking at the price of something. My tears left sticky marks on the glass.

*   *   *

314

We danced all evening at a private supper club (officers only) in Pall Mall. Like James, the men all wore uniform and, like me, the women were all trying madly to be gay and smart and carefree, when they were really just fed up to the back teeth with the war.

We got back to the blacked-out hotel at one, and went straight upstairs. James stood on the threshold between our two rooms, rotating his cap through his hands.

'A nightcap?'

'All right, a nightcap – why not?' I said brightly.

In fact I felt dog-tired, and when I had gulped down the brandy we ordered I said, 'If you don't mind, James, I think I'll turn in now.'

His face fell slightly, but he forced himself to smile. 'Right you are – well, sleep tight then.'

I assured him I would, and kissed him goodnight. Ten minutes later he was back dressed in pyjamas and dressing gown and knocking tentatively on the interconnecting door.

'I thought I might come in for a minute. Just to talk . . . I thought it might be nice to talk.'

Wearily, I switched on the reading light and patted the edge of the bed. 'Come on then.'

I don't remember what he talked about; something astoundingly trivial, no doubt. I was so sleepy I kept sliding down the pillows. I felt sorry for him, I know that. Poor James, having to barge his way into his fiancée's room under false pretences. I waited for him to do or say something decisive but he didn't, so in the end I just turned out the light.

Instantly his arm was around me.

'Well . . . ' he said.

'Well what?'

'Well, here we are.'

'Yes.' I waited, rigid against the pillows.

He reached across and fumbled with the straps of my nightgown. To speed things up, I slipped them off. He stroked my shoulders and nuzzled my neck awkwardly.

'Kitty . . . '

'Mmmm?'

'There's something I ought to tell you . . . something that happened in India.'

'What?'

'I had se—. . . I slept with someone.' He added in a tone that was clearly intended to indict him for even worse depravity, 'The wife of a superior officer, actually.'

Did he expect me to be upset? Angry? Before I could settle on the right response he was blurting out an explanation at breathless pace.

' . . . It was after a cocktail party, actually. Everyone was a bit tight, you know how these affairs are, I'd certainly had too much to drink, I know that, because when I arrived at the do it was the *last* thing on my mind, the last thing. But she – Myra – well, she was being a bit flirtatious that evening, hanging on my arm, and then we both ended up staying behind to clear up and before I know it I've been detailed to give her a lift home. God alone knows how, because I wasn't in a fit state to drive . . . anyway, she asked me to pull over by the side of the road and you can guess what happened . . . I won't insult you by telling you the details—'

'James,' I said calmly, 'it's all right. I mean . . .' I didn't want to sound as if I didn't give a damn. 'I mean, I understand. We've got a war to contend with, we're all under extraordinary pressure . . .'

'Thank God . . .' James embraced me. 'I've been feeling so bloody awful about it.'

I smiled in the dark. So the scores had been levelled somewhat. I wasn't the only one who had cause to feel guilty.

Having made his confession and received absolution, James showed no inclination to leave. I decided to get the business over and done with as soon as possible. I wrapped my arms tightly round James's neck and hauled him on top of me. In retrospect, our union can't have been much more satisfying than his roadside grope with the rapacious Myra. James kept his pyjamas on throughout. I was distracted by the background thumps and rattles and murmured comments of the other guests stumbling along the darkened corridor and trying to locate their keyholes. James was almost certainly distracted too, because after a struggle with a conscientiously produced French letter, it was all over in a rather damp rush. To his credit, James did not apologise.

He stayed in my bed for a while, just holding me, while an air-raid siren wailed in the distance. Like a real pair of wartime sweethearts. He said he felt happy. I sighed. He asked if I was happy. I nodded into the pillow.

In fact my thoughts were far, far from James, and the fact that he and I had just made love. I had to keep my face turned away, feigning sleepiness, so that he would not feel the tears that were running freely down my cheeks. At one point I thought a sob or a gasp would be sure to escape; the effort of holding them back was so great that I squeezed James's hand, hard. He interpreted this as a sign of affection, and squeezed mine in return.

*   *   *

316

James went back to India soon after our weekend in London was over, and nothing more was required of me except a weekly letter. His regiment was transferring to Burma, he told me after a few months, and he was hoping to see some action.

In the autumn, Irving returned to Russington for a while. There was none of his bluff good humour this time; he was openly tense and irritable, snapping at Clem when he came back for his half-term holiday and tried to attach himself to his older brother like a leech. Beattie put this behaviour down to grief over Jack, and to the fact that he had been pensioned off by the RAF and had nothing to do with his time. Both these things were probably true, but the fact that he wouldn't allow me to draw him into a private conversation suggested that he hadn't yet come to terms with his 'problem' and regretted confiding in me.

Margaret, the blonde WAAF, came to stay one weekend. I noticed how patient she was with Irving's moods, and I admired her for it.

I was angered by my aunt's treatment of her. She had decided that Margaret was not good enough for her son, and no rational argument would shake this belief.

'I agree, she's *perfectly* sweet. Perfectly sweet girl. She's just not suitable, dear, that's all.'

I hoped she would at least be able to keep her feelings to herself, but she proceeded to treat poor Margaret quite abominably.

'Irving, darling, you're invited to the Cawardines for dinner tomorrow night,' she anounced on the Friday they arrived.

'D'you hear that, Maggie? Hope you brought "long" ...'

'Well actually, darling, it's a teeny bit awkward ... I happen to know that Marjorie's expecting you on your own, and it would be awfully rude to mess up her numbers ... one could I suppose, but I wouldn't like to—'

'But Mother, I *told* you Margaret was coming with me!'

'So you did, dear, but it must have slipped my mind when I spoke to Marjorie about the dinner party. I am sorry.'

'I should think you are,' snapped Irving. He was so tense that the tendons in his neck stood out. He turned his napkin ring over and over, thumping it against the tablecloth. 'You're just going to have to phone Marjorie and tell her I can't bloody come.'

'Don't be silly dear ... ' Darling Beattie spoke as if he was ten years old. 'Of course you can go. Margaret won't mind, will you dear?'

'Of course not.' Margaret turned up the corners of her mouth in a smile.

'She can stay here and have a nice quiet read, or a game of cards with the girls ...'

And so it went, for the rest of the weekend. Beattie, whom I had never considered a spiteful person, contrived to exclude Margaret from the conversation in the nicest possible way; talking about people and events that she had no hope of knowing about. After that first evening, Irving stopped leaping to Margaret's defence and became morose, leaving her to look out for herself.

The following week, when they had left, I was to spend an afternoon in Oxford buying some rolls of film and other small necessities. This meant cadging a ride with Tony on a day when he was taking the Motor in for a service. There was no other reliable form of transport except for Jack's blue Bugatti. I couldn't drive that, nor did I want to.

I left the camera shop in Market Street and was walking down Turl Street when I remembered a friend of James's, Stuart Freeman, whom I had met on a couple of occasions. James had talked about him in London, said that he held a research post at Jesus College. His subject was human physiology.

I went into the college lodge and asked the porter to direct me to Doctor Freeman's rooms. Stuart was at his desk, poring over some indecipherable diagrams. He took off his spectacles and wiped them on his sweater, blinking at me in a puzzled fashion.

'Can I help you .. ?'

Then he broke into a broad grin. 'Kitty ..! Well, what a nice surprise! Sit down, and I'll phone for some tea. What brings you here?'

I didn't insult Stuart's intelligence by pretending mine was merely a social call. I told him, blushing a little, about Irving's predicament.

He was nodding as I spoke.

'It's all too common, you know. Similar symptoms have been well documented amongst the young men who returned from the Great War. Impotence is a symptom of shell-shock.'

He let the damning word hang there while he took a sip of his tea.

'But isn't there anything that can be done?'

'Nothing *you* can do, no.'

'What if he were to talk to someone?'

'A skull jockey? Hmmm ... ' Stuart took off his glasses and tapped them on the table. 'I'd be reluctant to suggest that, if he's already been under medical supervision. Probably had the forces doctors on to him.'

'So it's just a question of time, waiting for the problem to go away ... '

'Is he married?'

'No. He has a steady girlfriend.'

'Well there you are then. She's the only one who can help. By encouraging him, helping him to relax. Lots of non-sexual physical contact, that's what he needs. Massage, that sort of thing. Non-performance orientated stuff. That's my way of thinking anyway, though I know some people consider such things a bit ... modern.'

We talked some more, and I was left convinced that I could help Irving if only I could get Margaret on my side. She had gone back to her air-base in Wiltshire, though, and after the welcome she had just received at Russington, who was to say that she would want anything more to do with him?

The base was in the middle of nowhere, and the only possible way I could go to see her was by borrowing a car. If I took the Motor, I wouldn't be able to keep the visit a secret from the rest of the family, which was important.

After racking my brains for a couple of days, I thought of Pattie, the former Pattie Harman, now a respectable matron living in the village. I used to see her rattling around in a battered old Austin her husband had procured for her, only now she was getting very close to the birth of their first child, she wouldn't be needing it so much. I dropped in for tea, much as I had done with Stuart Freeman.

'Pattie ... d'you think I could borrow your car? I'd give you some money towards the running costs ... '

We struck up a deal: her car in return for the loan of my good raincoat, since she could no longer fasten her own coat over her bulging midriff. On a damp, gloomy October afternoon I muttered something to Darling Beattie about changing my library books, collected Pattie's Austin and set off in the direction of the Salisbury Plain.

Margaret was no fool, and she can't have believed my claim that I was just passing the base and thought I might drop in and say hello. With petrol as scarce as snow in the Sahara, people didn't drop in miles out of their way. But she just smiled and nodded, pert in her uniform, and asked some lesser WAAF to bring us some tea into the control room. We sat in front of a bank of complicated radio controls, next to a big window that looked on to the wind-swept landing strip.

Margaret dunked her shortbread biscuit into her tea and held it there for a few seconds. I noticed that she had very pretty hands; neat manicured nails painted sugar-pink.

'Everything all right at home, is it?'

'Yes. Yes, fine, thank you.'

'That's good. And yourself? Keeping busy. Taking any piccies?' The biscuit was removed from its dunking and popped delicately into Margaret's lipsticked mouth.

'When I get the time . . . ' There was a short anticipatory silence. 'Actually, I am a bit worried about Irving.'

'Oh?'

'He doesn't . . . he doesn't seem very happy with himself.'

'Because he can't get it up, you mean?' Our joint discomfiture provoked a wry smile from Margaret.

I smiled too, relieved. 'Yes, I suppose that's what I do mean.'

Margaret began to tell me her own side of the story, from the beginning. She was very calm, practical, and I felt this boded well.

'My aunt wasn't very nice to you. I was afraid her attitude might have driven you away. And that would have been disastrous for poor Irving. He'd never have got his confidence back.' I considered what I had just said and added, 'I hope that doesn't sound as though you're just being used?'

'Don't worry – it'd take more than your auntie to scare me off.' She flicked a crumb off the front of her immaculate uniform. 'Not that it's anyone's business but my own, but I do care about Irving, you know.'

I told her about my talk with Stuart Freeman and she said yes, that all sounded very sensible and perhaps she might go and see him sometime.

'Thanks for coming, Kitty. And don't worry about that great soft cousin of yours. I'll stand by him till he's better.'

Enough was enough. I was not going to interfere in my cousins' lives any more. It was time I put some thought into my own.

That winter my passion for photography reached a new intensity. I took shots of everyone and everything. No corner of the village, no quaint Cotswold scene escaped my modest collection of lenses. But shots of thatched cottages could only satisfy a fraction of the hunger I felt at that time. I wanted Hindu temples and desert sunsets and wide African plains. I wanted to be out there in the world practising my art, not sitting on my backside, waiting.

My personal frustrations were part of a general feeling of impatience. Everyone said the war would be ending soon, but when? As is the way with these things, when Churchill made his Victory in Europe speech, I didn't really believe it. What would we do without the war? I missed it, almost, as a force which held life in position. What on earth was going to happen to me now? Marriage to James?

There was an exuberant VE Day party in Russington village hall. Nim opened the proceedings with a squire-ish speech about the triumph of good over evil that I suspected he didn't believe in. People cheered anyway.

Irving came down, bringing Margaret and, in keeping with the spirit of the occasion, Darling Beattie called a truce. I didn't get a chance to talk privately with Margaret, but while she and Irving were jitterbugging to Glen Miller, she gave me a broad wink over his shoulder.

Shoes celebrated the occasion by smoking a cigarette openly, in front of her parents. She had her hair 'up' and was wearing a brand new pair of stilettoes. I thought how grown-up she looked.

'I suppose now the war's over, I'll have to come out,' she said, as we both watched the dancers ducking beneath balloons and streamers. 'What a bore!'

I remembered how Frannie and I had felt about the debutante circuit, and smiled. Reading my thoughts, Shoes said, 'Fran could be free now, couldn't she? In theory, I mean.'

She didn't sound any more convinced than I felt, but I was grateful to her all the same. There had been a lot of open speculation about Lexi's imminent return, but Shoes was the only one to mention Fran all evening.

I forgot all my goodwill towards Shoes the next morning when she banged on my bedroom door, interuptting my hangover.

'Kitty – phone call for you!'

I emerged, foul-breathed and groaning. 'Tell them to go away.'

'*It's a man!*' hissed Shoes, rolling her eyes. 'Don't you even want to find out who it is?'

'James? Is he back?'

'No, it's not James. Another man, you wicked thing, you. A man with a funny accent.'

I stomped downstairs and picked up the receiver. 'Hullo?'

'Kitty .. ? Kitty Conway? It's Harry Hoccleve here. *London Life* magazine.'

I was stunned, rigid.

'Please don't hang up ... I appreciate you may not have wanted

321

to hear from me, I understand that fully ... ' I could hear the familiar sound as he paused, the chomping of his teeth against a pipe stem. I could remember the smell of the tobacco he used, the smell of it in his clothes.

'... I was hoping I could do you a favour, actually. That is, if you're still taking pictures.'

'Yes,' I said faintly.

'Good. Now just listen. There's an American film crew going out to Germany to record the liberation of one of the camps. A concentration camp. They're making a documentary film, using the latest colour techniques. Now – I happen to know that there's room in their party for a stills photographer. Would you like to go along? The money'd be decent, and it'd be a unique professional opportunity. Would you like me to say you'll do it? One or two people have been quite impressed with your snaps of the bomb damage ...'

I hesitated only a fraction of a second. 'Yes. Please.'

'Good lass. Now, I'm not going to ask you to come into my office or anything. You're to take yourself along with your portfolio to the Ritz Hotel at seven o'clock tomorrow. The editor and the rest of the crew will meet you there.'

'All right.'

'Good... well...' More chomping. 'I'm proud of you.'

He hung up.

Harry Hoccleve could be crass, but he was not so crass that he would have talked about trying to 'make things up' to me. Nevertheless, I knew that was what he was trying to do. This gave me a sort of formal permission to let go of that sordid episode forever. If amends could be made, then the photographic opportunity of a lifetime was about the best he could have done.

'You're not going,' Darling Beattie said, when I told her.

'I don't see why not—'

'It's perfectly obvious, you foolish girl! We can't have you traipsing off, *bivouacking* with a group of men we don't even know. *American* men.'

'We don't know they're men. They could just as easily be other women.'

'Kitty, darling girl, have you considered the possibility that you've already done quite enough of this? Twice you've disappeared off to Europe for months on end, letting us think you were dead. Besides, you've a wedding to plan. What am I going to say to Gwen Peake-Taylor if—'

'It's only for a couple of weeks, Aunt Beattie. And I promise when I come back I'll—'

322

'No, it's out of the question, I'm afraid! You are not leaving this house unless it's to shop for a trousseau! There are times when one simply has to draw the line!'

Beattie put her small, solid foot well and truly down. Shoes was all set to create a ladder of sheets for me but, to my surprise, Nim spoke up against his wife, in my defence.

'The girl ought to go, it's as simple as that. She can't miss an opportunity like this. No one should − not to see what it's really like.'

I was very glad that we had watched the propaganda newsreel together. It wasn't mentioned, of course, but we both knew that it had influenced our decisions.

I collected together the most striking of my pictures from the past five years: occupied Paris, Nazis in the village in Normandy, bomb damage in the East End of London and in Berlin.

'That's one hell of a portfolio you've got,' said Walton Harker, the film editor I was going to be working with. 'No other war correspondent I've come across has covered quite this range; certainly no one as young as you are. I'll be glad to have you aboard with us.'

Beattie was right about one thing − the rest of the crew were all male. They were led by Walton Harker, who preferred to be known as Wally. Wally was from Chicago, thirty-eight-years old, a big, bear-like man with sandy hair and a good-looking, weather-beaten face. The other crew members made jokes about his tobacco chewing and his gravelly voice, but it was clear that they were somewhat in awe of him. He was very much a leader, and he singled me out for his special protection.

The other five men were understandably curious about me, but in a friendly way. After a little initial awkwardness they discovered that I was not made of china, not breakable, and they made an effort to include me in everything they did. To start with this meant playing endless crap games on the train to Munich. One of the men, Brad Gillan, had been at college with Charlie Olsen, and we quickly struck up a friendship. It was Brad who lent me a pair of khaki fatigue trousers, to help me feel less conspicuous. Amused by the idea of dressing me as a boy, the others chipped in too and soon I had a pair of thick-soled boots (two sizes too large), a battledress jacket and a forage cap.

The plan of action was as follows: we would spend our first night at a small inn near Augsburg, and at first light we would drive from there to the gates of Allenstadt camp, where we would liaise with a medical team and US army troops. We would then drive into the camp, in a convoy. No outsiders had set foot in the place since peace had been declared; no one knew exactly what we would find. There were whispered rumours of cholera, of intended revenge executions of the SS commanders in charge. I was frightened, but as a token man I dared not show it.

The inn we stayed at was sparse and clean, its owners unapologetic for the shortage of food. It was run by an elderly Saxon couple, grey and silent in the face of the Allied victory. They didn't care that Germany had lost the war, only that there was no food left, and no money. The old woman, dressed in a pair of shapeless trousers, tied sacking round her waist and went out at dusk to grub around in her meagre vegetable patch for something to feed us with. She made a passable stew and we provided tinned peaches for pudding and several bottles of bourbon.

The mood at the beginning of the evening was elated, a little wild even. We all drank too much, played some card games and sang camp-fire songs. But as the night wore on and the following day's ordeal grew ever nearer, voices were lowered and the conversation finally petered out altogether. Excuses were made, and one by one the men went up to their rooms.

I went outside into what must once have been a pretty garden, and was now no more than a glorified cabbage patch. Dark shapes loomed on the horizon and I realised for the first time that we were already near the camp, very near.

Wally came out, smoking a cheroot. He rested a heavy hand on my shoulder.

'That's it, kiddo. That's Allenstadt.'

We stood there and contemplated in silence, our eyes drawn irresistibly to the rows of posts with horizontal lines of barbed wire strung between them, and above them the silhouette of the watch-tower.

Three

Brad knocked on my door at six the next morning.

'Kitty – wake up! It's time we got moving.'

I was already awake, I had been for some time, but I was afraid to get up. I lay on my bed until the very last moment, not moving. Then, when I heard the men assembling outside the front of the inn, I jumped up and threw on my clothes.

We packed the film equipment into the back of a military jeep, and squeezed ourselves in around it. I busied myself with cleaning my lenses, the others fiddled with their movie cameras, creating their own diversions. No one spoke as we drove into the camp.

At first, I couldn't use my camera, I simply couldn't. There was too much horror to take in with the eye; it was quite literally blinding. Then Wally came to me and gently lifted my Leica up to my face.

'Use the camera to distance yourself from it.'

He was right: I would have to see the camp through the eyes of a photographer, not as a human observer with a heart, compassion.

I focused first on the worst sight I could find. It was a mountain, a heap some ten feet high, made up entirely of dead bodies. Naked dead bodies. Eyes were open, jaws slack. I moved in closer, changing to a shorter lens, taking in the details. The thrust of emaciated ribs, the grotesque, comic bulge of genitals. I worked rapidly, shooting several rolls of film. Every jab of my finger on the shutter was a small expression of my anger, my rage ...

But there were living victims, too, lying in rows by the roadside, too weak to move. Their stick-like bodies were draped in blue and white uniforms like striped pyjamas, loose and flapping. Their faces expressed no pleasure when they saw us, and when the medics approached they shrank back. It was explained, in whatever inadequate words came to hand, that we were here as their rescuers, their saviours. I think we wanted them to feel joy, but they didn't, couldn't. If they were past feeling pain, they were past feeling joy too.

At the time I thought their indifference the most terrible, the most shattering thing. But there was worse to come.

'D'you think you could do some shots of some of these guys?' asked Wally, pointing to the men stranded by the roadside, like fish on a beach.

I tried, but walking up to them with a camera, focusing dispassionately on the shrunken, defeated faces, seemed an outrageous imposition. If we gave in to our curiosity, then surely we were no better than the Germans? But I took the shots Wally wanted because I knew, as he did, that we had a duty to show the rest of the world exactly what we had found.

There was one man, an old man, who had been reduced to the size of a small child. Yet he held up his head with dignity when I pointed my camera at his face, tried to pose, almost. I had to lower the camera to wipe tears from my eye, my vision was blurred. The old man saw the tears and touched my hand.

'God bless you,' he said, in English.

Brad was at my side with his cine camera and the two of us worked our way along the row of faces together. Sharing the experience made it much easier. One of the men reached out and tugged at my sleeve as I passed.

Brad said, 'Hey, I think this guy knows you.'

The man, a young man, had a red star sewn on to his uniform, denoting a political prisoner. His hollow-eyed face, stubbly head and shrunken limbs were much like those of the other survivors.

But he did an extraordinary thing. He smiled.

'Prisoner Number 617169,' he said in a high, cracked voice. 'Jack Winstanley.'

The next few minutes were a blur. I tried to look at his face, but the features melted together before my eyes, my focus unravelling at the edges ...

I was on the ground with a thud, hurting my knees, but I did not lose consciousness, not quite.

'Brad!' I called weakly. 'Brad ..! Get Wally ... '

I was aware of footsteps running, people shouting for a stretcher. *It's a dream, some sort of dream, or I'm hallucinating...*

I shut my eyes, afraid to look at him, but somewhere in the background I could hear that familiar, broken voice saying, 'Old Jack wasn't such a bad fellow after all, eh?'

Jack was taken to the medical block, where a team of US army doctors were already hard at work. A typhoid epidemic had broken out in the last years of war, claiming many of the victims in the mountain of bodies. At first they were packed two to a coffin but when the disease had taken hold there was no space, no time to bury the corpses properly. They were just thrown into a heap to await interment in a mass grave, a lime pit.

Jack was diagnosed as having a severe chest infection, but otherwise was in better shape than many of the survivors. 'I weigh one hundred pounds,' he told me proudly. 'Most of them weigh no more than eighty-five.' He put this down to the fact that he was a political prisoner. Conditions were easier in the political block. There was more food.

The feeling of discovering that someone is alive after believing them to be dead is quite indescribable. For a while I stumbled around in a daze, overwhelmed. I felt blessed: I had discovered a seam of personal joy amongst all this misery and despair, a phoenix rising from the ashes of war.

My joy was to be short-lived. The troops who entered the camps with us had rounded up the camp commanders and were going to transport them in trucks to a place where they could await trial. Some of them had the gall to beg for mercy. They claimed they had not known what they were doing, that they had only been following orders. One of the young American soldiers, a Jew, was so crazed with anger that he aimed his rifle at the Germans and started to fire. He had to be forcibly restrained from killing those wretched men and women with his bare hands.

I was watching from the window of the clinic as they took them away. Jack was standing beside me. He ground his teeth together, making a terrible noise. Then suddenly he leaned forward, pointing, his whole body quivering with tension and his thin face suffused with red.

'That's the one! That's the bastard who shot her. YOU BASTARD! YOU FUCKING BASTARD!'

Jack was screaming at the top of his voice as he pointed to one of the handcuffed camp guards, a big, burly man with a sour expression.

'He's the one that shot her!'

One of the nurses had hurried over and was wiping Jack's forehead, assuming him to be delirious.

'Shot who? Who did he shoot?'

'Frannie.'

'Frannie .. ?' As I repeated her name I felt my lips going numb.

'Frannie was here, of course she was here.' Jack pushed the nurse away roughly. 'We were both sent here.'

'But ... ' I was bewildered. 'What happened? *Jack* – tell me what happened!'

But Jack went back to his bed, shaking his head. 'She was killed, that's all,' he said savagely. 'Just like all the rest of those poor bastards.'

I begged him to tell me more, but he said he couldn't, that he couldn't talk about it yet. I walked slowly to the barracks that had been allotted to us and sat down on the edge of my camp bed. In the portfolio of pictures I had brought with me was one of Frannie in her debutante's finery. I sat staring at it, at the image of her brave, funny face, and the tears coursed down my face, on to my neck, the backs of my hands, splashing down the front of my blouse.

You have to love good more than you hate evil ...

I wept at the thought of Frannie's shining whiteness extinguished in all that hellish filth. Then I went back to Jack and begged him to tell me what had happened to her. He would scarcely look at me.

'How can you still be alive while she's dead!' I shouted, my voice thick with tears. 'What did you do to get out of it? What lies did you tell?'

Jack turned away from me. He was playing Chinese chequers with the patient in the next bed. They were laughing.

'So you can still laugh,' I said in a low voice.

Jack turned round again. 'Oh yes. It's quite easy, you know, Kitty. After a few atrocities you don't feel anything any more.' He laughed again, to prove it.

Still weeping, I took hold of his shoulders and shook his thin body, as hard as I dared. 'I want you to cry, why don't you cry?'

My own tears had wet his cheeks. He wiped them off with the back of his hand. '*Cry?* What is there to cry about?'

Wally came to my room that evening and found me sitting there on my own.

328

'You OK?'

I nodded.

'Listen . . . ' He sat down beside me on the camp bed and it sagged so much that the mattress nearly touched the floor.

'I'm a little worried about you, you know? Your cousin turning out to be a prisoner here – that's a little rough.'

I forced a smile. 'Hardly. Not when I thought he was dead before.'

Wally pulled a cheroot out of his back pocket, looking hard at my face as he lit it. 'I still reckon it's rough. He may be alive, but after everything that's happened, could be that he's not the same person you knew before.'

'Yes, I know.'

Wally sighed. 'Kiddo, you don't have to stick this out, you know! I can see that stiff upper lip of yours at fifty paces. But what I'm saying is, you've done some good work already. If you want to call it quits, I'll arrange for you to go back to England.'

I shook my head. 'No, I couldn't do that. It's not just the work thing, it's Jack. I don't want to leave him.'

'But they'll be sending him back to England soon. No problem—'

'No, I don't want to leave him *now*.' I was vaguely aware of how stubborn I was sounding. 'It's difficult to explain . . . I've got to get him to talk to me first, that's all.'

Wally clapped me on the shoulder. 'Sure, I understand . . . Hey, listen, the guys are out there having a bit of a camp-fire. Why don't you come along?'

He seemed so desperate for me to cheer up that I agreed. The camp fire had been built in the *Appelplatz*, the square where roll-call had been taken twice a day. It was fuelled with furniture taken from the camp Kommandant's quarters. We warmed our hands before a blaze of burning walnut dining chairs, topped off with a portrait of the Führer, like a Guy Fawkes. The men passed round a bottle of rye and started to sing – nothing too rousing; negro spirituals and that sort of thing.

Wally came and sat close to me. After a little while he slipped his arm around me and pulled me close, so that I was resting against his chest. He stroked my hair gently.

I looked around the fire at the faces of the other men, anxious about their reactions, but they were all studiously ignoring Wally and me. They already regarded me as his special property. And when I had got over my initial embarrassment I enjoyed the physical contact, which did not seem sexually threatening in any way. When I stood up to retire to my room, I half expected Wally to follow me.

329

Silly that, since the last thing I wanted was to ... I was attracted to him, and this confused me. But he just blew me a kiss and let me go.

I went to the clinic again the next day, to visit Jack. The atmosphere there was gloomy. For a lot of the survivors, the cessation of the struggle acted as the final outrage and their bodies, previously driven on by some inbuilt sense of resistance, a survival instinct, could function no longer. These deaths were the saddest of all to me, the victims who had lived through years of hell and witnessed the liberation of the camp, only to prove too weak for freedom.

Those who had been relatively strong when we arrived were now seeing a rapid improvement in their physical condition. But their faces remained blank, defeated. I had talked to the American doctors and I knew that they feared the mental scars would never heal. I feared that too, when I looked at Jack. He could smile, and he could laugh, but that terrible expression never left his eyes.

As I sat making absurd small-talk with Jack, I became aware of Wally's large presence, hovering at the door to the ward. He was ostensibly there to discuss some interior shots of the clinic with the supervisor, but his eyes flicked constantly in my direction and I knew he was checking up on me.

'There's your lover boy,' said Jack sourly.

'He's not my—' I stopped myself just in time from taking the bait. 'Don't be ridiculous, Jack. He's too old for me! Come on – let's have a game of chequers.'

'Well he certainly fancies you. And that Brad Gillan. They're always running round after you, with their tongues hanging out!'

I continued with setting out the chequers board, pretending not to hear. It wasn't easy to ignore the bitterness in Jack's voice.

'... I suppose you think running round dressed as a little boy lets you off the hook? Well, it probably just turns them on. Just like their great big muscly chests turn you on! Well, why wouldn't you make sheep's eyes at a two-hundred-pound giant when the rest of the men round here can hardly lift a toothbrush. You probably don't even think of us as men ... '

So that was it. Jack's male pride was taking a battering now in the face of some imaginary contrast with these 'normal' outsiders. Jack, who had always been able to fell a girl with a mere smile.

'You'll put the weight on again,' I said briskly. 'Now – shall I start?'

'You know something ... ' Jack grabbed my hand and pulled me nearer to him, his eyes burning with some unvoiceable desire. 'You don't get over the things that happen to you, and you don't forget. I

330

never forget. I've never forgotten anything that's happened in our lives. I can remember the first day you came to Russington. I can remember the way you looked, what you wore. We stole some condensed milk, do you remember?'

'I remember.'

'You were so lovely.'

I looked down at the chequers board, confused.

'You know, I was always a little in love with you, Kitty.'

'What nonsense! You were nothing of the sort! Now for goodness' sake, Jack, let's get on with the game!'

I was laughing, but my hand trembled as I picked up the first counter. From then on I made sure I didn't appear too friendly with Wally and Brad when Jack was looking. I was prepared to be cold to them, if it meant sparing Jack pain. I liked Wally and Brad; I even found Wally physically attractive. But I was in love with Jack Winstanley. I always had been and I felt sure I always would be.

After a few days in the camp, we had come to know our way around. There was the looming bulk of the munitions factory, where the more able-bodied were put to work, making bombs. And we were familiar with the unloading ramps and the *Sortierungs-platz*, the square where the first selections were made; the undressing barracks where the new arrivals were stripped and washed and had their hair cut off; the cramped barracks for the *Totenjuden*, the Jewish work groups; and the latrine pits. We were able to distinguish the different classification of prisoners by the stars sewn on to the backs of their jackets; yellow for Jews, purple for Jehovah's Witnesses, green for criminals, red for politicals, pink for homosexuals ...

And we came to recognise, but never to accept, the 'baths'; the gas chambers which so frequently broke down and forced their victims to queue for hours at a time, and the roasting racks, like bread ovens, on which corpses were burnt.

Wally and the others filmed for a week, but after that the camp was to be evacuated and the prisoners moved on; either to hospitals, or – if they were well enough – to intermediate rehabilitation camps. Most of them were homeless, stateless. When I knew that we were about to return to Munich, and then to England, I tried to place a call to Lexi's house in Berlin. On my first few attempts there was no reply. Then a strange woman answered and told me that the *Fräulein* had gone away over a year ago, with the children. No, she didn't know where. And no, she didn't know

331

if they were coming back. I was no wiser than before, and could only pray that the three of them were safe.

On our last evening we had a celebratory dinner, a muted celebration in keeping with our surroundings. Wally had somehow managed to bribe a local farmer into parting with a pig, and that night we sat round the table in the staff dining room that had been allocated to us, feasting on roast pork and washing it down with peasant cider. Working under such extraordinary conditions had brought us all into a false intimacy. Glasses were raised in sentimental toasts and there were many promises to keep in touch, to hold a reunion in happier times.

'We're all going to turn up on Kitty's doorstep one day!' joked Wally. 'At that country mansion of hers!' He put his arm around my shoulders and hugged me against him, making me blush.

The door of the dining room opened and Jack walked in. He held himself upright, but he was still pitifully thin. His eyes moved quickly around the room, taking in the half-eaten pig, the empty jugs of cider, Wally's embrace. I waited for that sarcastic half-smile, but it didn't come.

'Kitty. I'm ready to talk now.'

Jack led me out of the dining room, out of the barricaded area of staff quarters, to the long, low block that housed the 'baths'. He motioned for me to sit down next to him on the steps. I didn't ask, 'Why here?' I knew he would have some private reason.

He took a squashed packet of Lucky Strikes from his shirt-pocket and lit two. I accepted the one he offered, even though I didn't want it, to recreate a sense of solidarity between us. He was about to commit an act of trust, after all.

'From the beginning then?' he asked.

'From the beginning.'

'I was picked up by the Gestapo in Lisieux, when I went to the market. I wasn't carrying anything; someone had shopped me. Maybe it was that bastard Fernand. I reckon he was jealous of my relationship with you. I was taken for questioning in Paris. Because I was English, they accused me of being a spy. Ridiculous . . . '

Jack laughed, then took another drag on his cigarette.

'They held me in the same detention centre as Frannie. We were kept in solitary cells, so I might never have found out if it hadn't been for one of the *souris grises* having a bit of a thing about me. She saw the name 'Winstanley' on both our files and came to tell me that there was a relative of mine there. When she was on duty at night she used to take me along to Fran's cell and let us talk for a few minutes. Just because she was sweet on me. Laughable, really ...

'That was when she told me about the baby. She'd given birth in custody, not long after she was arrested. One of the nurses in the hospital wing was sympathetic and helped smuggle the baby out in a laundry basket. Some of Fran's friends took her, but of course they were in danger themselves, and it was difficult for them to hide a baby. And to feed it. Frannie was worried out of her mind about it. So I asked my little Nazi sweetheart if Frannie could be allowed a visit from a friend, and she arranged it, in return for ... '

The half-smile flitted across Jack's face as he remembered some sordid little scene, in the dark, behind bars.

' ... Well, she arranged it. Frannie smuggled the note to her, the one that was to be pinned to Beatrice's clothes, and told her friend to send the baby up to Lisieux, having first sent a letter to the Lotys. That bit went well at least, didn't it?'

I nodded.

'Trouble was, the authorities had also latched on to the fact that we were brother and sister. As far as they were concerned, that set the seal on our guilt very nicely. A brother and sister team, with the sister married to a Jewish activist. We were found guilty of conspiracy and treason. Apparently so, anyway. We didn't find that out till later·– they never tell prisoners anything. We were both put on the next truck that was leaving for Allenstadt. And ... well, you can imagine what that was like.'

I looked down at the growing column of ash on my un-smoked Lucky Strike. 'Perhaps. But I still think you should tell me.'

Jack turned and looked over his shoulder, into the 'baths', empty now.

'I was a political, so I had it relatively easy ... ' He grimaced. 'It may not look like it now, with all these American hulks around, but it's true. We were allowed a little more freedom, given the better jobs to do ... better jobs, hah!'

His face twisted in an ugly laugh.

'But Frannie, because she married Simon, was given the status of Jew, a person of inferior race. She lived in one of those dreadful women's barracks, with bunks packed in layers. But you know Frannie ... we weren't allowed to talk, non-Jews and Jews weren't allowed to associate, but occasionally we had a chance. She tried very hard to be cheerful. "So-and-so's much worse off than me," she used to say, or "I feel really sorry for poor such-and-such." Never her own problems, though I know she had a bad chest infection in the winter and boils all over her body. She used to look after the others who were more feeble than she was. I think it made her feel better. Perhaps she was exercising her thwarted maternal instinct, I don't know. She only got to hold her own baby once, you know ...'

He glanced at me, but I was staring intently at my boot-laces, trying to hide my own feeble tears.

'... "Simon would be proud of me, don't you think?" That's what she used to say to me, time and time again. Good old Frannie, a dissident to the last. I used to wonder where on earth she got her ideas from. I'm still not sure I know. As a child she was always so divorced from the real world, scribbling away ...'

'She got them from a frustrated sense of justice,' I said quietly.

'I really wanted to help her, but it was impossible. I couldn't even smuggle her food. They shot you for that, and she wouldn't let me. Then one day a guard came and told me I was wanted at the house of the *hauptsturmführer*, the camp supervisor. They needed someone strong to chop logs, they said. I was round the side of the house, doing my best with a blunt axe, when a young Nazi came up to me, an officer. Was I Jack Winstanley? He spoke in English. He said his name was Kurt von Himpel, and he was a friend of yours. At first I thought it might be a trick.'

I shook my head slowly. 'I met him in Paris. I wondered what had happened to him.'

Jack avoided my eye. 'I decided I might as well trust him. He seemed genuine. Probably in love with Kitty, I thought, so why not? He said he could get me a pass, an exit visa. He showed me one. I would have to dress up a bit, change my identity. We would pretend I was a priest. What about my sister, I asked? He said he could really only do it once, so I told him to do one for Frannie instead.'

'It didn't work.' It was a statement, not a question.

'Poor old Kurt. He was a little naïve. The Gestapo had marked his card ages ago; they'd been watching him. He was arrested and sent before the firing squad.'

I hung my head. 'Before ... or after he got you the pass?'

'Before. But old Jacko here was prepared to be a bit resourceful. I'd seen one, remember, and I'd memorised it. I set about getting a forgery done. One or two of the men in our block were artists. They were allowed materials so they could make Christmas and Easter cards for the Nazis to send home to their families. Or sometimes they'd be commissioned to do a portrait from photographs of the guards' sweethearts. In return for extra food. So they had the ink and the paper and I got them working on a pass for Frannie.'

We were nearing, inevitably, the part of the narrative that I dreaded most. I took a second cigarette from the packet and lit it.

'Shall I go on?'

I nodded.

'She didn't get the chance to use the bloody thing.' Jack's voice faltered slightly. 'They ... She was caught giving her ration of food to another prisoner. They shot her on the spot, up against the fence.'

We sat in silence for a while. Then Jack said, 'I haven't told you about my job, have I?'

I recognised the edge in his voice. 'No, Jack, but I think we've both had enough—'

'Please. I want to tell you about it ... The block guards got me out of bed one morning and said they had a new job for me. I was going to serve here—' He pointed to the doorway behind us. 'In the gas chambers. Only the young and healthy were selected for this work. As long as we killed others, we could stay alive. I was told I was lucky. Lucky.'

'Don't, Jack ... '

'No, I have to tell you what it was like. I promised I would. It was an efficient way of bumping off the old and infirm, cutting down the numbers when new prisoners arrived. But they lied to them, when we brought them here, they told them they were going to have a shower. Why did they bother to lie? I still don't understand. No one had any choice ...

'On the worst days we had to get through three firings a day, four chambers used in a firing, fifteen hundred to a chamber ... Six thousand people, Kitty. That was my day's work, killing six thousand people. I had to tell them to tie their shoes together and fold their clothes neatly in a pile. I even had to say that the authorities would not be responsible if they mislaid their things. I gave them cakes of soap and towels, one each. *Lovely hot water*, some of them said, *I am so longing for a shower* ... And then I had to tell them that hot coffee would be served after the showers. Hot coffee! Dear God ... '

Jack's face twisted at the memory. He lit yet another cigarette.

'It was quick, I suppose one could say that for it. Three to five minutes. Their lungs ruptured.

'They said it would get easier as time went on, but it didn't, Kitty, it got harder ... One day I had had enough. I started to undress with the others, I was going to go in with them, to volunteer for extermination.

'But they wouldn't let me. Those women knew, you see. Not everyone believed the shower story, even though they pretended to believe. They stood there, naked, on the point of death and they talked me out of it.

"But I have several thousand deaths on my hands!" I told them. "Your own relatives, brothers, sons."

'"You have a duty to live," they said to me. "To live and to tell people. If you die, who will tell our story?" So I didn't do it.'

Jack took several deep breaths in and out. I waited. Gradually the tension in his body eased and his shoulders slumped.

I had one question to ask. 'After Frannie... you could have had the pass forged for you, used it yourself. Why didn't you?'

He thought for a moment. 'I told the artists not to bother, that I didn't have the spirit, the will, any more. That wasn't really true ... I'd like to say that it was a sense of decency; that I couldn't turn and run from the place once Frannie had met her death here. But it wasn't that either ...

'I suppose it's because I'm a Winstanley, and that stands for bloody-mindedness and perversity. I wanted the bastards to do their worst, to see what it took to wipe out a Winstanley ... '

He smiled at me, the first real smile.

' ... and they couldn't do it, could they? I survived.'

Four

On the day that we left Allenstadt, the American troops set fire to the munitions factory where the Jews had worked, razing it to the ground.

I stood and watched as Wally, Brad and the rest of the crew set up a camera to film the fire. Explosives were planted inside the building and lines laid to a detonator. The soldiers were experienced and they worked quickly. As the countdown began and the cameras started rolling, I looked around for Jack in the crowd that had gathered. I thought he would want to watch the place go up.

Suddenly, there he was, running out of the factory and towards the safe area where we were standing. The troops shouted at him angrily to get out of the way, and the excited crowd joined in, yelling and pointing.

He came to a halt at my side, panting heavily, just as the first blast rocked the building and sent a tongue of flame leaping towards the sky.

'*Jack! What the hell were you doing?*' I hissed at him.

Wally and Brad were frowning in his direction; his spectacular escape had interfered with the focus of their opening shot.

Jack was still weak enough for running a hundred yards to exhaust him, and it was a few minutes before he could speak.

'I went in to rescue these . . . ' He held out a tattered bundle of papers. 'I forgot about them until it was almost too late . . . '

'What are they?' I examined the fragments, which were covered in a tiny, pencilled scrawl.

'Frannie's diary. She used to keep it hidden in cracks in the factory wall. She risked her life to write about this place; I couldn't let it go up in flames, could I?'

'What do you want me to do with it?'

'Read it. And after that ... I'm sure you'll be able to think of the best thing to do with it.'

It was time to say goodbye to Jack, but only for a short while. The doctors had promised that he would be fit to travel to England in a few weeks' time. I helped the crew pack up their belongings and we were driven in a Red Cross van as far as Munich. Our train left for the coast that evening, so we spent our last night in Germany in the faded elegance of a hotel in the Prinzregentenplatz, where Adolf Hitler had once kept an apartment.

I declined Wally's invitation to go out and discover a *bierkellar* that still had some life to it. With a glass of schnapps from the bar, and a magnifying glass borrowed from an elderly waiter, I went alone to my room and sat on the edge of the bed, with the night light balanced precariously between my knees. Then slowly and with difficulty, I started to read Frannie's story.

3rd May 1943.

Last night, after it had gone dark, they took us out to the detention building and put us in a truck, like a cattle truck. It was already so full that we had to stand. We were so close to the other people that we couldn't even look at their faces. It was too dark in there to see them properly anyway.

We drove all through the night. I heard someone whisper that we were going over the border, into Germany. Standing up for hours on end quickly became too much for the older people. I felt so sorry for them. Several fainted. Someone else vomited. One woman was screaming to the driver to stop, that she needed to use the bathroom. Of course he didn't stop, so she had to relieve herself where she was, standing up. In the end we all had to do the same. When my legs began to wobble a bit, Jack let me lean on him for a while, then we changed positions.

By the end of the journey, no one spoke. No one was willing to put a name to what was happening. Jack said afterwards that it was the silence of collective despair. I said to him when we were in the truck that we should all sing to raise our spirits. He said, go on then, you start us off. How about 'Onward Christian Soldiers'? Even now he is capable of poking fun. But I pretended to take him at his word and started singing it. Not the best choice of hymn really, but some people joined in and others hummed along. I think it cheered people up.

338

After many, many hours, it started to get light outside; we could see little bits of light through cracks in the side of the truck. It was terrible really; even animals get treated better when they are transported to market. No point complaining, who are we to complain to? I suppose we tolerated it because we thought things could only get better, at least we would be outside, moving around, in the light.

They let us out in this place, Allenstadt. They call it a work camp. We are to be making munitions to kill the British with. And the Russians, I suppose. When we had left the truck, we queued up in a big yard and they divided us into groups. I was in a group with other women of the same age. We were taken into one of the buildings and they shouted something at us in German. I didn't understand, so I asked one of the Polish women who speaks very good English. She said we had been told to strip off. Everything. They pushed us into the showers and the guards came in and scrubbed us with vile soap, worse than carbolic. Not women guards, men. They scrubbed us hard, trying to hurt us. Then they examined us, squeezing and prodding all over. They made jokes and laughed while they were doing it. 'What are they saying?' I asked the Polish woman, when they pointed at me.

'They are saying, "Only lean pickings on that one".'

I suppose that was an insult. Apparently if you are pretty it can help, you get better jobs, things like that. Anyway, I don't mind the fact that I'm working in the factory. At least you can talk a bit, when the guards are in a good mood.

None of us looks very pretty now. They cut all our hair off, leaving little whorls sticking out in different directions like the fur on the guinea pig Clem used to have. Still, it's probably for the best, since there's no such thing as shampoo here.

One girl, Tereza, had the most beautiful hair, silvery ash-blonde and very thick. The guards took pity on her and left her more than the rest of us. All the other women came and stroked her stubble afterwards, admiring it and saying how much prettier she looked than the rest of us. They hate their own dark hair, and say it is ugly. It's as if Hitler and his crew have made them believe all the propaganda about their uncleanliness and inferiority. About Himmler being physically ill if he laid eyes on anyone with black hair. They have lost pride in Judaism. I'm glad Simon is not here to see what has happened to his people. Anyway, Tereza is a Jewess too; she just happens to have blonde hair.

339

I'm writing this in the latrine hut. I have to work very quickly. Apparently when the guards are bored they decide to have some fun at our expense and stand outside timing us with a big clock. If you're not out on time, they force down the door. (Jack was not impressed; he said they used to play childish games like that at his prep school.) They took away all personal belongings when we arrived. I didn't have any anyway, I wasn't allowed any in Paris. So I asked around in the dormitory if anyone had pen and paper. I was shushed instantly. If you're caught in possession of a pencil, they execute you. But one girl who has already been here a few months had a pencil that she stole when she was working as a maid up at the Kommandant's house. She said she was happy for me to have it if I would write about what this place was like. She gave me this piece of paper, too, and says she can get some more.

Tuesday. Tereza, the blonde girl, sleeps on the bunk below mine. Last night I could hear her crying, very softly, trying not to disturb anyone. I asked her what was wrong. She said she was thinking about her children. Tomas aged four and Irena aged three. She had to hide them in a basement so that they would be safe, and it worked – when the Gestapo came to the ghetto they assumed she was childless. Now Vera has just told her that they are sending trucks round the ghettos, rounding up children in hiding and taking them to camps. I told her that Vera was just being spiteful and saying it to scare her. Vera is the block leader. That means she has to liaise with the guards and the officers, pass on any complaints or requests. Not that they do anything. Apparently they just use her as a spy, and to stir up trouble so that we are afraid to trust one another.

I talked to Tereza about her children, and that seemed to make her feel better. I didn't say anything about Beatrice. If only I could hold her, just once! If only I could be sure she was safe. I can't remember what she looks like, yet I can't drag my thoughts away from her. But I must. It's dangerous to dwell on those things. Longing for her will make me weaker, and then I'll never survive. Jack says we have to eliminate anything about us that might make us weak, even sympathy for our fellow prisoners.

At least I haven't had to live through the ghettos. I talked to Tereza about it. They sound terrible. But I have heard some women saying that it would have been better if they had died when the ghettos were burnt.

340

I think it's Friday. Difficult to keep track of what day it is. I'm so tired, all the time. I sleep for a few hours each night, but it's never enough. Or perhaps I'm not really asleep. My body is tensed all the time, waiting for something to happen.
Sometimes I can hear Tereza crying.

Jack says that we won't be here long, that someone will find out what they are doing to us and come and rescue us. That would be nice. Nice to see my daughter again.

In the factory, the powder that we pack into the shells makes our hands sore. Like burns. We asked the supervisor if we could have gloves. He laughed and called us 'dirty Jews'. Were we afraid of getting our hands even dirtier than they were already?, he wanted to know.

Some of the women talk in Yiddish, so the guards can't understand what they are saying. They don't like this, so they've forbidden it. When they caught some of the Dutch girls speaking in Yiddish they took them outside and beat them.
The Germans seem to be afraid of our ability to communicate.

Vera says there will be more prisoners arriving soon. Where will they go? We're packed to the rafters. They'll have to find room for them somehow.

I can't write about what's happening here, it's too painful ...
Oh but I must, I must! I heard the rumours but I didn't believe them, I thought the other women were just being hysterical. Then I saw the smoke coming from the big chimney stack, and the smell, like burning chickens' feathers. I asked Jack about it. He said the gas canisters arrived in a Red Cross Ambulance.

I will try to believe that they are better off, the ones that are dead. If they are, what does that mean for the rest of us?

Tereza said they wanted to just wipe us out, destroy us completely. I told her that we can't be destroyed completely, that something of the human spirit will remain.

She doesn't know about the New Testament of course, so I told her the parable about the rich man going to heaven being harder than a camel passing through the eye of a needle. She didn't understand at first. I explained that the more we suffer on earth, the greater our reward in heaven. The Germans can't do anything about that.

I don't know what day it is, or what month. I haven't been

341

able to get paper for a long time. It's getting much colder, anyway. Our feet have chilblains and our fingers are too numb to handle the powder. The pile of bodies waiting to be buried has a thin layer of snow on it, like a dusting of icing sugar.

Trying to think how old Beatrice is now. Can't remember. She must be one, more than one. I hope darling Kitty has her.

I gave some of my paper to Tereza so she could draw. She studied at an art college in Salzburg. She drew herself, on her bunk, holding out her arms, with an angel flying down to rescue her. She draws very well.

She also sings, beautifully. Vera was sent round to ask if anyone could sing. Tereza said she could. They told her she was to sing for the *hauptsturmführer*, in his house. They gave her a new dress for the occasion. It was red velvet, with gold braid, but it didn't fit properly. She stood in the drawing room and sang, for the officers and their wives. They wanted Mozart's 'Ave Maria'. Afterwards they clapped and gave her some bread and jam. She saved me a little.

Jack managed to speak to me when I came out of the factory today. He seemed very excited, apparently a German friend of Kitty's has been transferred to the camp command, and he thinks he might be able to help us. Jack tried to give me some of his food, but I wouldn't take it. It's too dangerous for him if he's caught.

Yesterday Tereza was very quiet; she would hardly speak at all. After the lights were out I asked her what was wrong. I thought perhaps Vera had been bullying her again. She told me about the last time she had been to sing for the *hauptsturmführer*. The wives weren't there this time, only the men, and they had had too much to drink. She started to sing, but they stopped her and said they knew of a way that she could improve her performance. They told her to take her dress off. She stood there in her underwear; she said she was shivering. They laughed and told her to come closer to the fire, i.e. closer to them. Then one of them said that she would sound best of all if she took off her underwear too. She wanted to refuse, but what would have been the point? They had guns and they could have shot her on the spot without anyone

342

caring. They knew that and she knew that. So she sang for them naked while they rejoiced in her humiliation.

Afterwards the *hauptsturmführer* said he was pleased and ordered the maid to bring her some cake.

It's bitterly cold. Jack's friend, Kurt, was shot for collaboration. Jack says we should still try and get out. I'm not so sure. I've been having trouble with these wretched boils. I went to the hospital block and a Jewish doctor lanced one of them for me. He was nice. So cheerful, considering the dreadful things he sees.

Tereza is ill. She has a chest infection. I hear it all night, the rhythmic wheezing. It soothes me.

The problem for Tereza, for all of us, is that we don't have enough to eat. Our bodies have no hope of fighting off infection. Tereza used to do better than most of us because of the bread and jam at the *hauptsturmführer's*. But now she's too ill to sing, so she doesn't get the extra food. I gave her some paper so that she could draw. She drew her children, standing on the edge of a deep pit.

This morning, when it was time to go to the factory, Tereza couldn't get up. She was too weak to stand. Vera came over; she was angry. She said we'd have to get her out of bed somehow, or they'd take her away. That scared us. One of the Dutch girls and I managed to get her to the factory, leaning against our shoulders. She said she felt better later on, but she was very red, flushed.

Tereza is much worse. She should be in the hospital. She shouts and mumbles all the time, calling out her children's names. I could hear it all night – 'Tomas ... Irena ... Tomas ...' I put my jacket over my head and stuffed paper in my ears so that I couldn't hear.

When I finally fell asleep, I dreamed I was at Russington. They were all standing there on the steps; Mummy, Nim, Kitty, welcoming me home. Flash was there too. All the flowers were out. It looked so pretty.

Tereza needs more food. Tomorrow I'll save my ration and give it to her.

Five

It didn't take me long to read Frannie's diary, there were not very many pages. But I did sit and hold it in my hand for a long time, hours perhaps.

I kept hearing Frannie's voice, reading the last line of a fairy tale when we were very young.

All good things come to an end ... is this true, Kitty ..?

I was overwhelmingly glad that Jack had rescued this testimony to his sister's courage and unselfishness. One day everyone would be able to read it and know what sort of human being she was. And one day I would be able to consign Frannie's life to the past. Soon – very soon.

I had no sleep that night. I was still sitting on my bed, fully clothed, when dawn broke and it was time to go to the station and catch the train for the coast. I stumbled along with the others in a stupor of exhaustion, unable to explain to them why I was behaving like a zombie, yet feeling somehow at peace with myself. For me, the war had only just ended.

I was so exhausted that I thought I was dreaming when a hand clutched at my sleeve and a familiar voice whispered,

'Kitty ... *Kitty*!'

There – looking infinitely healthier than she had done when I last saw her – was Lexi. She had both the boys with her, and a mountain of luggage.

I hugged her, laughing and crying. 'Thank God you're all right! I tried to get in touch but you'd vanished ...'

'I couldn't stay in Berlin after you left. I took the boys down to the Black Forest and we stayed at a wonderful farm, with the most lovely family ... and here we all are ..! Oh, Kitty!'

She hugged me again, crushing the breath out of me, and for a few moments we were quite unable to speak. Then she said, 'If you can, I'd like to hear about why you're here ...'

We started to talk on the train, and continued almost as far as Dover. I told Lexi as much as I could about the past two years: Jack and Frannie and little Bea, James and myself, Irving and Margaret. She took the news of Frannie's death calmly, some might have said coolly, if they did not know what Lexi had already suffered in the war. I decided I would show her the diary, but later, after the memories of Berlin had had a chance to fade.

'I was afraid something like that had happened to her,' she said quietly. 'Poor darling Piggy Eyes ... still, fancy old Jack turning up like that. Talk about the bad penny. He must be the original.'

'Who's Jack?' asked Paul.

Lexi brightened visibly. 'Your Uncle Jack, darling, you'll meet him soon. Now – tell me all about this photographic assignment of yours. I must say, one or two of your American friends do look divine ...'

Later, when we were on the deck of the passenger steamer staring out over the bleak grey expanse of the Channel, Lexi said, 'You must have done this journey so often in the last six years! Really, you've done so much more than the rest of us. Your life's been so exciting.'

I laughed. 'I always thought I was rather dull next to you Winstanleys.'

'Nonsense! You actually got on and did things. We just talked about doing them, and rather noisily, I seem to remember.'

'But I wanted to be more like all of you.'

'Just as well you weren't!' Lexi spoke with her old briskness. 'We're all riddled with faults, great big glaring ones. Anyway, it's your being different that's enabled you to hold us all together.' She became serious again. 'Because that's what you've done, Kitty. Helping me during ... well, during the bad times. Rescuing Frannie's baby. Finding Jack ... I was going to say keeping Jack out of trouble but no one can do that ... sorting out Irving. God knows what we would have done without you.'

I smiled at her and slipped my arm round her waist. 'Look on it as grateful thanks. For providing me with a family.'

'And now what lies ahead for you? A career? Marriage to a Bleak-Wailer?'

'Marriage to James . . . yes. A career . . . I don't know. I hope so.'

'Is that what you want? The marriage part, I mean?'

'I think so.' I turned away so that Lexi's sharp eyes wouldn't see the traces of doubt. 'I'd rather be married to James than most men I've met.' Paul and Alexander thundered past me up the deck. I smiled at them. 'And it would be nice to have a home of my own, and children . . . '

'Hmm . . .' Lexi looked as though she might argue, then changed her mind and went after the boys instead.

I felt oppressed during the journey by the dual responsibility I had to the rest of the family; to break news simultaneously of Jack's miraculous resurrection and Frannie's death. But at least I wasn't returning alone this time, there was Lexi to help me share the burden, and her two children to help distract. As I became quieter and more restrained at the prospect of returning to Russington, so Lexi brightened to the point of glee. She could hardly sit still on the familiar journey to Finstock, and as soon as the train came to a halt she was on her feet and leaning out of the window.

'Dear God, is that the beastly old Motor I see sitting there . . ? I don't believe it! *Plus ça change*, eh Kitty? Kitty . . ?'

I was still sitting in my seat, suddenly too tired to stand up. Lexi took one of my hands and beckoned to Paul to take the other

'Come on, darling, give poor Aunt Kitty a hand. We're going to take her home.'

'D'you think we should ask Gerald Arboyne to the wedding?' Darling Beattie enquired through a mouthful of pins.

I was standing on a chair in her bedroom, with both my aunt and the village dressmaker circling me, pinning up the hem of my wedding dress. It was made from Brussels lace left over from Lexi's unused bridal attire, which Darling Beattie had stored in the attic.

'Gerald Arboyne?' I queried.

'You know, darling!' chided Beattie. She lowered her voice to a stage-whisper that was supposed to prevent the dressmaker from overhearing. '*Lexi's ex-fiancé* . . . *only, he's Terribly Well-Connected.*'

'I shouldn't do that,' said Lexi, who was watching the whole procedure from the doorway. 'He might recognise the second-hand lace and think you're being cheap.'

'Oh, do run along Lexi, dear . . . can't you go and supervise the children, or something . . ? Turn round, Kitty, your rear's sagging.'

346

Darling Beattie's attempts to help were only thwarting the dressmaker's efforts, and in the end she realised this and sat down on the bed. She had her handbag with her and she rummaged through it. 'Where did I put my lists .. ?'

Triumphant, she pulled out an assortment of jottings, the dreaded lists. 'Right Kitty. Flowers ... we've been through that. Food. Do you think lobster is going to look a little bourgeois? Should we just stick with the salmon?'

I shrugged. 'I don't know. Do what you think's best.'

'Very well ...' Beattie pursed her lips. 'Transport ... we've done that one as well. Presents! Ah yes, presents. Now, they're already starting to arrive, so I thought if you opened the first ones without James, you could start on your thank-you letters now and that would save you an awful lot of time later.'

I pulled a face above the head of the dressmaker, who was sticking pins in my chest.

'I *know* it's nicer to open them together, but if we still don't have a date for James getting back from the Far East and we've got everything still to do here before August 24th, then we'll jolly well have to get on with it without him. We don't even know whether Jack's going to get here in time.'

'He said he'd come,' I pointed out.

'I know he *says* he'll be here on the 22nd, in his letter, but the boy's so unreliable ... anyway, where were we? Presents ... I thought people bringing them on the day (though it's really not done) could leave them on a side table in the hall. What do you think, dear?'

'I really don't mind.'

Beattie lowered her lists and directed a reproving glance in my direction. 'You might be a little more enthusiastic, Kitty dear. It is your wedding, and a lot of people are going to a lot of trouble.'

I pretended to study the satin-covered buttons on my cuffs.

'What's the matter? You do want to get married, don't you?'

'Of course,' I said quickly. 'I'm just not that bothered about the details, that's all.'

'In that case you'd better leave them to me,' said Beattie in a pained tone.

The dressmaker had finished her work on the hem, and I was relieved to take off the tight, scratchy dress and go outside for some fresh air. I played on the lawn with Lexi and the three children, throwing a ball for Ripper the collie and a new labrador pup called Baskerville. The children scampered to and fro, screaming, and Lexi and I laughed as we tried to outwit the dogs. It was a normal, happy game, because that was what we were at last, a normal, happy family. The new generation had brought an air of harmony and rejuvenation to Russington. Nim had even revived his correspondence with the nincompoop at *The Times*, lauding the national sweet-rationing as a welcome discipline for the savages who called themselves his grandchildren. And Shoes was proving a thorn in the flesh, giving her parents plenty of the sort of argument that I was convinced they secretly loved. She had not only refused to do a London season, but had announced her intention to train as a motor mechanic, influenced by some of the dubious friends she had made in the village.

Darling Beattie appeared on the terrace steps. At first I thought she had come out to watch our game, then I saw that she was waving. 'She wants to talk to you!' shouted Lexi.

'Oh Kitty, dear ... ' My aunt seemed agitated. 'Gwen Peake-Taylor was just on the telephone ... there's been some bad news about James ...'

I stopped in my tracks. 'What sort of bad news?'

'Oh, goodness me, nothing like that! Gwen says you're not to worry. He's been taken ill, that's all, with some sort of a tummy thing. It's going to delay his return by a few days, that's all, but he said to tell you to go ahead with the plans regardless, and he'd do his best to be back, if not on the 24th then a few days afterwards. I'm sure the vicar ... Kitty? Kitty!'

I had pushed past her and was racing up the stairs to my room. Damn James, damn him! As if things weren't bad enough with everyone clucking around me and making a fuss, and all the arrangements being left up to me, now I didn't even know if the bridegroom was going to show up. There might be a wedding on August 24th, there might not.

I slammed about my room in a distracted fashion for a while, ostensibly tidying it, but really I was moving my belongings around to try to deflect some of my anger and frustration. All the time the thought at the back of my mind was: I shouldn't be feeling like this, I should just be looking forward to James getting back, whenever he comes.

I opened my desk and started leafing through the papers I found there, inspecting each one and either throwing it to one side or scrumpling it in a ball and tossing it on the floor. There were draft guest lists, invoices for photographic developing, bills for items of my trousseau ... A tattered white envelope fell out of the pile. I opened it up and a ball of grubby cotton wool dropped on to my lap. Inside it, brown and desiccated, was the four-leaf clover that Jack had given me for my ninth birthday. Lexi had told me that it was a five-leaf clover with one leaf pulled off. I turned it over and over in my fingers, remembering how much the gift had pleased me, fake or not.

There was a tap on my door and my aunt's voice said, 'Kitty .. ?'

I put the four-leaf clover back in my desk. 'Come in.'

'I just wanted to make sure you were all right, dear. You seemed so upset ... '

'Yes, I'm all right ... I'm sorry, Aunt Beattie. I suppose it's just pre-wedding nerves.'

'Of course it is, dear, it's only to be expected.' She sat down heavily on my bed and the seams of her tweed skirt creaked. 'All brides get nervous ... except your cousin Lexi, of course, but then look what happened to her ...'

'I just wish it were all over.'

'All over?'

'The wedding. So that James and I can get on and have some sort of normal life. At the moment everything seems to be getting in the way.'

Beattie smiled uncertainly. 'I'm not sure I know what you mean.'

She looked at me with her head on one side, and it occurred to me that she was waiting for some sort of confession. I floundered on, 'Everything's uncertain. I mean, we don't even know where we're going to be living, or where James is going to be working ...'

'There are advantages to it, you know,' Beattie said suddenly.

'To what?'

'To not marrying for love.'

I blushed. 'I've never said—'

'Love is all very well in the beginning, it's like a new amusing pastime one has discovered, but growing away from someone you've been in love with is the worst sort of growing apart there is. No, on the whole marrying for friendship and security and the right sort of position in life is by far the best thing to do. Much more comfortable, don't you think?'

I turned and faced my aunt directly, trying to look past that rather vague smile to the private person who lurked beneath and who had once been ravishingly pretty, feminine and sought-after.

'How much of this advice is based on your own experience, Aunt Beattie?' I asked, baldly curious.

'That's hardly the point dear ... ' She stood up to leave. 'I'm saying this: that there is a place for passion and marriage is not that place. And if it makes any difference to you, I approve of what you're doing.'

*   *   *

The news reached us two days before the wedding, on the day that James was due to return.

James wasn't coming. The 'stomach trouble' contracted in Burma was dysentery and he worsened rapidly after the message to say that he might be late home. Although his condition wasn't life-threatening, it would be weeks, possibly months before he could return to England. The wedding would have to be cancelled.

We had hardly had time to digest this news when a taxi drew up outside and discharged Jack and his meagre amount of luggage. I was standing at the top of the stairs when he came into the hall. Still very thin, but with a sheen on his hair and some of the old brightness about his eyes.

He flung open his arms when he saw me. 'Here I am, Kit − just in time to see you given away to the Bleak-Wailers!'

I turned and fled, leaving the others to make the necessary explanations.

Later he came up to my room. I was lying on my bed, dry-eyed, staring at the ceiling. The wedding dress hung on the wardrobe door in its cellophane sheath.

'Glad you're not crying, old girl.' He gave my shoulder a brisk pat. 'Anyway, according to Ma, it's just a postponement, not a cancellation.'

I sighed.

'Want to tell your Uncle Jacko all about it?'

'I just feel so guilty, Jack!' I twisted round on to my side so that I was facing him. 'It was supposed to be the most important day of my life and all I can feel is relief that it's not going to happen.'

Jack narrowed his eyes. 'Are you saying that if he had turned up, you wouldn't have gone through with it?'

'I don't know! I don't know what I'm saying. I'm so confused . . .'

' . . . Because he will come back in the end, you know.' He went over to the wedding dress and fingered the edge of a lace cuff. 'And then you'll have to choose.'

'*Choose?*' I challenged him.

But he let the word drop. 'If you want my opinion, I can't see you settling down to be a provincial wife after the sort of life you've led during the war. You're far too independent. And you've got a photographic career ahead of you.'

'Can't I have both?' I demanded. 'A career and love?'

'Ah . . . love! Is that what we're talking about . .?' An odd look came over his face briefly. Then he grinned. 'Typical of a Bleak-Wailer though, isn't it? Prevented from claiming the girl of his dreams by a dose of the squits.'

'*Jack!*'

He inspected the wreath of silk flowers that hung over the dress, making it look like a decapitated corpse. 'Pity though ... I was rather looking forward to seeing you as a bride.'

'Do you know what the worst thing is?' I said, sitting up. 'The worst, most unforgivable thing?' Jack still had his back to me, making it easier to say what I wanted to say. 'I'm glad. That it's you who's here and James who's ill. Isn't that wicked? If I were forced to—'

'Sshh!' Jack put his finger on his lips. 'You'd better not talk like that – God might hear you.' He stooped and kissed me, swiftly, on the mouth. 'But for what it's worth – I'm glad you're glad.'

Irving and Margaret arrived a few days later to spend the weekend, and after discussing the matter with me first, they put a very controversial suggestion to Nim and Beattie.

They wanted to get married, they said, as soon as possible. They wondered if they might make use of the dress that had been made for me, and the cake, and all the other trimmings that had been provided before the wedding was finally cancelled.

Nim laughed at their nerve, and said he saw no reason why all that money should go to waste. And since the bride's family were supposed to pay, perhaps he might bill Margaret's parents for a consideration. Beattie was harder to convince, clinging firmly as she did to the idea that James and I would wed eventually. She claimed to be shocked when she learned that the scheme had my blessing.

'I don't know ... Whatever will you come up with next? Digging up the family burial plot and making people share graves ..? And what on earth am I going to say to Gwen Peake-Taylor ..?'

But in the end she was forced to admit that it would be sad to see all her hard work go to waste, and this way the wedding could be held in Russington which was much preferable to the dubious recesses of Surrey or Essex, or wherever it was that Margaret's family came from.

She even went so far as to hold a dinner party for the bridal couple on the eve of the ceremony, which was to be a very small, quiet one, in keeping with recent events. Getting ready for the dinner was just like old times. Lexi and I loafed around in our dressing gowns, unable to decide what to wear.

'What d'you think, Kit?' Lexi mumbled through a cigarette clamped firmly between her lips. She was holding up an old dove-grey dress that had been made for her years earlier. 'It's a bit ...' She squinted at it. '... a bit *pre-war*, isn't it? Anyway, I probably couldn't get into it now, not after two kids. But you could try it; it might fit you.'

'I was thinking about this old red thing.'

'Hmmm ... ' Lexi held it against me. 'Red is a good colour for you, and I've got just the lipstick to lend you ... But maybe the grey is more Suitable for the Disappointed Bride.' She waited to see if I was going to laugh, and when I did she added, 'More spinsterly.'

I stood in front of the mirror with both dresses, unable to decide which to wear.

'Why don't you go and ask Jack which one he thinks is best?' suggested Lexi.

I draped the dresses over one arm and went down the passage to his room. He was sitting on the edge of his bed in his undershorts and shirt.

'Jack – whatever's wrong?'

'Look!' he said savagely. 'Look at this! How am I supposed to wear it?'

He wrenched his dinner suit down from its hanger and put it on. He was still two stones lighter than he had been when it was made for him, and it hung loosely from his body, a potent symbol of fatter, happier times. And a reminder of all he had suffered.

I opened my mouth to say that it wasn't so bad, then quickly shut it again. As he contemplated his reflection in the looking glass, two tears appeared on his cheeks and rolled slowly down to his chin. For the first time since his internment in Allenstadt concentration camp – and, as far I was aware, the first time in his life – Jack Winstanley was able to cry.

I cried copiously at Irving's wedding, as did Lexi, Shoes and Darling Beattie. It was, as they say, a lovely wedding. Margaret made a far better bride than I would have done. There was a glow of happiness about her that I could never have produced, however smoothly things might have gone. But then she was in love with Irving.

Afterwards there was a small reception at the house for close friends and family. Aunt Griz came for the day, from the nursing home nearby where she was now living. She was in a wheelchair and minus Dearest, who had pre-deceased her, but on the whole seemed much happier now that she was no longer a burden to Darling Beattie. The three children ran around pilfering other

352

people's *petits fours* and behaving as antisocially as we would have done twenty years earlier.

The bride's father made a speech that was too long and rather boring, but Margaret still had the good grace to blush prettily and clutch her new husband's hand, as brides are supposed to.

'She looks lovely, doesn't she?' Lexi whispered to me.

'Mmm ... My dress suits her. In fact, it's much better on her than it would have been on me.'

Lexi reflected for a moment and then gave my hand a squeeze. 'Yes, I think you're probably right.'

The wedding helped to dispel any traces of doubt. I knew I wouldn't marry James now, whenever he came back. And it was time for me to move on, to leave Russington for a while and become an adult again. My pictures of Allenstadt had been published to quiet acclaim, and a new American magazine called *Photoworld* had asked me to be their London stringer.

I sorted and re-sorted all my prints and negatives for the final time, putting aside my favourite family pictures. I intended to mount them in a special album and give them to Nim and Beattie as a sort of goodbye present.

I spread out a collection of potential inclusions on my faded candlewick bedspread. There was my earliest attempt, with the whole family on the terrace steps and Flash a white blur in the middle. Then Lexi, Frannie and I in our rag-bag finery on the night of the dinner party Beattie gave for Mireille. Jack under the pergola in the villa in Rome, his young face mysterious and beautiful. Clem and Flash dozing at our picnic on the banks of the Windrush. Frannie in her coming-out dress. Lexi half-hidden beneath a slope-brimmed hat, smoking a cigarette in the Romanisches Café. Jack in the garden of Madame Loty's house, with his arm round her shoulders. Young Paul, tobogganning in the snow-bound streets of Berlin.

I considered myself lucky, privileged to have made this record of the family, following their griefs and triumphs, however petty. It was fitting that of all of us, I should have become the photographer. I had been the Winstanleys' observer from the day I first entered their world, at the age of eight. Standing on the edge of their charmed circle as I did, I was in a position to mediate. But not to judge; I knew that now.

Jack came in to the room and sat looking at the photographs for a long time, no doubt fitting them into private memories of his own.

'So, Kitty ...' he said at last. 'You're off to London then?'

'Yes. What about you?'

'It's London for me too. I'm afraid you can't get rid of old Jack that easily ... time I did a bit of business, a bit of wheeling and dealing. Thought I might go into property.'

I chose my next words carefully. 'I hope we'll be able to see one another sometimes?'

Jack grinned. 'Oh, I expect we will. And if I have anything to do with it, it'll be more than just sometimes.'

I smiled back but, through force of old habit, did not allow myself to feel too pleased. After all, with Jack one never knew quite what to believe.

I stood at the window looking down at the garden. Paul and Alexander were playing some wild and inventive game on the lawn below while Lexi took little Bea for a stroll in her pram. Jack stood beside me and watched them.

'The terrible thing about childhood,' he told me, 'is that you don't know at the time how happy you are ...'

I nodded my agreement.

'... So – time those evil young nephews of ours were toughened up a bit, eh?' He took my hand in his. 'You and I are going to go and teach them to Hunt the Snark ...'